BLUE IN GREEN™

IN COLOR The finest since 1992

BLUE IN GREEN. First Printing. October 2020. Published by Image Comics, Inc. Office of publication: 2701 NW Vaughn St, Ste 780, Portland, OR 97210. Copyright © 2020 Ram Venkatesan & Anand Radhakrishnan. All rights reserved. BLUE IN GREEN, and the likenesses of all characters herein or hereon are trademarks of Ram Venkatesan & Anand Radhakrishnan, unless expressly indicated. IMAGE and the Image Comics logos are registered trademarks of Image Comics, Inc. No part of this publication may be reproduced or transmitted in any form or by any means (except for short excerpts for journalistic or review purposes), without the express written permission of Ram Venkatesan & Anand Radhakrishnan or Image Comics, Inc. All names, characters, events, and places herein are entirely fictional. Any resemblance to actual persons (living or dead), events, or places, without satiric intent, is coincidental. Printed in the USA. For international rights, contact: foreignlicensing@imagecomics.com. ISBN: 978-1-5343-1713-0.

BLUE IN GREEN™

RAM V, writer; **ANAND RK**, artist;
JOHN PEARSON, color artist;
ADITYA BIDIKAR, letterer; **TOM MULLER**, designer;
RYAN BREWER, production artist.

IMAGE COMICS, INC.
Todd McFarlane: President
Jim Valentino: Vice President
Marc Silvestri: Chief Executive Officer
Erik Larsen: Chief Financial Officer
Robert Kirkman: Chief Operating Officer

Eric Stephenson: Publisher / Chief Creative Officer
Shanna Matuszak: Editorial Coordinator
Marla Eizik: Talent Liaison

Nicole Lapalme: Controller
Leanna Caunter: Accounting Analyst
Sue Korpela: Accounting & HR Manager

Jeff Boison: Director of Sales & Publishing Planning
Dirk Wood: Director of International Sales & Licensing
Alex Cox: Director of Direct Market & Speciality Sales
Chloe Ramos-Peterson: Book Market & Library Sales Manager
Emilio Bautista: Digital Sales Coordinator

Kat Salazar: Director of PR & Marketing
Drew Fitzgerald: Marketing Content Associate

Heather Doornink: Production Director
Drew Gill: Art Director
Hilary DiLoreto: Print Manager
Tricia Ramos: Traffic Manager
Erika Schnatz: Senior Production Artist
Ryan Brewer: Production Artist
Deanna Phelps: Production Artist

CHAPTER 1

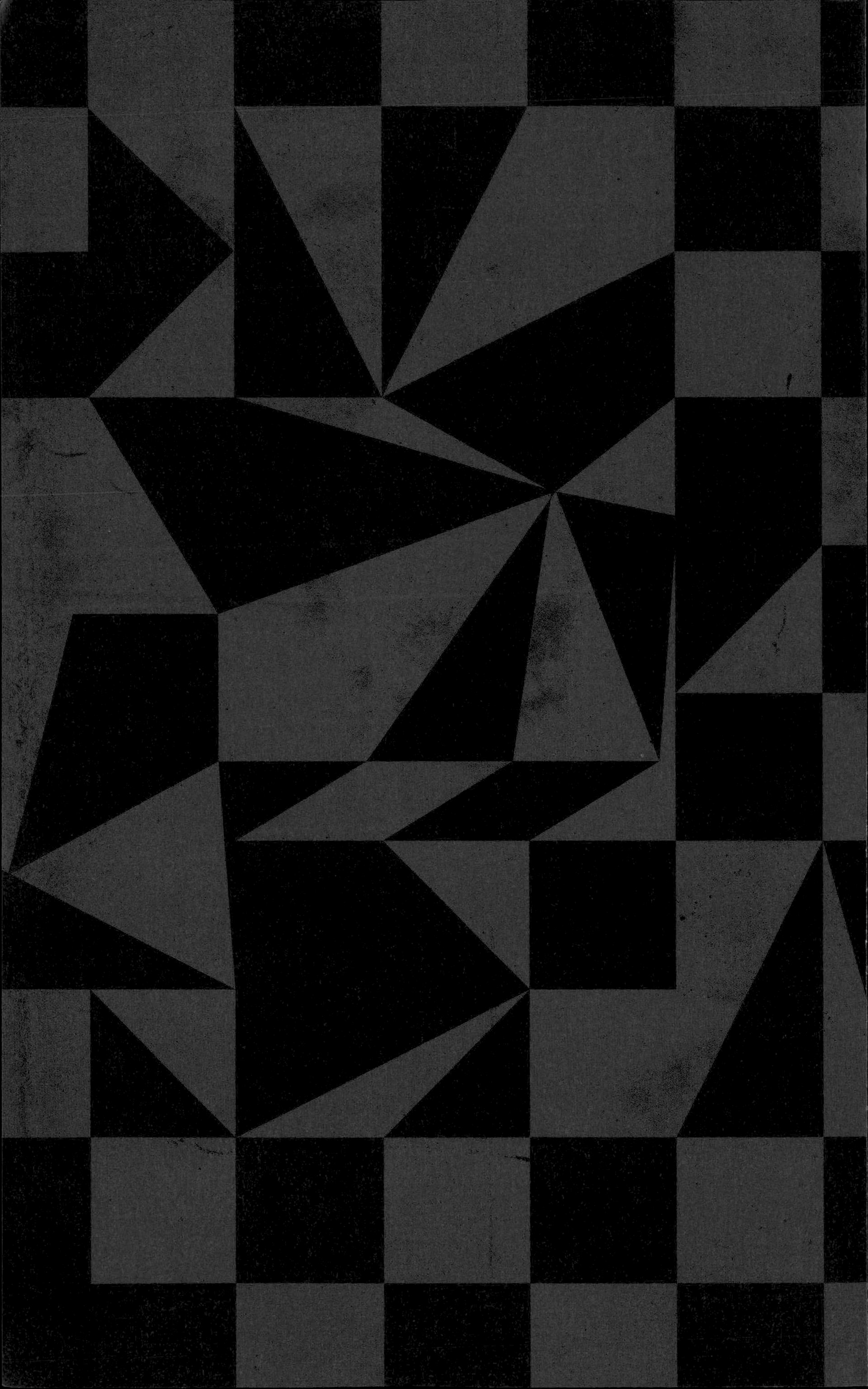

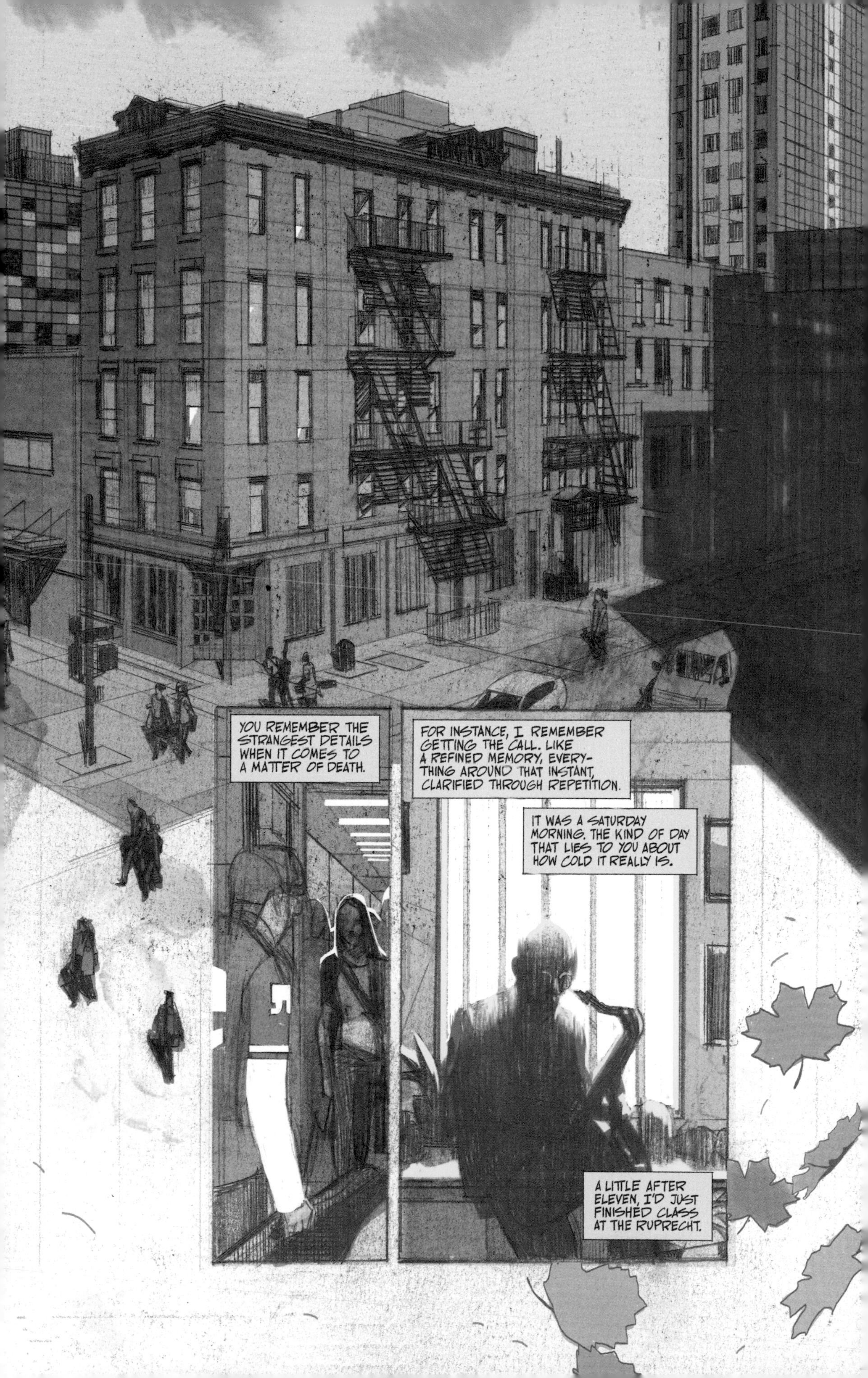
YOU REMEMBER THE STRANGEST DETAILS WHEN IT COMES TO A MATTER OF DEATH.
FOR INSTANCE, I REMEMBER GETTING THE CALL. LIKE A REFINED MEMORY, EVERYTHING AROUND THAT INSTANT, CLARIFIED THROUGH REPETITION.
IT WAS A SATURDAY MORNING. THE KIND OF DAY THAT LIES TO YOU ABOUT HOW COLD IT REALLY IS.
A LITTLE AFTER ELEVEN, I'D JUST FINISHED CLASS AT THE RUPRECHT.

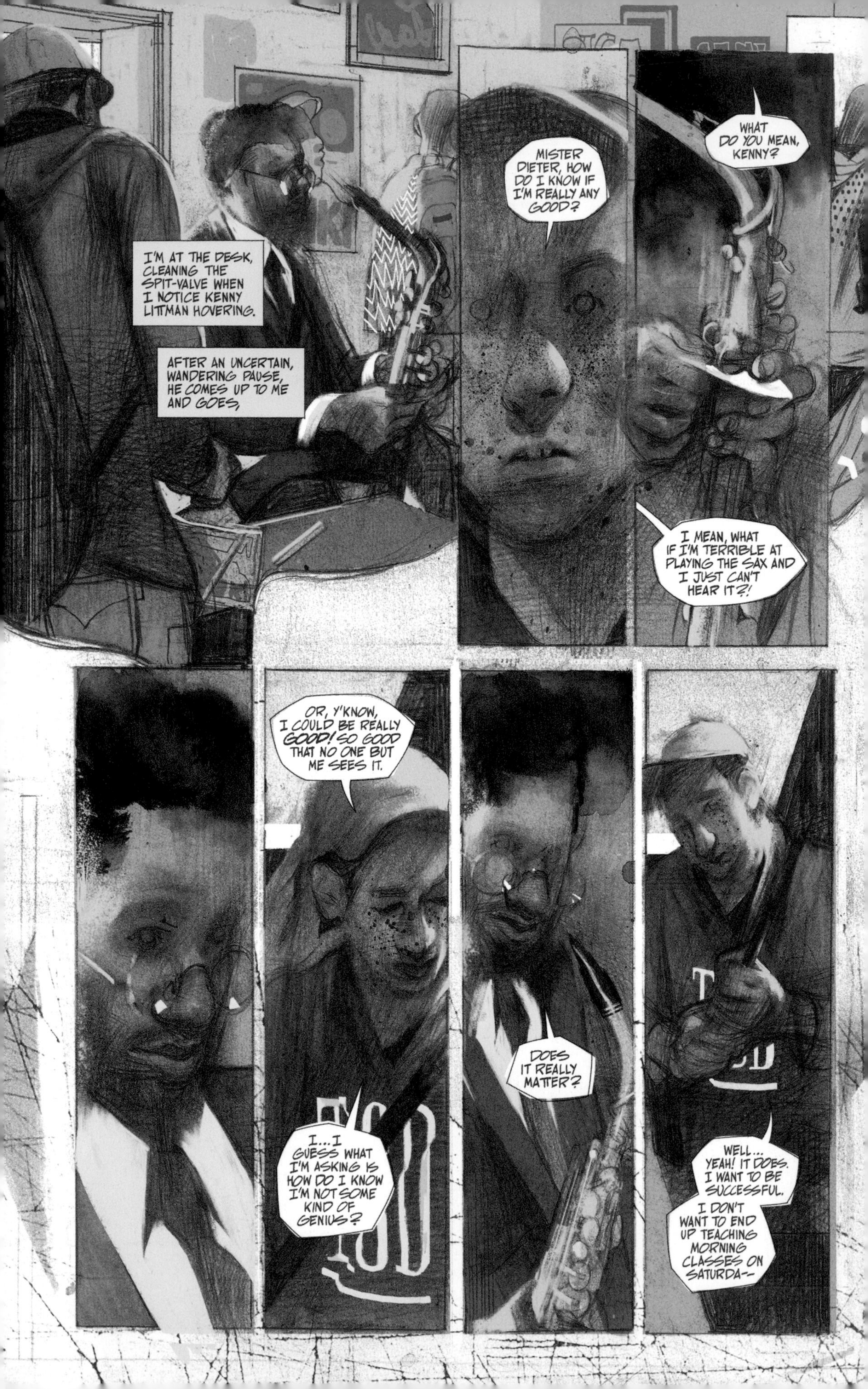
I'M AT THE DESK, CLEANING THE SPIT-VALVE WHEN I NOTICE KENNY LITTMAN HOVERING.
AFTER AN UNCERTAIN, WANDERING PAUSE, HE COMES UP TO ME AND GOES,
MISTER DIETER, HOW DO I KNOW IF I'M REALLY ANY GOOD?
WHAT DO YOU MEAN, KENNY?
I MEAN, WHAT IF I'M TERRIBLE AT PLAYING THE SAX AND I JUST CAN'T HEAR IT?!
OR, Y'KNOW, I COULD BE REALLY GOOD! SO GOOD THAT NO ONE BUT ME SEES IT.
I...I GUESS WHAT I'M ASKING IS HOW DO I KNOW I'M NOT SOME KIND OF GENIUS?
DOES IT REALLY MATTER?
WELL... YEAH! IT DOES. I WANT TO BE SUCCESSFUL.
I DON'T WANT TO END UP TEACHING MORNING CLASSES ON SATURDA--

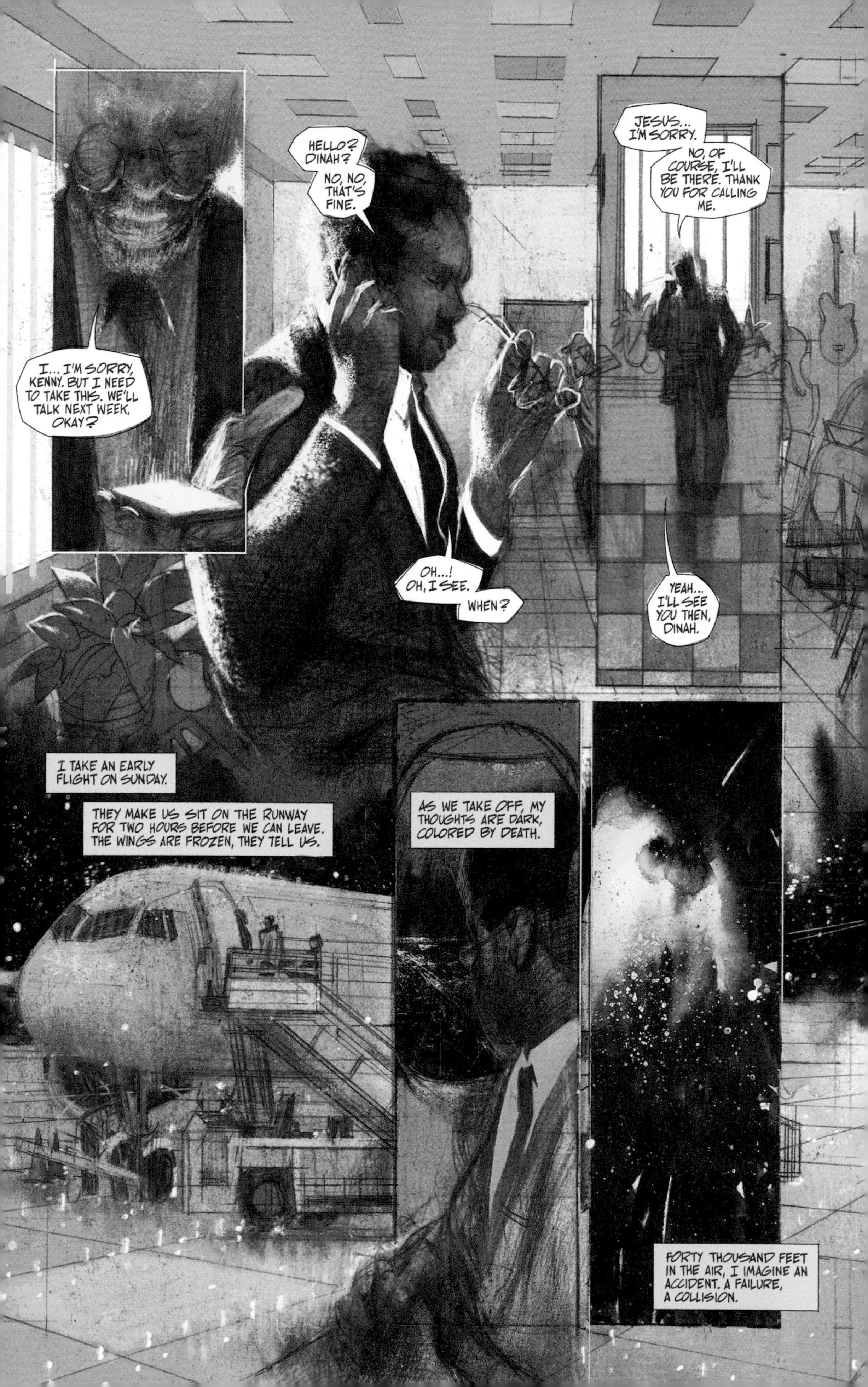
HELLO? DINAH?
NO, NO, THAT'S FINE.
I... I'M SORRY, KENNY. BUT I NEED TO TAKE THIS. WE'LL TALK NEXT WEEK, OKAY?
OH...! OH, I SEE.
WHEN?
JESUS... I'M SORRY.
NO, OF COURSE, I'LL BE THERE. THANK YOU FOR CALLING ME.
YEAH... I'LL SEE YOU THEN, DINAH.
I TAKE AN EARLY FLIGHT ON SUNDAY.
THEY MAKE US SIT ON THE RUNWAY FOR TWO HOURS BEFORE WE CAN LEAVE. THE WINGS ARE FROZEN, THEY TELL US.
AS WE TAKE OFF, MY THOUGHTS ARE DARK, COLORED BY DEATH.
FORTY THOUSAND FEET IN THE AIR, I IMAGINE AN ACCIDENT. A FAILURE, A COLLISION.

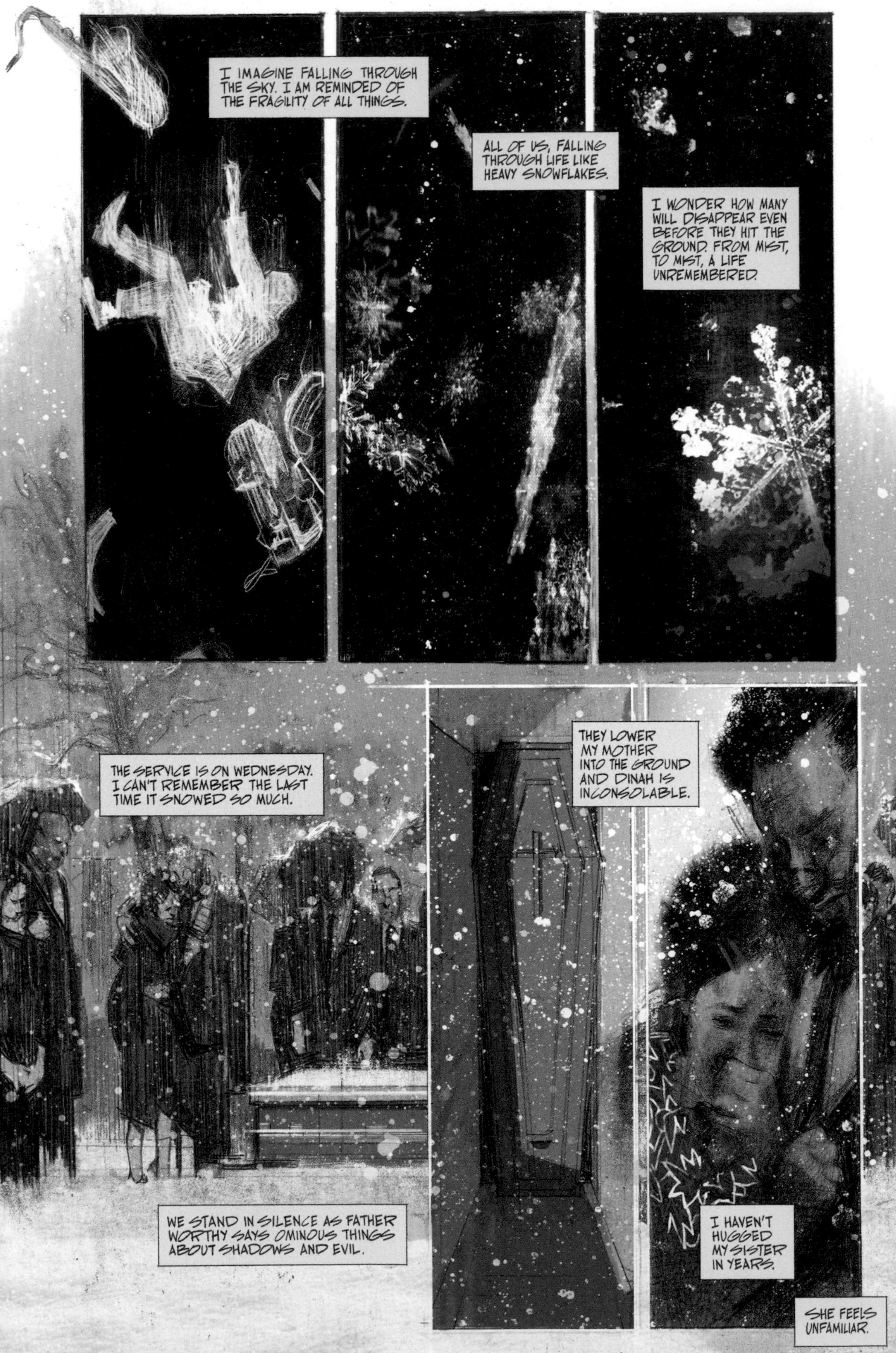
I IMAGINE FALLING THROUGH THE SKY. I AM REMINDED OF THE FRAGILITY OF ALL THINGS.
ALL OF US, FALLING THROUGH LIFE LIKE HEAVY SNOWFLAKES.
I WONDER HOW MANY WILL DISAPPEAR EVEN BEFORE THEY HIT THE GROUND. FROM MIST, TO MIST, A LIFE UNREMEMBERED.
THE SERVICE IS ON WEDNESDAY. I CAN'T REMEMBER THE LAST TIME IT SNOWED SO MUCH.
WE STAND IN SILENCE AS FATHER WORTHY SAYS OMINOUS THINGS ABOUT SHADOWS AND EVIL.
THEY LOWER MY MOTHER INTO THE GROUND AND DINAH IS INCONSOLABLE.
I HAVEN'T HUGGED MY SISTER IN YEARS.
SHE FEELS UNFAMILIAR.

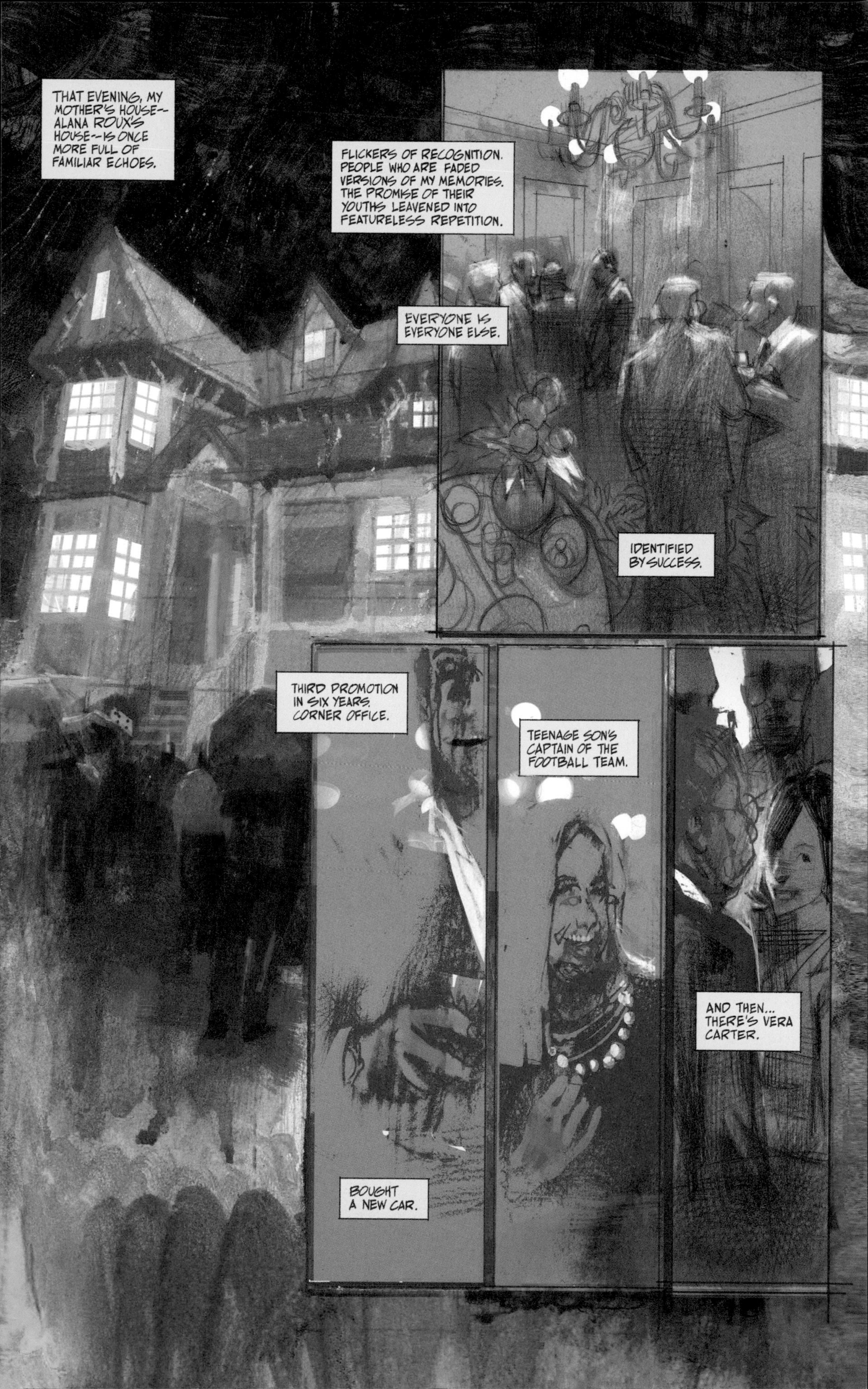
THAT EVENING, MY MOTHER'S HOUSE--ALANA ROUX'S HOUSE--IS ONCE MORE FULL OF FAMILIAR ECHOES.
FLICKERS OF RECOGNITION. PEOPLE WHO ARE FADED VERSIONS OF MY MEMORIES. THE PROMISE OF THEIR YOUTHS LEAVENED INTO FEATURELESS REPETITION.
EVERYONE IS EVERYONE ELSE.
IDENTIFIED BY SUCCESS.
THIRD PROMOTION IN SIX YEARS. CORNER OFFICE.
BOUGHT A NEW CAR.
TEENAGE SON'S CAPTAIN OF THE FOOTBALL TEAM.
AND THEN... THERE'S VERA CARTER.

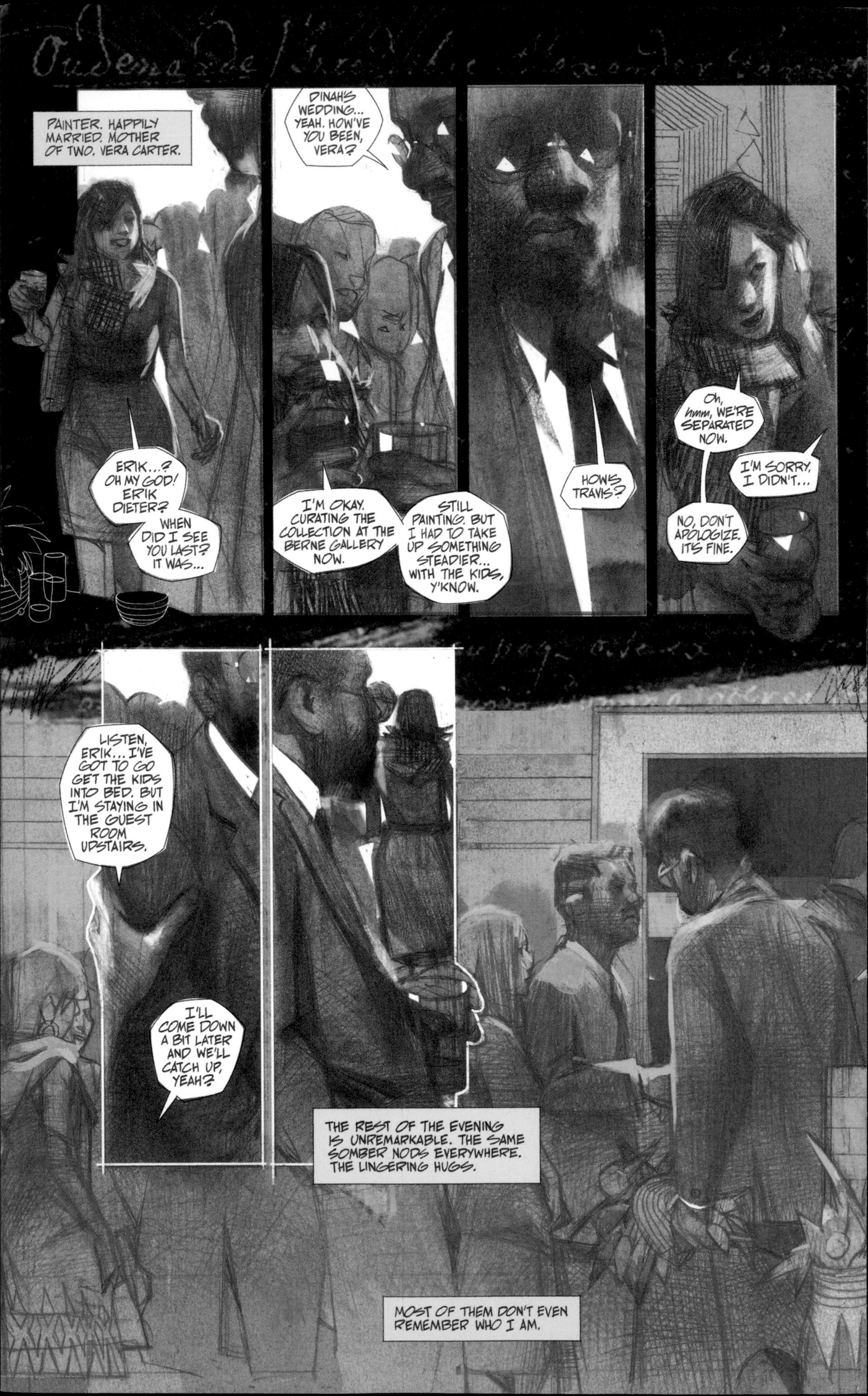
PAINTER. HAPPILY MARRIED. MOTHER OF TWO. VERA CARTER.
ERIK...? OH MY GOD! ERIK DIETER?
WHEN DID I SEE YOU LAST? IT WAS...
DINAH'S WEDDING... YEAH. HOW'VE YOU BEEN, VERA?
I'M OKAY. CURATING THE COLLECTION AT THE BERNE GALLERY NOW.
STILL PAINTING. BUT I HAD TO TAKE UP SOMETHING STEADIER... WITH THE KIDS, Y'KNOW.
HOW'S TRAVIS?
Oh, hmm, WE'RE SEPARATED NOW.
I'M SORRY, I DIDN'T...
NO, DON'T APOLOGIZE. IT'S FINE.
LISTEN, ERIK... I'VE GOT TO GO GET THE KIDS INTO BED. BUT I'M STAYING IN THE GUEST ROOM UPSTAIRS.
I'LL COME DOWN A BIT LATER AND WE'LL CATCH UP, YEAH?
THE REST OF THE EVENING IS UNREMARKABLE. THE SAME SOMBER NODS EVERYWHERE. THE LINGERING HUGS.
MOST OF THEM DON'T EVEN REMEMBER WHO I AM.

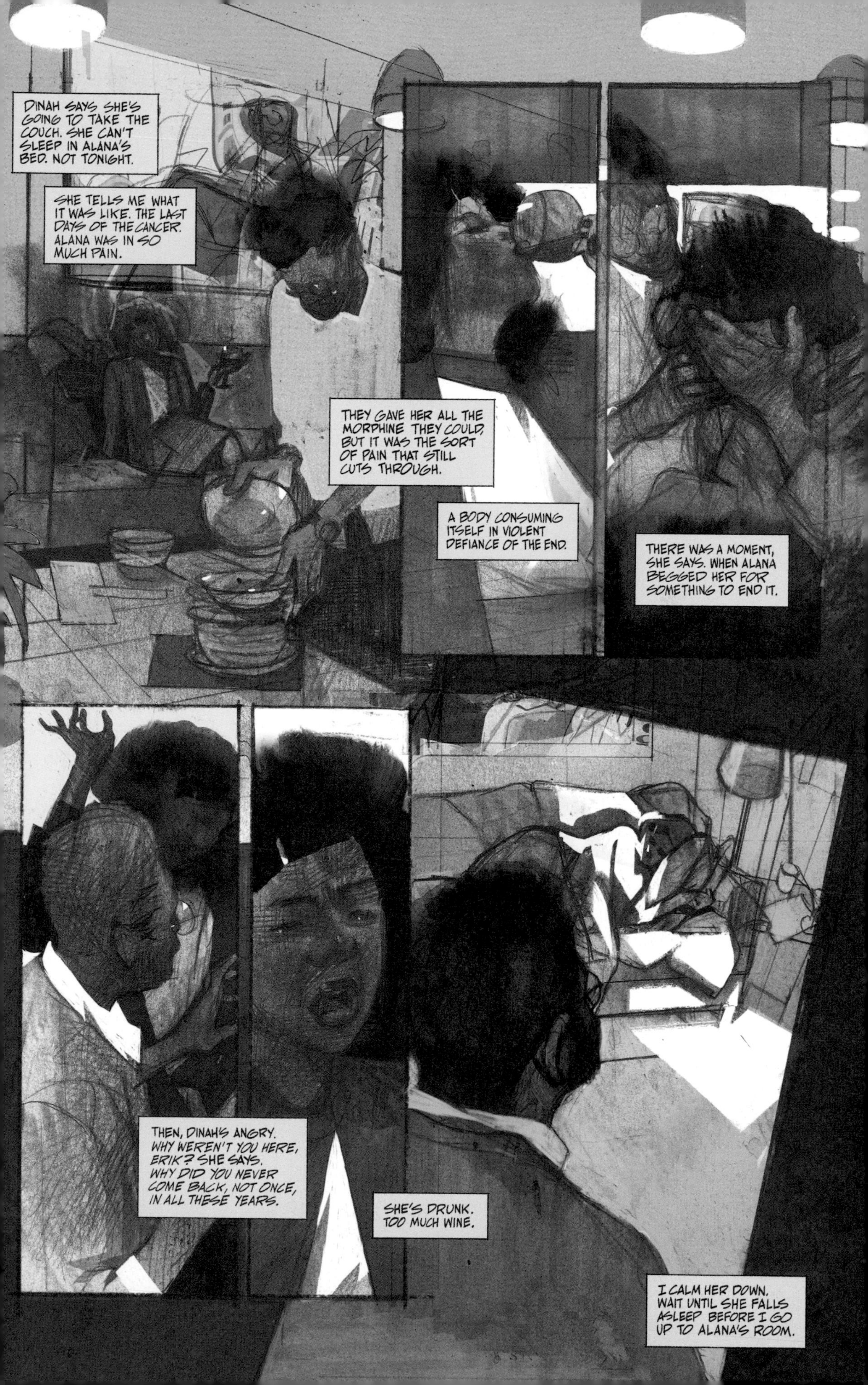
DINAH SAYS SHE'S GOING TO TAKE THE COUCH. SHE CAN'T SLEEP IN ALANA'S BED. NOT TONIGHT.
SHE TELLS ME WHAT IT WAS LIKE. THE LAST DAYS OF THE CANCER. ALANA WAS IN SO MUCH PAIN.
THEY GAVE HER ALL THE MORPHINE THEY COULD, BUT IT WAS THE SORT OF PAIN THAT STILL CUTS THROUGH.
A BODY CONSUMING ITSELF IN VIOLENT DEFIANCE OF THE END.
THERE WAS A MOMENT, SHE SAYS. WHEN ALANA BEGGED HER FOR SOMETHING TO END IT.
THEN, DINAH'S ANGRY. WHY WEREN'T YOU HERE, ERIK? SHE SAYS. WHY DID YOU NEVER COME BACK, NOT ONCE, IN ALL THESE YEARS.
SHE'S DRUNK. TOO MUCH WINE.
I CALM HER DOWN. WAIT UNTIL SHE FALLS ASLEEP BEFORE I GO UP TO ALANA'S ROOM.

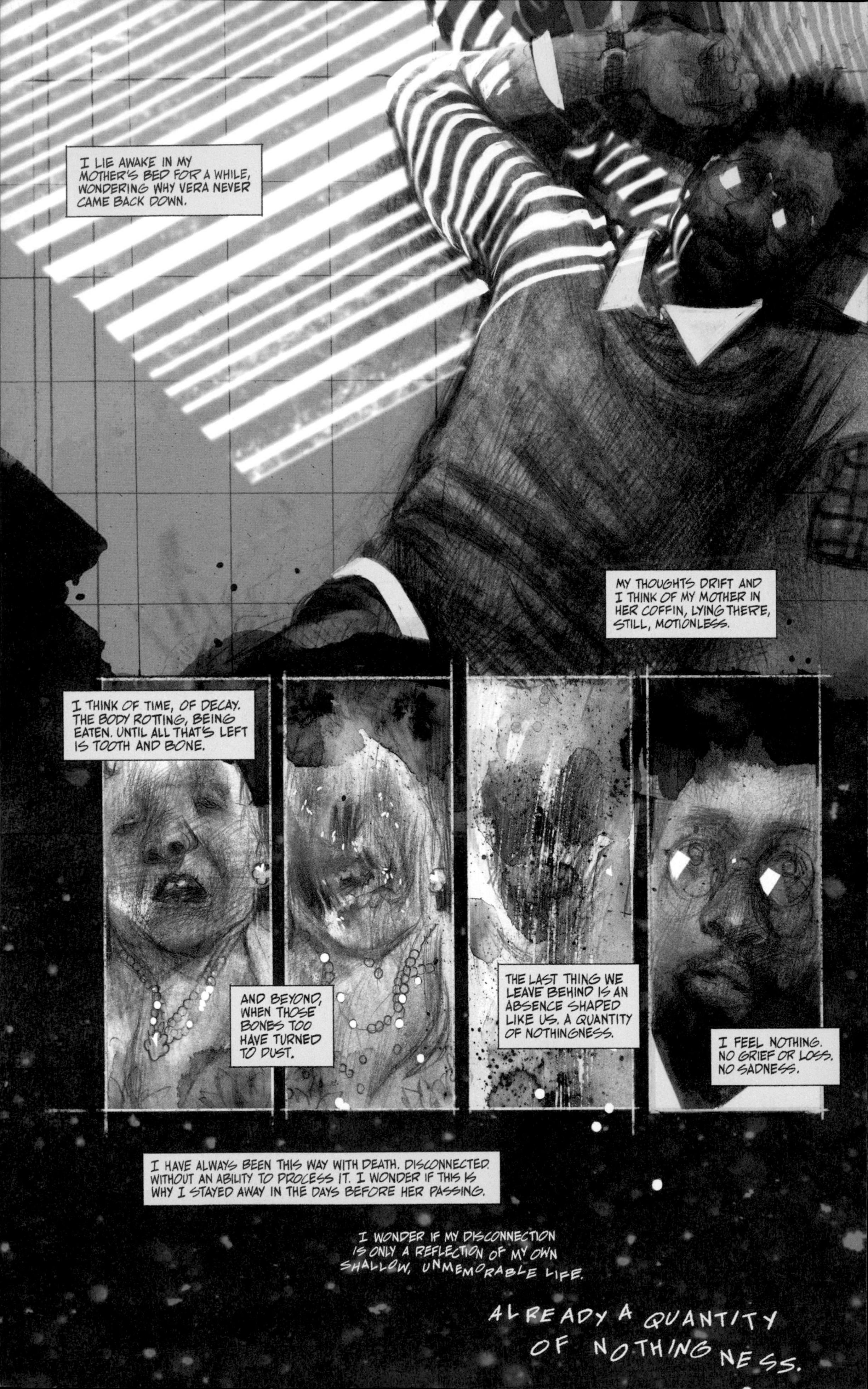

I LIE AWAKE IN MY MOTHER'S BED FOR A WHILE, WONDERING WHY VERA NEVER CAME BACK DOWN.
MY THOUGHTS DRIFT AND I THINK OF MY MOTHER IN HER COFFIN, LYING THERE, STILL, MOTIONLESS.
I THINK OF TIME, OF DECAY. THE BODY ROTTING, BEING EATEN. UNTIL ALL THAT'S LEFT IS TOOTH AND BONE.
AND BEYOND, WHEN THOSE BONES TOO HAVE TURNED TO DUST.
THE LAST THING WE LEAVE BEHIND IS AN ABSENCE SHAPED LIKE US. A QUANTITY OF NOTHINGNESS.
I FEEL NOTHING. NO GRIEF OR LOSS. NO SADNESS.
I HAVE ALWAYS BEEN THIS WAY WITH DEATH. DISCONNECTED. WITHOUT AN ABILITY TO PROCESS IT. I WONDER IF THIS IS WHY I STAYED AWAY IN THE DAYS BEFORE HER PASSING.
I WONDER IF MY DISCONNECTION IS ONLY A REFLECTION OF MY OWN SHALLOW, UNMEMORABLE LIFE.
ALREADY A QUANTITY OF NOTHINGNESS.

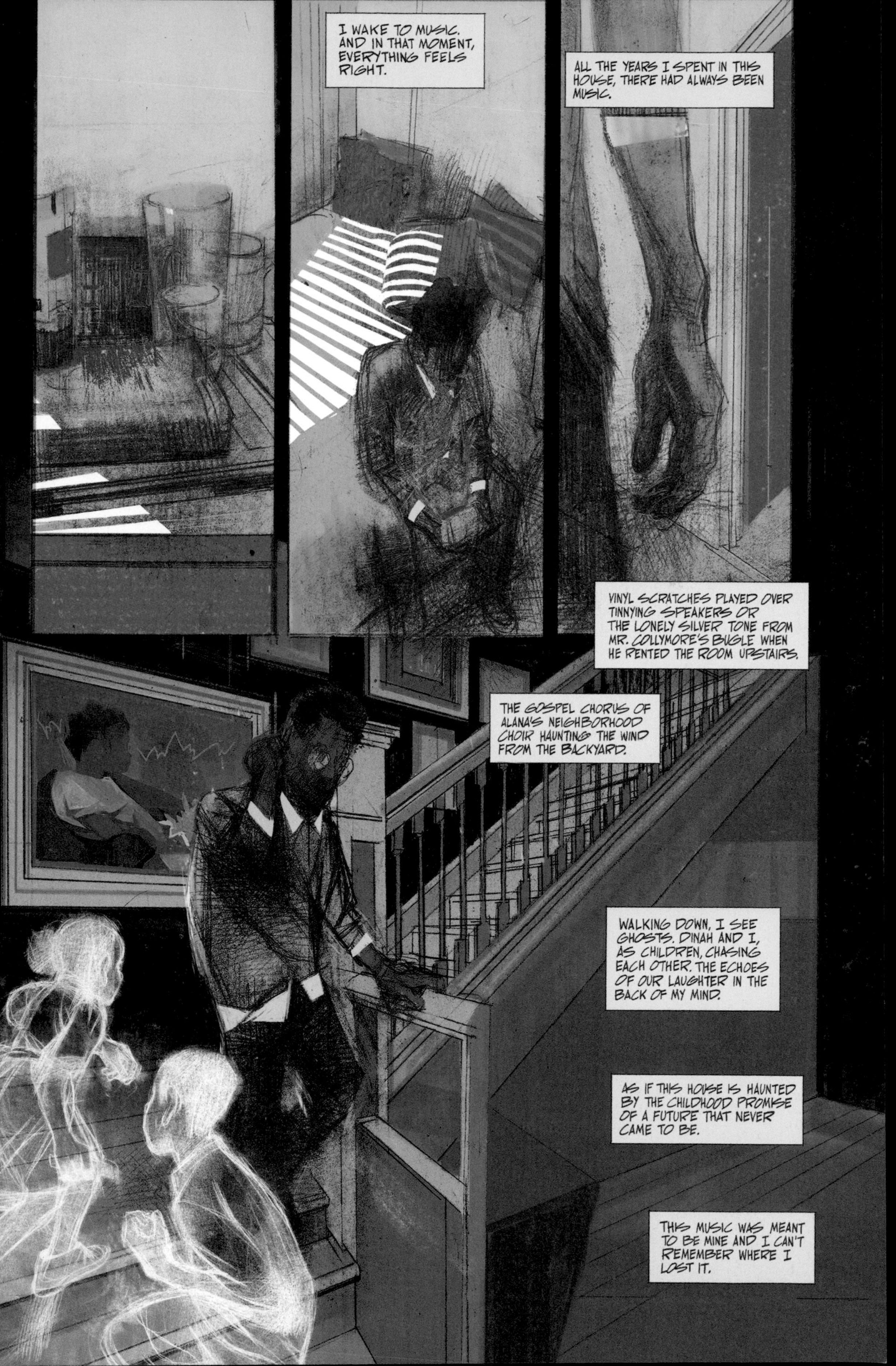
I WAKE TO MUSIC. AND IN THAT MOMENT, EVERYTHING FEELS RIGHT.
ALL THE YEARS I SPENT IN THIS HOUSE, THERE HAD ALWAYS BEEN MUSIC.
VINYL SCRATCHES PLAYED OVER TINNYING SPEAKERS OR THE LONELY SILVER TONE FROM MR. COLLYMORE'S BUGLE WHEN HE RENTED THE ROOM UPSTAIRS.
THE GOSPEL CHORUS OF ALANA'S NEIGHBORHOOD CHOIR HAUNTING THE WIND FROM THE BACKYARD.
WALKING DOWN, I SEE GHOSTS. DINAH AND I, AS CHILDREN, CHASING EACH OTHER. THE ECHOES OF OUR LAUGHTER IN THE BACK OF MY MIND.
AS IF THIS HOUSE IS HAUNTED BY THE CHILDHOOD PROMISE OF A FUTURE THAT NEVER CAME TO BE.
THIS MUSIC WAS MEANT TO BE MINE AND I CAN'T REMEMBER WHERE I LOST IT.

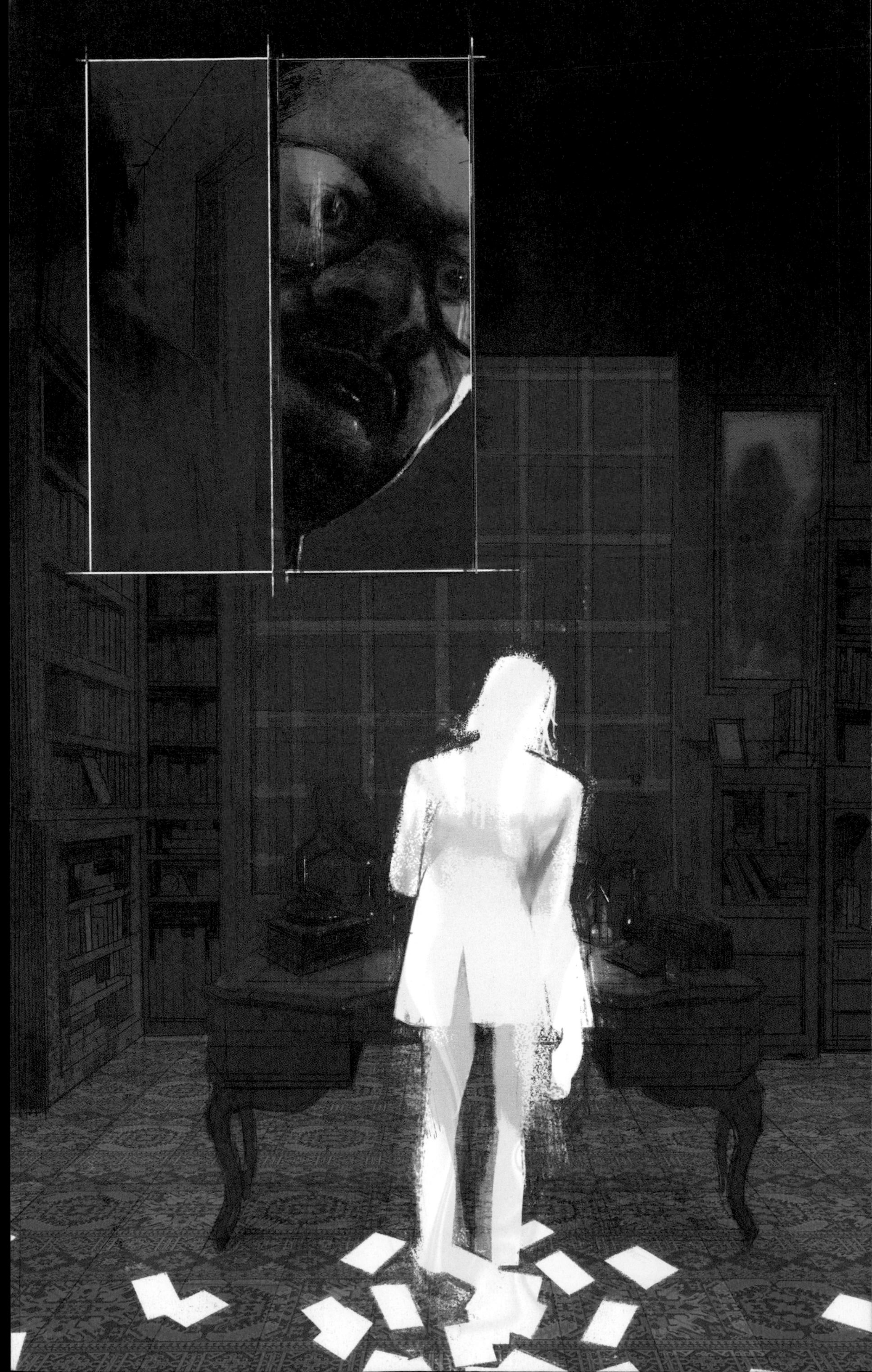

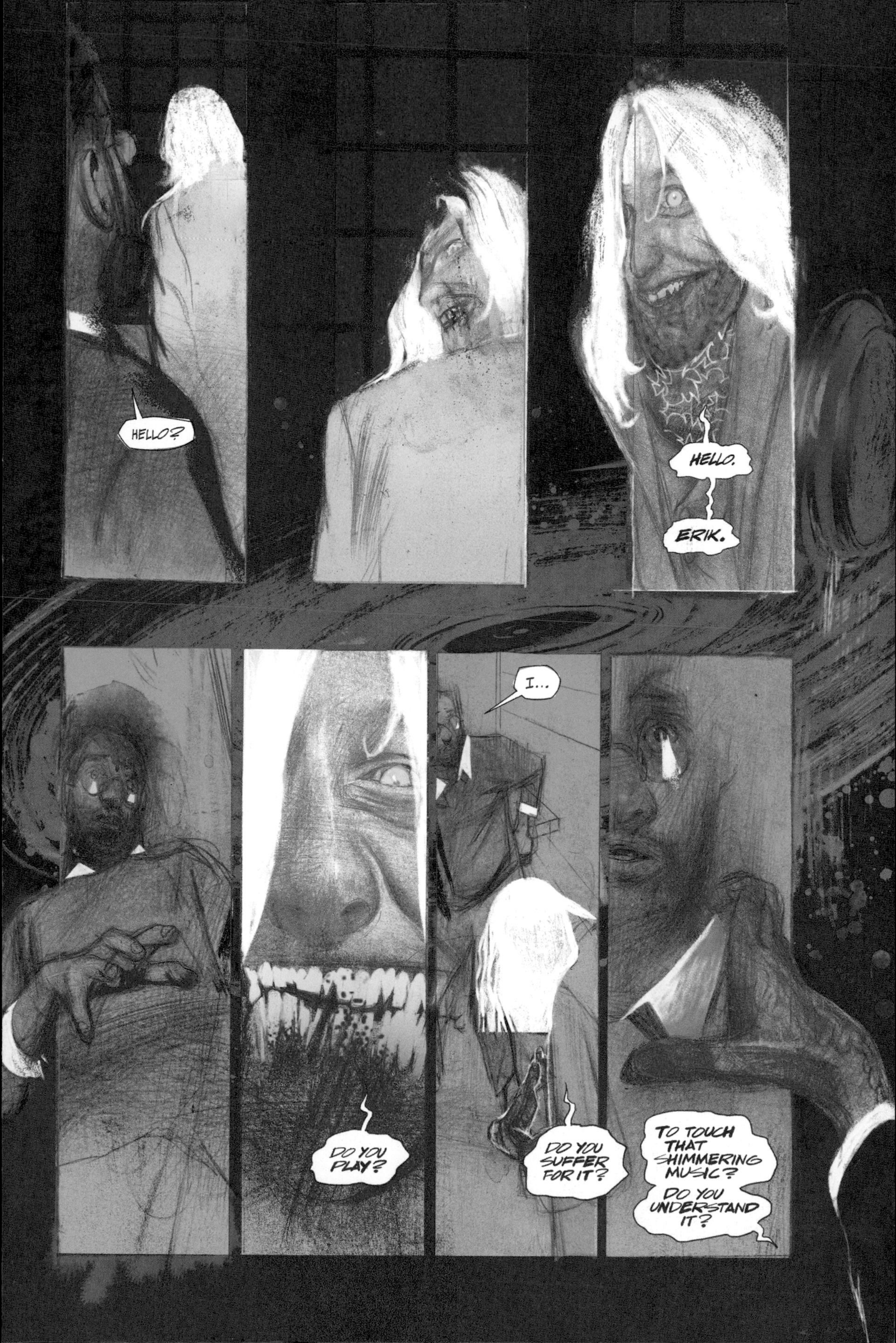
HELLO?
HELLO.
ERIK.
I...
DO YOU PLAY?
DO YOU SUFFER FOR IT?
TO TOUCH THAT SHIMMERING MUSIC?
DO YOU UNDERSTAND IT?

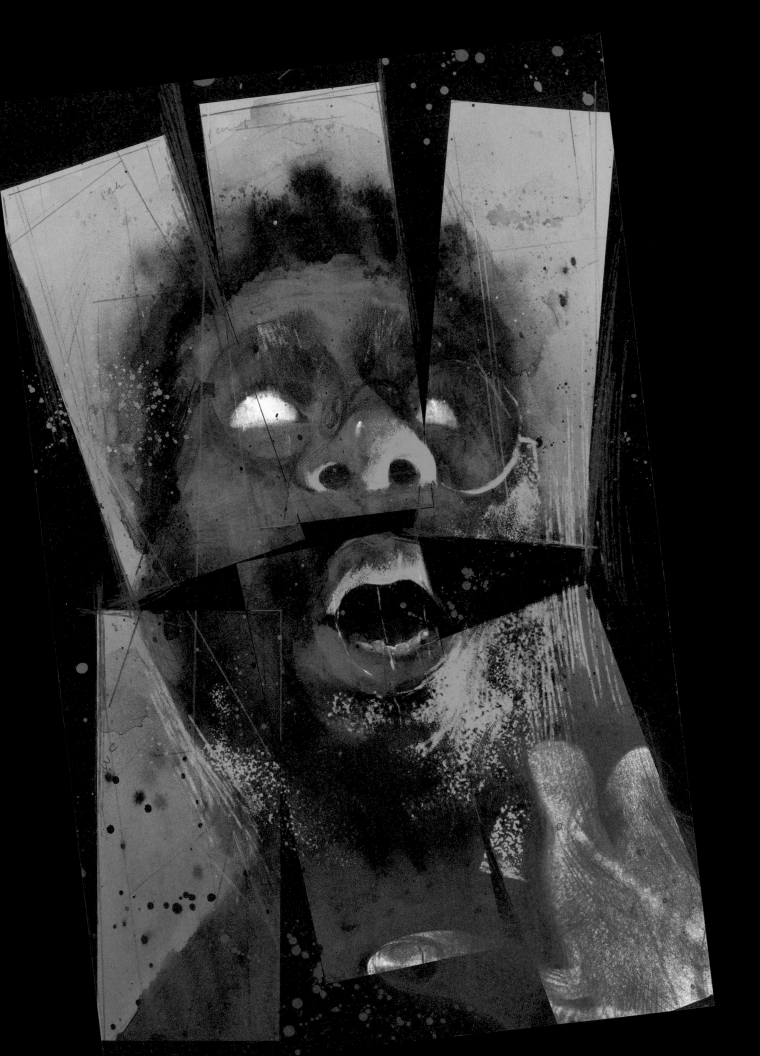

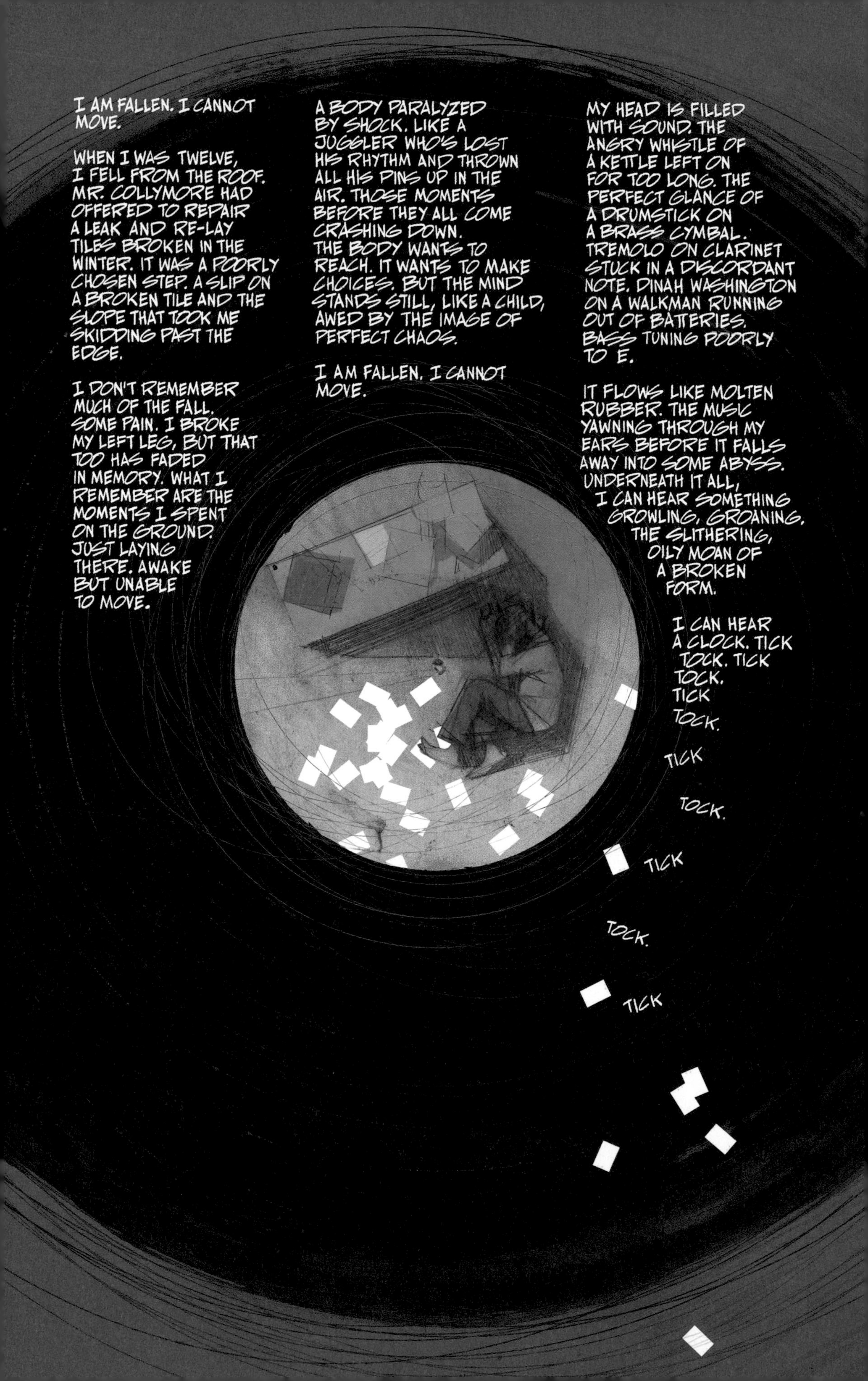

I AM FALLEN. I CANNOT MOVE.
WHEN I WAS TWELVE, I FELL FROM THE ROOF. MR. COLLYMORE HAD OFFERED TO REPAIR A LEAK AND RE-LAY TILES BROKEN IN THE WINTER. IT WAS A POORLY CHOSEN STEP. A SLIP ON A BROKEN TILE AND THE SLOPE THAT TOOK ME SKIDDING PAST THE EDGE.
I DON'T REMEMBER MUCH OF THE FALL. SOME PAIN. I BROKE MY LEFT LEG, BUT THAT TOO HAS FADED IN MEMORY. WHAT I REMEMBER ARE THE MOMENTS I SPENT ON THE GROUND. JUST LAYING THERE. AWAKE BUT UNABLE TO MOVE.
A BODY PARALYZED BY SHOCK. LIKE A JUGGLER WHO'S LOST HIS RHYTHM AND THROWN ALL HIS PINS UP IN THE AIR. THOSE MOMENTS BEFORE THEY ALL COME CRASHING DOWN.
THE BODY WANTS TO REACH. IT WANTS TO MAKE CHOICES. BUT THE MIND STANDS STILL, LIKE A CHILD, AWED BY THE IMAGE OF PERFECT CHAOS.
I AM FALLEN. I CANNOT MOVE.
MY HEAD IS FILLED WITH SOUND. THE ANGRY WHISTLE OF A KETTLE LEFT ON FOR TOO LONG. THE PERFECT GLANCE OF A DRUMSTICK ON A BRASS CYMBAL. TREMOLO ON CLARINET STUCK IN A DISCORDANT NOTE. DINAH WASHINGTON ON A WALKMAN RUNNING OUT OF BATTERIES. BASS TUNING POORLY TO E.
IT FLOWS LIKE MOLTEN RUBBER. THE MUSIC YAWNING THROUGH MY EARS BEFORE IT FALLS AWAY INTO SOME ABYSS. UNDERNEATH IT ALL, I CAN HEAR SOMETHING GROWLING, GROANING. THE SLITHERING, OILY MOAN OF A BROKEN FORM.
I CAN HEAR A CLOCK. TICK TOCK. TICK TOCK.
TICK
TOCK.
TICK
TOCK.
TICK
TOCK.
TICK

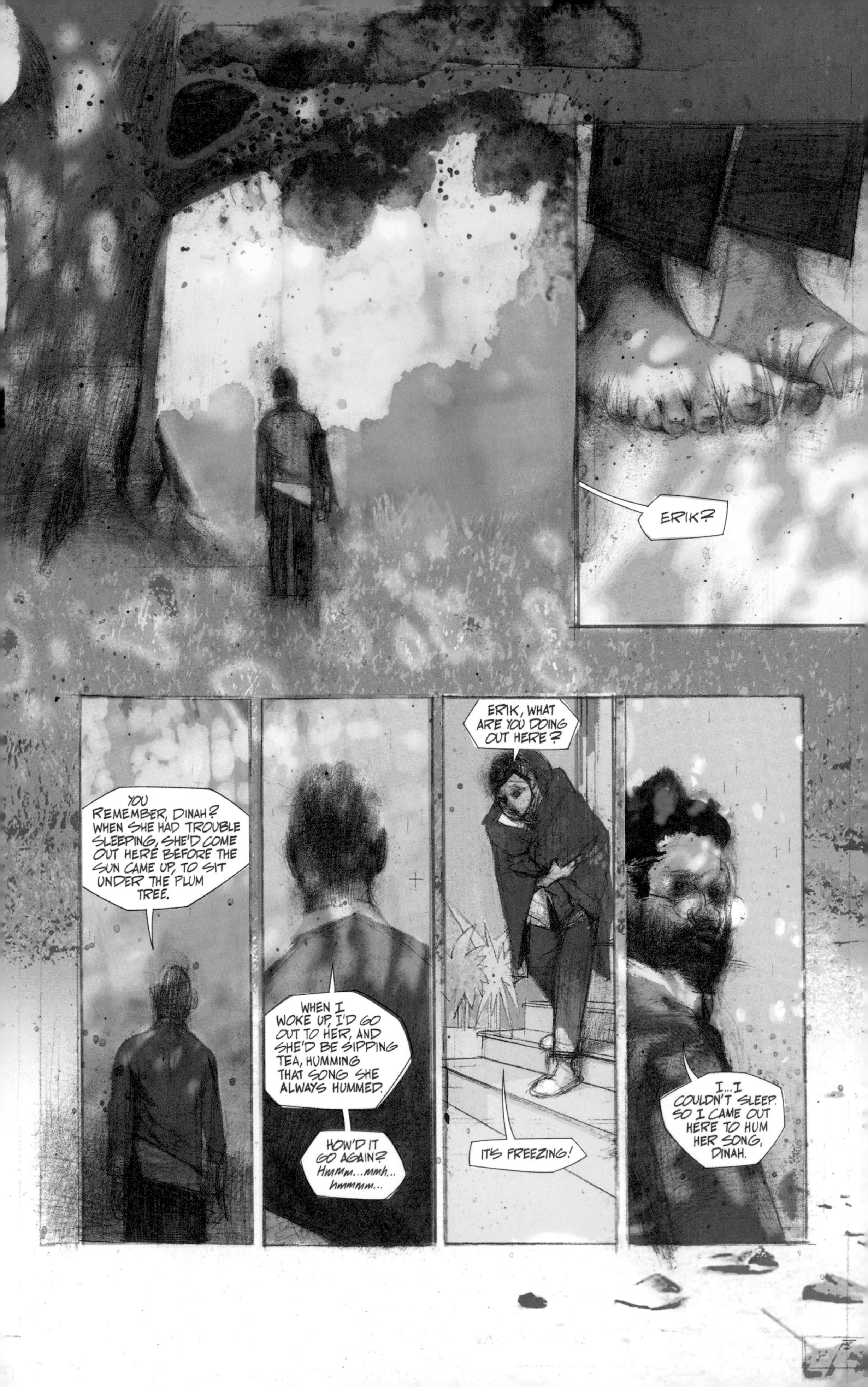
ERIK?
YOU REMEMBER, DINAH? WHEN SHE HAD TROUBLE SLEEPING, SHE'D COME OUT HERE BEFORE THE SUN CAME UP, TO SIT UNDER THE PLUM TREE.
WHEN I WOKE UP, I'D GO OUT TO HER, AND SHE'D BE SIPPING TEA, HUMMING THAT SONG SHE ALWAYS HUMMED.
HOW'D IT GO AGAIN? Hmmm...mmh... hmmmm...
ERIK, WHAT ARE YOU DOING OUT HERE?
IT'S FREEZING!
I...I COULDN'T SLEEP. SO I CAME OUT HERE TO HUM HER SONG, DINAH.

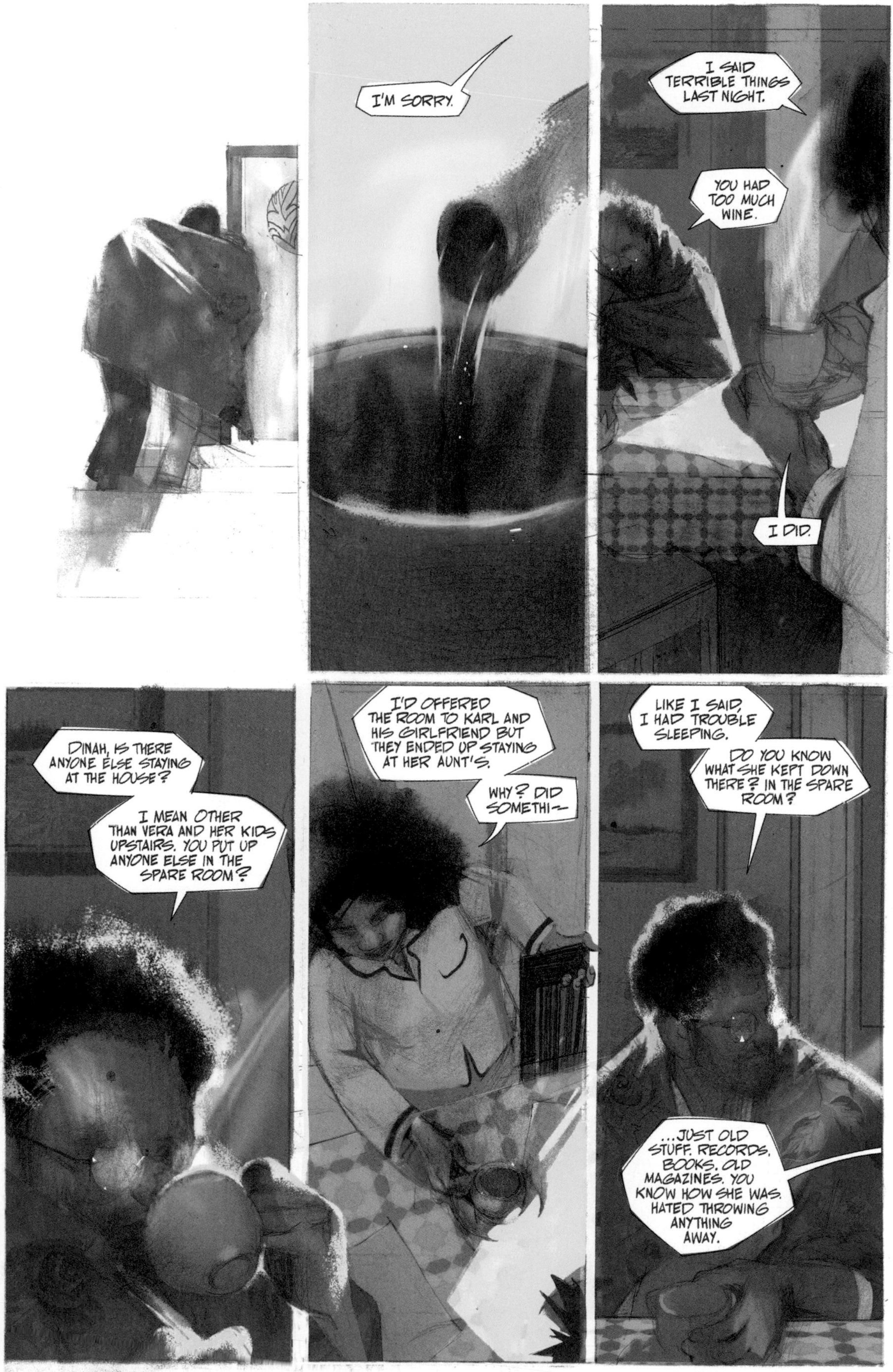
I'M SORRY.
I SAID TERRIBLE THINGS LAST NIGHT.
YOU HAD TOO MUCH WINE.
I DID.
DINAH, IS THERE ANYONE ELSE STAYING AT THE HOUSE?
I MEAN OTHER THAN VERA AND HER KIDS UPSTAIRS. YOU PUT UP ANYONE ELSE IN THE SPARE ROOM?
I'D OFFERED THE ROOM TO KARL AND HIS GIRLFRIEND BUT THEY ENDED UP STAYING AT HER AUNT'S.
WHY? DID SOMETHI--
LIKE I SAID, I HAD TROUBLE SLEEPING.
DO YOU KNOW WHAT SHE KEPT DOWN THERE? IN THE SPARE ROOM?
...JUST OLD STUFF. RECORDS, BOOKS. OLD MAGAZINES. YOU KNOW HOW SHE WAS. HATED THROWING ANYTHING AWAY.

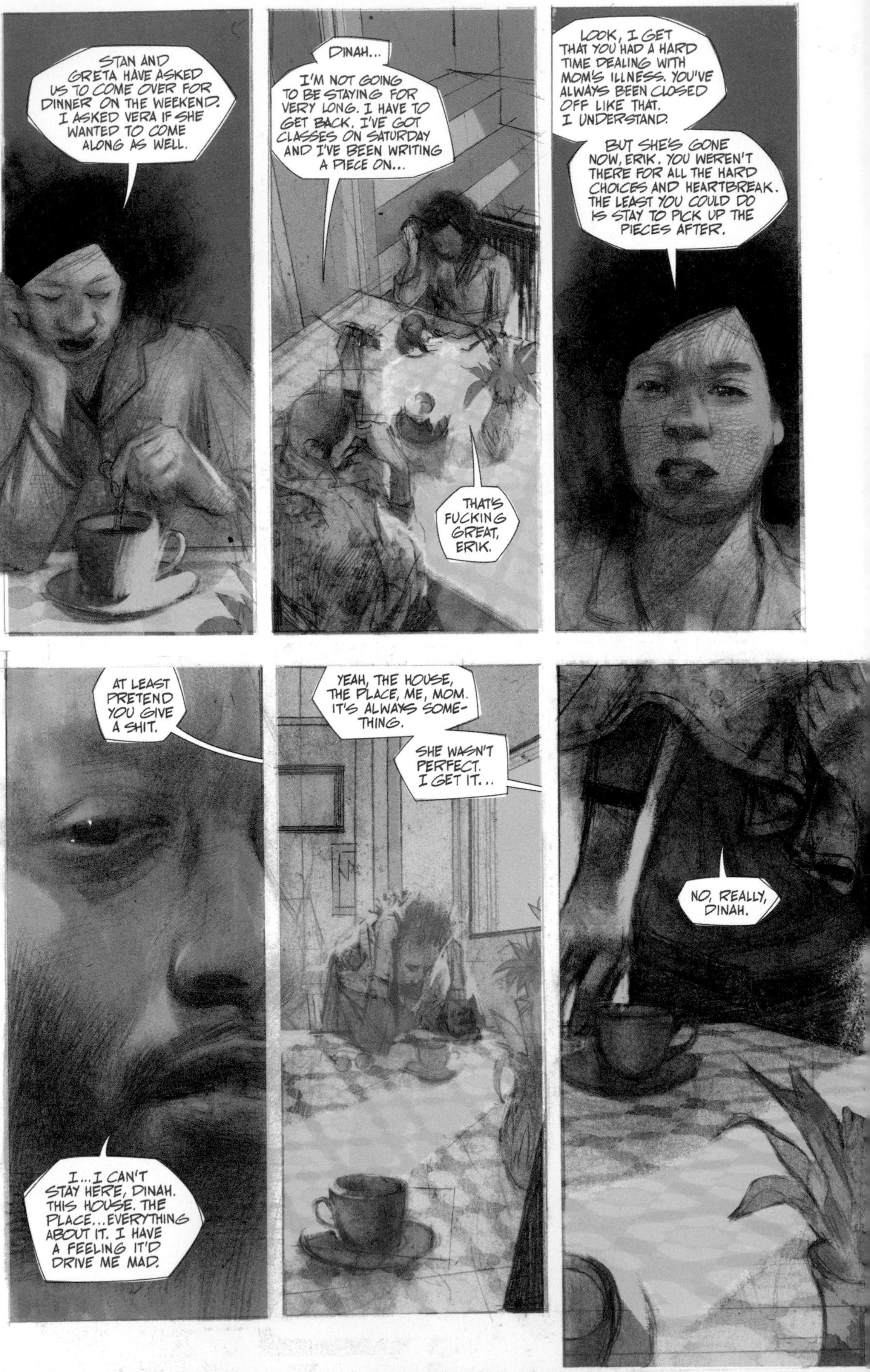
STAN AND GRETA HAVE ASKED US TO COME OVER FOR DINNER ON THE WEEKEND. I ASKED VERA IF SHE WANTED TO COME ALONG AS WELL.
DINAH...
I'M NOT GOING TO BE STAYING FOR VERY LONG. I HAVE TO GET BACK. I'VE GOT CLASSES ON SATURDAY AND I'VE BEEN WRITING A PIECE ON...
THAT'S FUCKING GREAT, ERIK.
LOOK, I GET THAT YOU HAD A HARD TIME DEALING WITH MOM'S ILLNESS. YOU'VE ALWAYS BEEN CLOSED OFF LIKE THAT. I UNDERSTAND.
BUT SHE'S GONE NOW, ERIK. YOU WEREN'T THERE FOR ALL THE HARD CHOICES AND HEARTBREAK. THE LEAST YOU COULD DO IS STAY TO PICK UP THE PIECES AFTER.
AT LEAST PRETEND YOU GIVE A SHIT.
I...I CAN'T STAY HERE, DINAH. THIS HOUSE. THE PLACE...EVERYTHING ABOUT IT. I HAVE A FEELING IT'D DRIVE ME MAD.
YEAH, THE HOUSE, THE PLACE, ME, MOM. IT'S ALWAYS SOME-THING.
SHE WASN'T PERFECT. I GET IT...
NO, REALLY, DINAH.

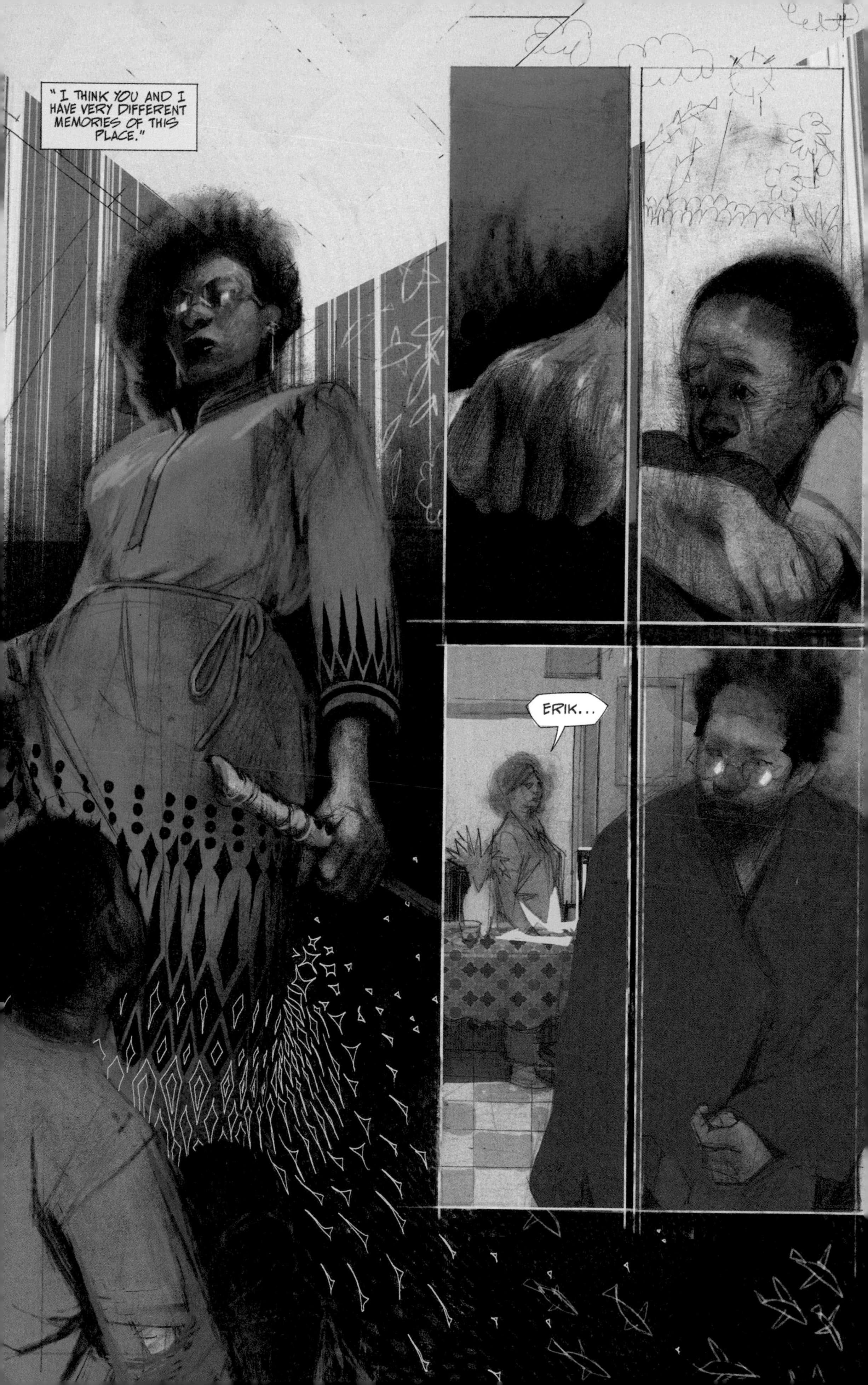
"I THINK YOU AND I HAVE VERY DIFFERENT MEMORIES OF THIS PLACE."
ERIK...

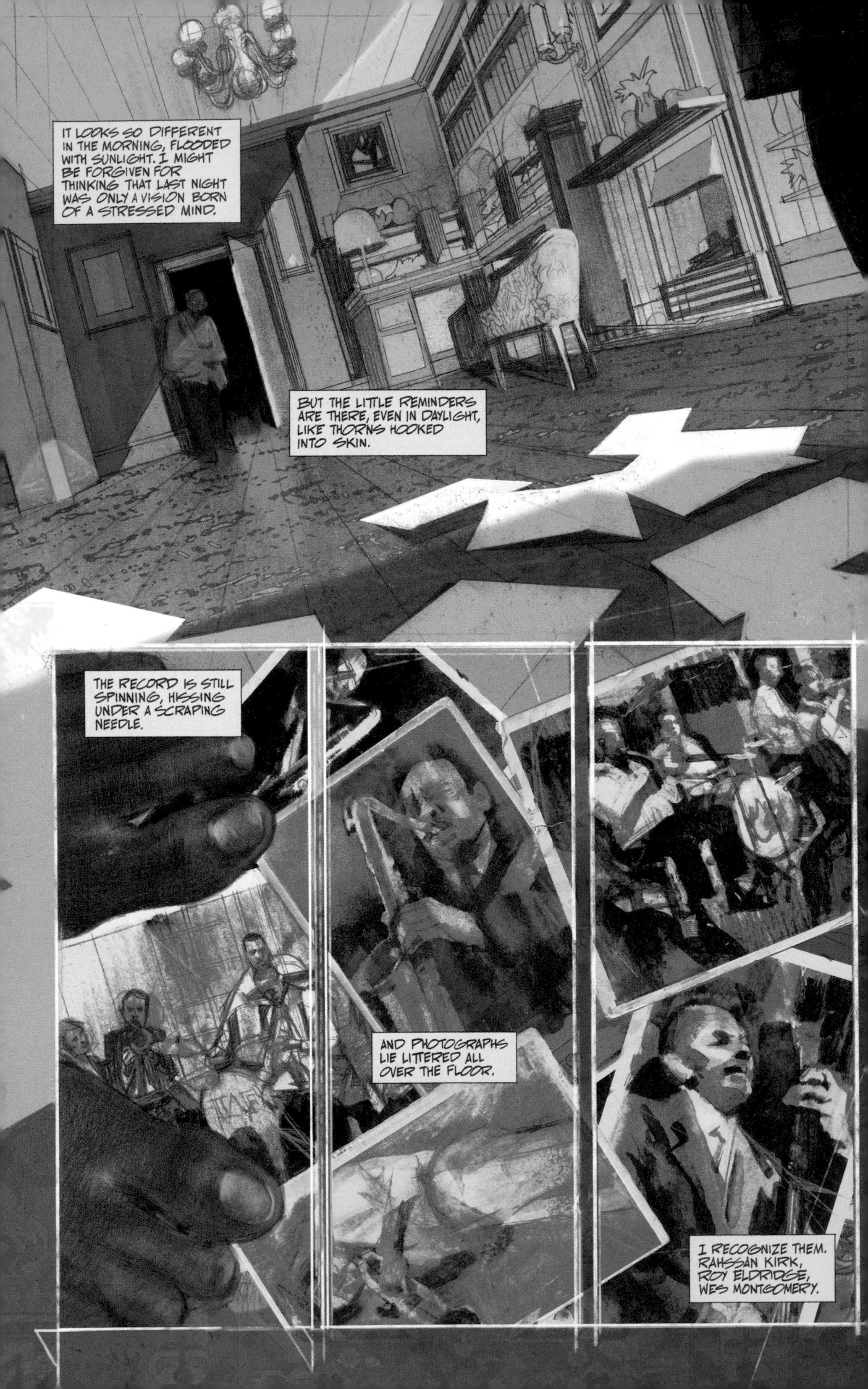
IT LOOKS SO DIFFERENT IN THE MORNING, FLOODED WITH SUNLIGHT. I MIGHT BE FORGIVEN FOR THINKING THAT LAST NIGHT WAS ONLY A VISION BORN OF A STRESSED MIND.
BUT THE LITTLE REMINDERS ARE THERE, EVEN IN DAYLIGHT, LIKE THORNS HOOKED INTO SKIN.
THE RECORD IS STILL SPINNING, HISSING UNDER A SCRAPING NEEDLE.
AND PHOTOGRAPHS LIE LITTERED ALL OVER THE FLOOR.
I RECOGNIZE THEM. RAHSSAN KIRK, ROY ELDRIDGE, WES MONTGOMERY.

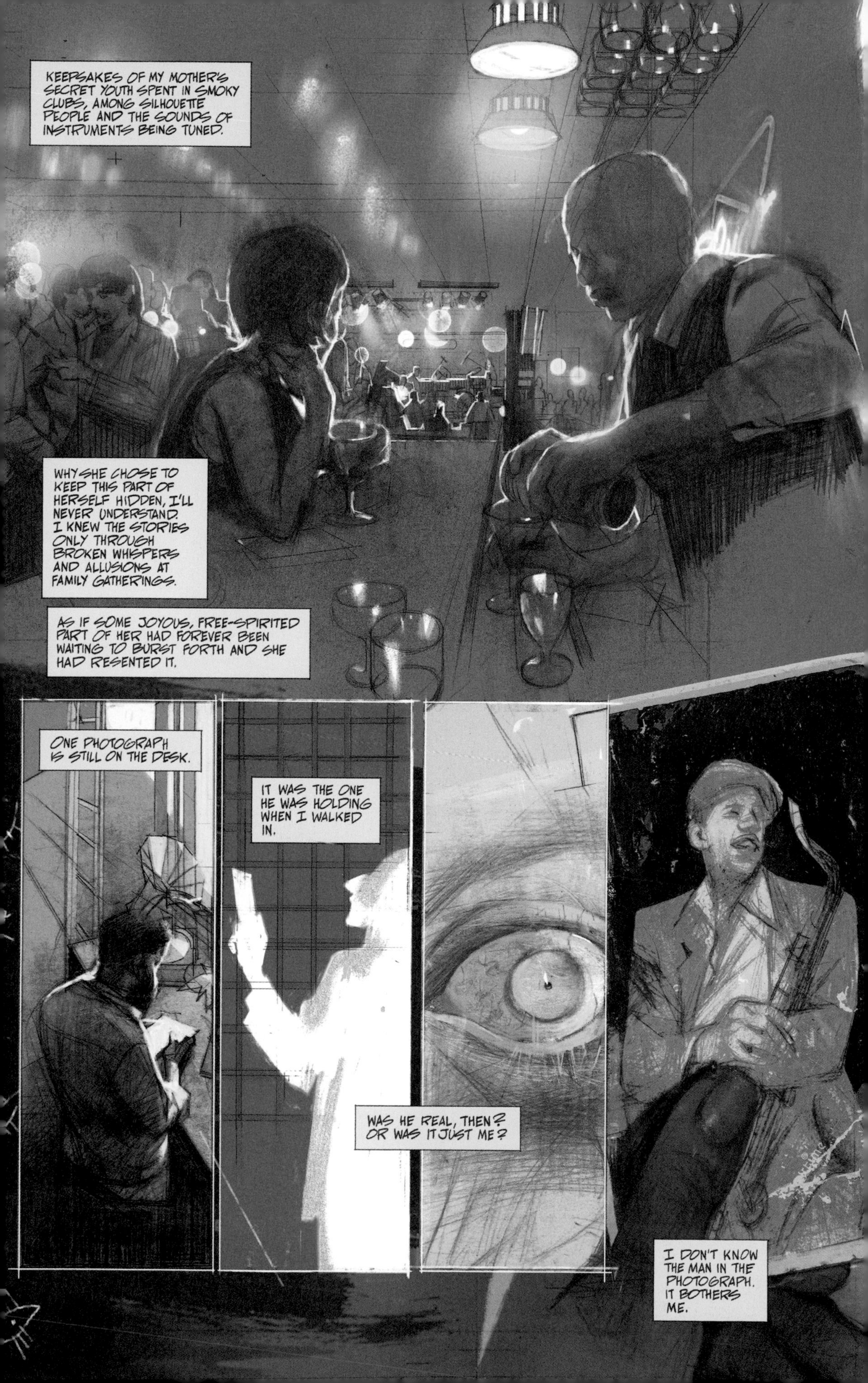
KEEPSAKES OF MY MOTHER'S SECRET YOUTH SPENT IN SMOKY CLUBS, AMONG SILHOUETTE PEOPLE AND THE SOUNDS OF INSTRUMENTS BEING TUNED.
WHY SHE CHOSE TO KEEP THIS PART OF HERSELF HIDDEN, I'LL NEVER UNDERSTAND. I KNEW THE STORIES ONLY THROUGH BROKEN WHISPERS AND ALLUSIONS AT FAMILY GATHERINGS.
AS IF SOME JOYOUS, FREE-SPIRITED PART OF HER HAD FOREVER BEEN WAITING TO BURST FORTH AND SHE HAD RESENTED IT.
ONE PHOTOGRAPH IS STILL ON THE DESK.
IT WAS THE ONE HE WAS HOLDING WHEN I WALKED IN.
WAS HE REAL, THEN? OR WAS IT JUST ME?
I DON'T KNOW THE MAN IN THE PHOTOGRAPH. IT BOTHERS ME.

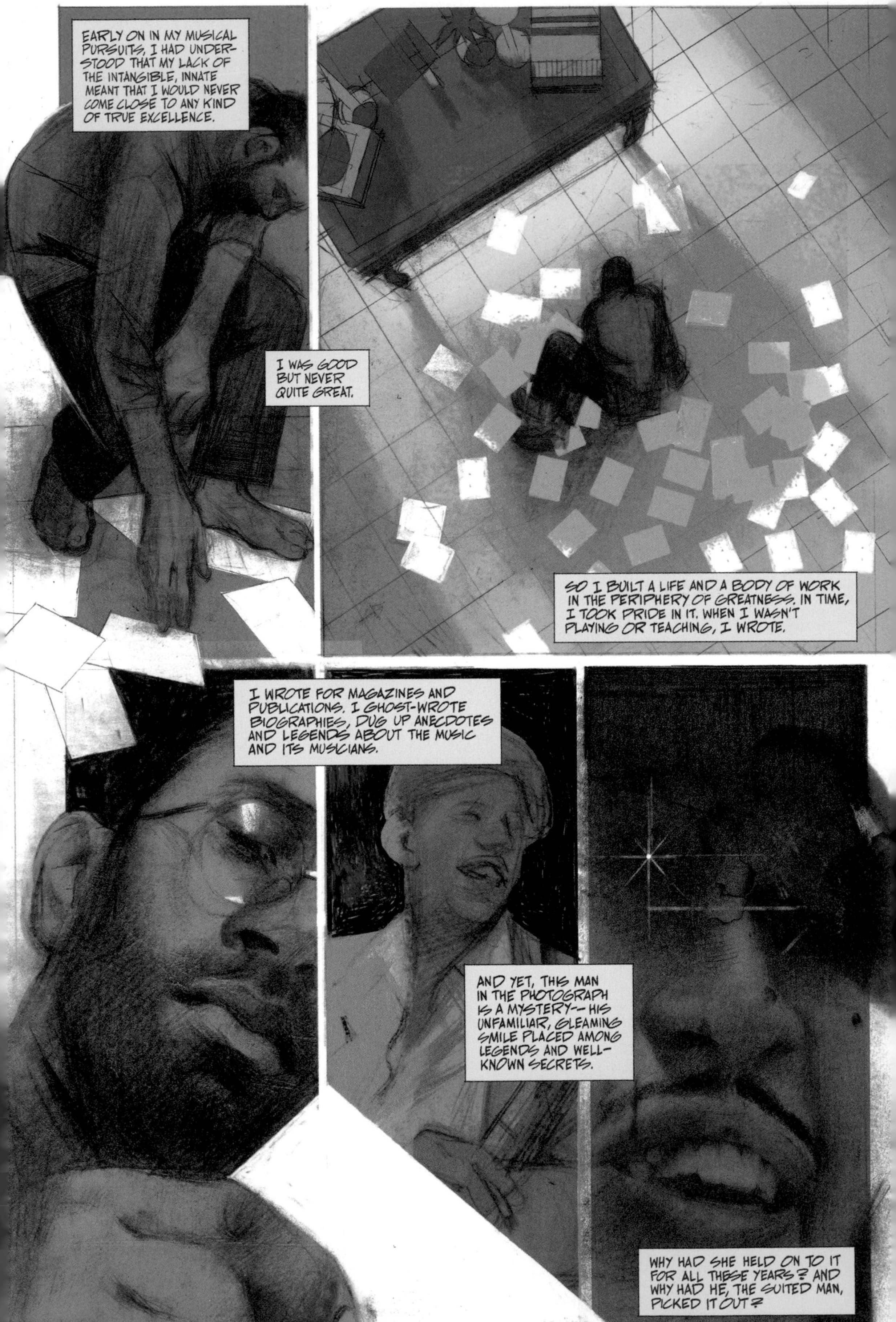
EARLY ON IN MY MUSICAL PURSUITS, I HAD UNDERSTOOD THAT MY LACK OF THE INTANGIBLE, INNATE MEANT THAT I WOULD NEVER COME CLOSE TO ANY KIND OF TRUE EXCELLENCE.
I WAS GOOD BUT NEVER QUITE GREAT.
SO I BUILT A LIFE AND A BODY OF WORK IN THE PERIPHERY OF GREATNESS. IN TIME, I TOOK PRIDE IN IT. WHEN I WASN'T PLAYING OR TEACHING, I WROTE.
I WROTE FOR MAGAZINES AND PUBLICATIONS. I GHOST-WROTE BIOGRAPHIES, DUG UP ANECDOTES AND LEGENDS ABOUT THE MUSIC AND ITS MUSICIANS.
AND YET, THIS MAN IN THE PHOTOGRAPH IS A MYSTERY-- HIS UNFAMILIAR, GLEAMING SMILE PLACED AMONG LEGENDS AND WELL-KNOWN SECRETS.
WHY HAD SHE HELD ON TO IT FOR ALL THESE YEARS? AND WHY HAD HE, THE SUITED MAN, PICKED IT OUT?

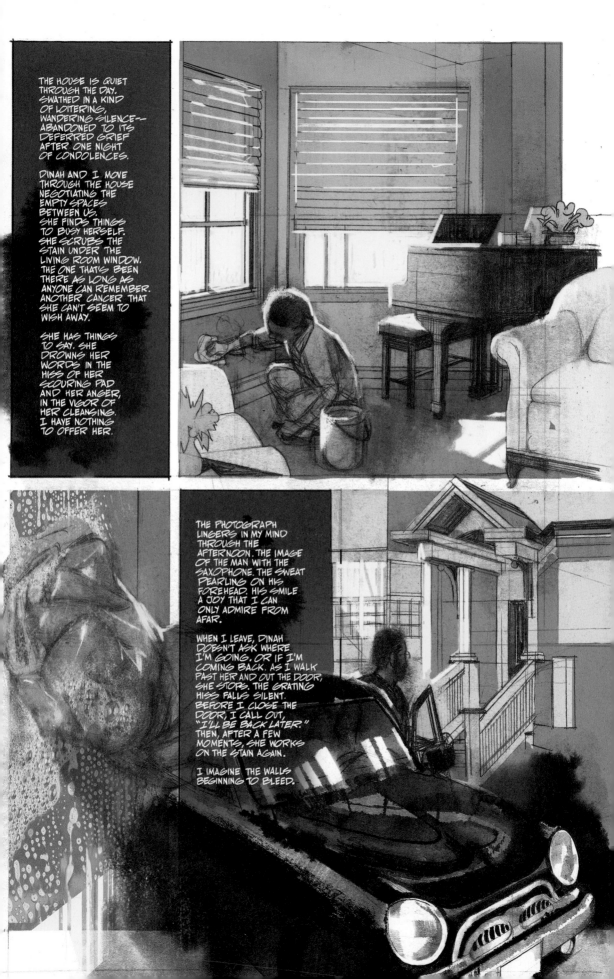

THE HOUSE IS QUIET THROUGH THE DAY. SWATHED IN A KIND OF LOITERING, WANDERING SILENCE-- ABANDONED TO ITS DEFERRED GRIEF AFTER ONE NIGHT OF CONDOLENCES.

DINAH AND I MOVE THROUGH THE HOUSE NEGOTIATING THE EMPTY SPACES BETWEEN US. SHE FINDS THINGS TO BUSY HERSELF. SHE SCRUBS THE STAIN UNDER THE LIVING ROOM WINDOW. THE ONE THAT'S BEEN THERE AS LONG AS ANYONE CAN REMEMBER. ANOTHER CANCER THAT SHE CAN'T SEEM TO WISH AWAY.

SHE HAS THINGS TO SAY. SHE DROWNS HER WORDS IN THE HISS OF HER SCOURING PAD AND HER ANGER, IN THE VIGOR OF HER CLEANSING. I HAVE NOTHING TO OFFER HER.

THE PHOTOGRAPH LINGERS IN MY MIND THROUGH THE AFTERNOON. THE IMAGE OF THE MAN WITH THE SAXOPHONE. THE SWEAT PEARLING ON HIS FOREHEAD. HIS SMILE A JOY THAT I CAN ONLY ADMIRE FROM AFAR.

WHEN I LEAVE, DINAH DOESN'T ASK WHERE I'M GOING. OR IF I'M COMING BACK. AS I WALK PAST HER AND OUT THE DOOR, SHE STOPS. THE GRATING HISS FALLS SILENT. BEFORE I CLOSE THE DOOR, I CALL OUT, "I'LL BE BACK LATER." THEN, AFTER A FEW MOMENTS, SHE WORKS ON THE STAIN AGAIN.

I IMAGINE THE WALLS BEGINNING TO BLEED.

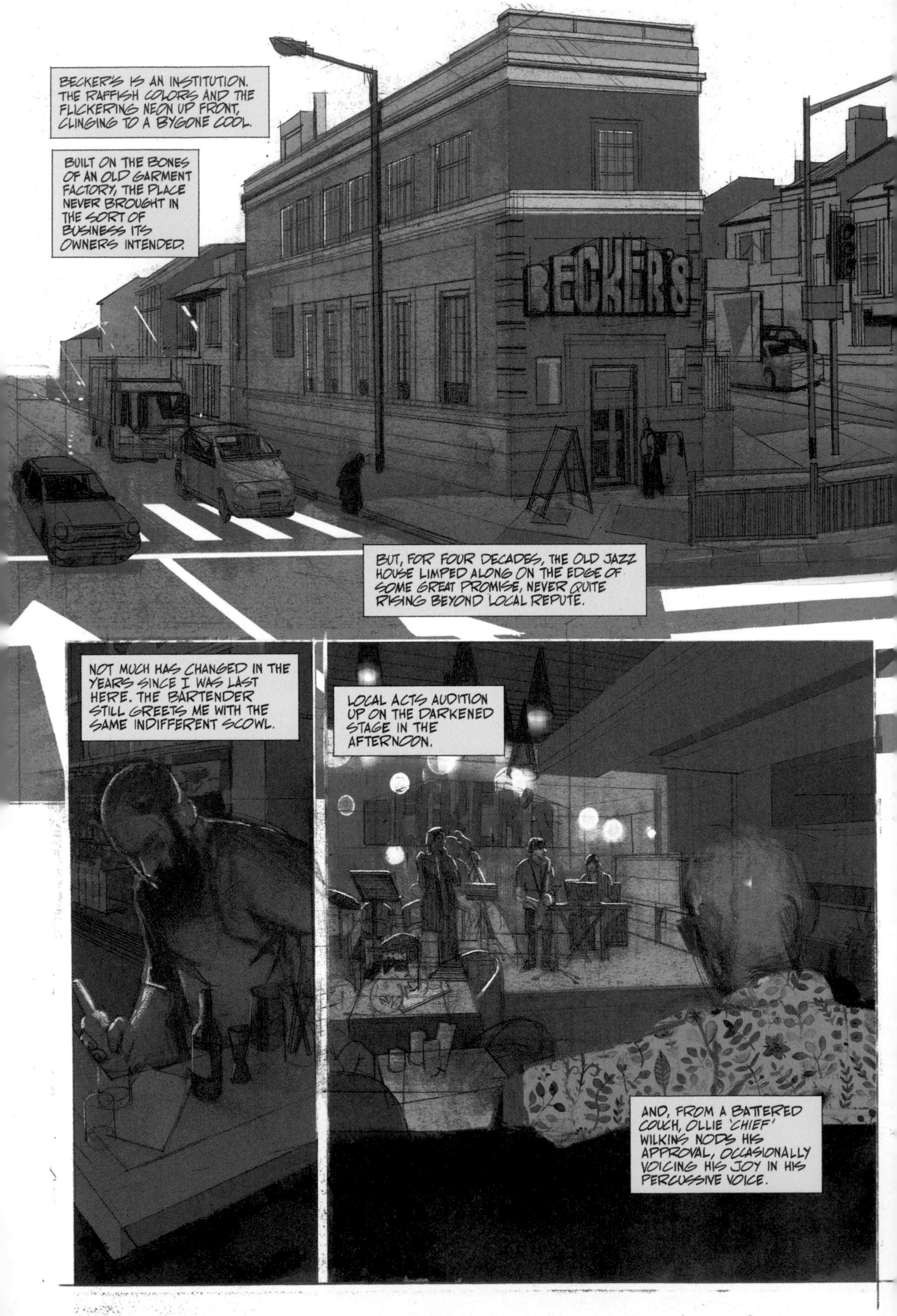
BECKER'S IS AN INSTITUTION. THE RAFFISH COLORS AND THE FLICKERING NEON UP FRONT, CLINGING TO A BYGONE COOL.
BUILT ON THE BONES OF AN OLD GARMENT FACTORY, THE PLACE NEVER BROUGHT IN THE SORT OF BUSINESS ITS OWNERS INTENDED.
BECKER'S
BUT, FOR FOUR DECADES, THE OLD JAZZ HOUSE LIMPED ALONG ON THE EDGE OF SOME GREAT PROMISE, NEVER QUITE RISING BEYOND LOCAL REPUTE.
NOT MUCH HAS CHANGED IN THE YEARS SINCE I WAS LAST HERE. THE BARTENDER STILL GREETS ME WITH THE SAME INDIFFERENT SCOWL.
LOCAL ACTS AUDITION UP ON THE DARKENED STAGE IN THE AFTERNOON.
AND, FROM A BATTERED COUCH, OLLIE 'CHIEF' WILKINS NODS HIS APPROVAL, OCCASIONALLY VOICING HIS JOY IN HIS PERCUSSIVE VOICE.

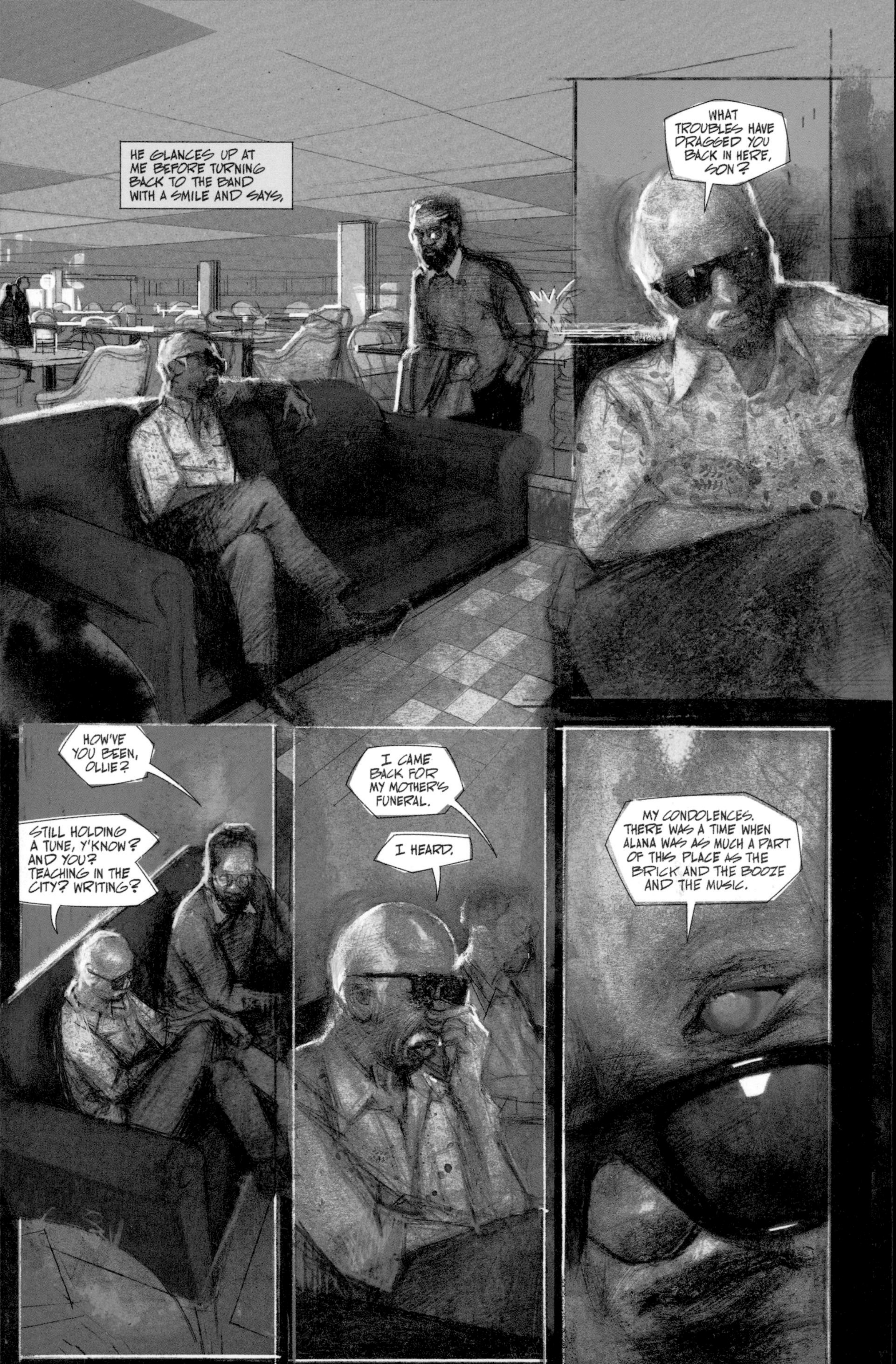
HE GLANCES UP AT ME BEFORE TURNING BACK TO THE BAND WITH A SMILE AND SAYS,
WHAT TROUBLES HAVE DRAGGED YOU BACK IN HERE, SON?
HOW'VE YOU BEEN, OLLIE?
STILL HOLDING A TUNE, Y'KNOW? AND YOU? TEACHING IN THE CITY? WRITING?
I CAME BACK FOR MY MOTHER'S FUNERAL.
I HEARD.
MY CONDOLENCES. THERE WAS A TIME WHEN ALANA WAS AS MUCH A PART OF THIS PLACE AS THE BRICK AND THE BOOZE AND THE MUSIC.

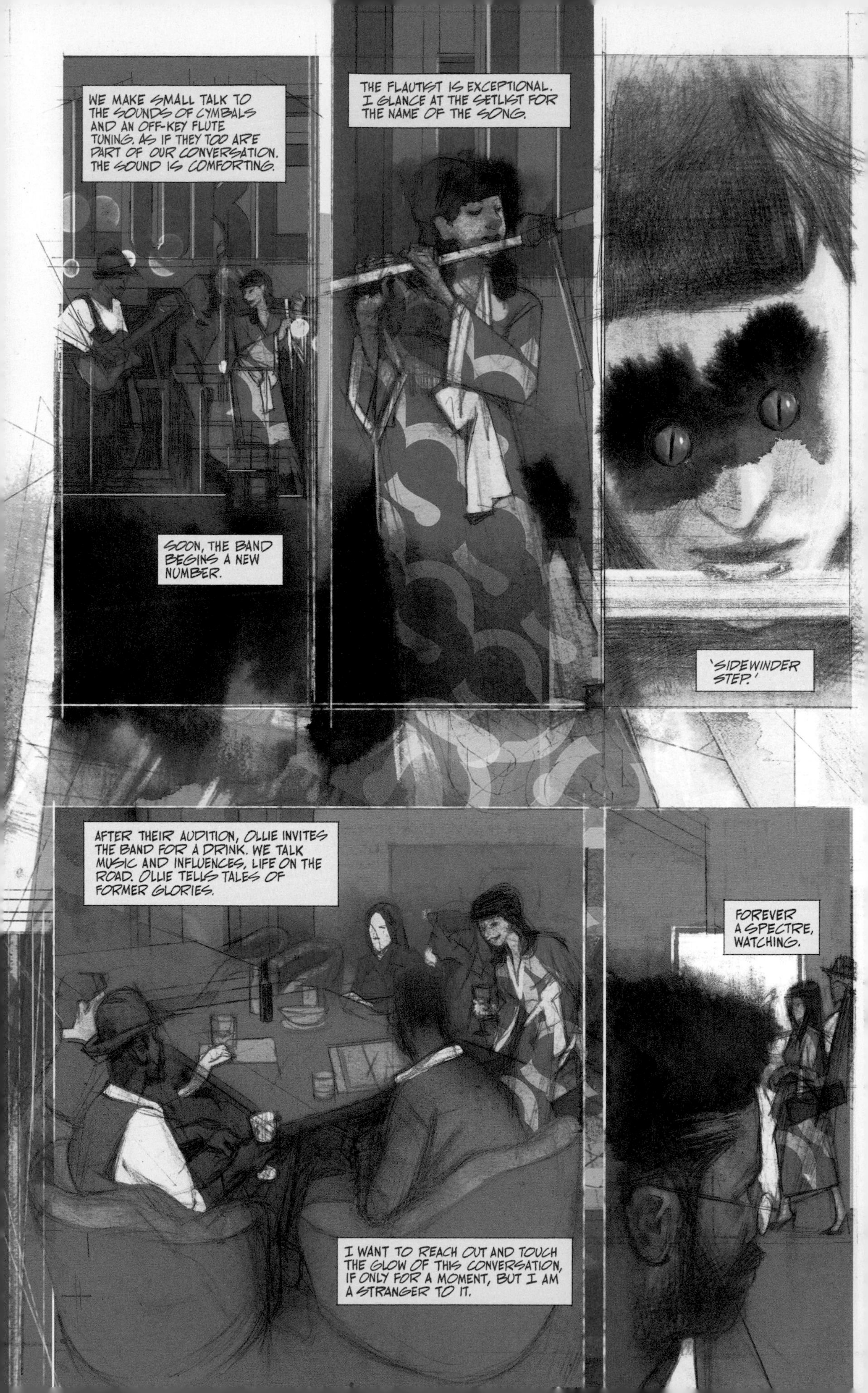
WE MAKE SMALL TALK TO THE SOUNDS OF CYMBALS AND AN OFF-KEY FLUTE TUNING. AS IF THEY TOO ARE PART OF OUR CONVERSATION. THE SOUND IS COMFORTING.
SOON, THE BAND BEGINS A NEW NUMBER.
THE FLAUTIST IS EXCEPTIONAL. I GLANCE AT THE SETLIST FOR THE NAME OF THE SONG.
'SIDEWINDER STEP.'
AFTER THEIR AUDITION, OLLIE INVITES THE BAND FOR A DRINK. WE TALK MUSIC AND INFLUENCES, LIFE ON THE ROAD. OLLIE TELLS TALES OF FORMER GLORIES.
I WANT TO REACH OUT AND TOUCH THE GLOW OF THIS CONVERSATION, IF ONLY FOR A MOMENT, BUT I AM A STRANGER TO IT.
FOREVER A SPECTRE, WATCHING.

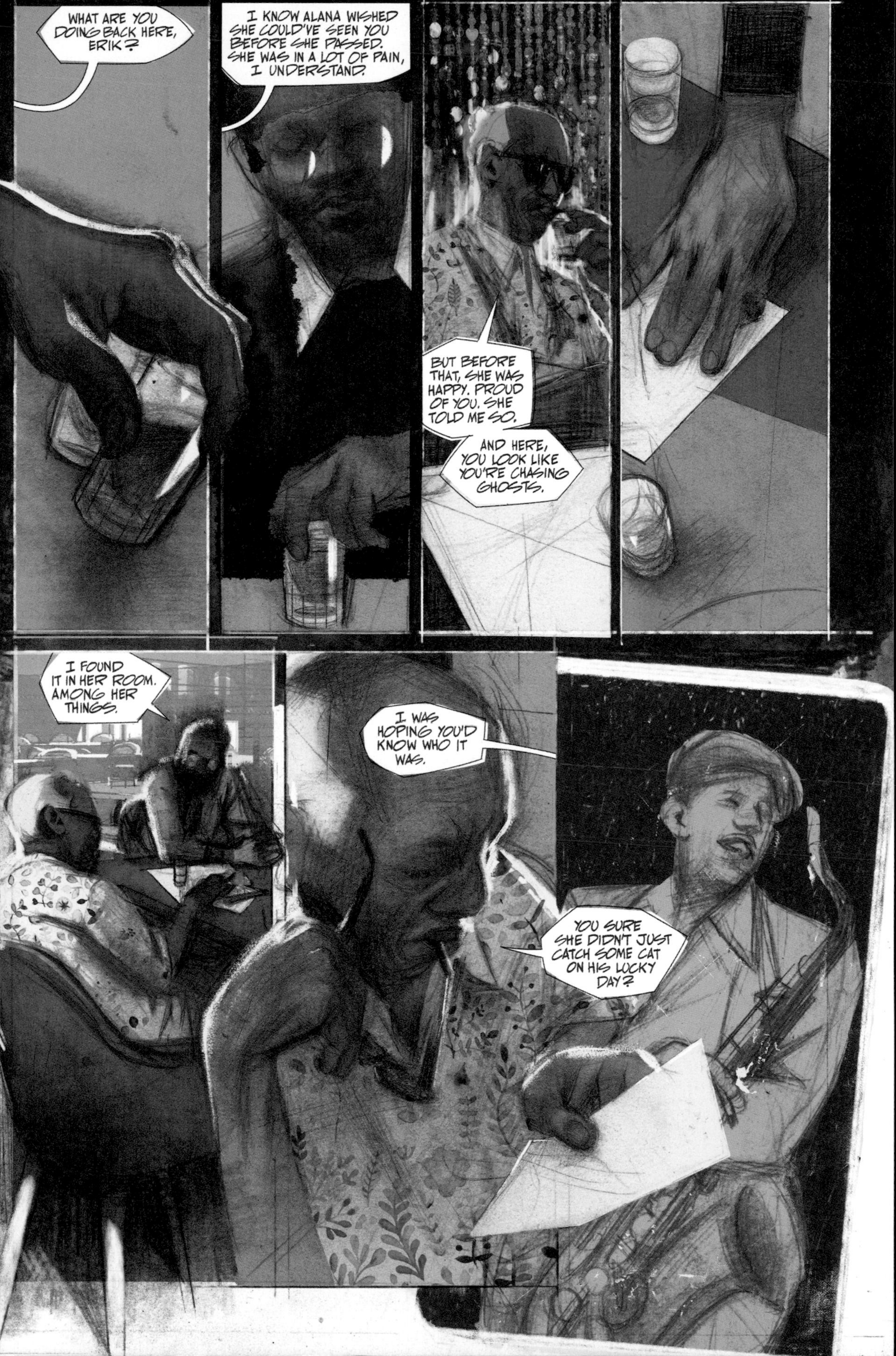
WHAT ARE YOU DOING BACK HERE, ERIK?
I KNOW ALANA WISHED SHE COULD'VE SEEN YOU BEFORE SHE PASSED. SHE WAS IN A LOT OF PAIN, I UNDERSTAND.
BUT BEFORE THAT, SHE WAS HAPPY. PROUD OF YOU. SHE TOLD ME SO.
AND HERE, YOU LOOK LIKE YOU'RE CHASING GHOSTS.
I FOUND IT IN HER ROOM. AMONG HER THINGS.
I WAS HOPING YOU'D KNOW WHO IT WAS.
YOU SURE SHE DIDN'T JUST CATCH SOME CAT ON HIS LUCKY DAY?

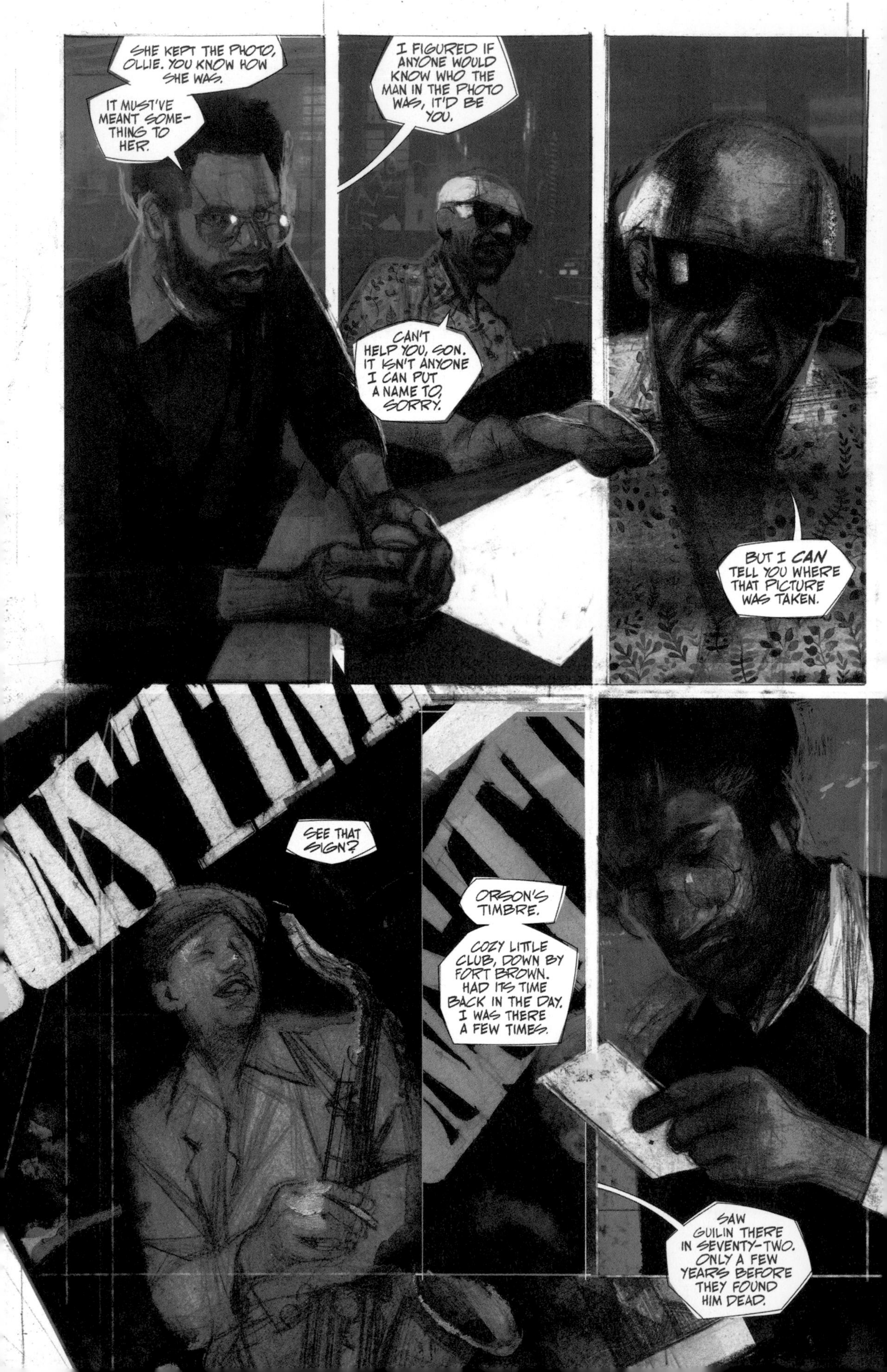
SHE KEPT THE PHOTO, OLLIE. YOU KNOW HOW SHE WAS.
IT MUST'VE MEANT SOME-THING TO HER.
I FIGURED IF ANYONE WOULD KNOW WHO THE MAN IN THE PHOTO WAS, IT'D BE YOU.
CAN'T HELP YOU, SON. IT ISN'T ANYONE I CAN PUT A NAME TO, SORRY.
BUT I CAN TELL YOU WHERE THAT PICTURE WAS TAKEN.
SEE THAT SIGN?
ORSON'S TIMBRE.
COZY LITTLE CLUB, DOWN BY FORT BROWN. HAD ITS TIME BACK IN THE DAY. I WAS THERE A FEW TIMES.
SAW GUILIN THERE IN SEVENTY-TWO. ONLY A FEW YEARS BEFORE THEY FOUND HIM DEAD.

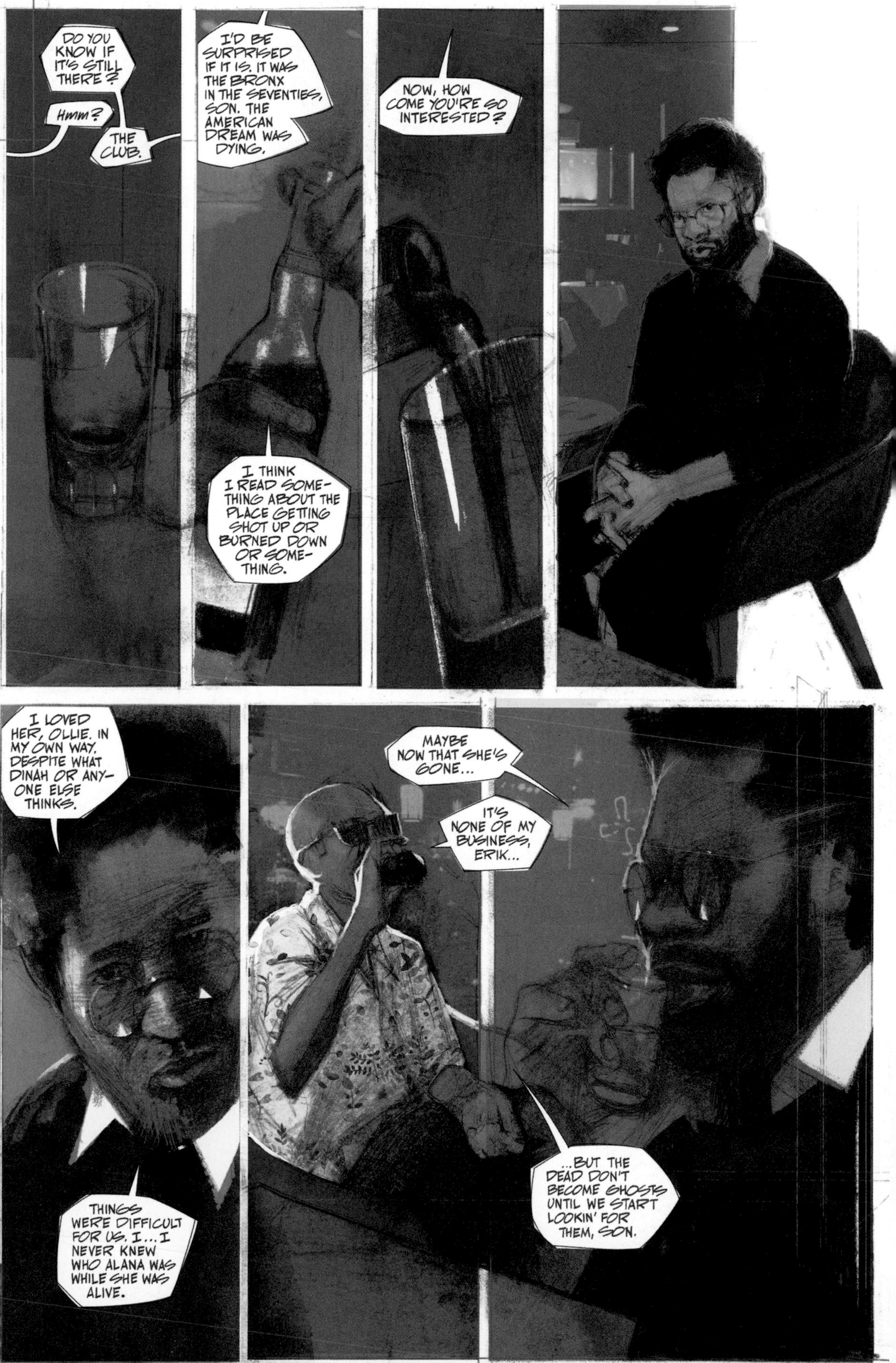
DO YOU KNOW IF IT'S STILL THERE?
HMM?
THE CLUB.
I'D BE SURPRISED IF IT IS. IT WAS THE BRONX IN THE SEVENTIES, SON. THE AMERICAN DREAM WAS DYING.
I THINK I READ SOMETHING ABOUT THE PLACE GETTING SHOT UP OR BURNED DOWN OR SOMETHING.
NOW, HOW COME YOU'RE SO INTERESTED?
I LOVED HER, OLLIE. IN MY OWN WAY. DESPITE WHAT DINAH OR ANYONE ELSE THINKS.
THINGS WERE DIFFICULT FOR US. I... I NEVER KNEW WHO ALANA WAS WHILE SHE WAS ALIVE.
MAYBE NOW THAT SHE'S GONE...
IT'S NONE OF MY BUSINESS, ERIK...
...BUT THE DEAD DON'T BECOME GHOSTS UNTIL WE START LOOKIN' FOR THEM, SON.

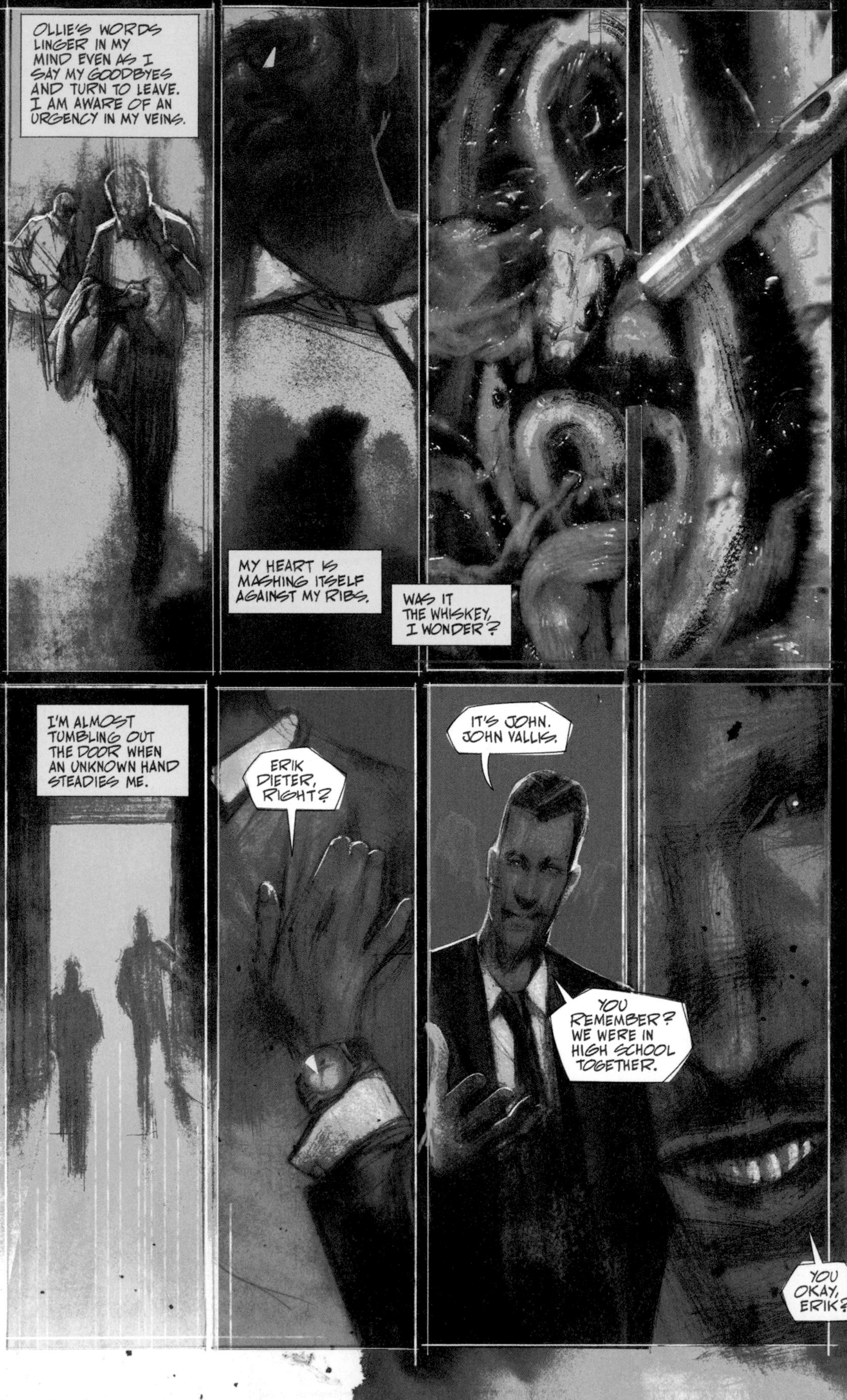
OLLIE'S WORDS LINGER IN MY MIND EVEN AS I SAY MY GOODBYES AND TURN TO LEAVE. I AM AWARE OF AN URGENCY IN MY VEINS.
MY HEART IS MASHING ITSELF AGAINST MY RIBS.
WAS IT THE WHISKEY, I WONDER?
I'M ALMOST TUMBLING OUT THE DOOR WHEN AN UNKNOWN HAND STEADIES ME.
ERIK DIETER, RIGHT?
IT'S JOHN. JOHN VALLIS.
YOU REMEMBER? WE WERE IN HIGH SCHOOL TOGETHER.
YOU OKAY, ERIK?

I, uhh... YEAH. JUST NEED SOME AIR.
RIGHT... SORRY. I'M JUST SURPRISED! WHAT'RE THE CHANCES? RUNNING INTO YOU HERE OF ALL PLACES?
YOU KNOW I OWN IT?
OLLIE HERE TALKS ABOUT YOU ALL THE TIME. YOU'RE PRETTY GOOD WITH A SAX, RIGHT?
WEREN'T YOU SOME KINDA MUSIC WHIZ KID BACK IN HIGH SCHOOL?
I... I JUST TEACH AT A MUSIC COLLEGE IN THE WEST VILLAGE. LISTEN, JOHN... I REALLY HAVE TO GO.
RIGHT. RIGHT, OF COURSE. LISTEN, I OWN A FEW OTHER PLACES LIKE THIS ONE. SOME IN THE CITY.
YOU EVER DECIDE YOU WANT TO PLAY SOME NIGHTS AT ONE OF THE CLUBS, YOU GIVE ME A CALL, ALRIGHT?
SURE. T-THANKS.
BECKER'S
IT'S GOOD TO SEE YOU, ERIK.

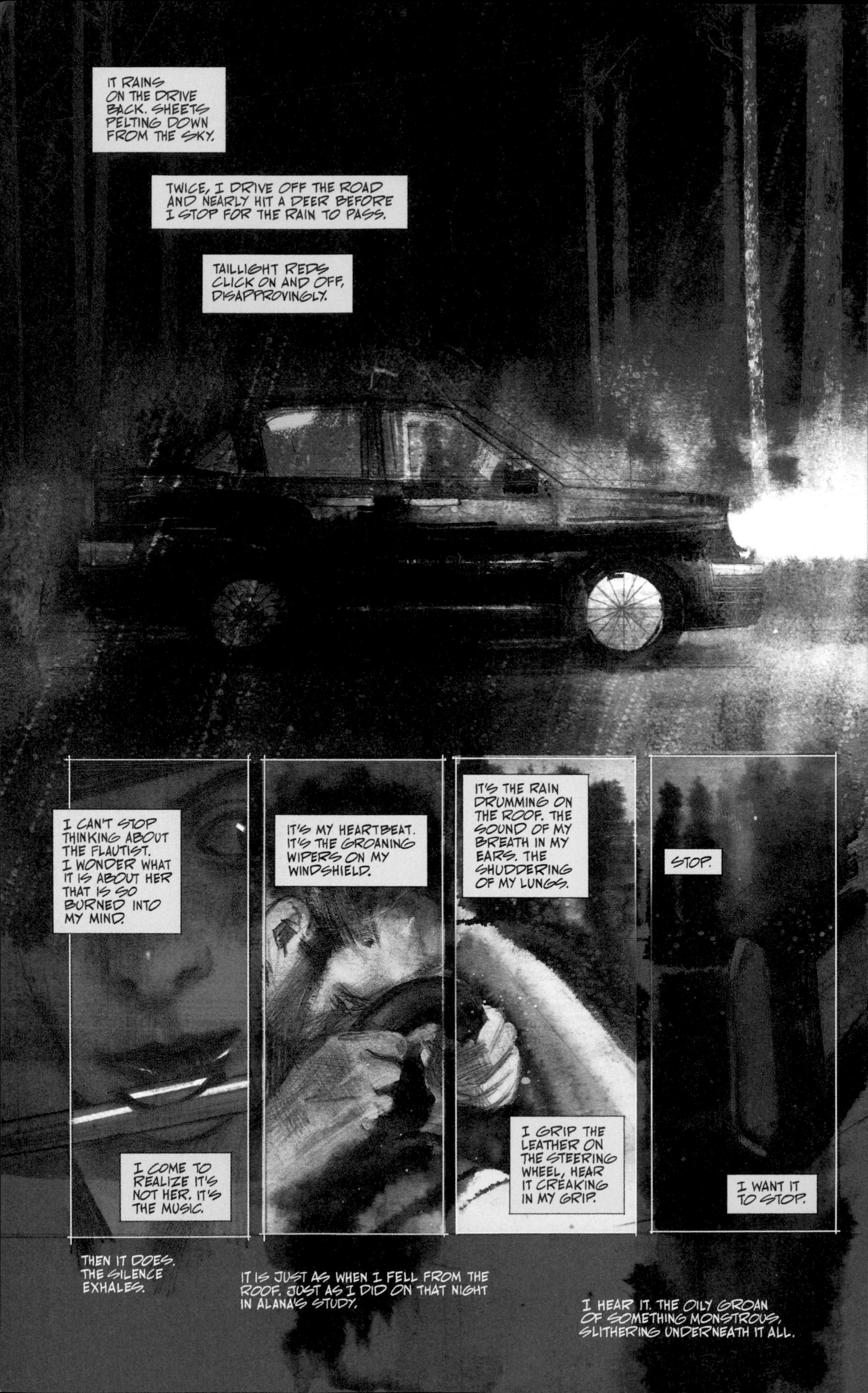
IT RAINS ON THE DRIVE BACK. SHEETS PELTING DOWN FROM THE SKY.
TWICE, I DRIVE OFF THE ROAD AND NEARLY HIT A DEER BEFORE I STOP FOR THE RAIN TO PASS.
TAILLIGHT REDS CLICK ON AND OFF, DISAPPROVINGLY.
I CAN'T STOP THINKING ABOUT THE FLAUTIST. I WONDER WHAT IT IS ABOUT HER THAT IS SO BURNED INTO MY MIND.
I COME TO REALIZE IT'S NOT HER. IT'S THE MUSIC.
IT'S MY HEARTBEAT. IT'S THE GROANING WIPERS ON MY WINDSHIELD.
IT'S THE RAIN DRUMMING ON THE ROOF. THE SOUND OF MY BREATH IN MY EARS. THE SHUDDERING OF MY LUNGS.
I GRIP THE LEATHER ON THE STEERING WHEEL, HEAR IT CREAKING IN MY GRIP.
STOP.
I WANT IT TO STOP.
THEN IT DOES. THE SILENCE EXHALES.
IT IS JUST AS WHEN I FELL FROM THE ROOF. JUST AS I DID ON THAT NIGHT IN ALANA'S STUDY.
I HEAR IT. THE OILY GROAN OF SOMETHING MONSTROUS, SLITHERING UNDERNEATH IT ALL.

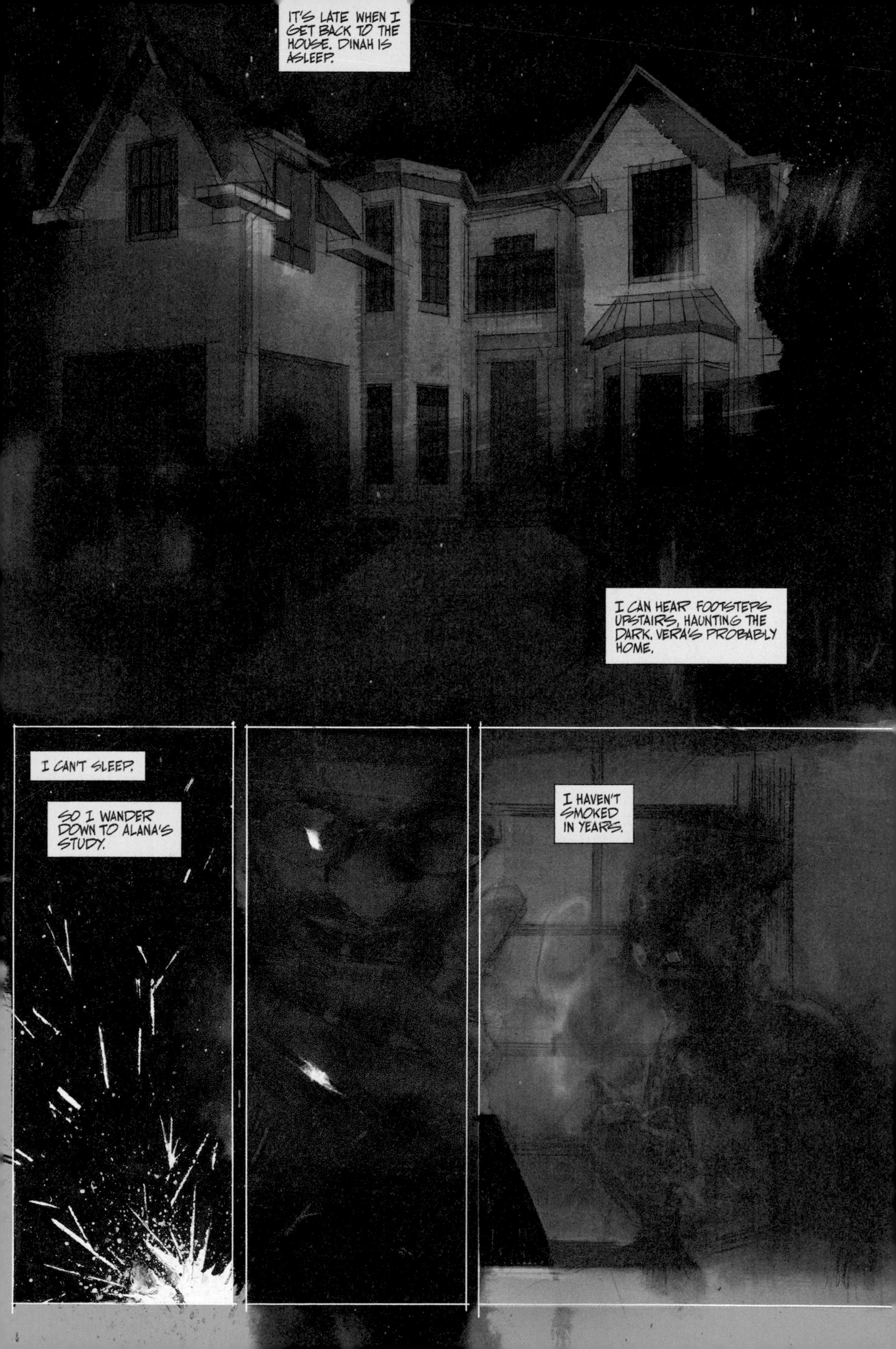
IT'S LATE WHEN I GET BACK TO THE HOUSE. DINAH IS ASLEEP.
I CAN HEAR FOOTSTEPS UPSTAIRS, HAUNTING THE DARK. VERA'S PROBABLY HOME.
I CAN'T SLEEP.
SO I WANDER DOWN TO ALANA'S STUDY.
I HAVEN'T SMOKED IN YEARS.

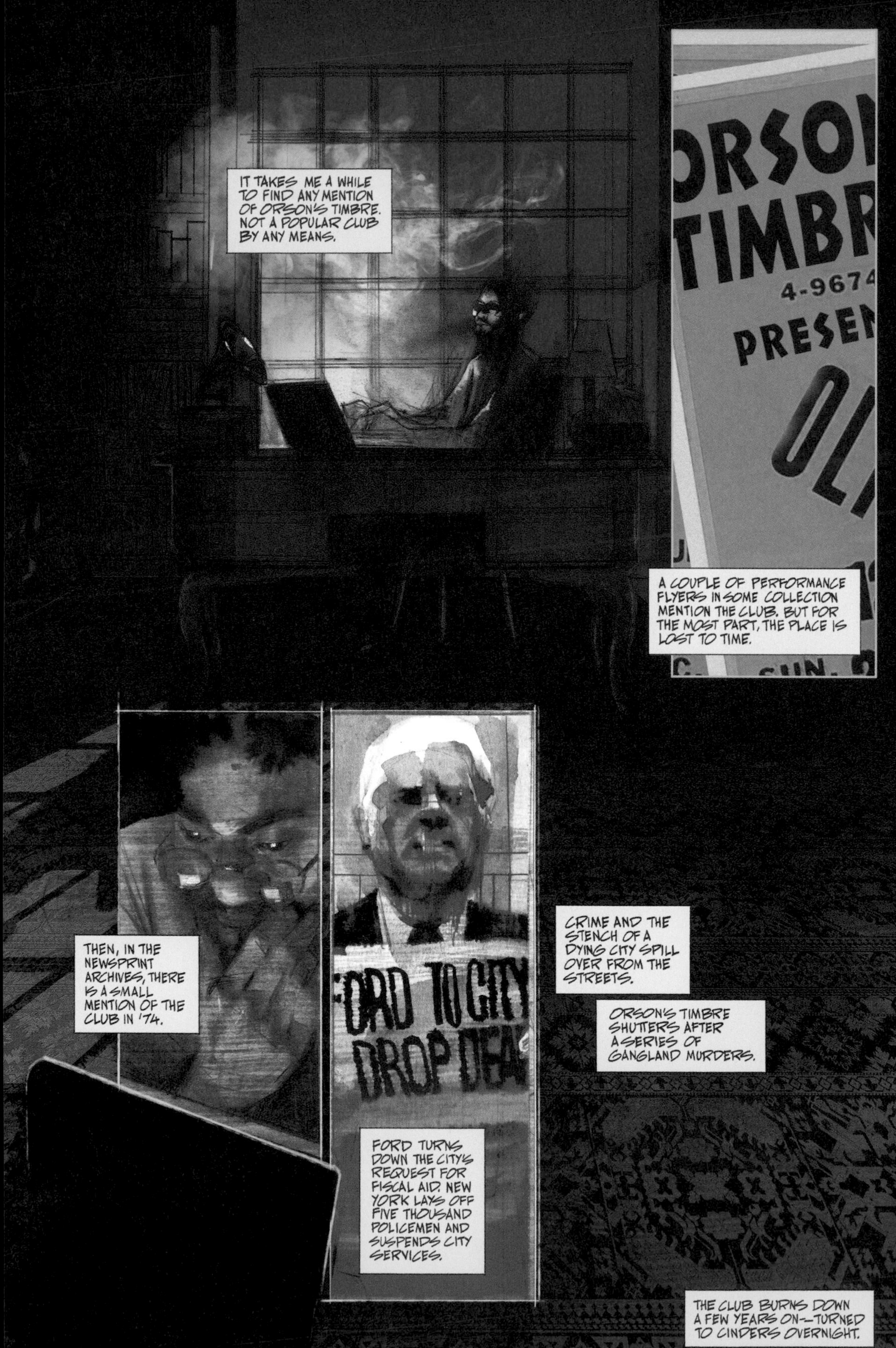
IT TAKES ME A WHILE TO FIND ANY MENTION OF ORSON'S TIMBRE. NOT A POPULAR CLUB BY ANY MEANS.
ORSON TIMBR
4-9674
PRESEN
A COUPLE OF PERFORMANCE FLYERS IN SOME COLLECTION MENTION THE CLUB. BUT FOR THE MOST PART, THE PLACE IS LOST TO TIME.
THEN, IN THE NEWSPRINT ARCHIVES, THERE IS A SMALL MENTION OF THE CLUB IN '74.
ORD TO CITY DROP DEA
FORD TURNS DOWN THE CITY'S REQUEST FOR FISCAL AID. NEW YORK LAYS OFF FIVE THOUSAND POLICEMEN AND SUSPENDS CITY SERVICES.
CRIME AND THE STENCH OF A DYING CITY SPILL OVER FROM THE STREETS.
ORSON'S TIMBRE SHUTTERS AFTER A SERIES OF GANGLAND MURDERS.
THE CLUB BURNS DOWN A FEW YEARS ON--TURNED TO CINDERS OVERNIGHT.

A DEAD END.

Mob Violence Fla...

I LOOK AROUND THE STUDY. THERE ISN'T A SINGLE PICTURE OF ALANA AND ME. NO KEEPSAKES, NO MEMORIES TO HOLD ON TO. NOT ONE THING THAT WE HELD TOGETHER.

IT TAKES ME A MOMENT TO REGISTER THAT SHE ACTUALLY KEPT IT. I THOUGHT SHE MIGHT HAVE SOLD THE OLD THING.

THE BATTERED OLD TENOR. MY FIRST... ALL THOSE YEARS AGO.

SHE CARED FOR IT.

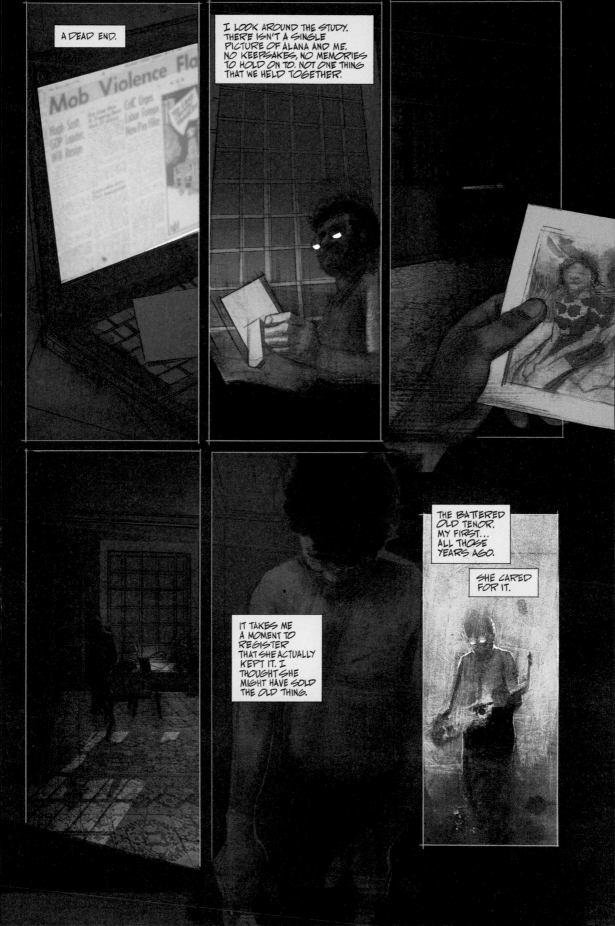

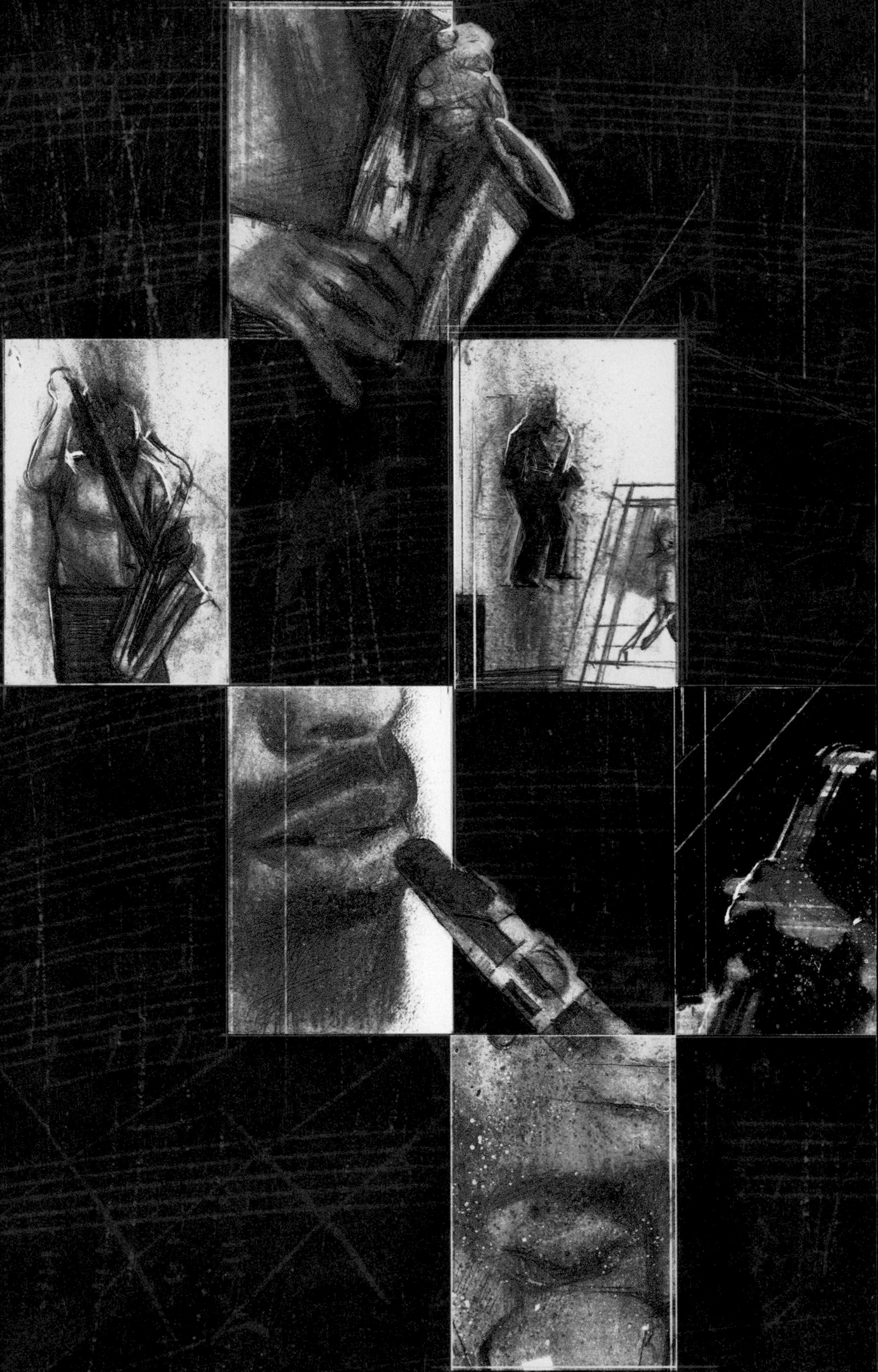

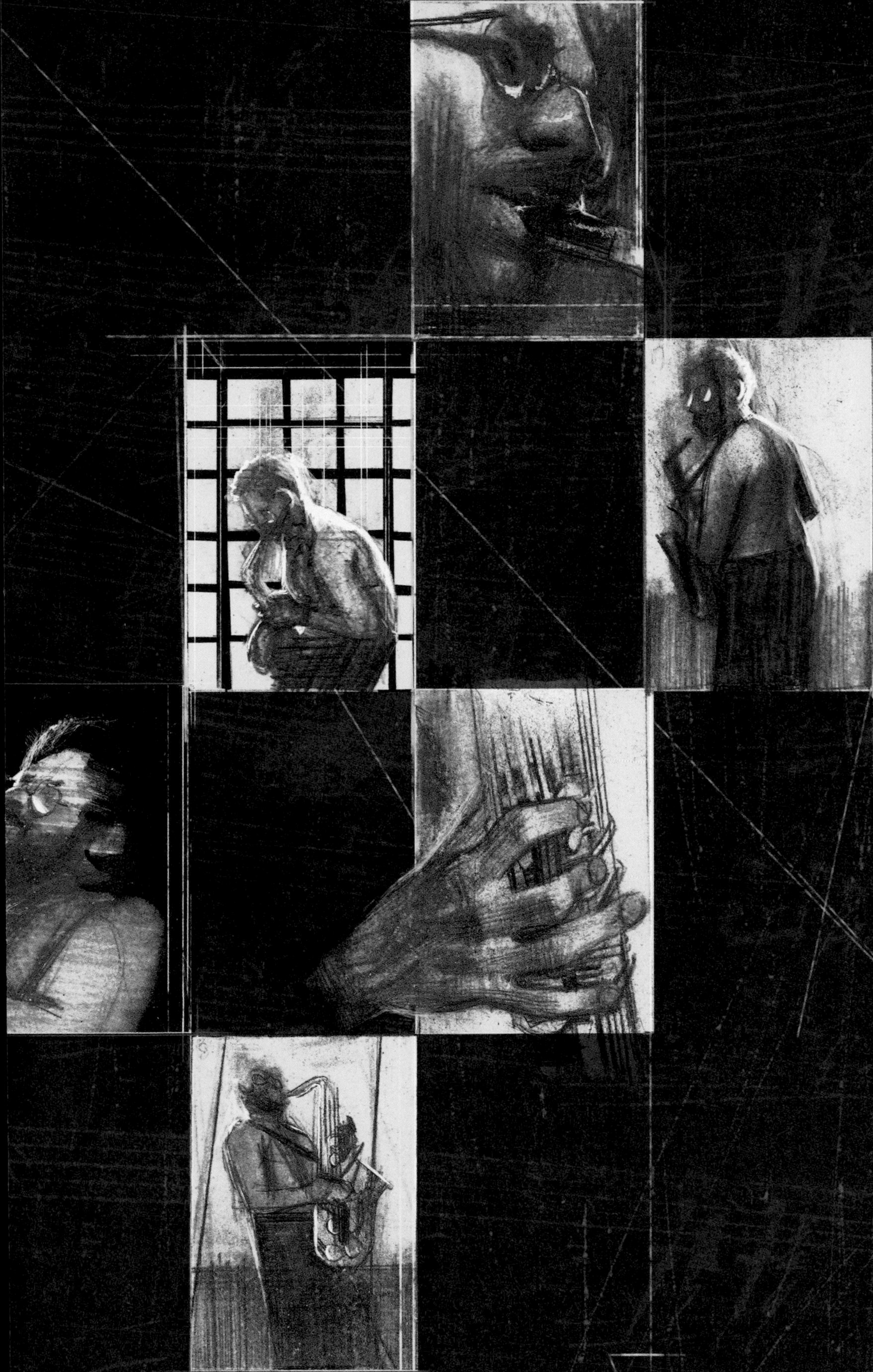

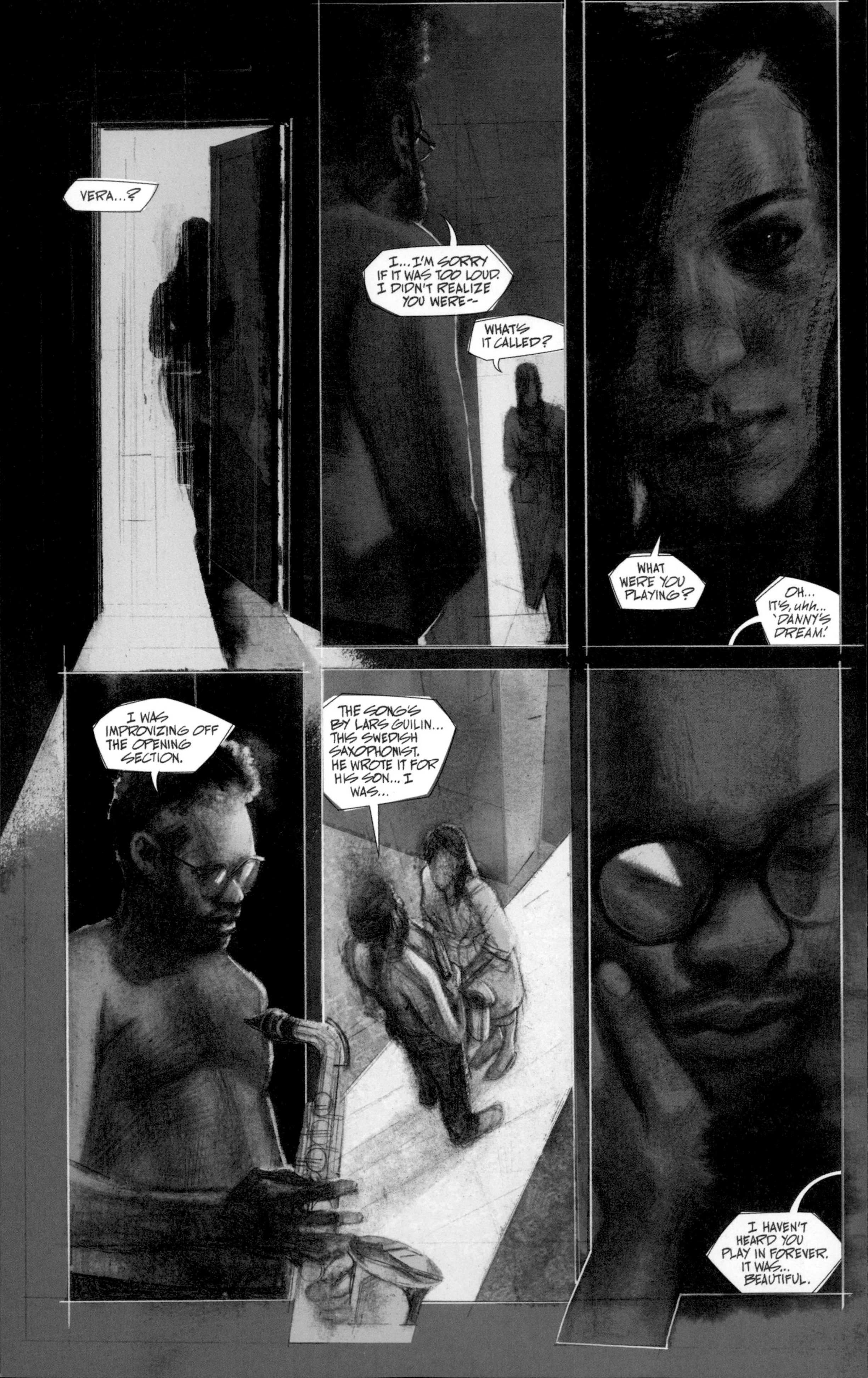
VERA...?
I... I'M SORRY IF IT WAS TOO LOUD. I DIDN'T REALIZE YOU WERE--
WHAT'S IT CALLED?
WHAT WERE YOU PLAYING?
OH... IT'S, uhh... 'DANNY'S DREAM.'
I WAS IMPROVIZING OFF THE OPENING SECTION.
THE SONG'S BY LARS GUILIN... THIS SWEDISH SAXOPHONIST. HE WROTE IT FOR HIS SON... I WAS...
I HAVEN'T HEARD YOU PLAY IN FOREVER. IT WAS... BEAUTIFUL.

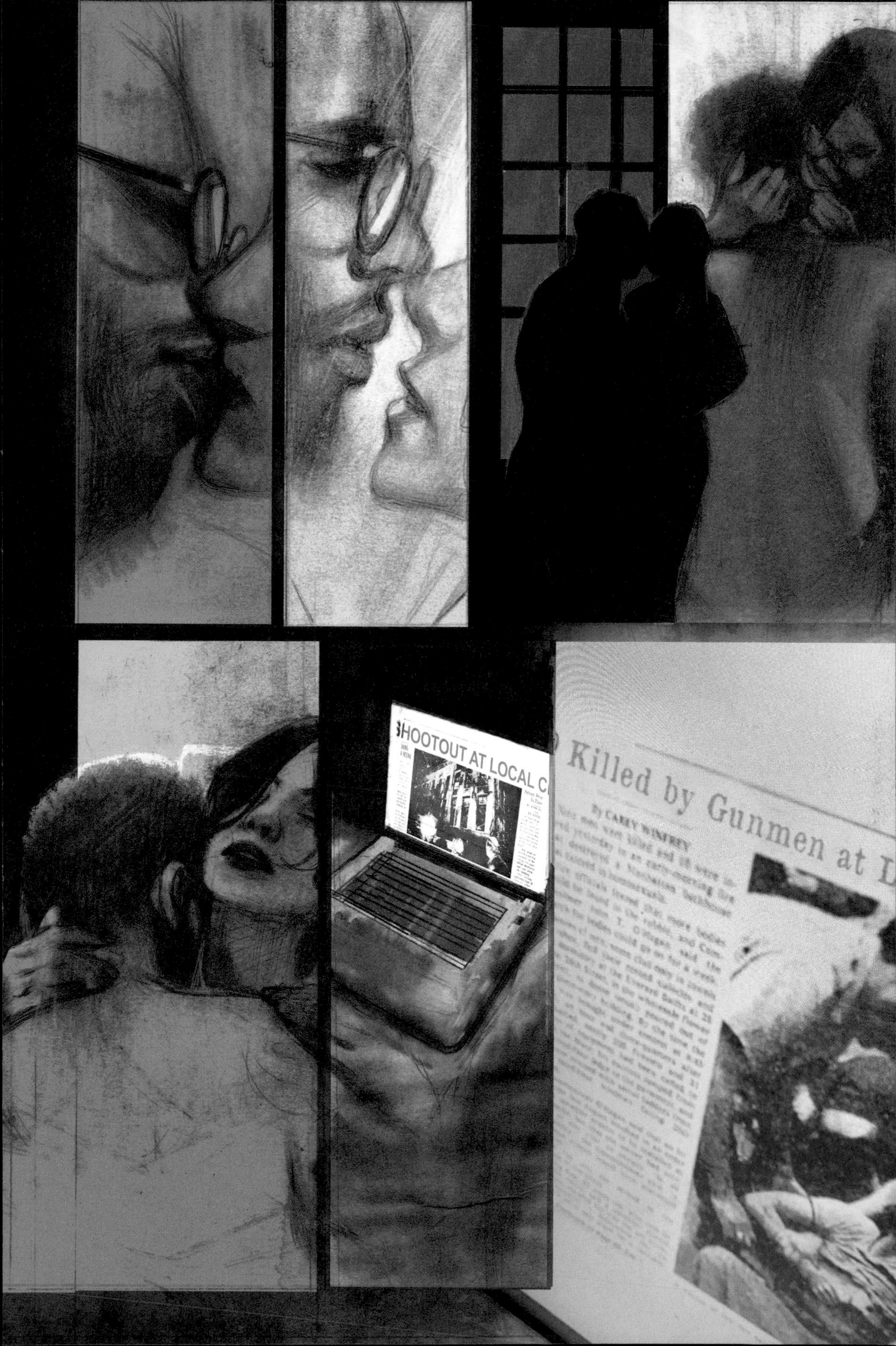
HOOTOUT AT LOCAL
Killed by Gunmen at

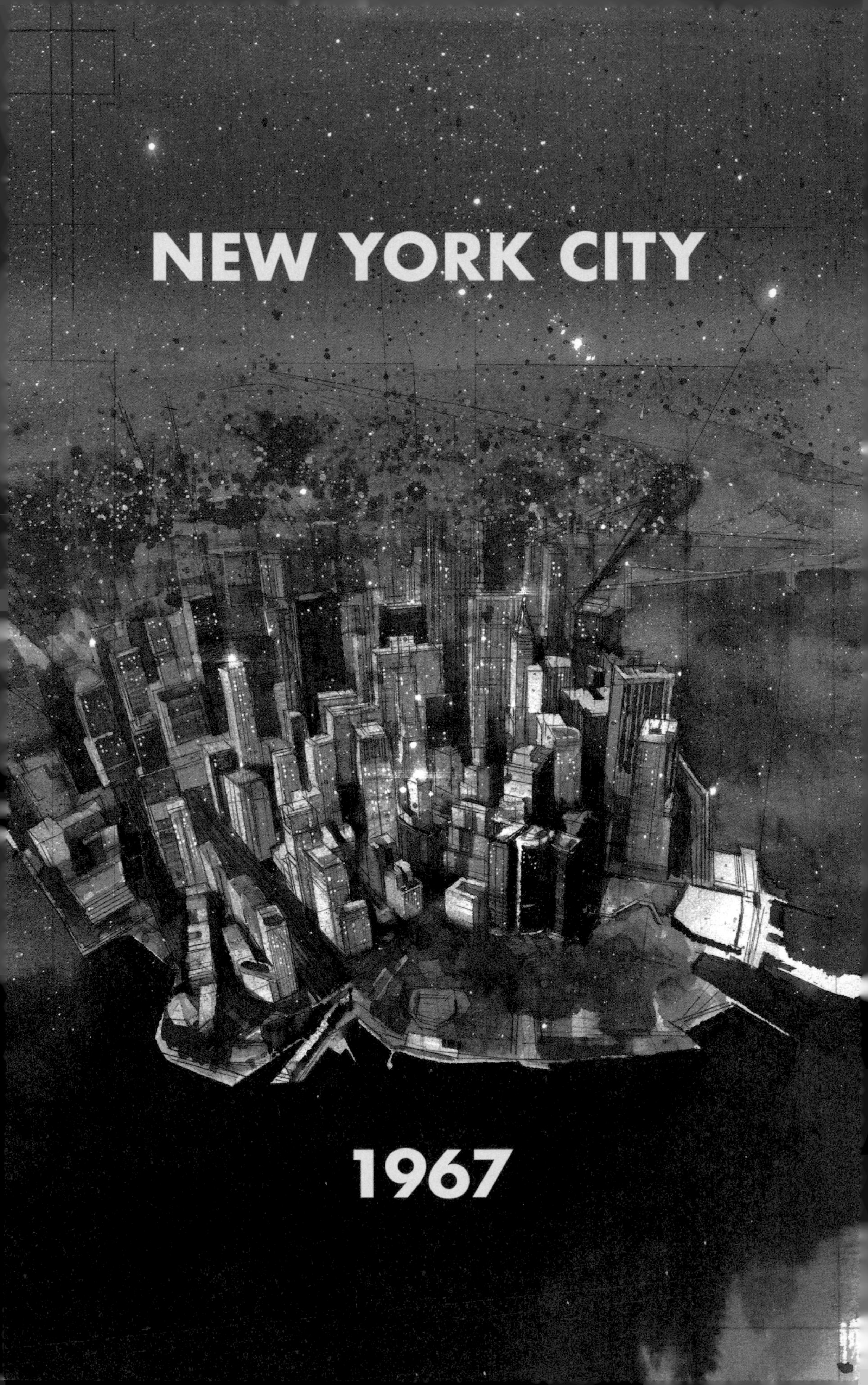
NEW YORK CITY
1967

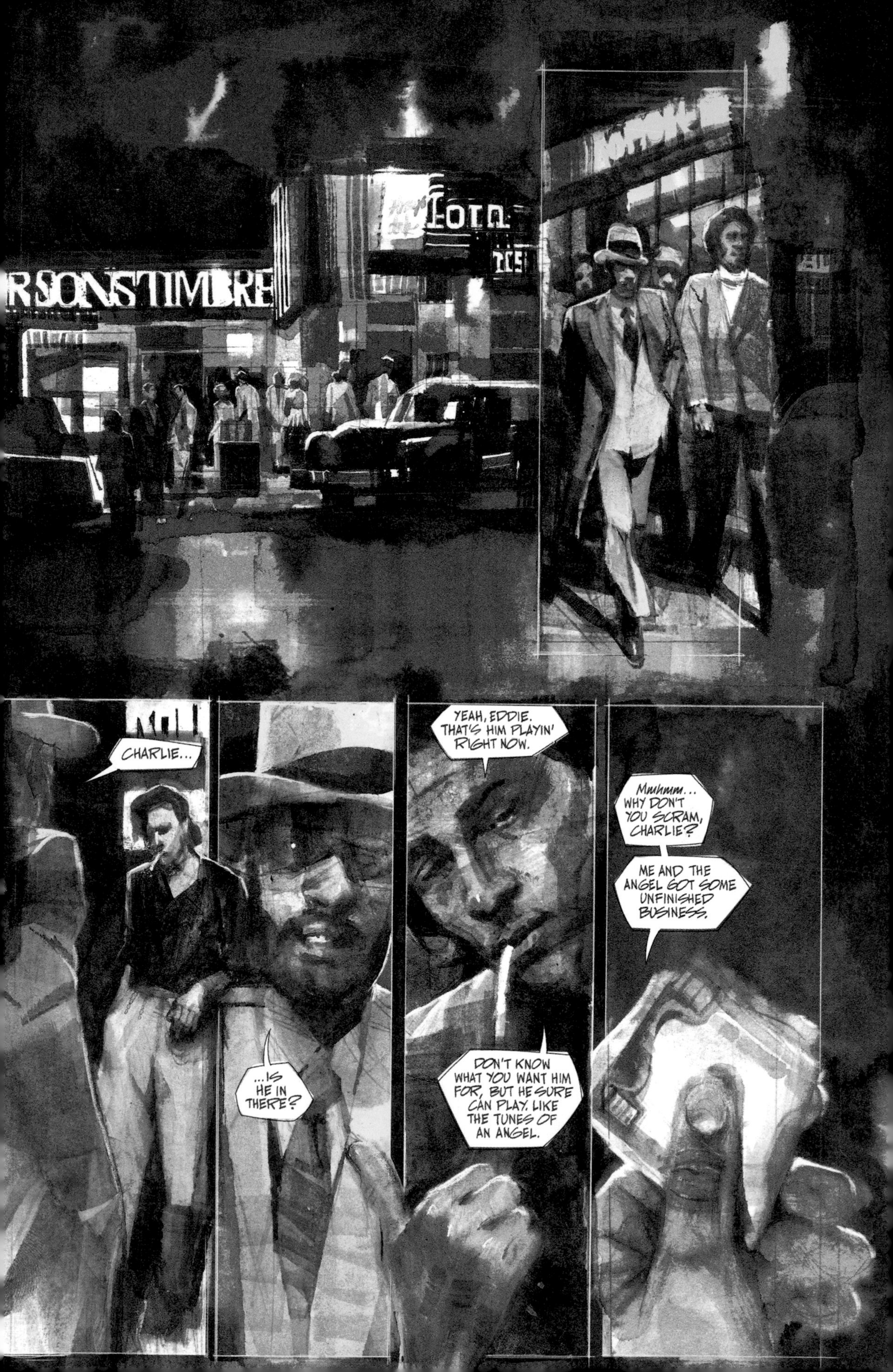
RSONSTIMBRE
CHARLIE...
...IS HE IN THERE?
YEAH, EDDIE. THAT'S HIM PLAYIN' RIGHT NOW.
DON'T KNOW WHAT YOU WANT HIM FOR, BUT HE SURE CAN PLAY. LIKE THE TUNES OF AN ANGEL.
Mmhmm... WHY DON'T YOU SCRAM, CHARLIE?
ME AND THE ANGEL GOT SOME UNFINISHED BUSINESS.

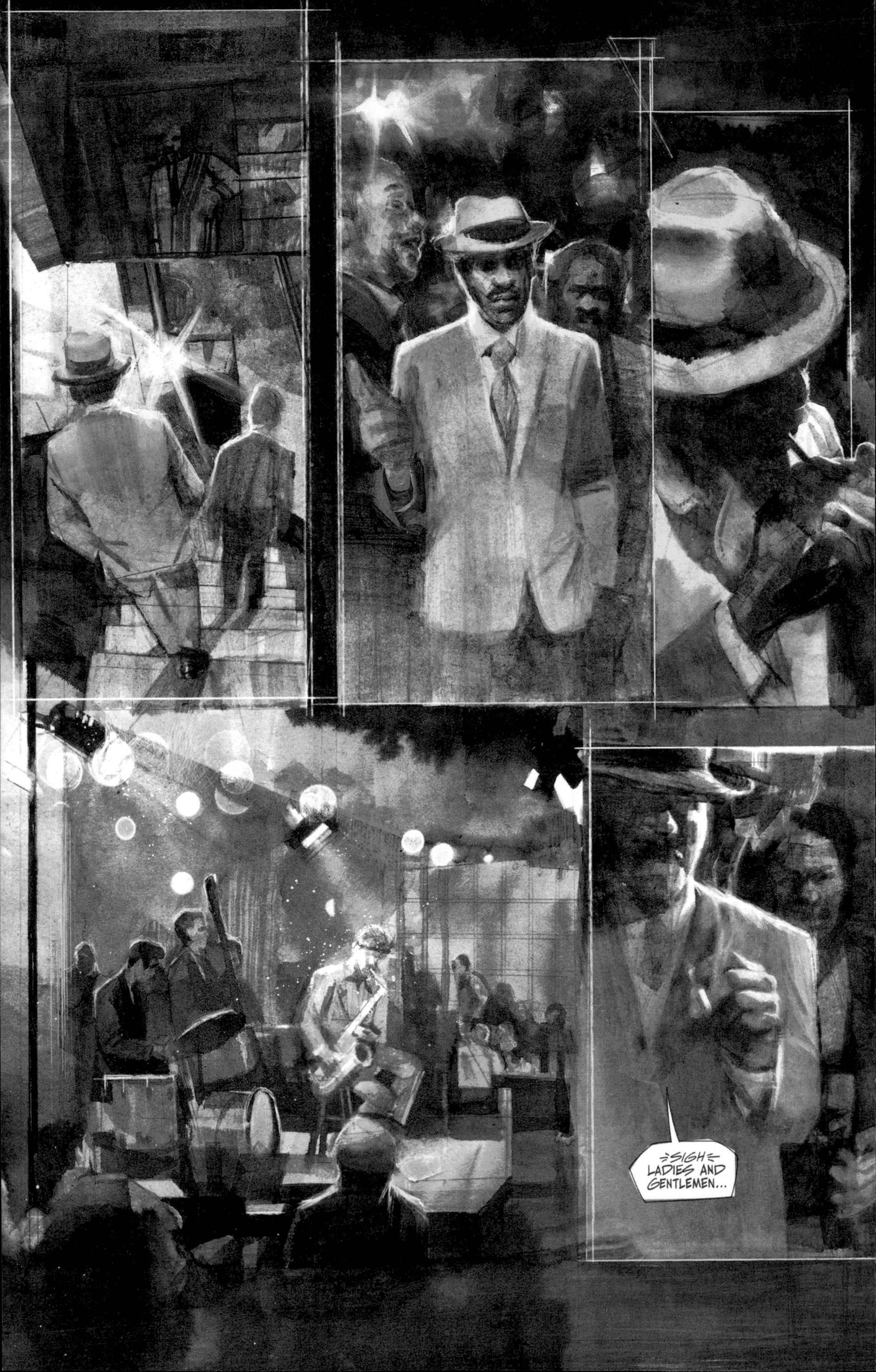
SIGH
LADIES AND GENTLEMEN...

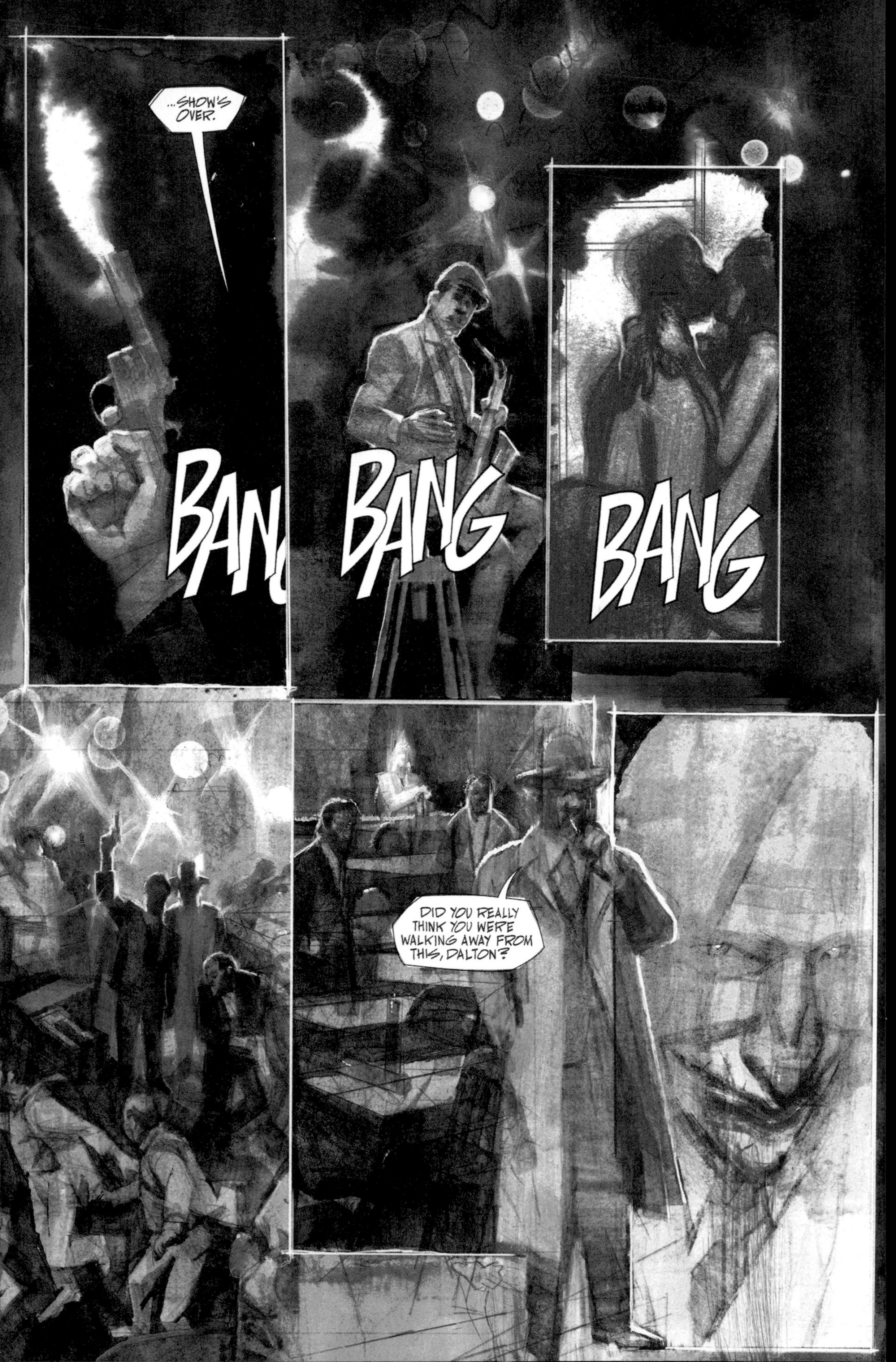
...SHOW'S OVER.
BANG
BANG
BANG
DID YOU REALLY THINK YOU WERE WALKING AWAY FROM THIS, DALTON?

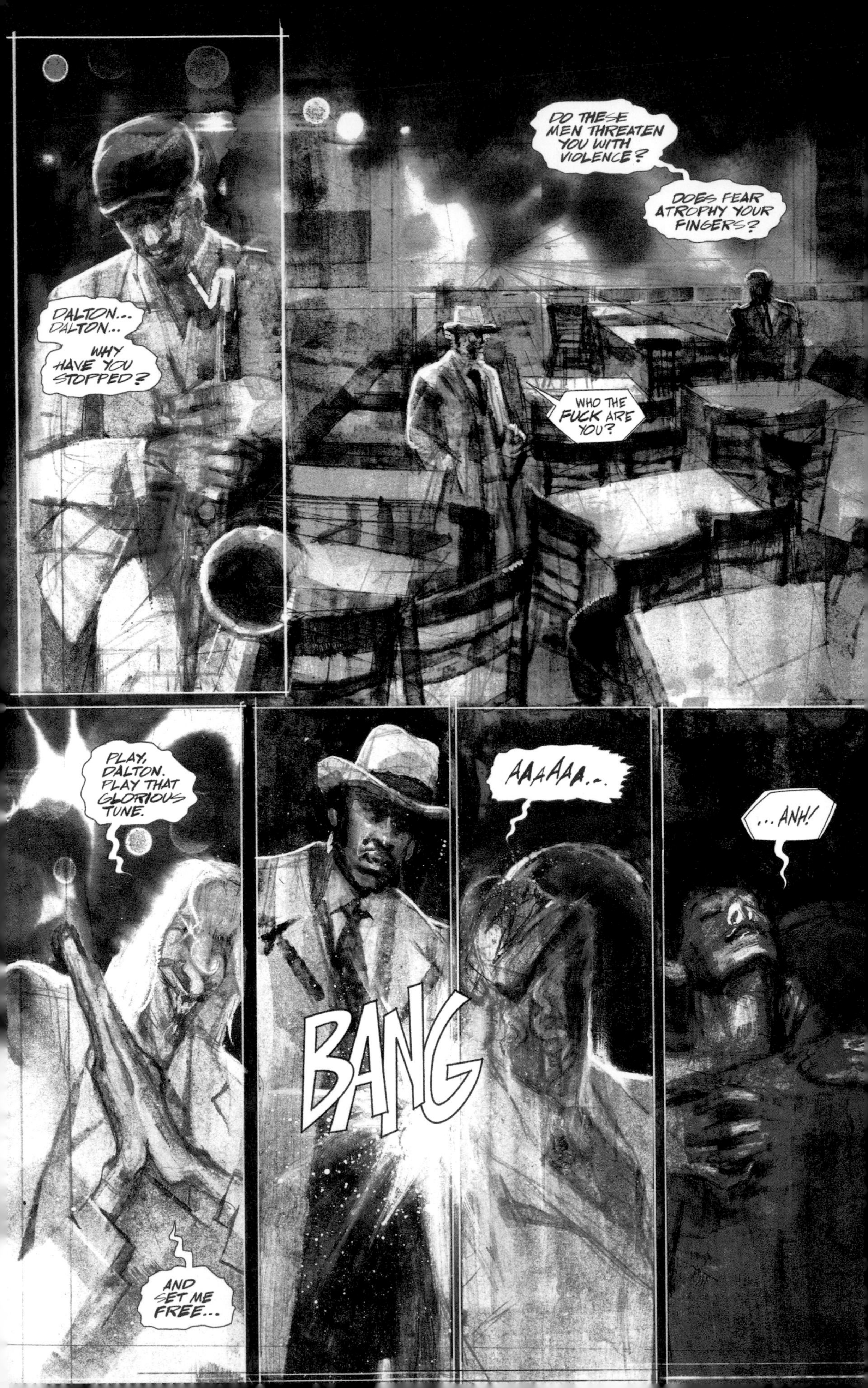
DALTON... DALTON... WHY HAVE YOU STOPPED?
DO THESE MEN THREATEN YOU WITH VIOLENCE?
DOES FEAR ATROPHY YOUR FINGERS?
WHO THE FUCK ARE YOU?
PLAY, DALTON. PLAY THAT GLORIOUS TUNE.
AND SET ME FREE...
BANG
AAAAAA...
...ANH!

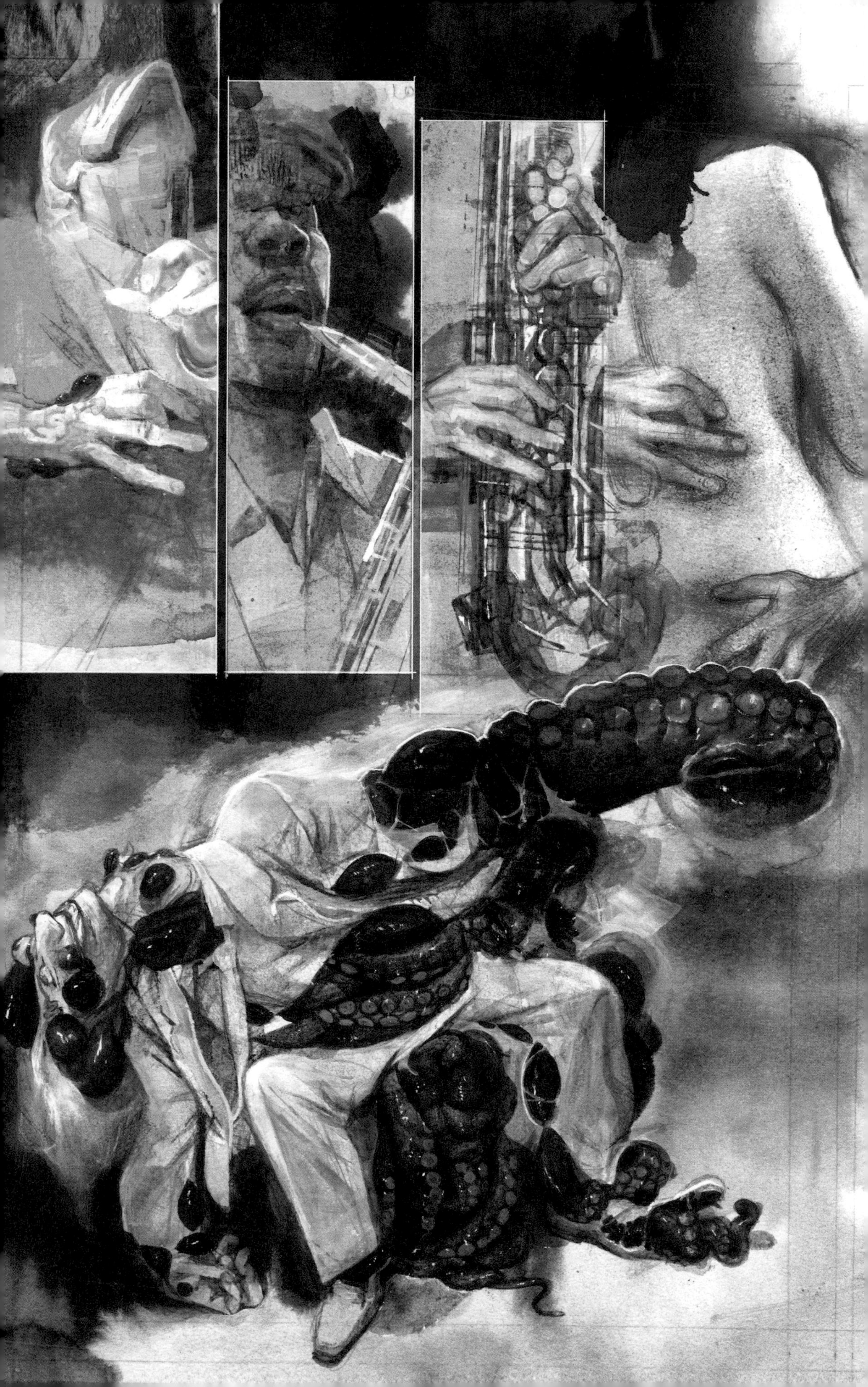

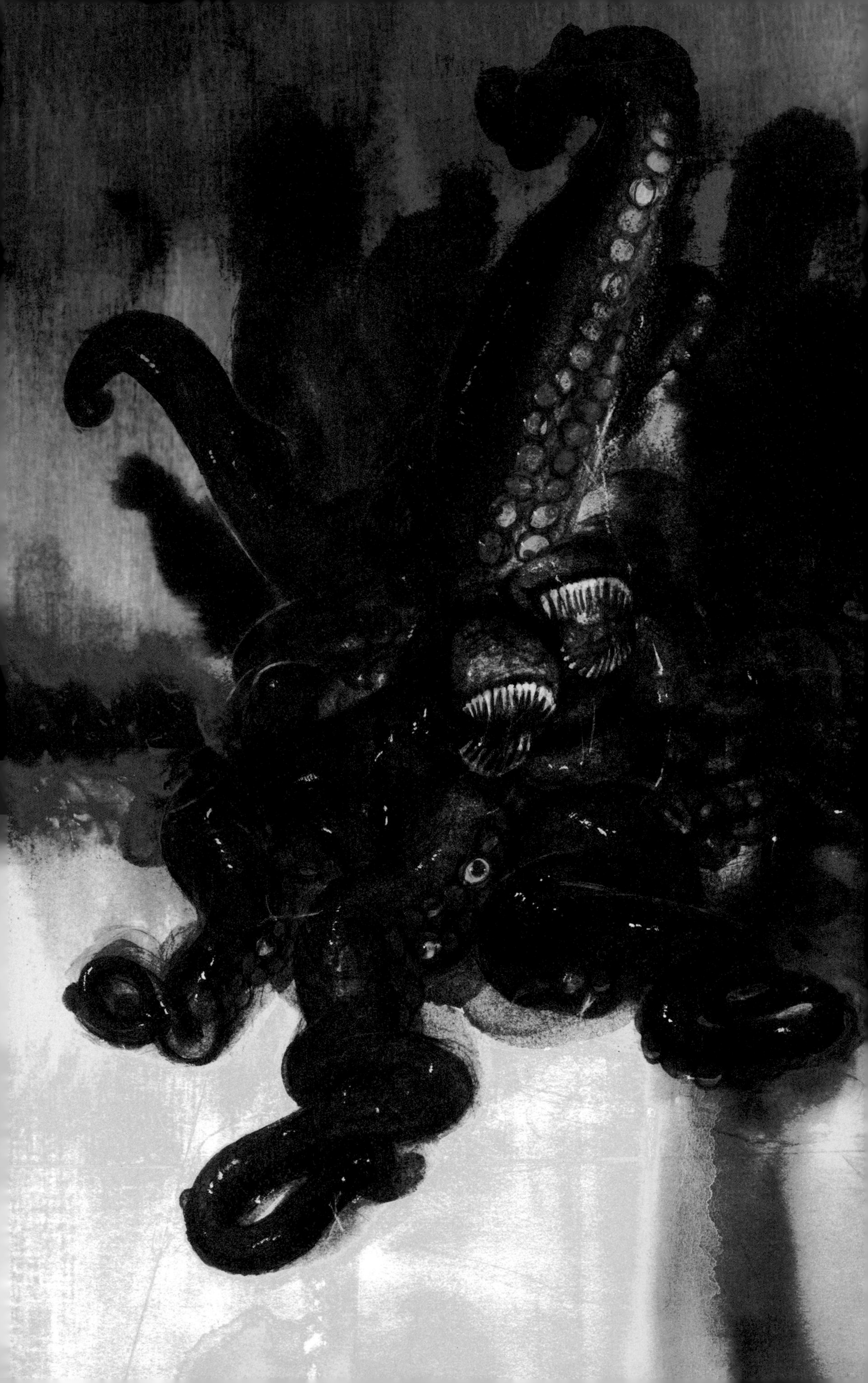

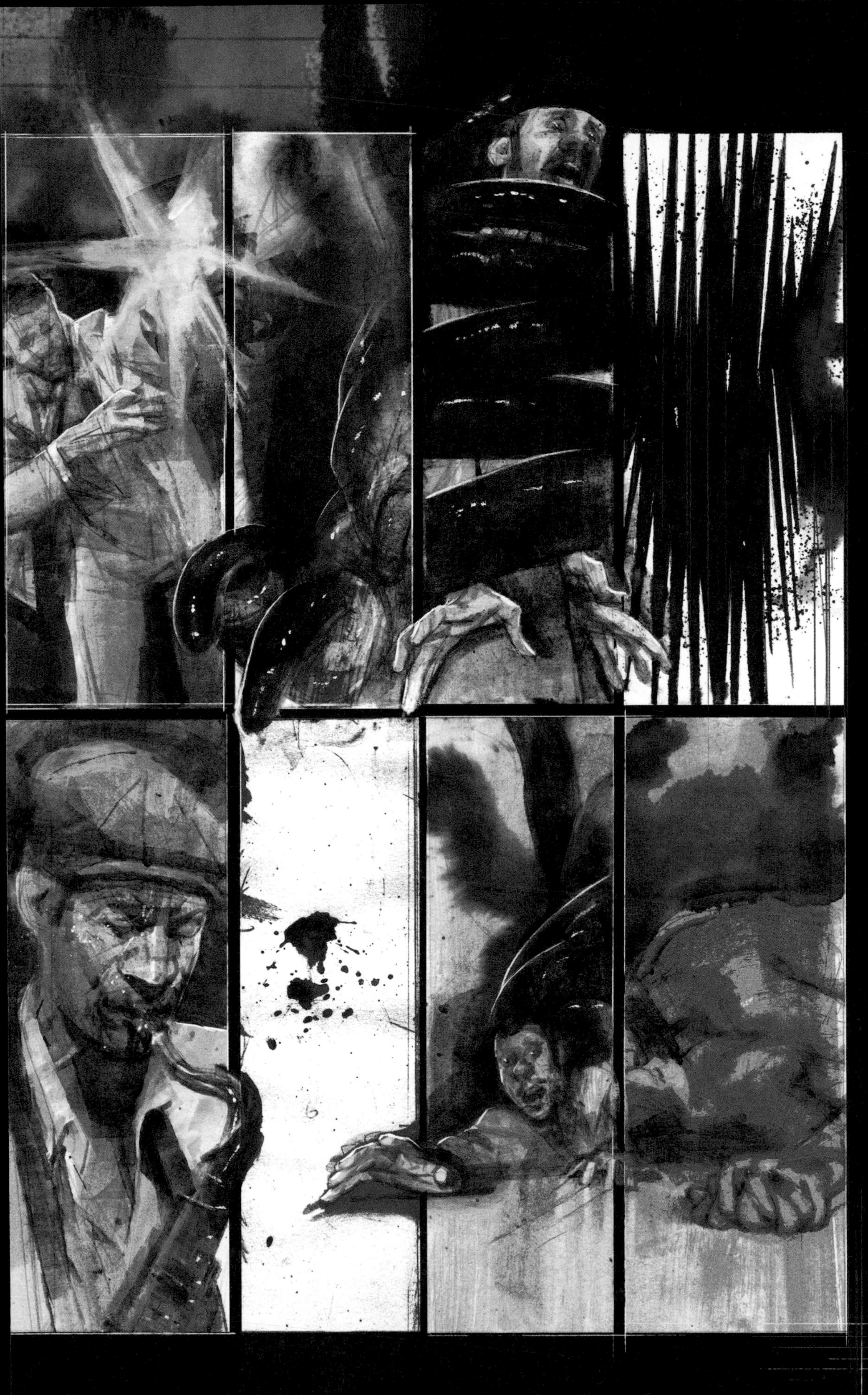

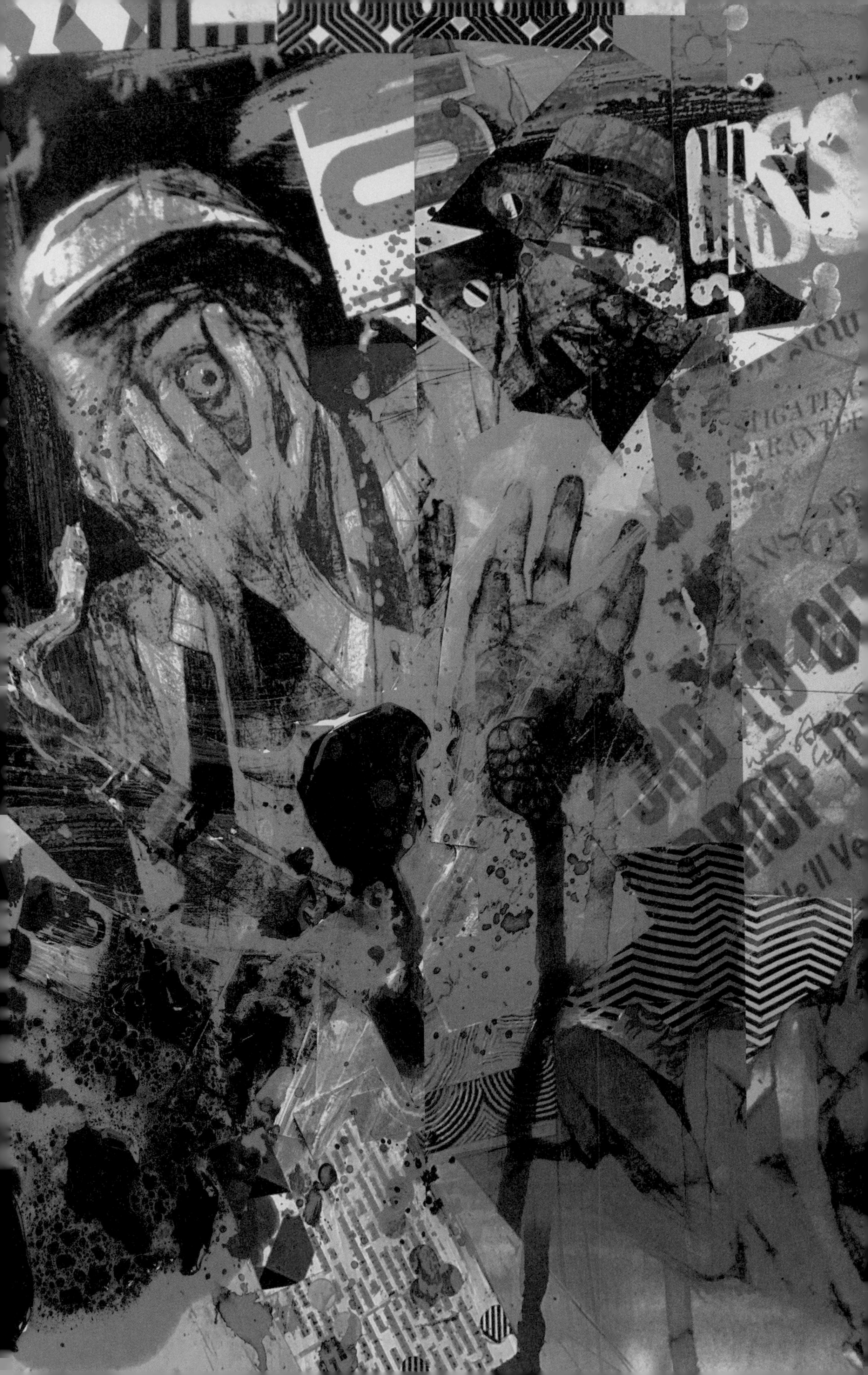

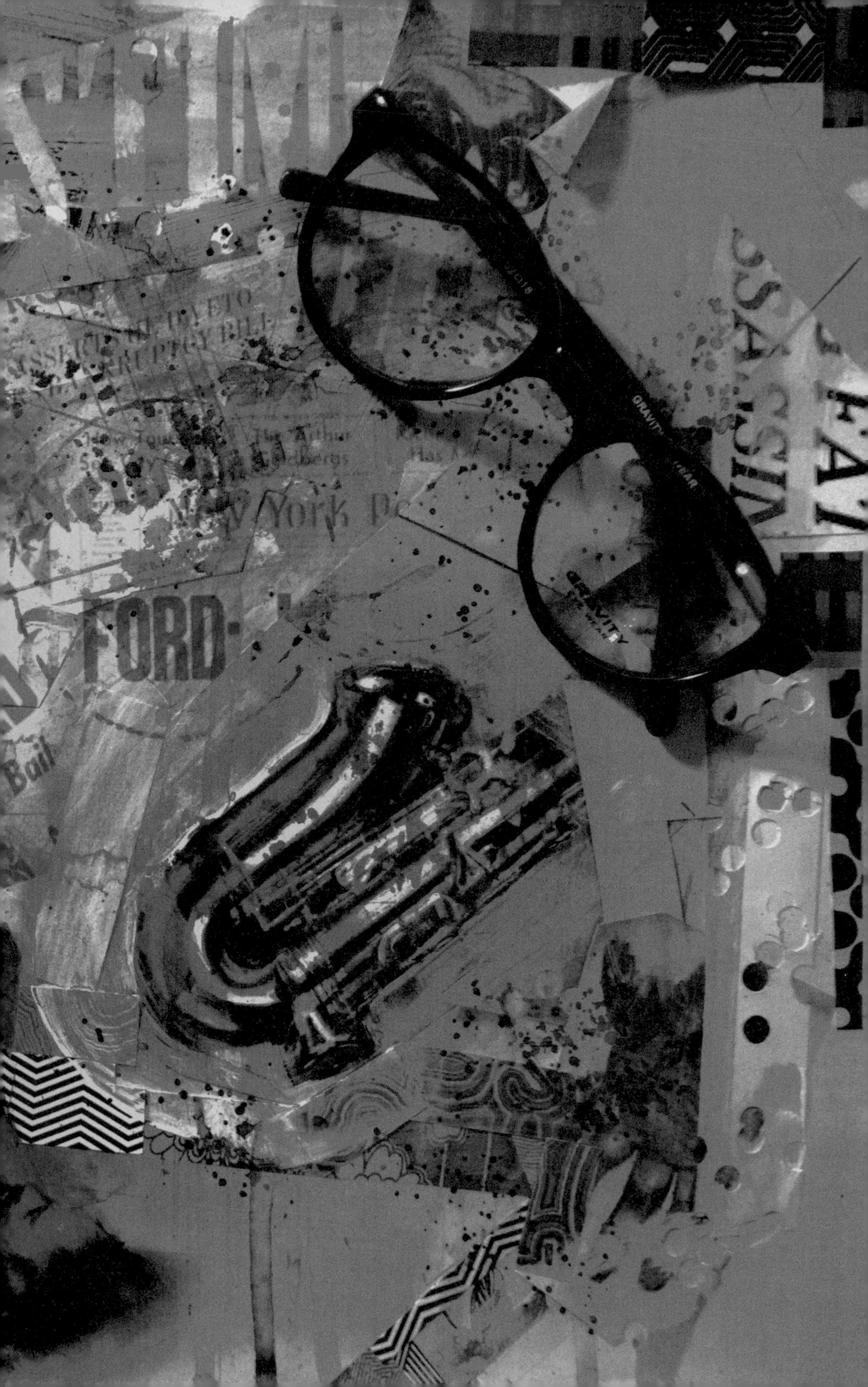
New York
FORD-

[redacted]

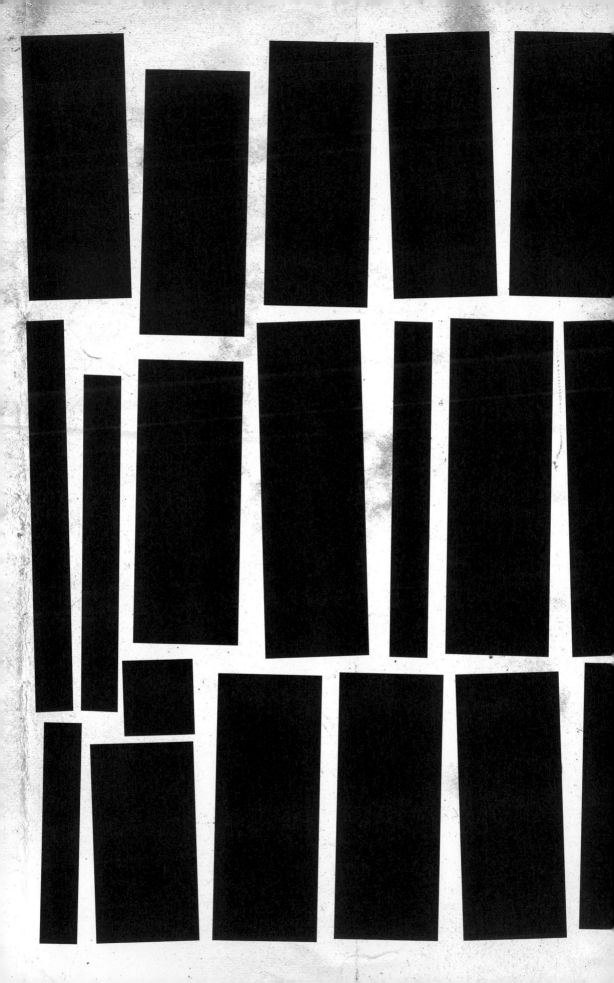

CHAPTER 2

I'VE STOOD AT THE WINDOW SINCE I AWOKE, WATCHING THE SUNLIGHT CARESS HER FORM BENEATH THE SHEETS.

VERA CARTER—AFTER ALL THESE YEARS.

IT WAS SPONTANEOUS LAST NIGHT. UNQUESTIONED. DRIVEN BY DESIRE.

THIS MORNING, ALL I CAN THINK OF IS WHAT HAPPENS WHEN SHE AWAKES?

I AGONIZE ABOUT IT. I REMEMBER WHEN WE BROKE UP. JUST A YEAR BEFORE I LEFT THIS HOUSE.

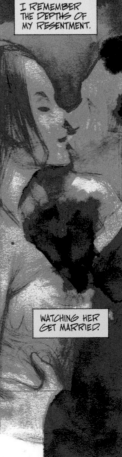

I REMEMBER THE DEPTHS OF MY RESENTMENT.

WATCHING HER GET MARRIED.

PICTURES OF HER KIDS.

HOW DID WE END UP HERE?

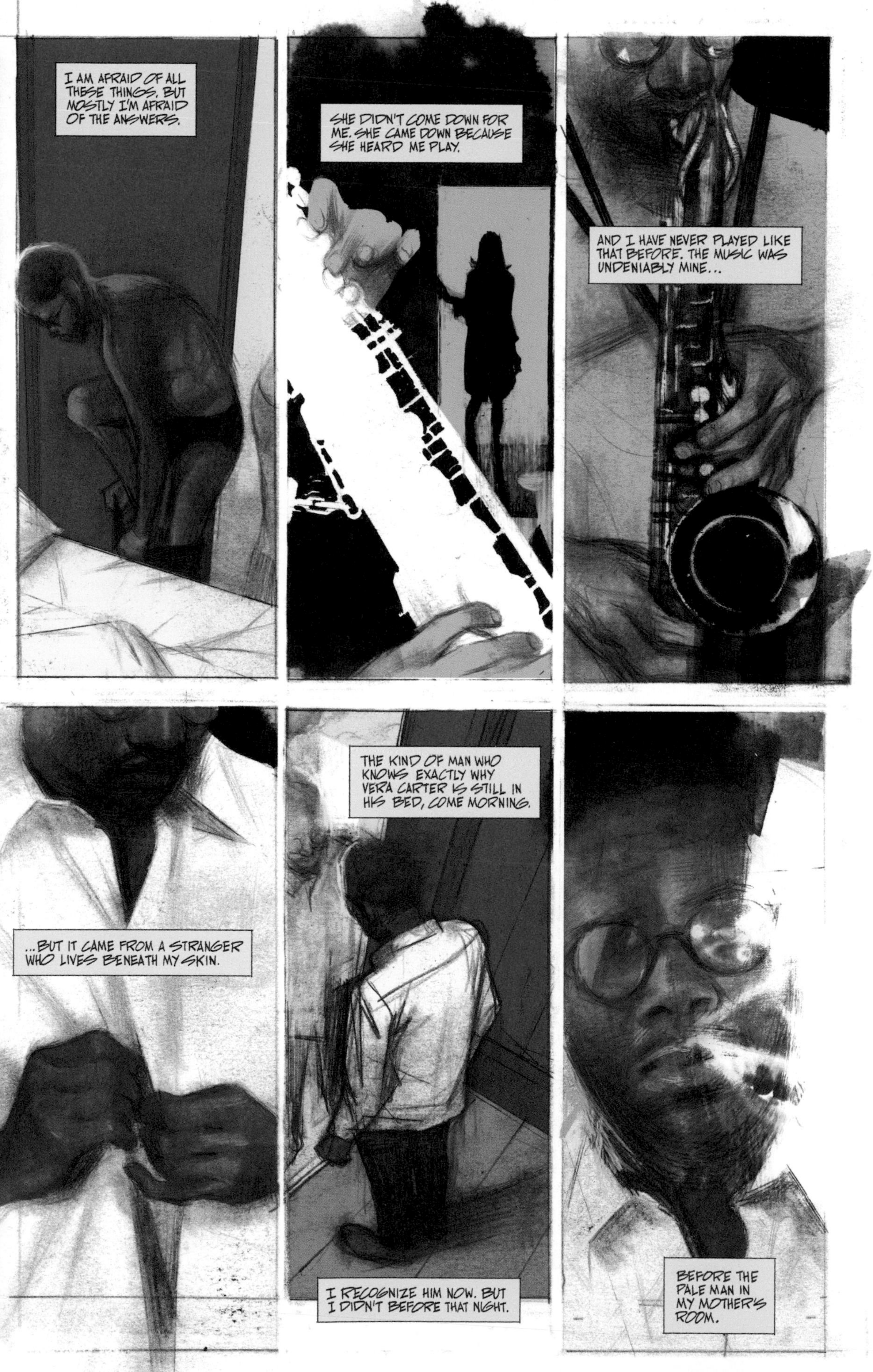
I AM AFRAID OF ALL THESE THINGS, BUT MOSTLY I'M AFRAID OF THE ANSWERS.
SHE DIDN'T COME DOWN FOR ME. SHE CAME DOWN BECAUSE SHE HEARD ME PLAY.
AND I HAVE NEVER PLAYED LIKE THAT BEFORE. THE MUSIC WAS UNDENIABLY MINE...
...BUT IT CAME FROM A STRANGER WHO LIVES BENEATH MY SKIN.
THE KIND OF MAN WHO KNOWS EXACTLY WHY VERA CARTER IS STILL IN HIS BED, COME MORNING.
I RECOGNIZE HIM NOW. BUT I DIDN'T BEFORE THAT NIGHT.
BEFORE THE PALE MAN IN MY MOTHER'S ROOM.

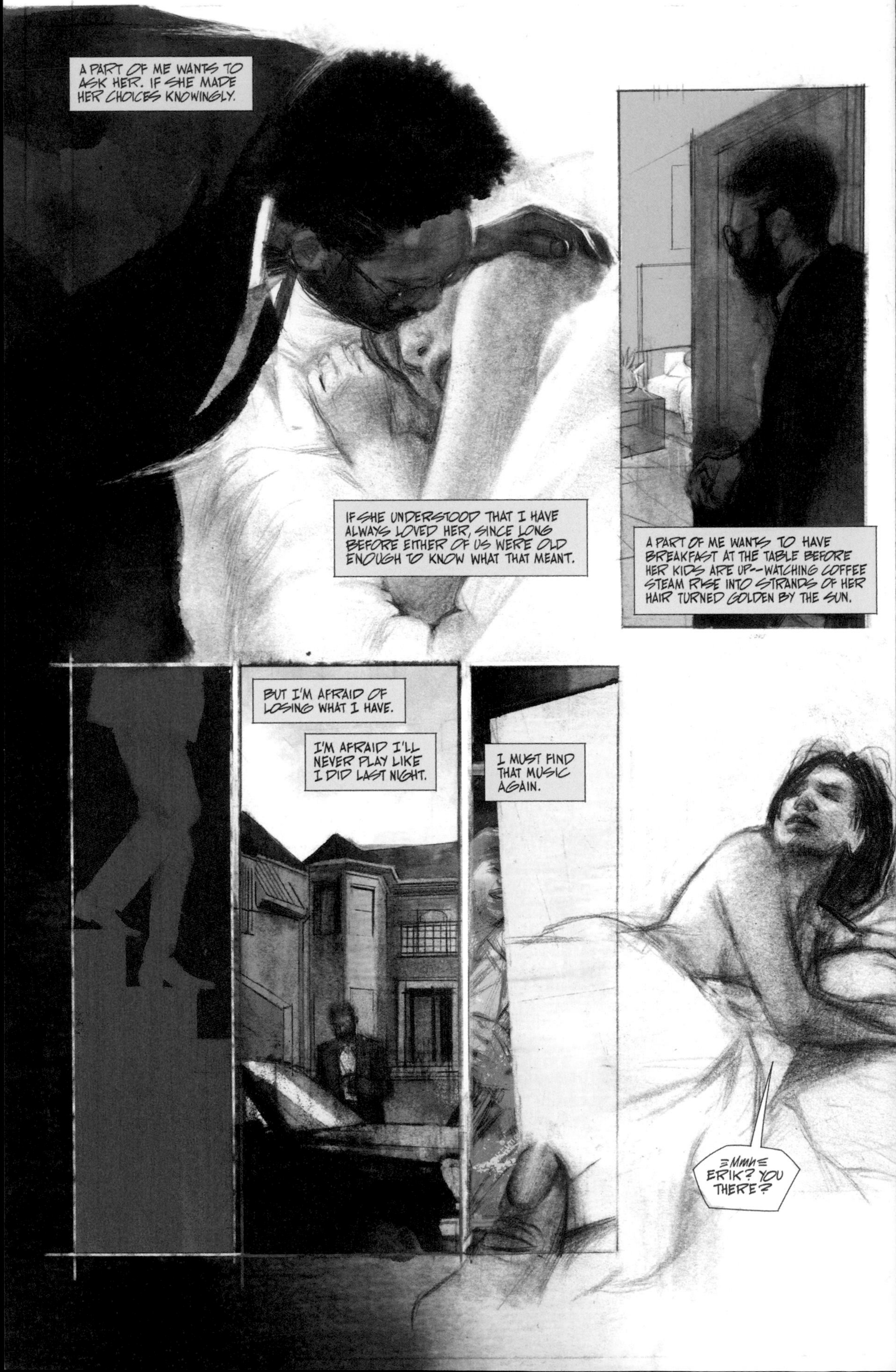
A PART OF ME WANTS TO ASK HER. IF SHE MADE HER CHOICES KNOWINGLY.
IF SHE UNDERSTOOD THAT I HAVE ALWAYS LOVED HER, SINCE LONG BEFORE EITHER OF US WERE OLD ENOUGH TO KNOW WHAT THAT MEANT.
A PART OF ME WANTS TO HAVE BREAKFAST AT THE TABLE BEFORE HER KIDS ARE UP--WATCHING COFFEE STEAM RISE INTO STRANDS OF HER HAIR TURNED GOLDEN BY THE SUN.
BUT I'M AFRAID OF LOSING WHAT I HAVE.
I'M AFRAID I'LL NEVER PLAY LIKE I DID LAST NIGHT.
I MUST FIND THAT MUSIC AGAIN.
=Mmh= ERIK? YOU THERE?

IT USED TO BE A KOREAN TAKEOUT.
YOU THE ONE WHO CALLED ABOUT THE PLACE?
YEAH... ERIK.
MORRIS.
WELL, IT AIN'T A JAZZ CLUB NO MORE. IT'S BEEN A LAUNDRY, AND A GARAGE BEFORE THAT.
FIRE, ROBBERY, BUSINESSES GOIN' BELLY UP. ALWAYS SOMETHING WITH THIS DAMN PLACE.
THE CLUB SHUT DOWN FROM A FIRE, RIGHT?
I DON'T KNOW, MAN. MY MOTHER-IN-LAW RAN THE CLUB BACK THEN. SHE LOVED THAT JOINT. IT'S THE ONLY REASON SHE DOESN'T SELL THE FUCKIN' LOT.

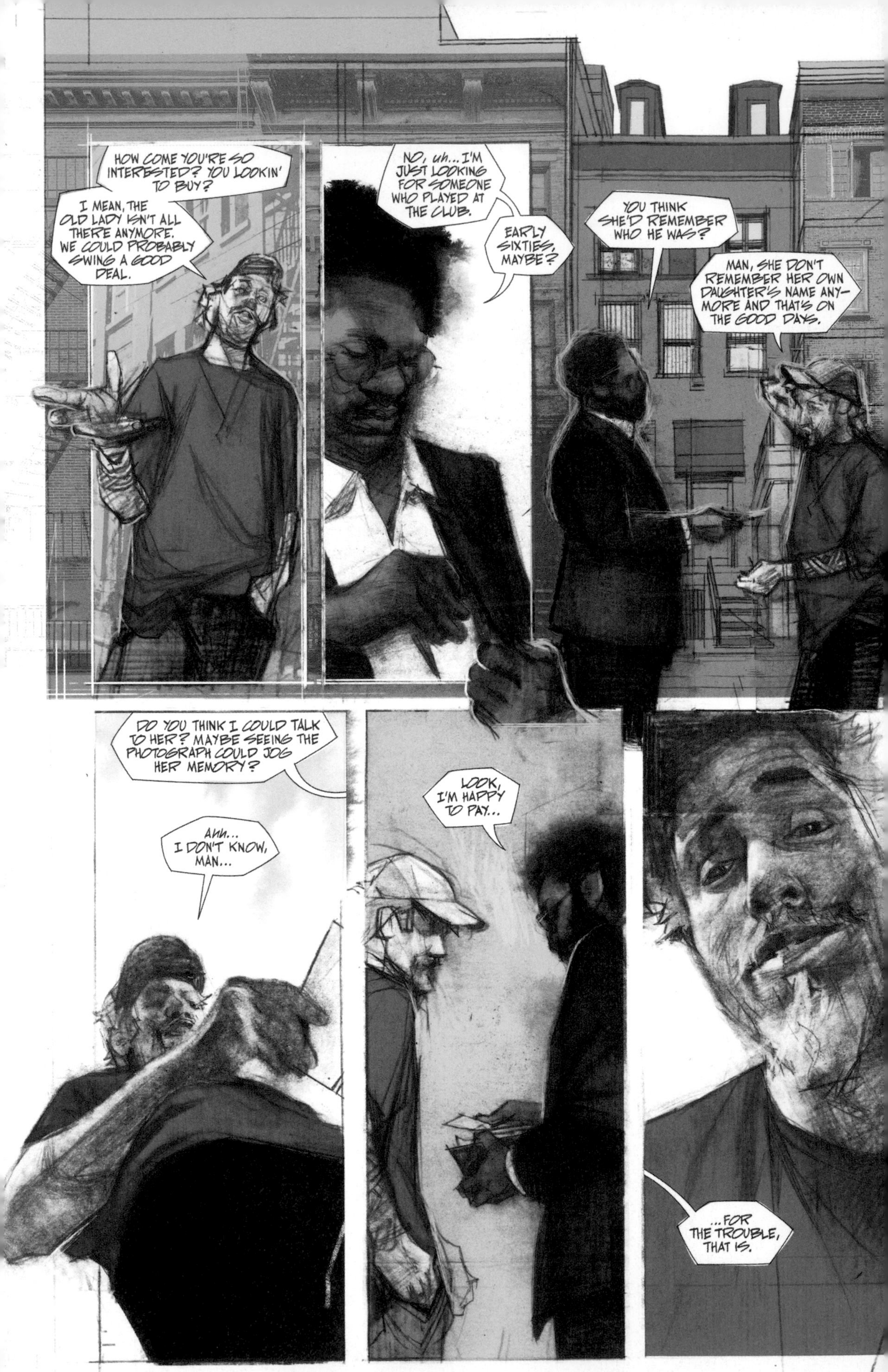
HOW COME YOU'RE SO INTERESTED? YOU LOOKIN' TO BUY?
I MEAN, THE OLD LADY ISN'T ALL THERE ANYMORE. WE COULD PROBABLY SWING A GOOD DEAL.
NO, uh... I'M JUST LOOKING FOR SOMEONE WHO PLAYED AT THE CLUB.
EARLY SIXTIES, MAYBE?
YOU THINK SHE'D REMEMBER WHO HE WAS?
MAN, SHE DON'T REMEMBER HER OWN DAUGHTER'S NAME ANYMORE AND THAT'S ON THE GOOD DAYS.
DO YOU THINK I COULD TALK TO HER? MAYBE SEEING THE PHOTOGRAPH COULD JOG HER MEMORY?
Ahh... I DON'T KNOW, MAN...
LOOK, I'M HAPPY TO PAY...
...FOR THE TROUBLE, THAT IS.

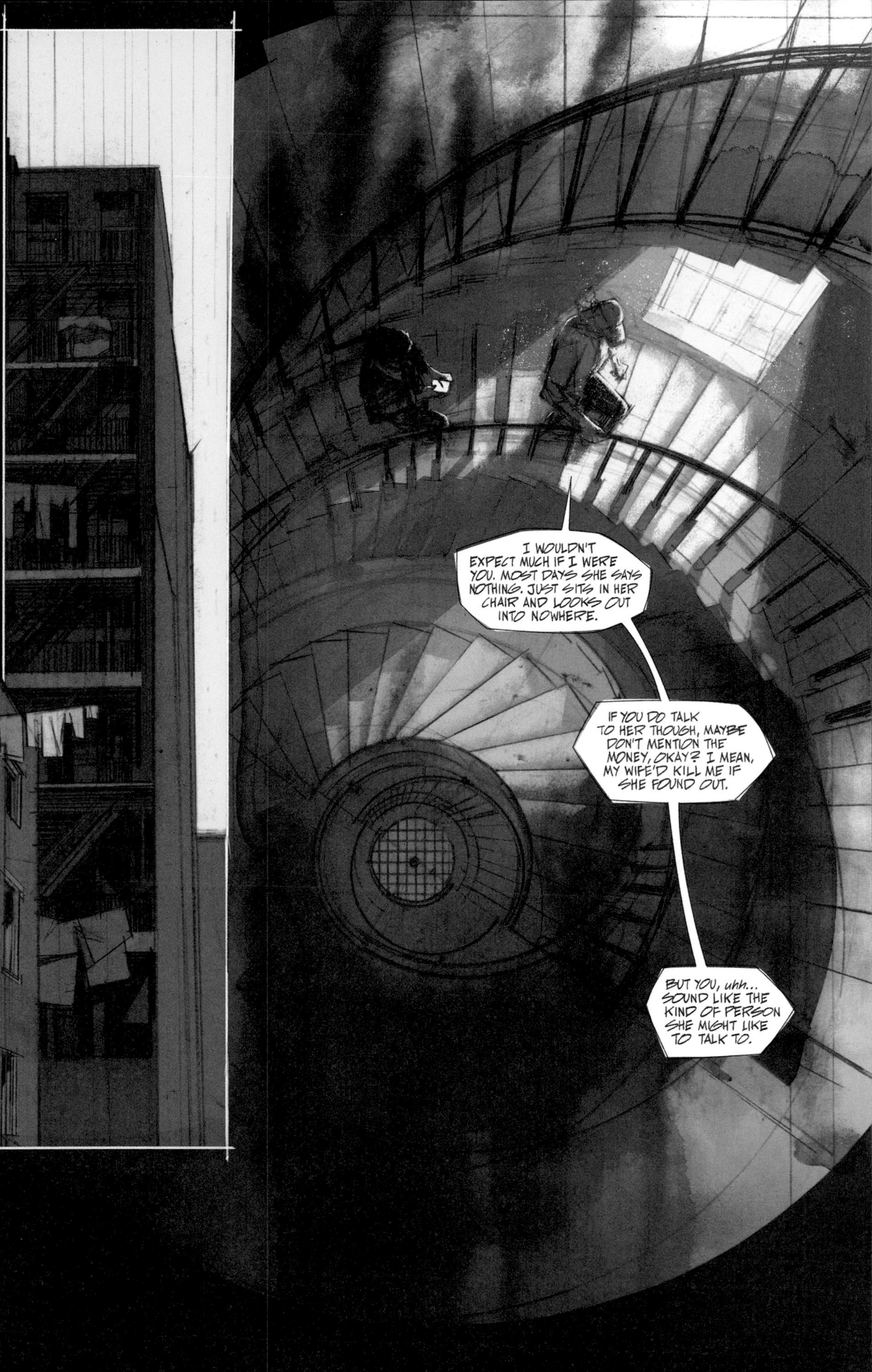
I WOULDN'T EXPECT MUCH IF I WERE YOU. MOST DAYS SHE SAYS NOTHING. JUST SITS IN HER CHAIR AND LOOKS OUT INTO NOWHERE.
IF YOU DO TALK TO HER THOUGH, MAYBE DON'T MENTION THE MONEY, OKAY? I MEAN, MY WIFE'D KILL ME IF SHE FOUND OUT.
BUT YOU, uhh... SOUND LIKE THE KIND OF PERSON SHE MIGHT LIKE TO TALK TO.

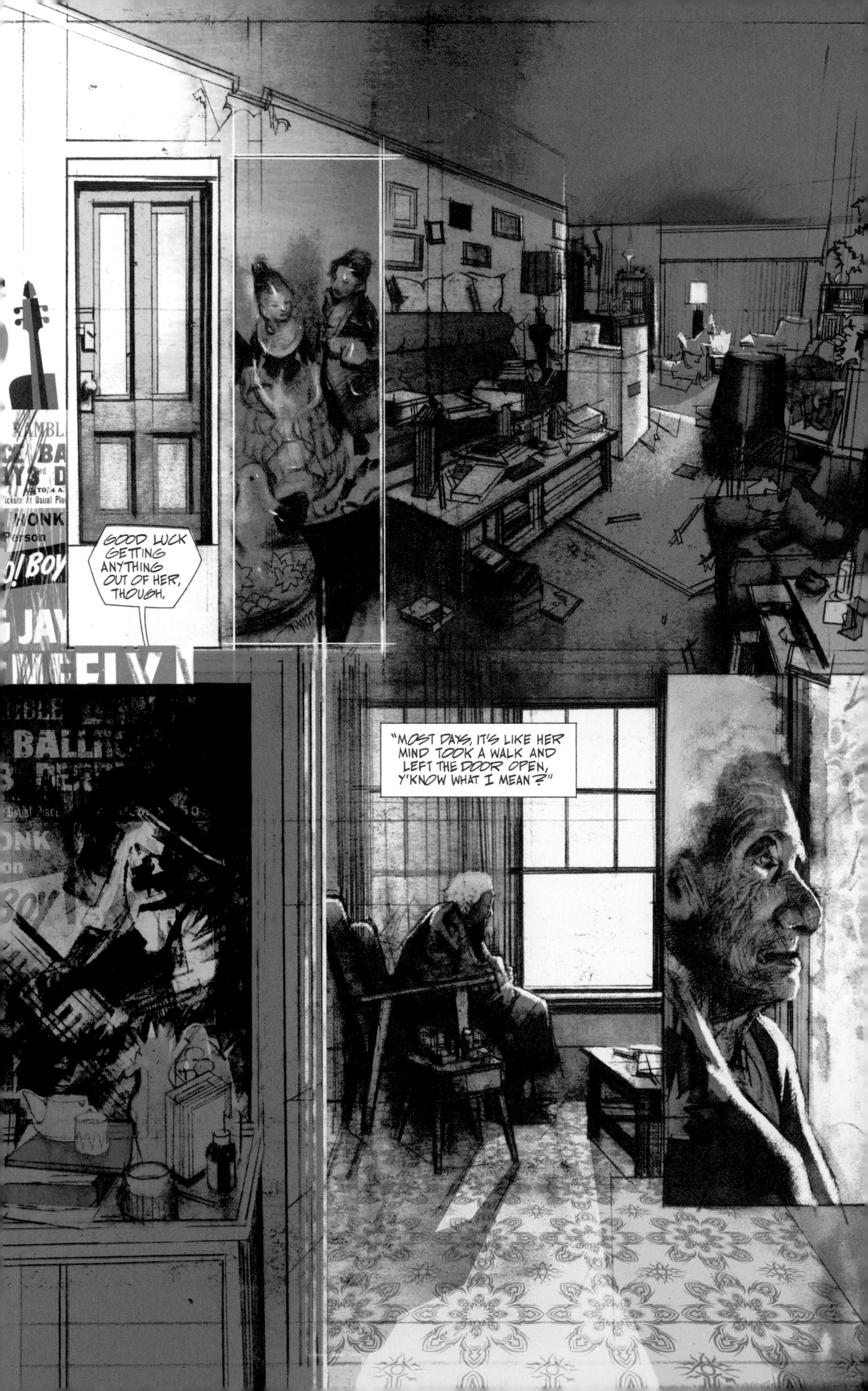
GOOD LUCK GETTING ANYTHING OUT OF HER, THOUGH.
"MOST DAYS, IT'S LIKE HER MIND TOOK A WALK AND LEFT THE DOOR OPEN, Y'KNOW WHAT I MEAN?"

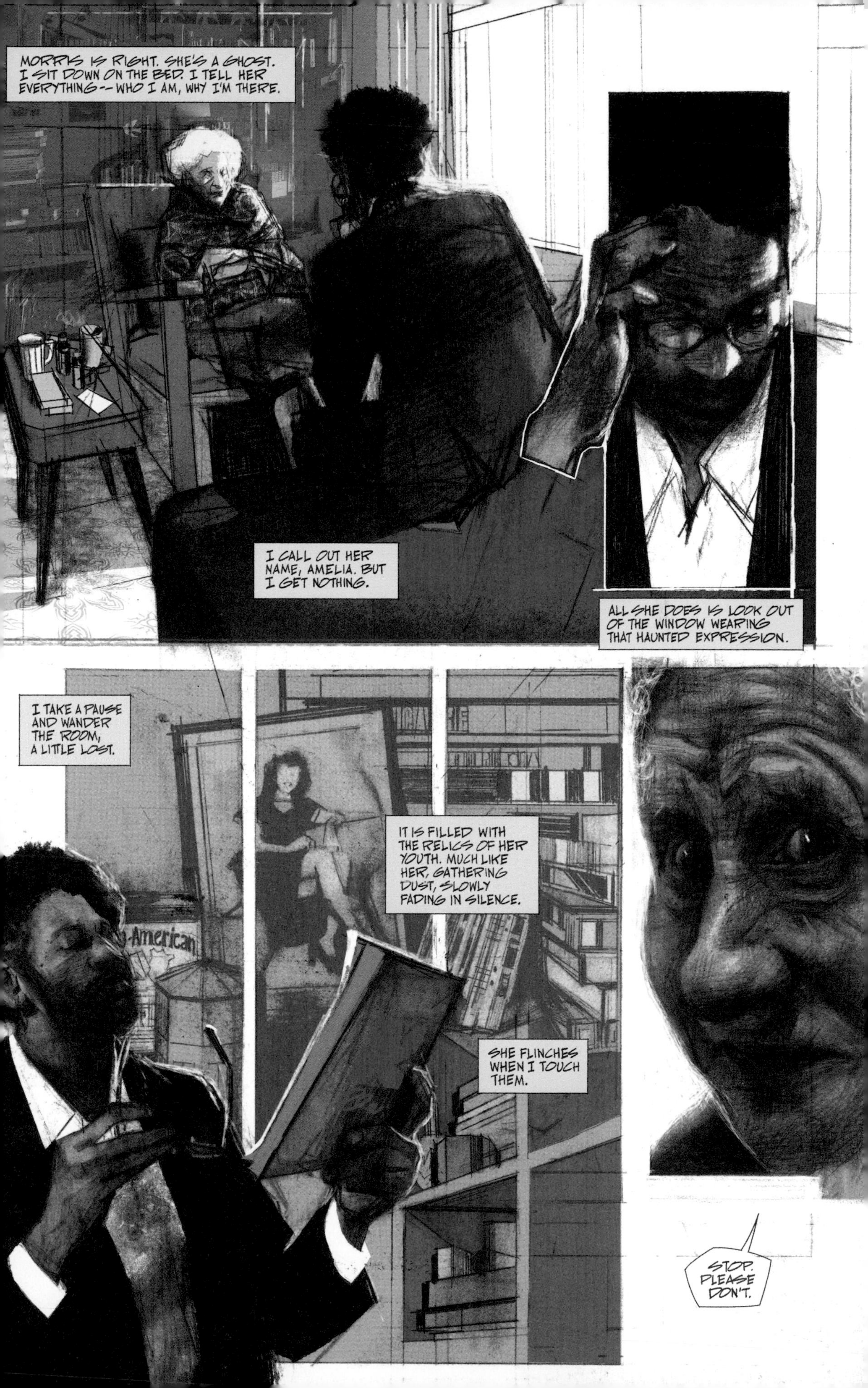
MORRIS IS RIGHT. SHE'S A GHOST. I SIT DOWN ON THE BED. I TELL HER EVERYTHING-- WHO I AM, WHY I'M THERE.
I CALL OUT HER NAME, AMELIA. BUT I GET NOTHING.
ALL SHE DOES IS LOOK OUT OF THE WINDOW WEARING THAT HAUNTED EXPRESSION.
I TAKE A PAUSE AND WANDER THE ROOM, A LITTLE LOST.
IT IS FILLED WITH THE RELICS OF HER YOUTH. MUCH LIKE HER, GATHERING DUST, SLOWLY FADING IN SILENCE.
SHE FLINCHES WHEN I TOUCH THEM.
STOP. PLEASE DON'T.

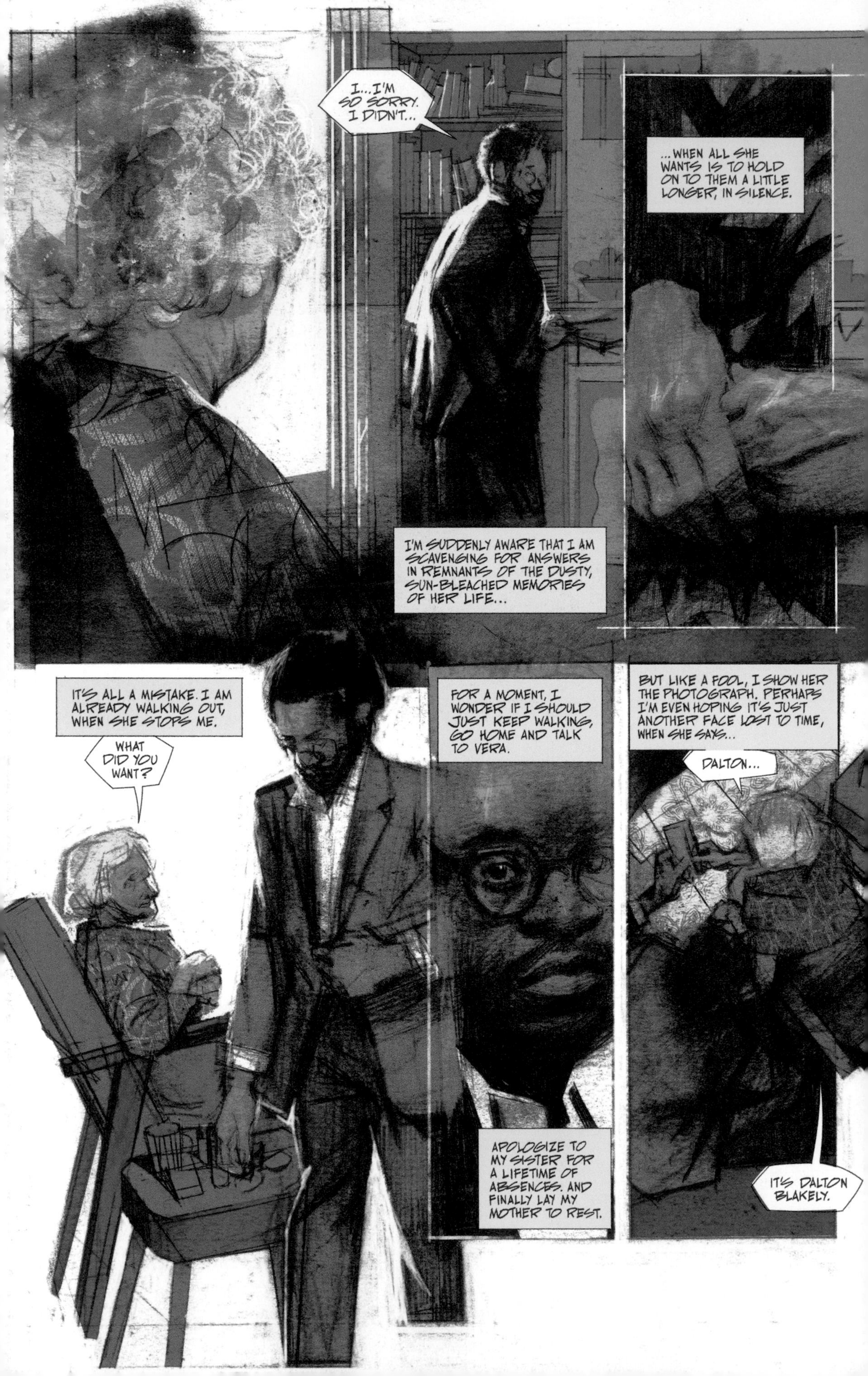
I... I'M SO SORRY. I DIDN'T...
...WHEN ALL SHE WANTS IS TO HOLD ON TO THEM A LITTLE LONGER, IN SILENCE.
I'M SUDDENLY AWARE THAT I AM SCAVENGING FOR ANSWERS IN REMNANTS OF THE DUSTY, SUN-BLEACHED MEMORIES OF HER LIFE...
IT'S ALL A MISTAKE. I AM ALREADY WALKING OUT, WHEN SHE STOPS ME.
WHAT DID YOU WANT?
FOR A MOMENT, I WONDER IF I SHOULD JUST KEEP WALKING, GO HOME AND TALK TO VERA.
APOLOGIZE TO MY SISTER FOR A LIFETIME OF ABSENCES. AND FINALLY LAY MY MOTHER TO REST.
BUT LIKE A FOOL, I SHOW HER THE PHOTOGRAPH. PERHAPS I'M EVEN HOPING IT'S JUST ANOTHER FACE LOST TO TIME, WHEN SHE SAYS...
DALTON...
IT'S DALTON BLAKELY.

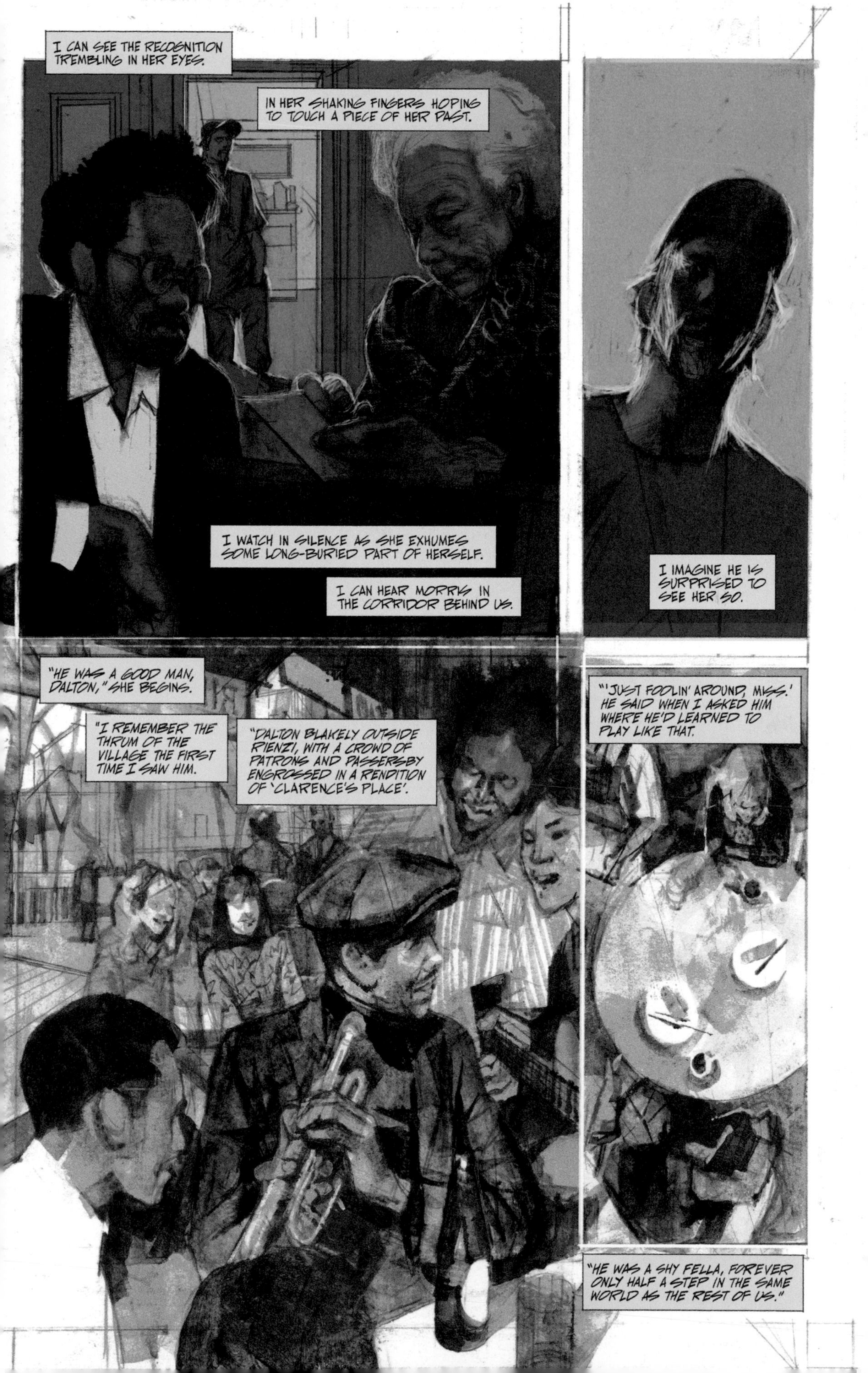
I CAN SEE THE RECOGNITION TREMBLING IN HER EYES.
IN HER SHAKING FINGERS HOPING TO TOUCH A PIECE OF HER PAST.
I WATCH IN SILENCE AS SHE EXHUMES SOME LONG-BURIED PART OF HERSELF.
I CAN HEAR MORRIS IN THE CORRIDOR BEHIND US.
I IMAGINE HE IS SURPRISED TO SEE HER SO.
"HE WAS A GOOD MAN, DALTON," SHE BEGINS.
"I REMEMBER THE THRUM OF THE VILLAGE THE FIRST TIME I SAW HIM.
"DALTON BLAKELY OUTSIDE RIENZI, WITH A CROWD OF PATRONS AND PASSERSBY ENGROSSED IN A RENDITION OF 'CLARENCE'S PLACE'.
"'JUST FOOLIN' AROUND, MISS.' HE SAID WHEN I ASKED HIM WHERE HE'D LEARNED TO PLAY LIKE THAT.
"HE WAS A SHY FELLA, FOREVER ONLY HALF A STEP IN THE SAME WORLD AS THE REST OF US."

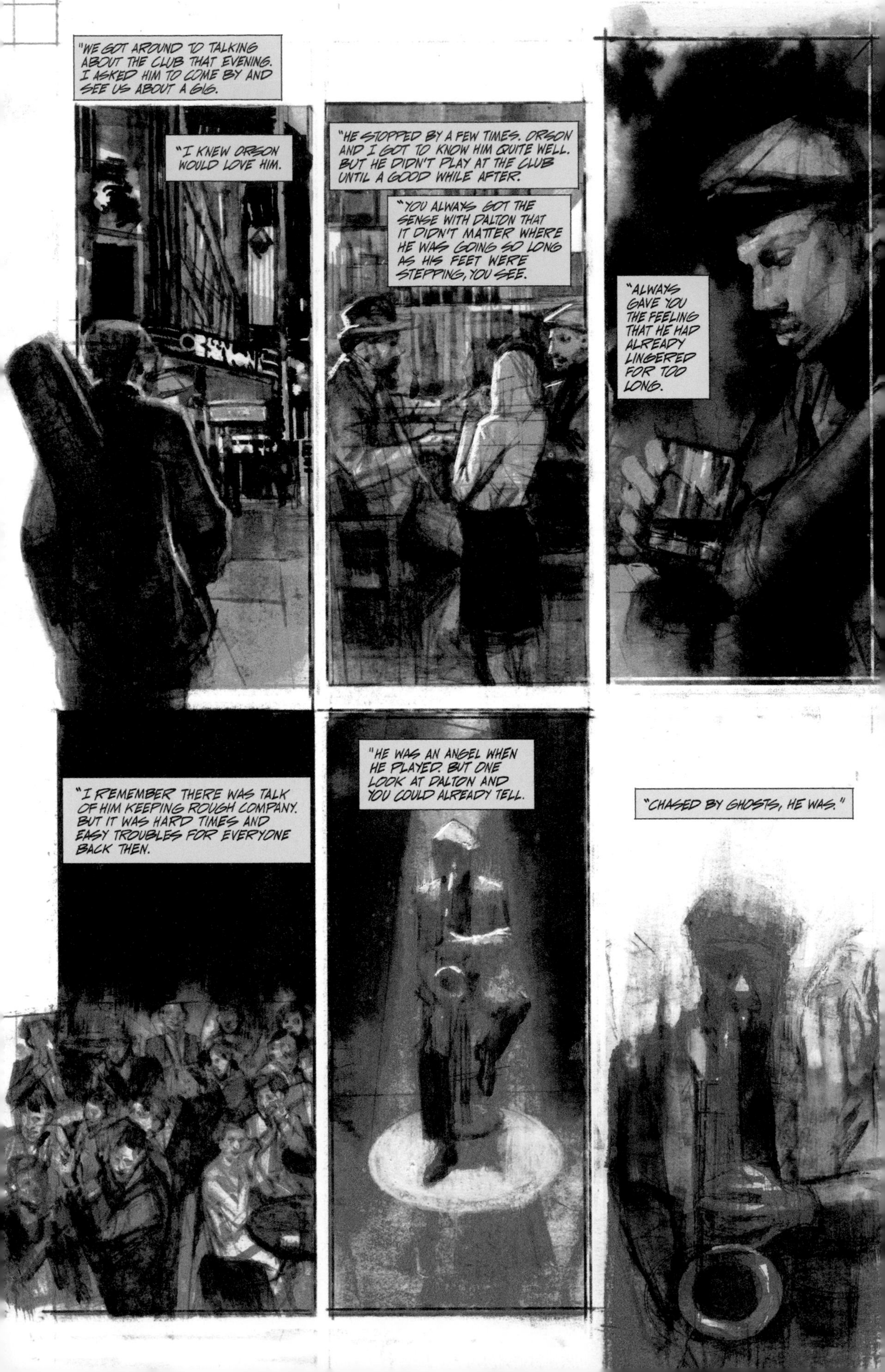
"WE GOT AROUND TO TALKING ABOUT THE CLUB THAT EVENING. I ASKED HIM TO COME BY AND SEE US ABOUT A GIG.
"I KNEW ORSON WOULD LOVE HIM.
"HE STOPPED BY A FEW TIMES. ORSON AND I GOT TO KNOW HIM QUITE WELL. BUT HE DIDN'T PLAY AT THE CLUB UNTIL A GOOD WHILE AFTER.
"YOU ALWAYS GOT THE SENSE WITH DALTON THAT IT DIDN'T MATTER WHERE HE WAS GOING SO LONG AS HIS FEET WERE STEPPING, YOU SEE.
"ALWAYS GAVE YOU THE FEELING THAT HE HAD ALREADY LINGERED FOR TOO LONG.
"I REMEMBER THERE WAS TALK OF HIM KEEPING ROUGH COMPANY. BUT IT WAS HARD TIMES AND EASY TROUBLES FOR EVERYONE BACK THEN.
"HE WAS AN ANGEL WHEN HE PLAYED. BUT ONE LOOK AT DALTON AND YOU COULD ALREADY TELL.
"CHASED BY GHOSTS, HE WAS."

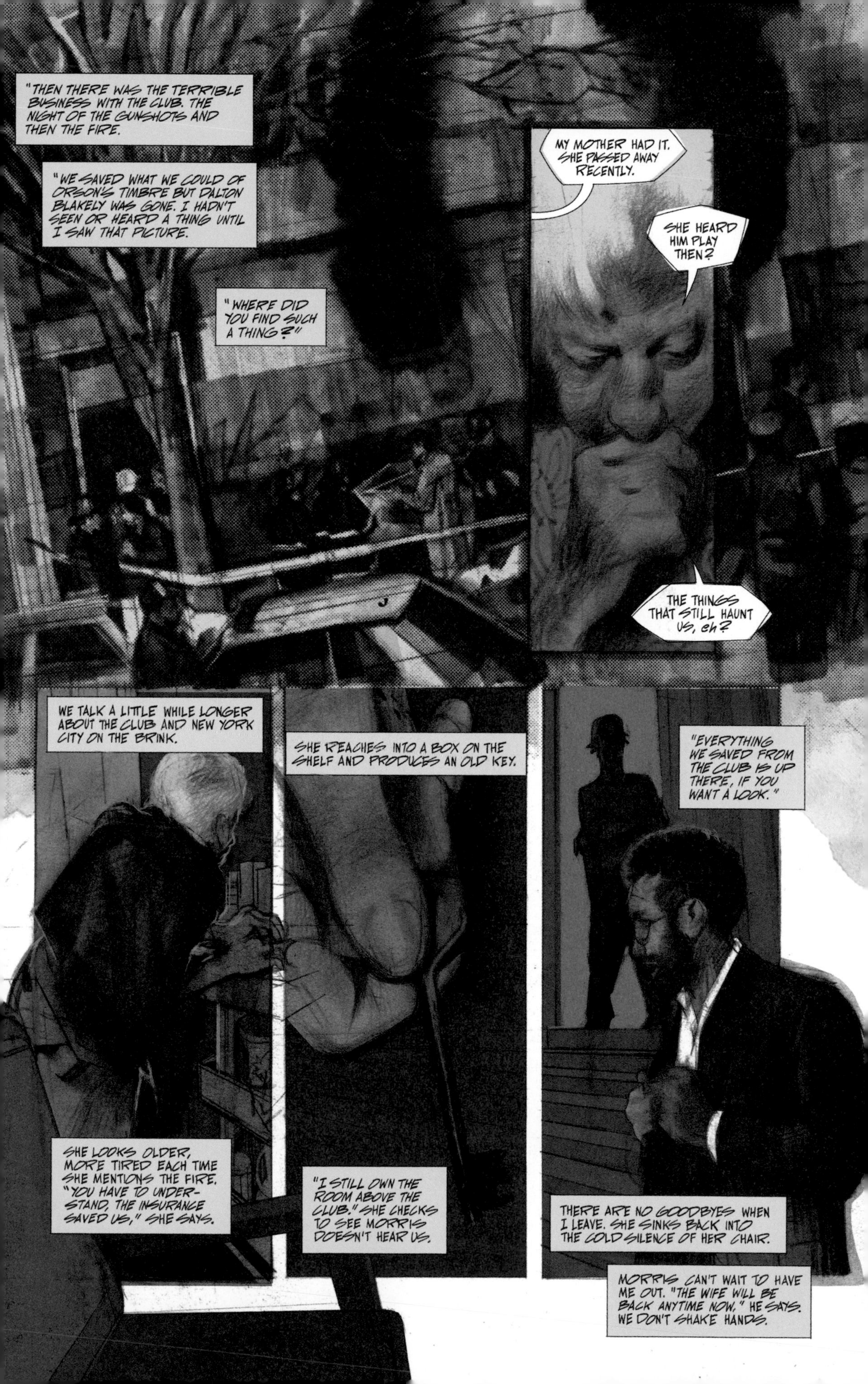
"THEN THERE WAS THE TERRIBLE BUSINESS WITH THE CLUB. THE NIGHT OF THE GUNSHOTS AND THEN THE FIRE.
"WE SAVED WHAT WE COULD OF ORSON'S TIMBRE BUT DALTON BLAKELY WAS GONE. I HADN'T SEEN OR HEARD A THING UNTIL I SAW THAT PICTURE.
"WHERE DID YOU FIND SUCH A THING?"
MY MOTHER HAD IT. SHE PASSED AWAY RECENTLY.
SHE HEARD HIM PLAY THEN?
THE THINGS THAT STILL HAUNT US, eh?
WE TALK A LITTLE WHILE LONGER ABOUT THE CLUB AND NEW YORK CITY ON THE BRINK.
SHE LOOKS OLDER, MORE TIRED EACH TIME SHE MENTIONS THE FIRE. "YOU HAVE TO UNDERSTAND, THE INSURANCE SAVED US," SHE SAYS.
SHE REACHES INTO A BOX ON THE SHELF AND PRODUCES AN OLD KEY.
"I STILL OWN THE ROOM ABOVE THE CLUB." SHE CHECKS TO SEE MORRIS DOESN'T HEAR US.
"EVERYTHING WE SAVED FROM THE CLUB IS UP THERE, IF YOU WANT A LOOK."
THERE ARE NO GOODBYES WHEN I LEAVE. SHE SINKS BACK INTO THE COLD SILENCE OF HER CHAIR.
MORRIS CAN'T WAIT TO HAVE ME OUT. "THE WIFE WILL BE BACK ANYTIME NOW," HE SAYS. WE DON'T SHAKE HANDS.

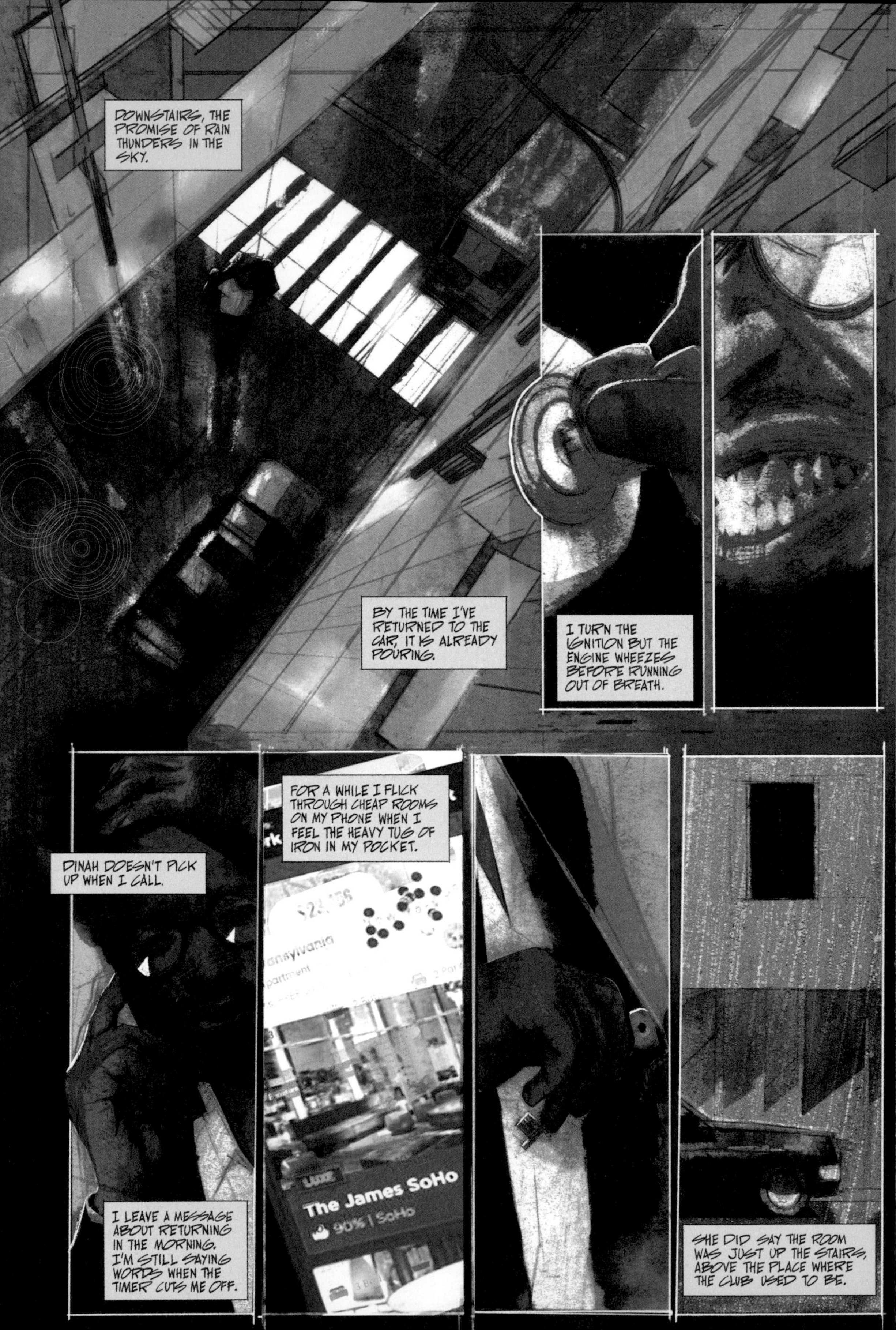
DOWNSTAIRS, THE PROMISE OF RAIN THUNDERS IN THE SKY.
BY THE TIME I'VE RETURNED TO THE CAR, IT IS ALREADY POURING.
I TURN THE IGNITION BUT THE ENGINE WHEEZES BEFORE RUNNING OUT OF BREATH.
DINAH DOESN'T PICK UP WHEN I CALL.
I LEAVE A MESSAGE ABOUT RETURNING IN THE MORNING. I'M STILL SAYING WORDS WHEN THE TIMER CUTS ME OFF.
FOR A WHILE I FLICK THROUGH CHEAP ROOMS ON MY PHONE WHEN I FEEL THE HEAVY TUG OF IRON IN MY POCKET.
The James SoHo
90% | SoHo
SHE DID SAY THE ROOM WAS JUST UP THE STAIRS, ABOVE THE PLACE WHERE THE CLUB USED TO BE.

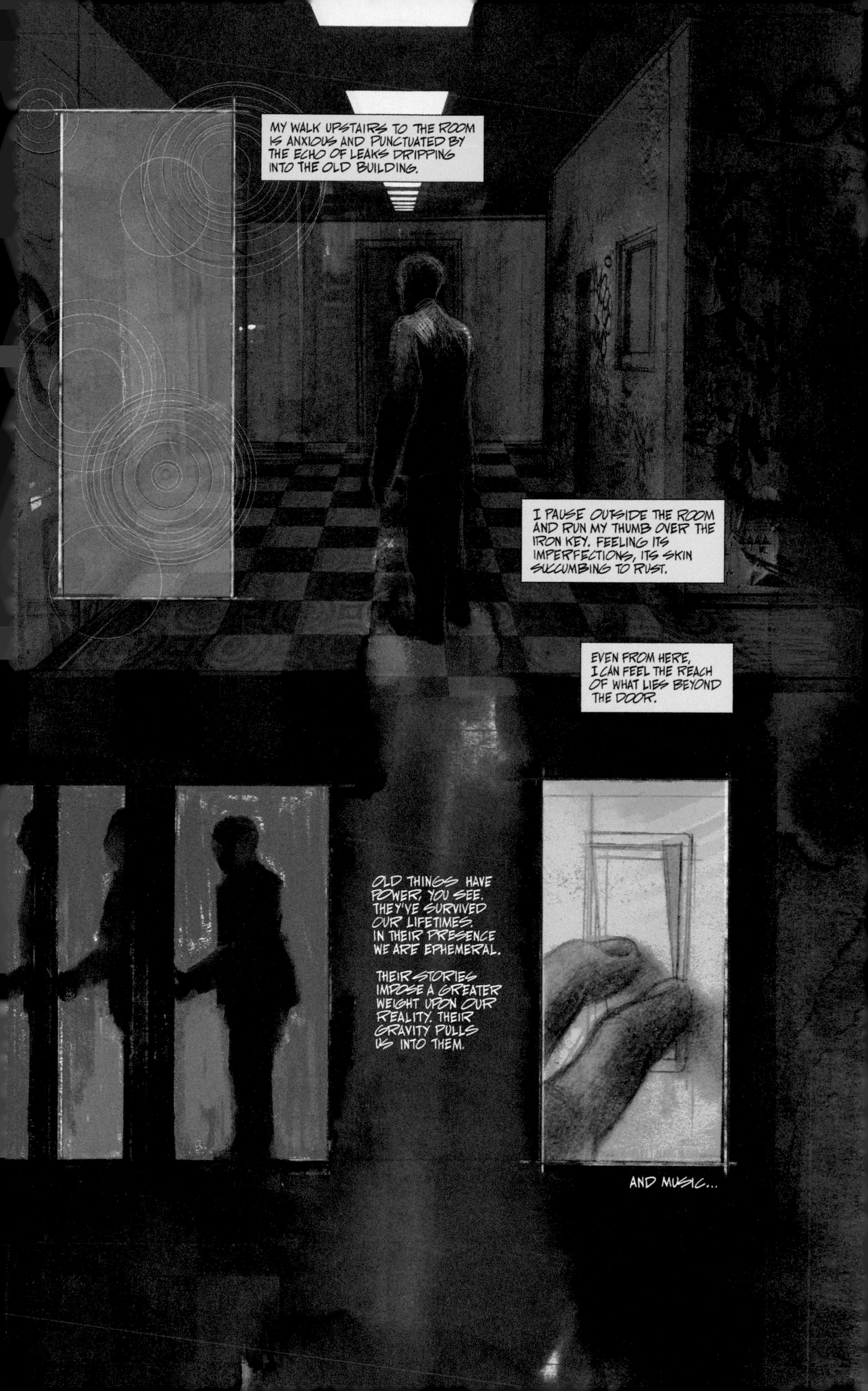
MY WALK UPSTAIRS TO THE ROOM IS ANXIOUS AND PUNCTUATED BY THE ECHO OF LEAKS DRIPPING INTO THE OLD BUILDING.
I PAUSE OUTSIDE THE ROOM AND RUN MY THUMB OVER THE IRON KEY. FEELING ITS IMPERFECTIONS, ITS SKIN SUCCUMBING TO RUST.
EVEN FROM HERE, I CAN FEEL THE REACH OF WHAT LIES BEYOND THE DOOR.
OLD THINGS HAVE POWER, YOU SEE. THEY'VE SURVIVED OUR LIFETIMES. IN THEIR PRESENCE WE ARE EPHEMERAL.
THEIR STORIES IMPOSE A GREATER WEIGHT UPON OUR REALITY. THEIR GRAVITY PULLS US INTO THEM.
AND MUSIC...

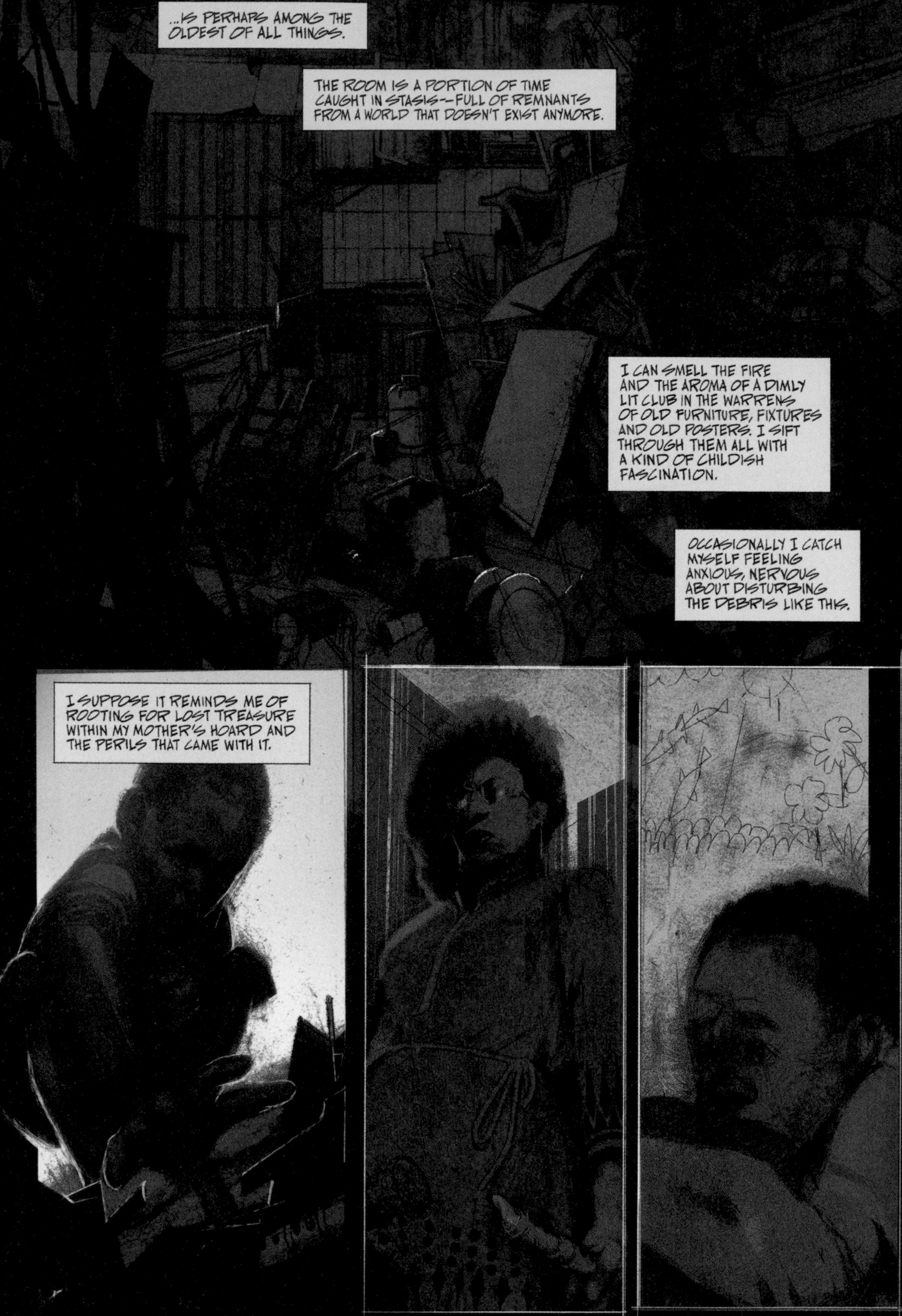
...IS PERHAPS AMONG THE OLDEST OF ALL THINGS.
THE ROOM IS A PORTION OF TIME CAUGHT IN STASIS--FULL OF REMNANTS FROM A WORLD THAT DOESN'T EXIST ANYMORE.
I CAN SMELL THE FIRE AND THE AROMA OF A DIMLY LIT CLUB IN THE WARRENS OF OLD FURNITURE, FIXTURES AND OLD POSTERS. I SIFT THROUGH THEM ALL WITH A KIND OF CHILDISH FASCINATION.
OCCASIONALLY I CATCH MYSELF FEELING ANXIOUS, NERVOUS ABOUT DISTURBING THE DEBRIS LIKE THIS.
I SUPPOSE IT REMINDS ME OF ROOTING FOR LOST TREASURE WITHIN MY MOTHER'S HOARD AND THE PERILS THAT CAME WITH IT.

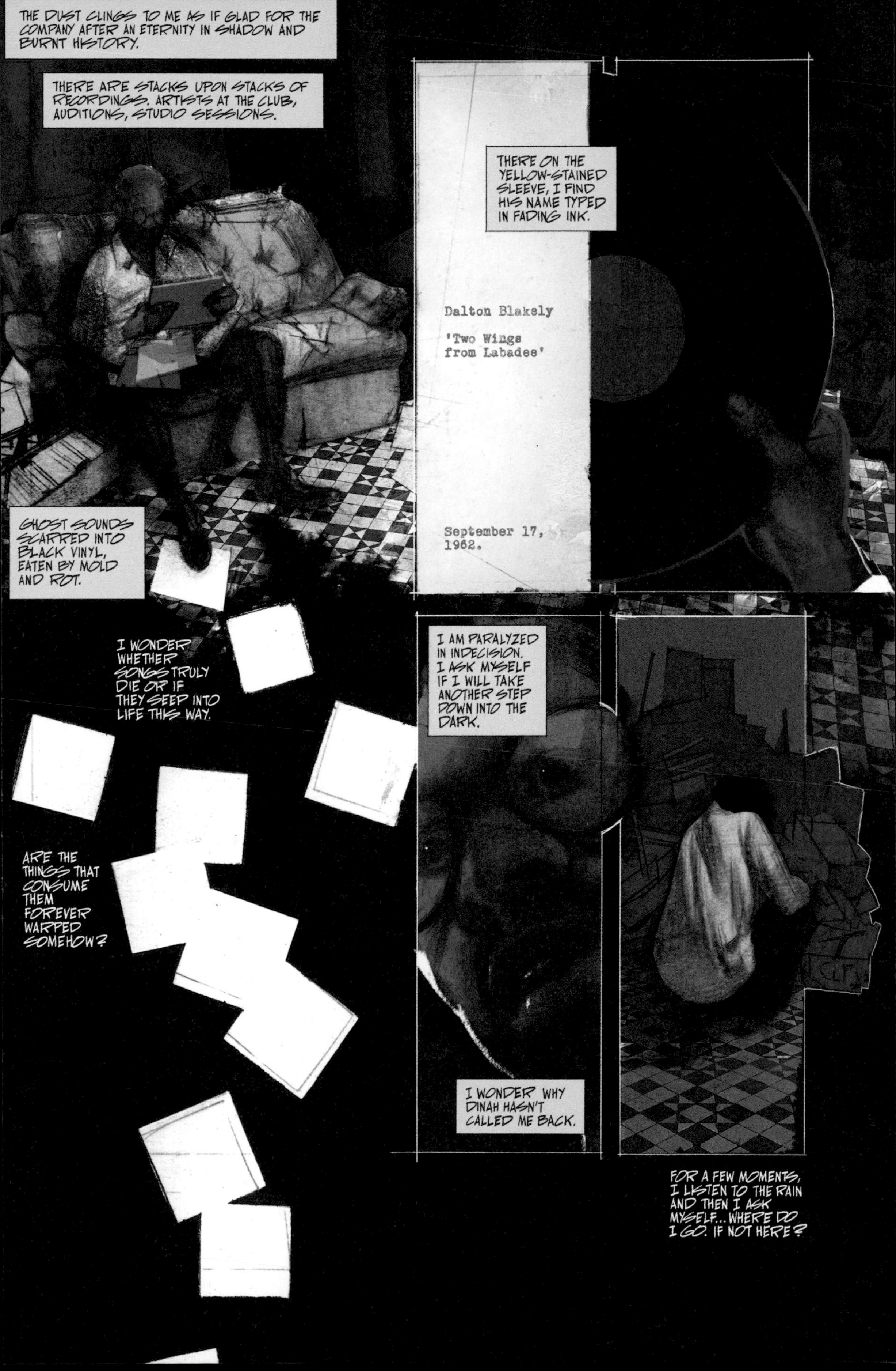
THE DUST CLINGS TO ME AS IF GLAD FOR THE COMPANY AFTER AN ETERNITY IN SHADOW AND BURNT HISTORY.
THERE ARE STACKS UPON STACKS OF RECORDINGS. ARTISTS AT THE CLUB, AUDITIONS, STUDIO SESSIONS.
THERE ON THE YELLOW-STAINED SLEEVE, I FIND HIS NAME TYPED IN FADING INK.
Dalton Blakely
'Two Wings from Labadee'
September 17, 1962.
GHOST SOUNDS SCARRED INTO BLACK VINYL, EATEN BY MOLD AND ROT.
I WONDER WHETHER SONGS TRULY DIE OR IF THEY SEEP INTO LIFE THIS WAY.
ARE THE THINGS THAT CONSUME THEM FOREVER WARPED SOMEHOW?
I AM PARALYZED IN INDECISION. I ASK MYSELF IF I WILL TAKE ANOTHER STEP DOWN INTO THE DARK.
I WONDER WHY DINAH HASN'T CALLED ME BACK.
FOR A FEW MOMENTS, I LISTEN TO THE RAIN AND THEN I ASK MYSELF... WHERE DO I GO. IF NOT HERE?

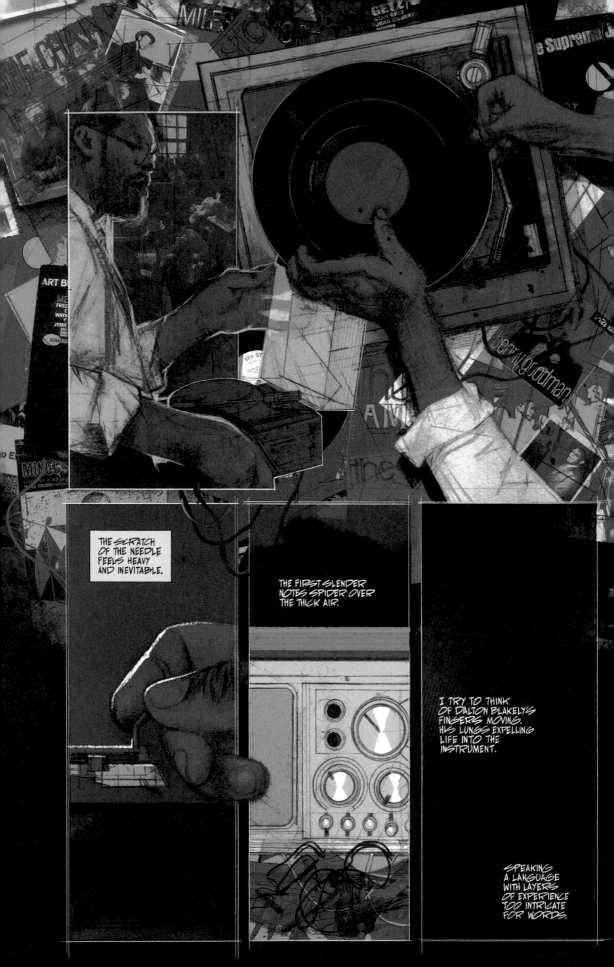

THE SCRATCH OF THE NEEDLE FEELS HEAVY AND INEVITABLE.

THE FIRST SLENDER NOTES SPIDER OVER THE THICK AIR.

I TRY TO THINK OF DALTON BLAKELY'S FINGERS MOVING. HIS LUNGS EXPELLING LIFE INTO THE INSTRUMENT.

SPEAKING A LANGUAGE WITH LAYERS OF EXPERIENCE TOO INTRICATE FOR WORDS.

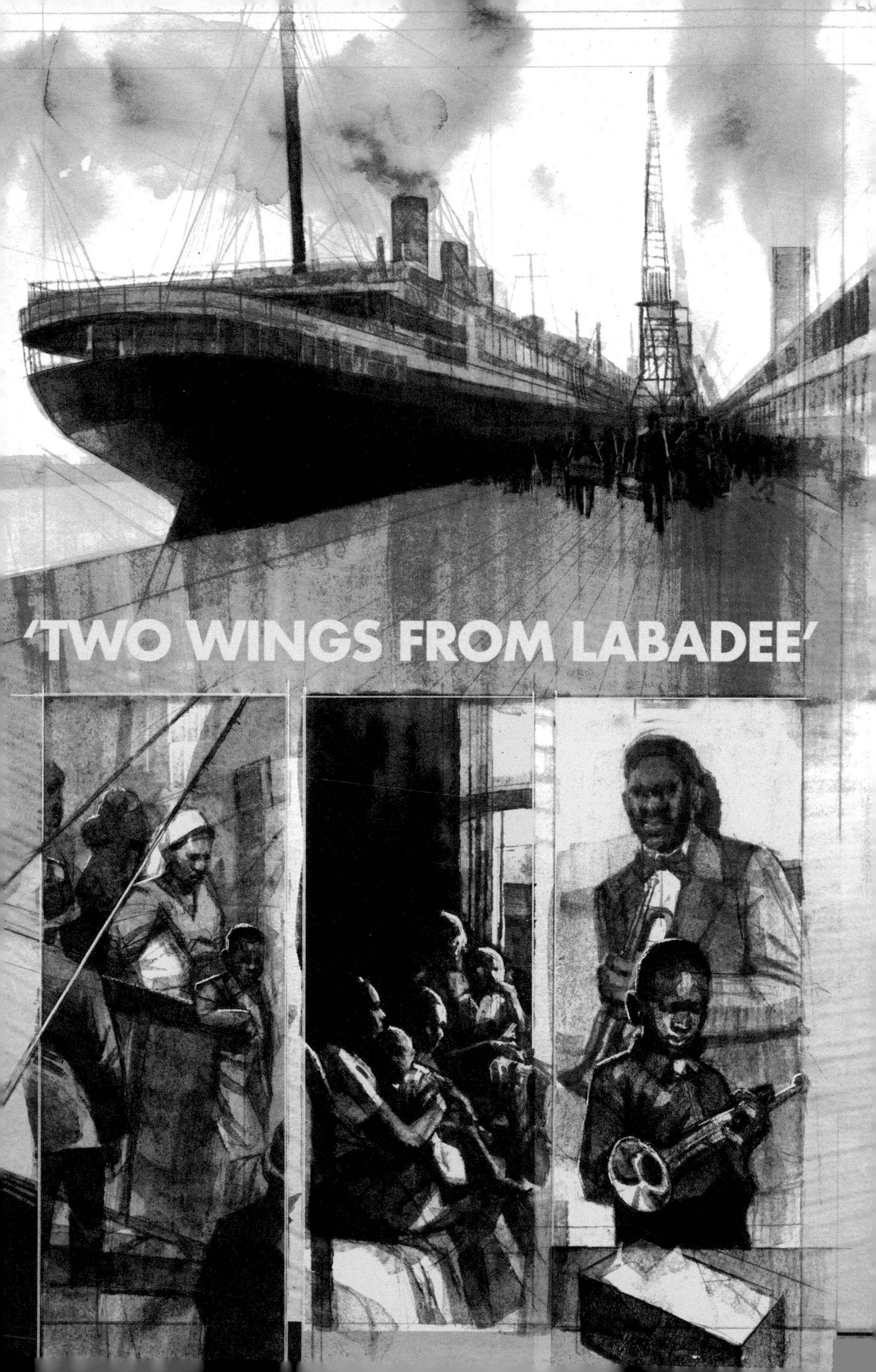
'TWO WINGS FROM LABADEE'

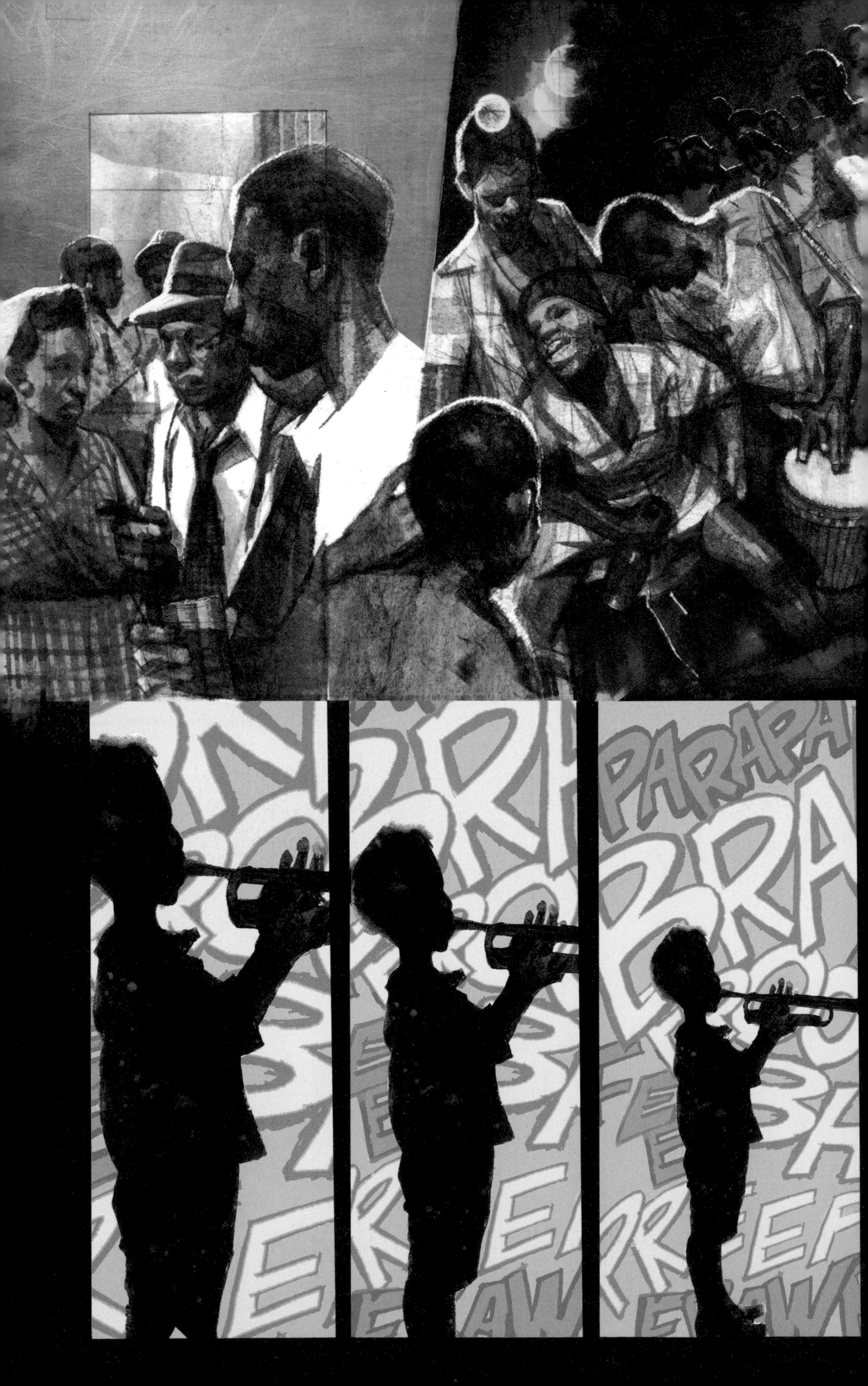
PARAPA

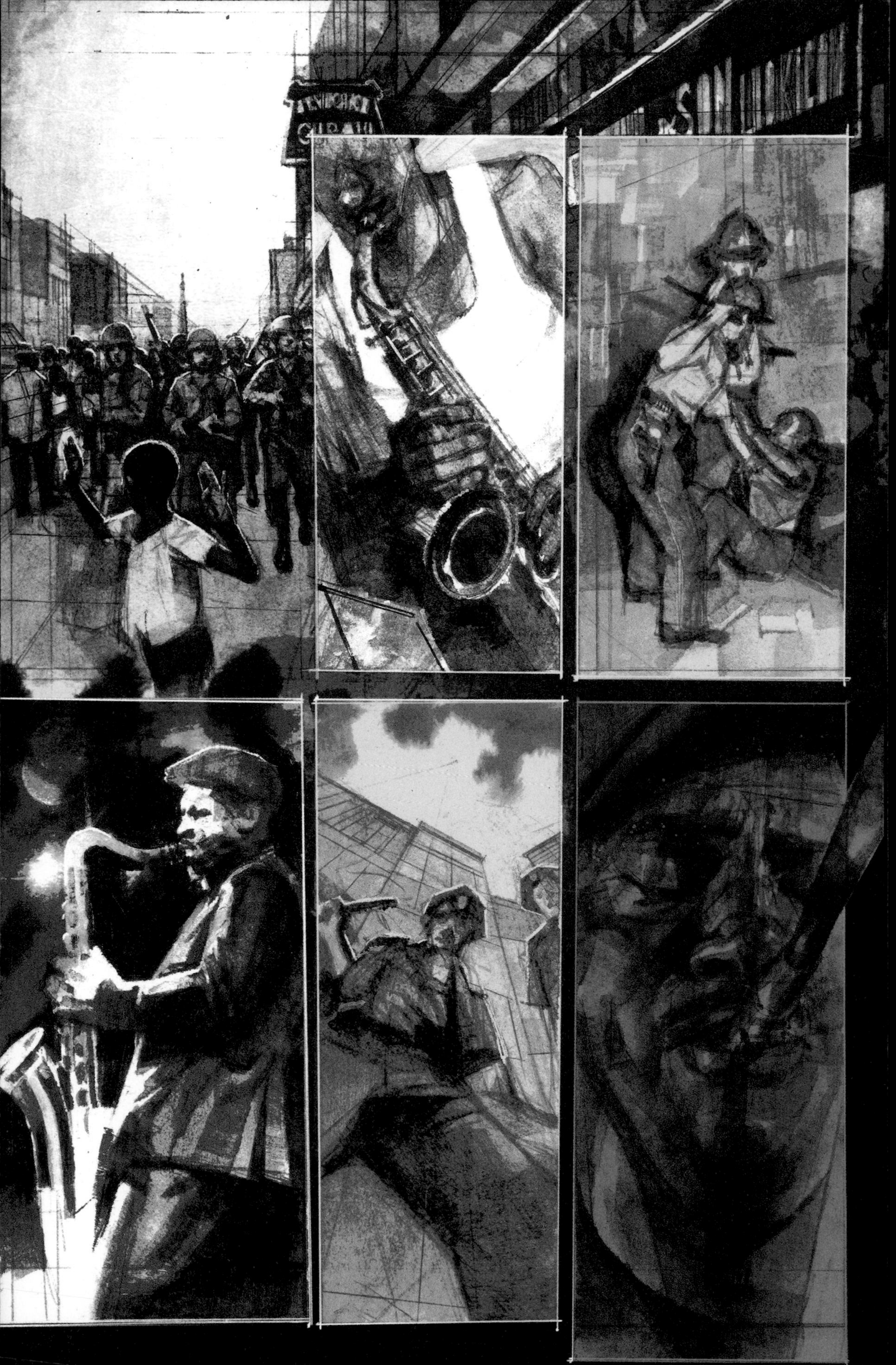

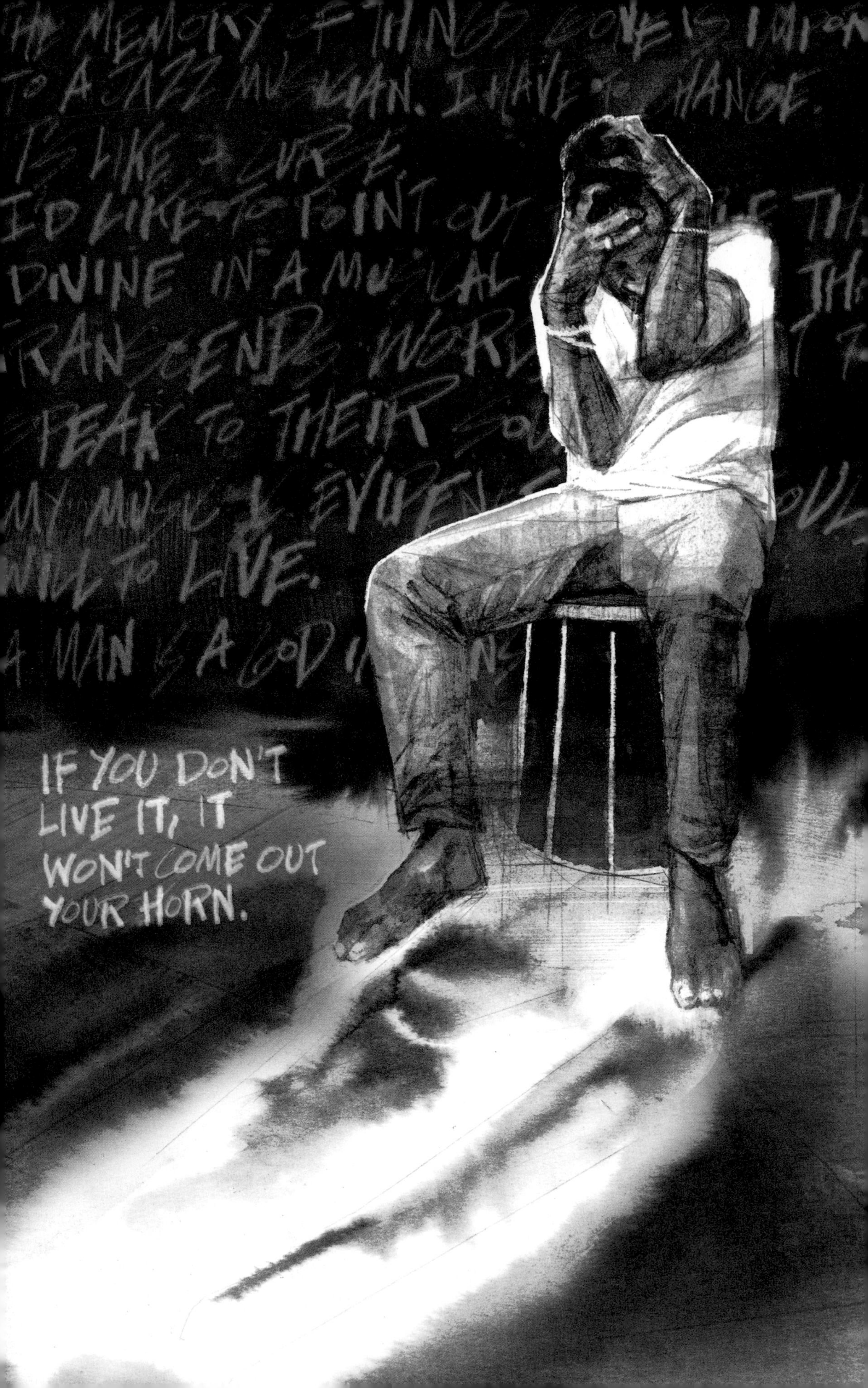
IF YOU DON'T LIVE IT, IT WON'T COME OUT YOUR HORN.

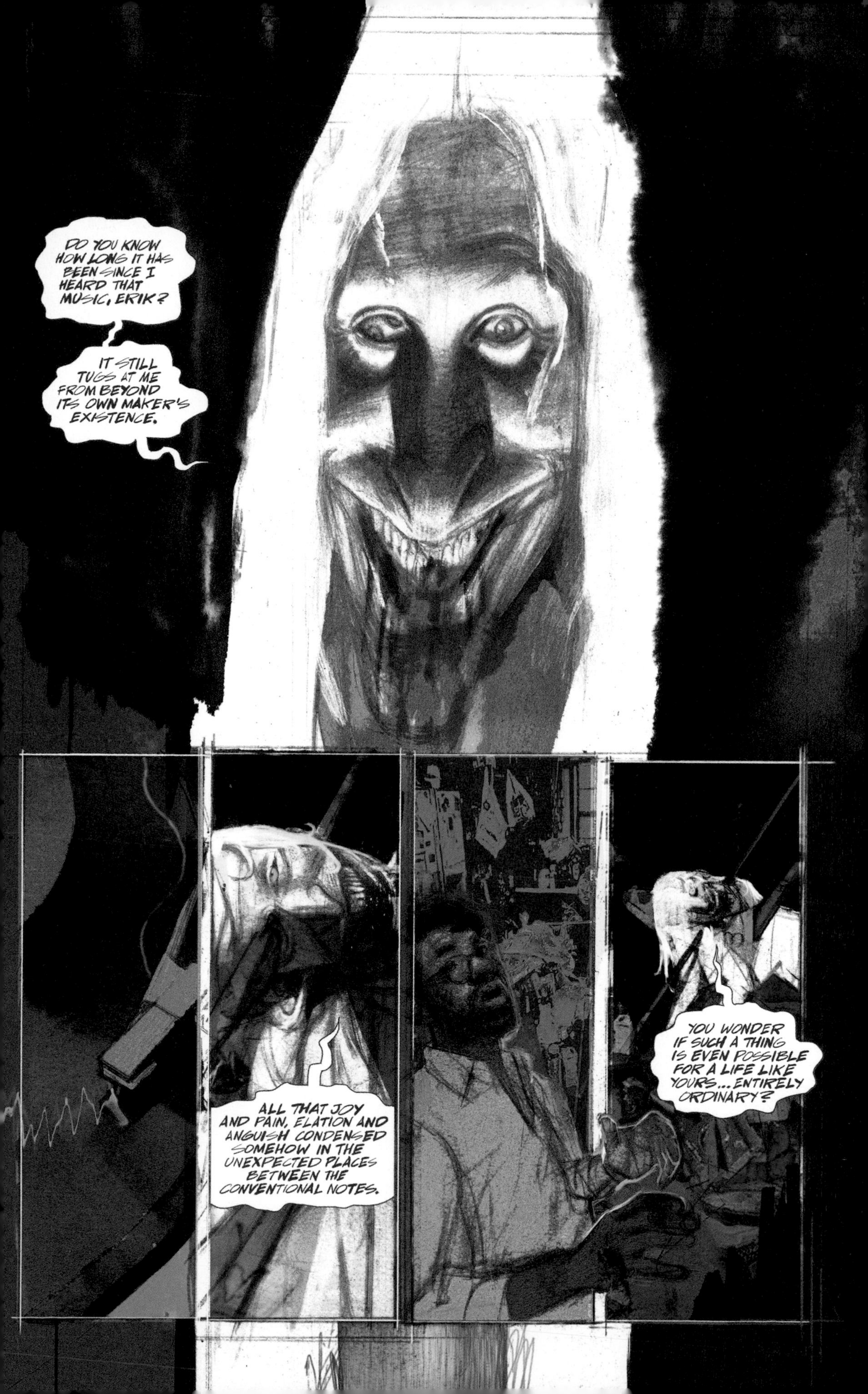
DO YOU KNOW HOW LONG IT HAS BEEN SINCE I HEARD THAT MUSIC, ERIK?
IT STILL TUGS AT ME FROM BEYOND ITS OWN MAKER'S EXISTENCE.
ALL THAT JOY AND PAIN, ELATION AND ANGUISH CONDENSED SOMEHOW IN THE UNEXPECTED PLACES BETWEEN THE CONVENTIONAL NOTES.
YOU WONDER IF SUCH A THING IS EVEN POSSIBLE FOR A LIFE LIKE YOURS... ENTIRELY ORDINARY?

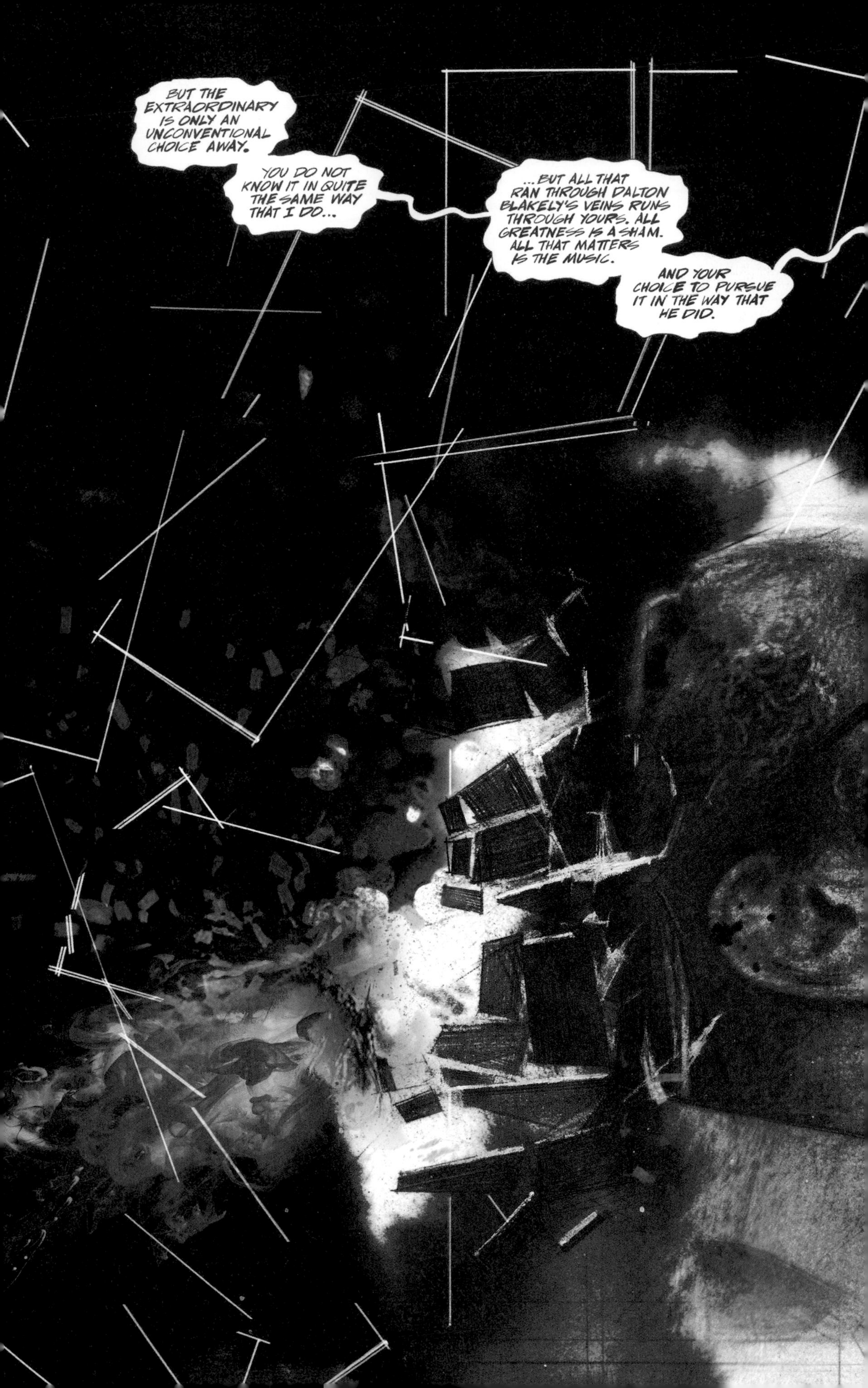
BUT THE EXTRAORDINARY IS ONLY AN UNCONVENTIONAL CHOICE AWAY.
YOU DO NOT KNOW IT IN QUITE THE SAME WAY THAT I DO...
...BUT ALL THAT RAN THROUGH DALTON BLAKELY'S VEINS RUNS THROUGH YOURS. ALL GREATNESS IS A SHAM. ALL THAT MATTERS IS THE MUSIC.
AND YOUR CHOICE TO PURSUE IT IN THE WAY THAT HE DID.

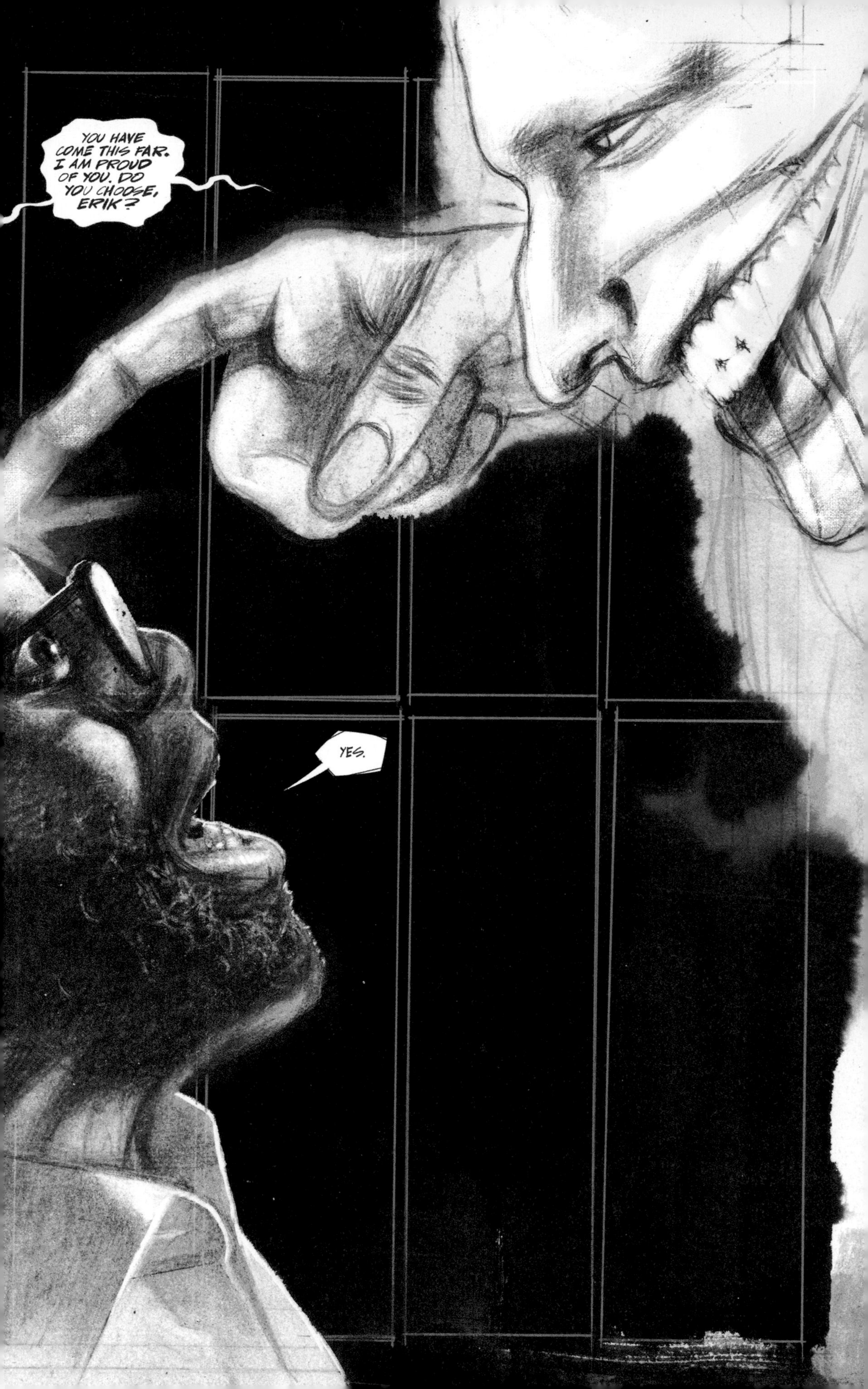
YOU HAVE COME THIS FAR. I AM PROUD OF YOU. DO YOU CHOOSE, ERIK?
YES.

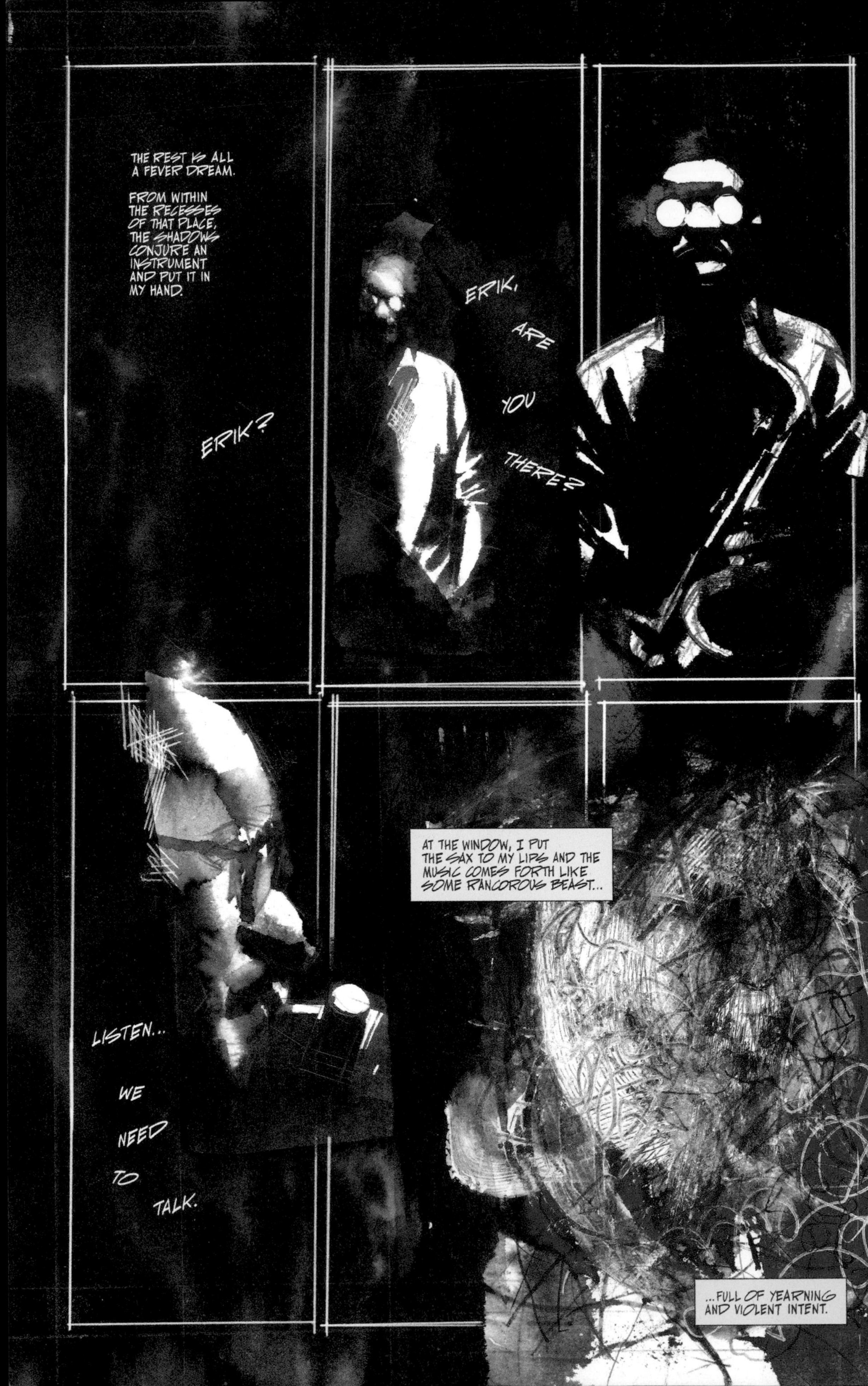
THE REST IS ALL A FEVER DREAM.
FROM WITHIN THE RECESSES OF THAT PLACE, THE SHADOWS CONJURE AN INSTRUMENT AND PUT IT IN MY HAND.
ERIK?
ERIK, ARE YOU THERE?
LISTEN... WE NEED TO TALK.
AT THE WINDOW, I PUT THE SAX TO MY LIPS AND THE MUSIC COMES FORTH LIKE SOME RANCOROUS BEAST...
...FULL OF YEARNING AND VIOLENT INTENT.

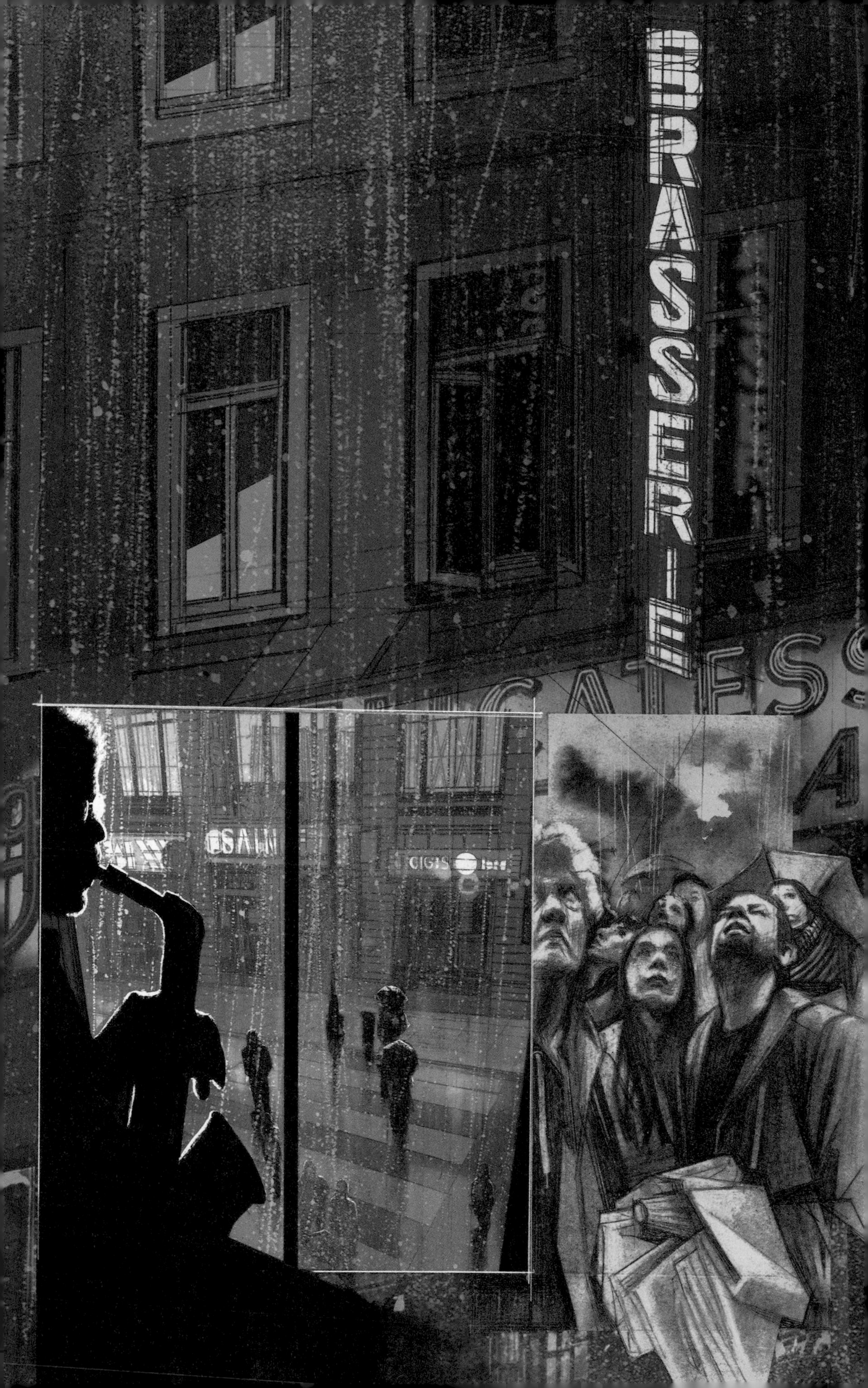
BRASSERIE

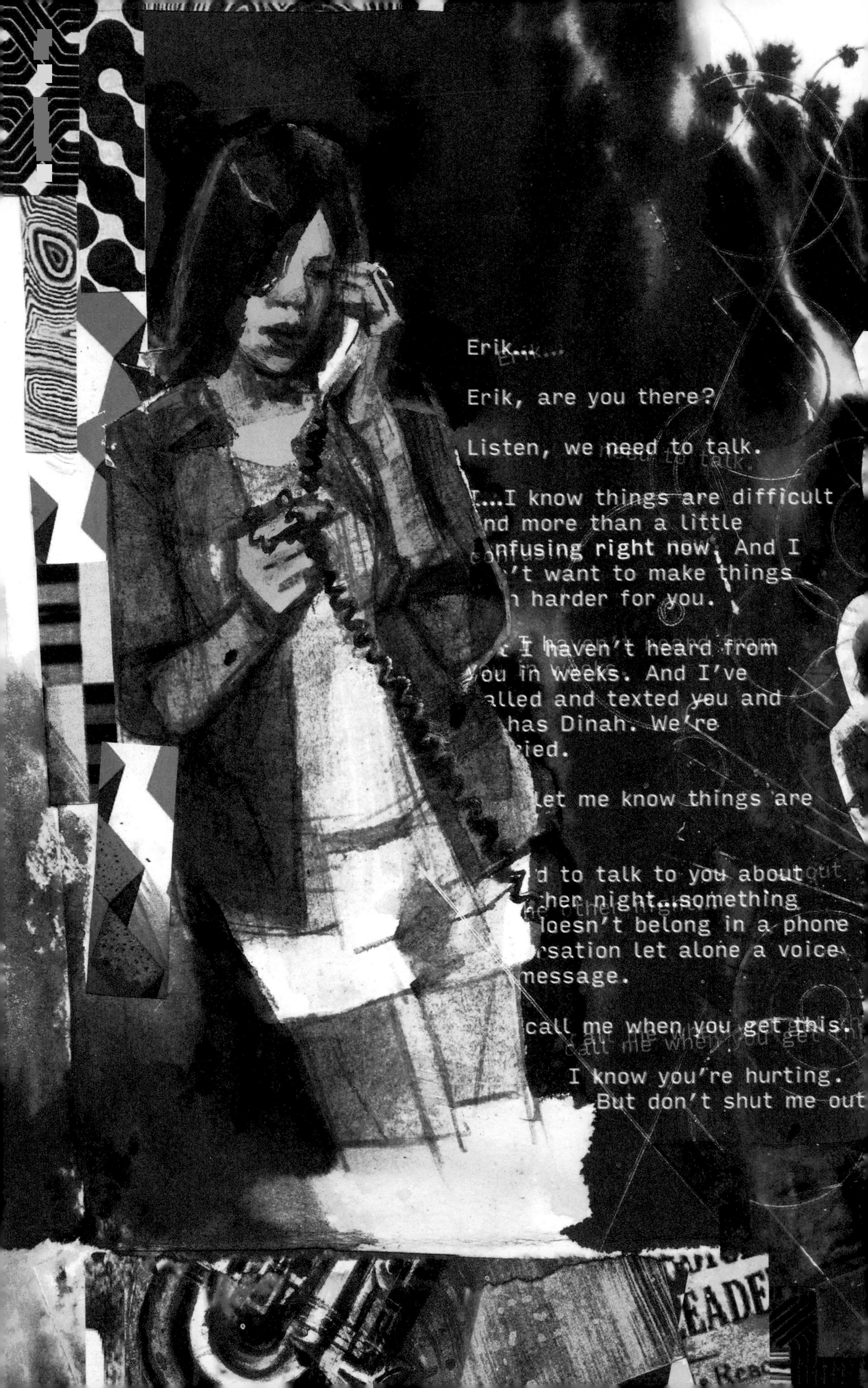
Erik...
Erik, are you there?
Listen, we need to talk.
I...I know things are difficult
nd more than a little
nfusing right now. And I
't want to make things
harder for you.
I haven't heard from
you in weeks. And I've
alled and texted you and
has Dinah. We're
ied.
let me know things are
d to talk to you about
her night...something
loesn't belong in a phone
rsation let alone a voice
message.
call me when you get this.
I know you're hurting.
But don't shut me out

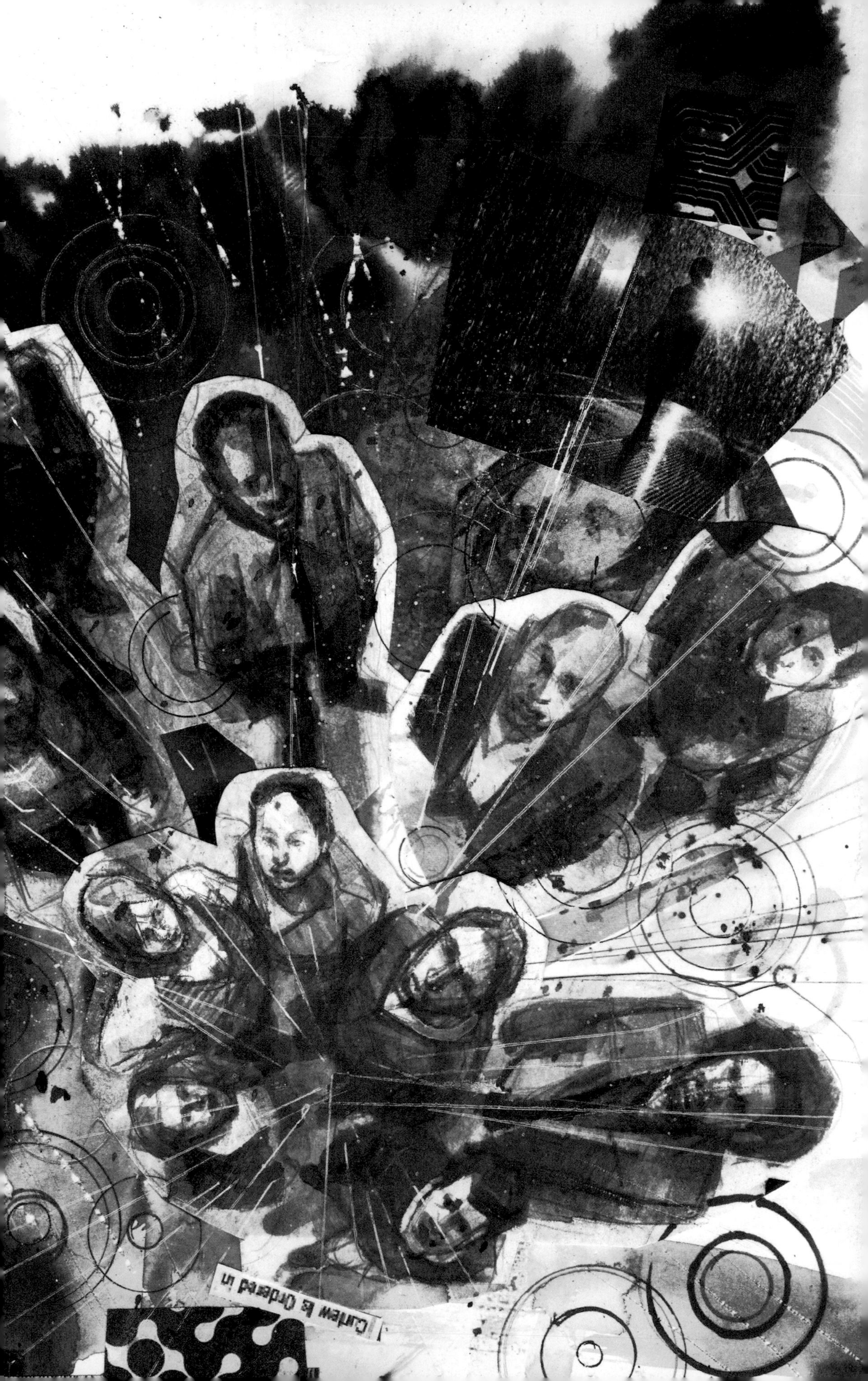
Curfew Is Ordered in

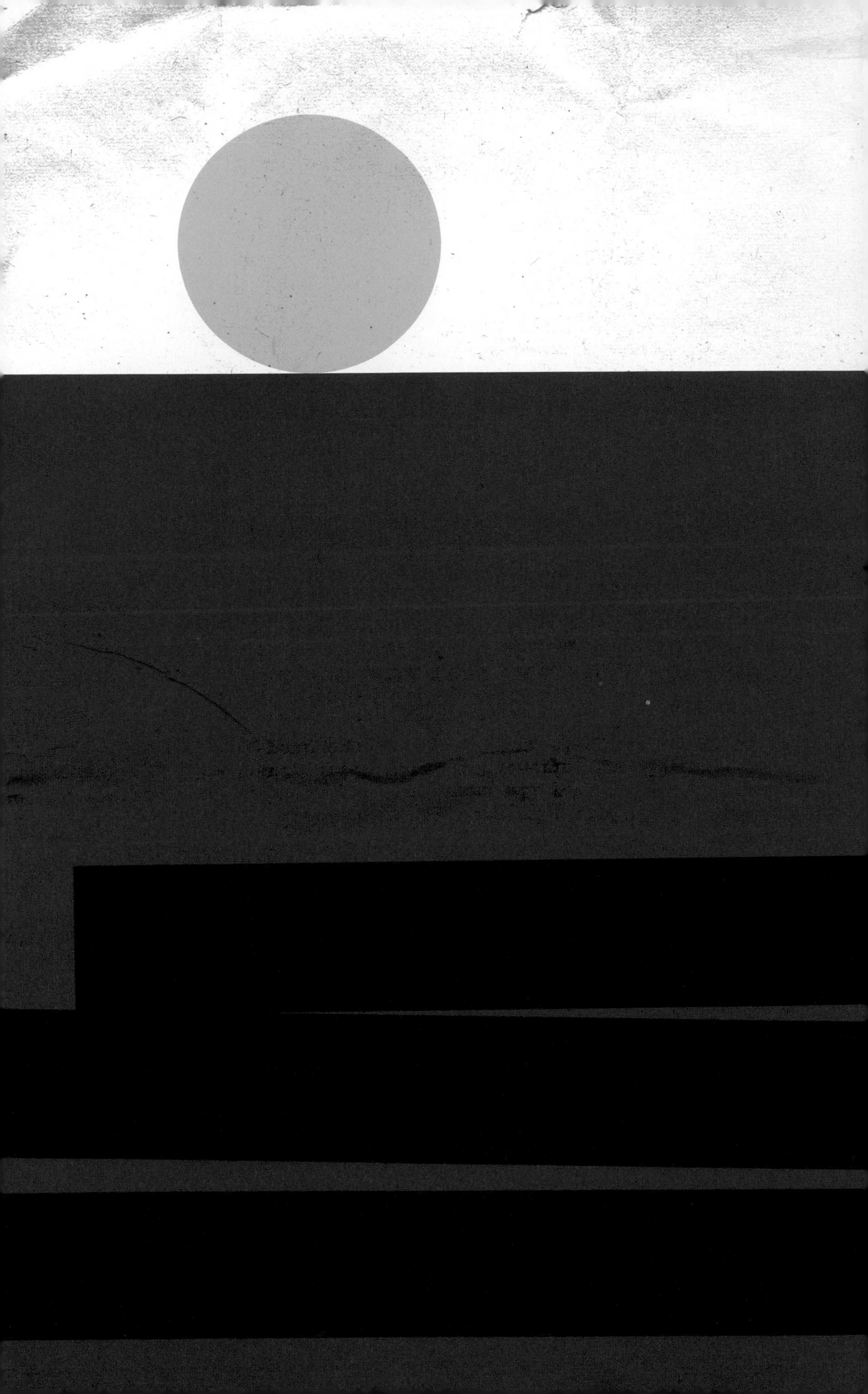

CHAPTER 3

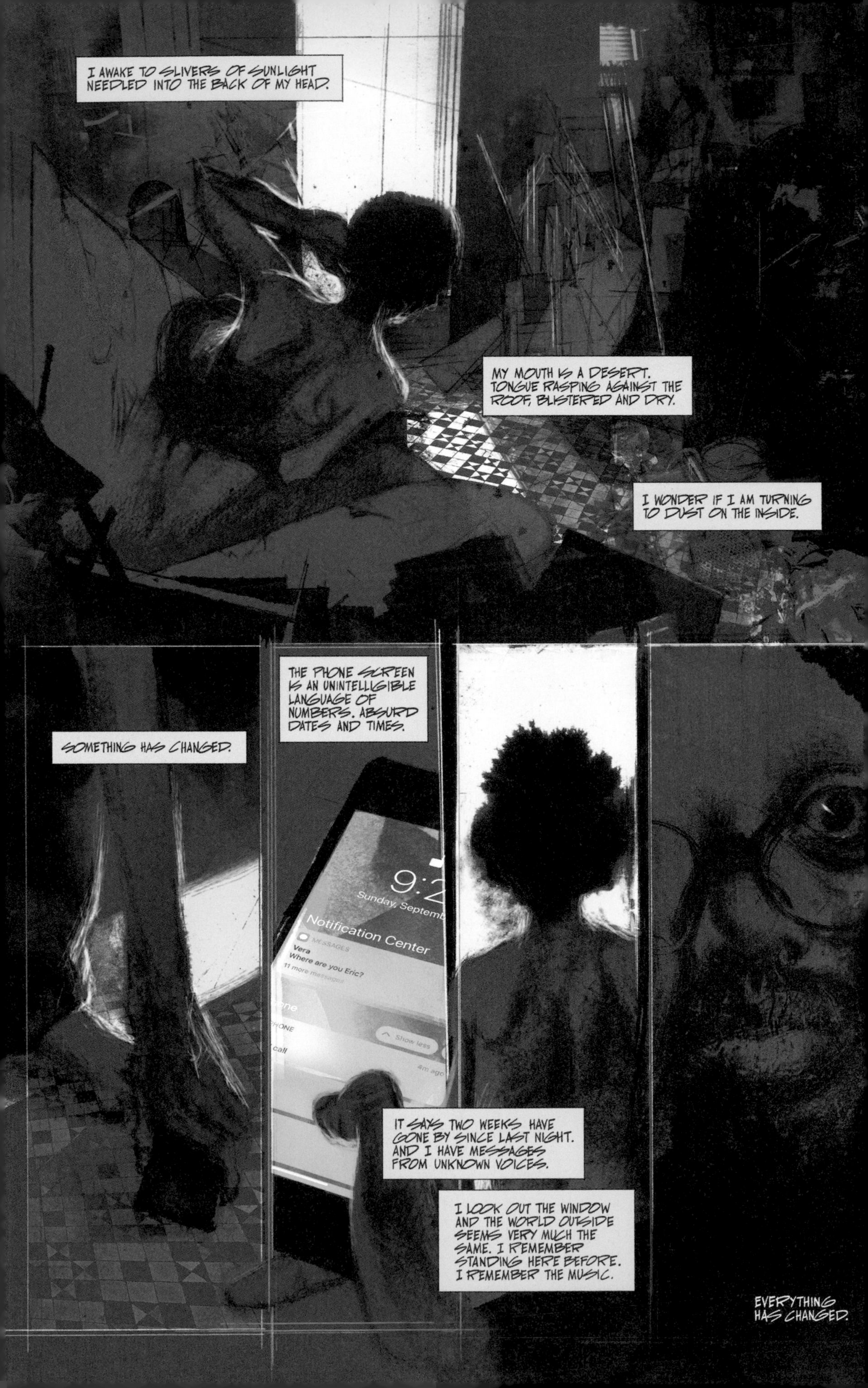
I AWAKE TO SLIVERS OF SUNLIGHT NEEDLED INTO THE BACK OF MY HEAD.
MY MOUTH IS A DESERT. TONGUE RASPING AGAINST THE ROOF, BLISTERED AND DRY.
I WONDER IF I AM TURNING TO DUST ON THE INSIDE.
SOMETHING HAS CHANGED.
THE PHONE SCREEN IS AN UNINTELLIGIBLE LANGUAGE OF NUMBERS. ABSURD DATES AND TIMES.
Notification Center
MESSAGES
Vera
Where are you Eric?
Show less
IT SAYS TWO WEEKS HAVE GONE BY SINCE LAST NIGHT. AND I HAVE MESSAGES FROM UNKNOWN VOICES.
I LOOK OUT THE WINDOW AND THE WORLD OUTSIDE SEEMS VERY MUCH THE SAME. I REMEMBER STANDING HERE BEFORE. I REMEMBER THE MUSIC.
EVERYTHING HAS CHANGED.

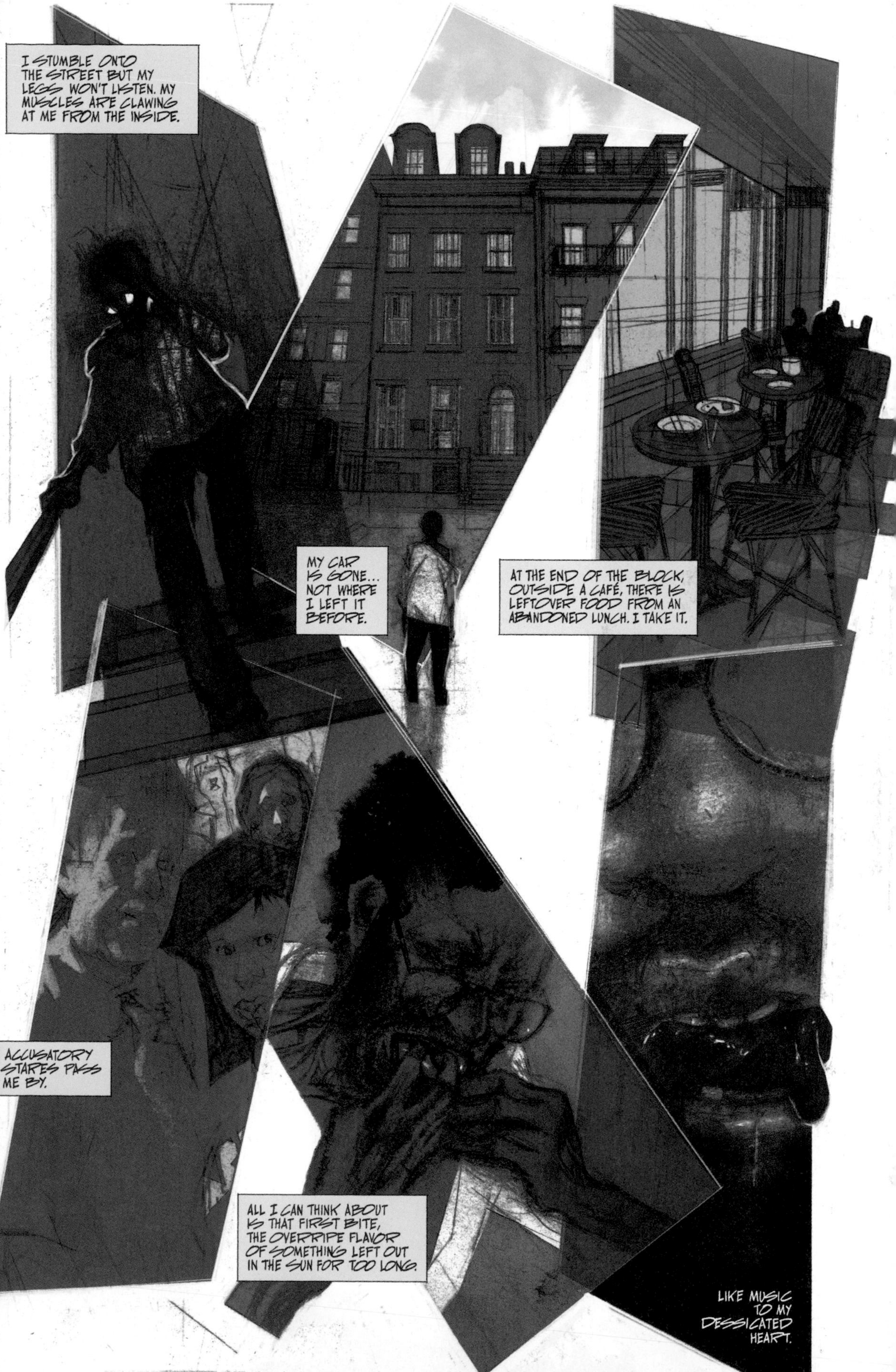
I STUMBLE ONTO THE STREET BUT MY LEGS WON'T LISTEN. MY MUSCLES ARE CLAWING AT ME FROM THE INSIDE.
MY CAR IS GONE... NOT WHERE I LEFT IT BEFORE.
AT THE END OF THE BLOCK, OUTSIDE A CAFÉ, THERE IS LEFTOVER FOOD FROM AN ABANDONED LUNCH. I TAKE IT.
ACCUSATORY STARES PASS ME BY.
ALL I CAN THINK ABOUT IS THAT FIRST BITE, THE OVERRIPE FLAVOR OF SOMETHING LEFT OUT IN THE SUN FOR TOO LONG.
LIKE MUSIC TO MY DESSICATED HEART.

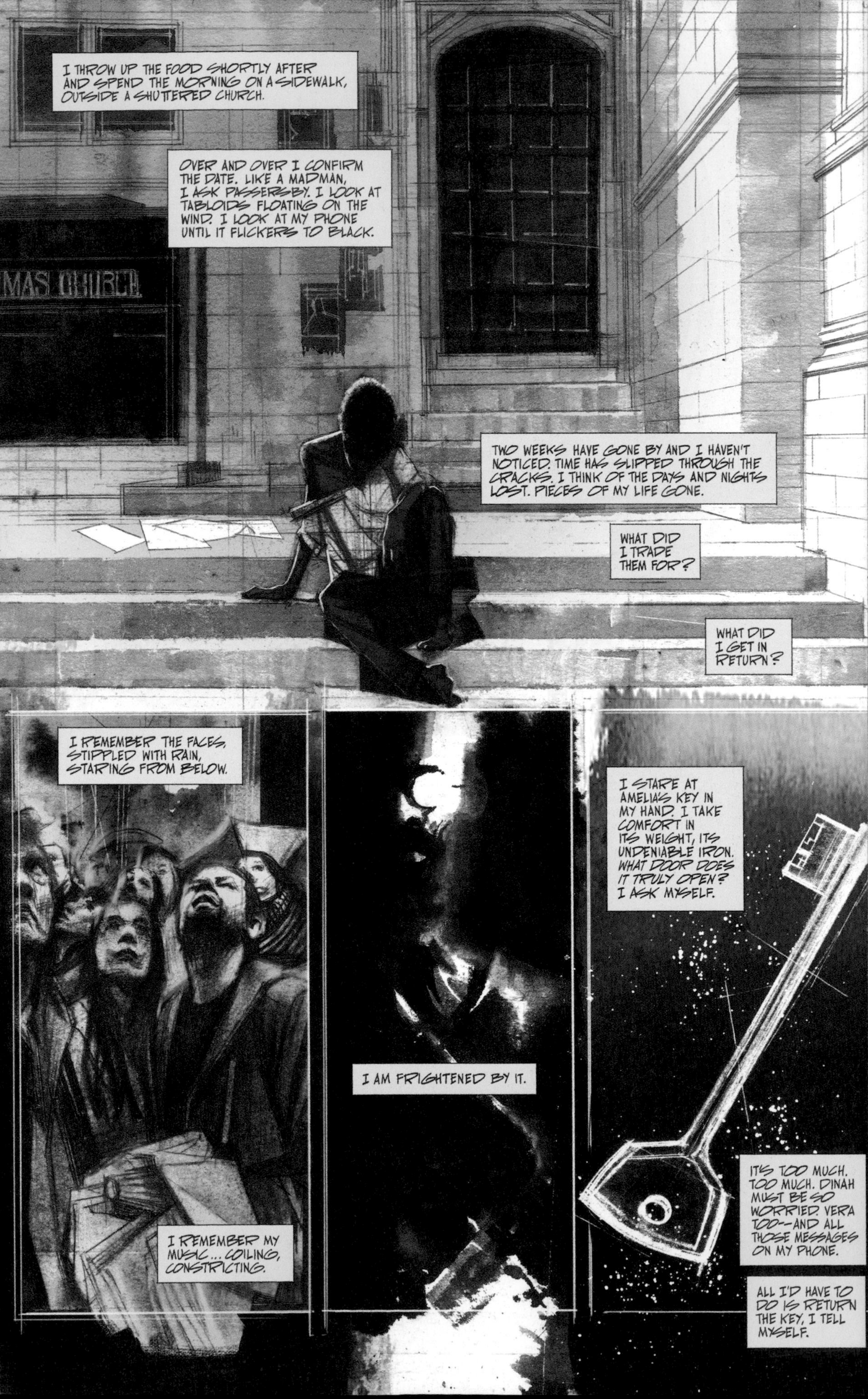
I THROW UP THE FOOD SHORTLY AFTER AND SPEND THE MORNING ON A SIDEWALK, OUTSIDE A SHUTTERED CHURCH.
OVER AND OVER I CONFIRM THE DATE. LIKE A MADMAN, I ASK PASSERSBY. I LOOK AT TABLOIDS FLOATING ON THE WIND. I LOOK AT MY PHONE UNTIL IT FLICKERS TO BLACK.
MAS CHURCH
TWO WEEKS HAVE GONE BY AND I HAVEN'T NOTICED. TIME HAS SLIPPED THROUGH THE CRACKS. I THINK OF THE DAYS AND NIGHTS LOST. PIECES OF MY LIFE GONE.
WHAT DID I TRADE THEM FOR?
WHAT DID I GET IN RETURN?
I REMEMBER THE FACES, STIPPLED WITH RAIN, STARING FROM BELOW.
I REMEMBER MY MUSIC... COILING, CONSTRICTING.
I AM FRIGHTENED BY IT.
I STARE AT AMELIA'S KEY IN MY HAND. I TAKE COMFORT IN ITS WEIGHT, ITS UNDENIABLE IRON. WHAT DOOR DOES IT TRULY OPEN? I ASK MYSELF.
IT'S TOO MUCH. TOO MUCH. DINAH MUST BE SO WORRIED. VERA TOO--AND ALL THOSE MESSAGES ON MY PHONE.
ALL I'D HAVE TO DO IS RETURN THE KEY, I TELL MYSELF.

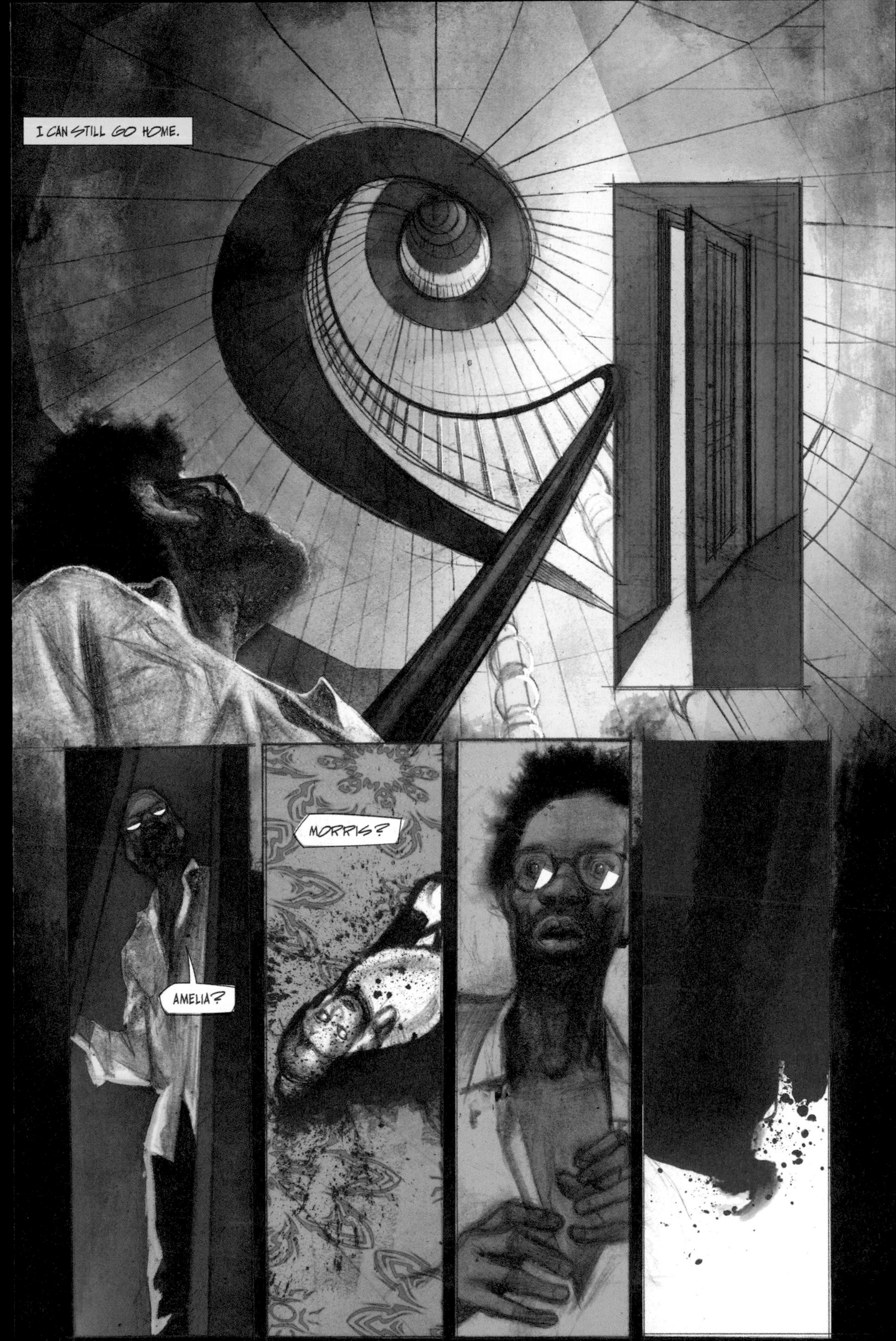
I CAN STILL GO HOME.
AMELIA?
MORRIS?

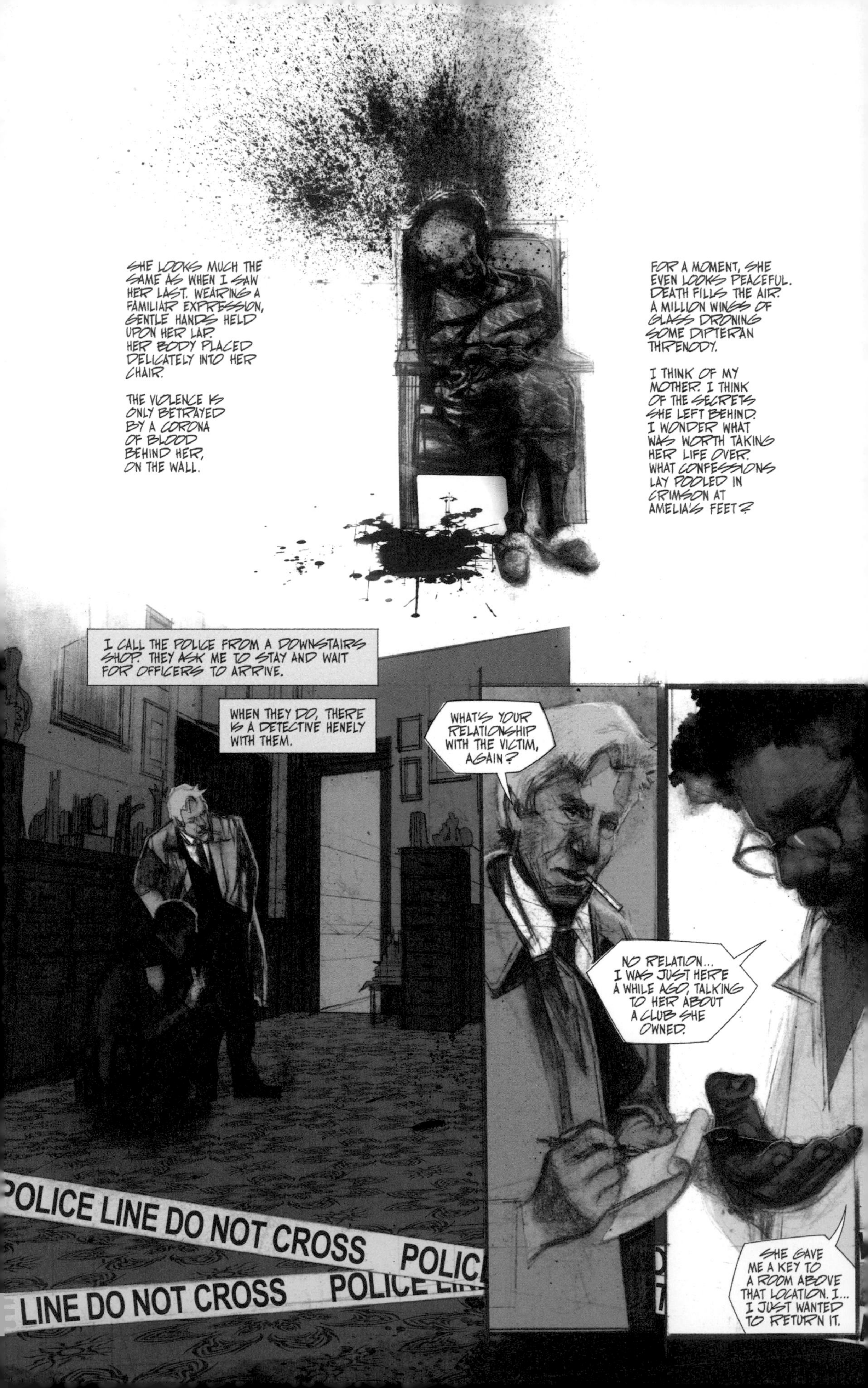
SHE LOOKS MUCH THE SAME AS WHEN I SAW HER LAST. WEARING A FAMILIAR EXPRESSION, GENTLE HANDS HELD UPON HER LAP. HER BODY PLACED DELICATELY INTO HER CHAIR.
THE VIOLENCE IS ONLY BETRAYED BY A CORONA OF BLOOD BEHIND HER, ON THE WALL.
FOR A MOMENT, SHE EVEN LOOKS PEACEFUL. DEATH FILLS THE AIR. A MILLION WINGS OF GLASS DRONING SOME DIPTERAN THRENODY.
I THINK OF MY MOTHER. I THINK OF THE SECRETS SHE LEFT BEHIND. I WONDER WHAT WAS WORTH TAKING HER LIFE OVER. WHAT CONFESSIONS LAY POOLED IN CRIMSON AT AMELIA'S FEET?
I CALL THE POLICE FROM A DOWNSTAIRS SHOP. THEY ASK ME TO STAY AND WAIT FOR OFFICERS TO ARRIVE.
WHEN THEY DO, THERE IS A DETECTIVE HENELY WITH THEM.
POLICE LINE DO NOT CROSS
POLICE
LINE DO NOT CROSS
POLICE
WHAT'S YOUR RELATIONSHIP WITH THE VICTIM, AGAIN?
NO RELATION... I WAS JUST HERE A WHILE AGO, TALKING TO HER ABOUT A CLUB SHE OWNED.
SHE GAVE ME A KEY TO A ROOM ABOVE THAT LOCATION. I... I JUST WANTED TO RETURN IT.

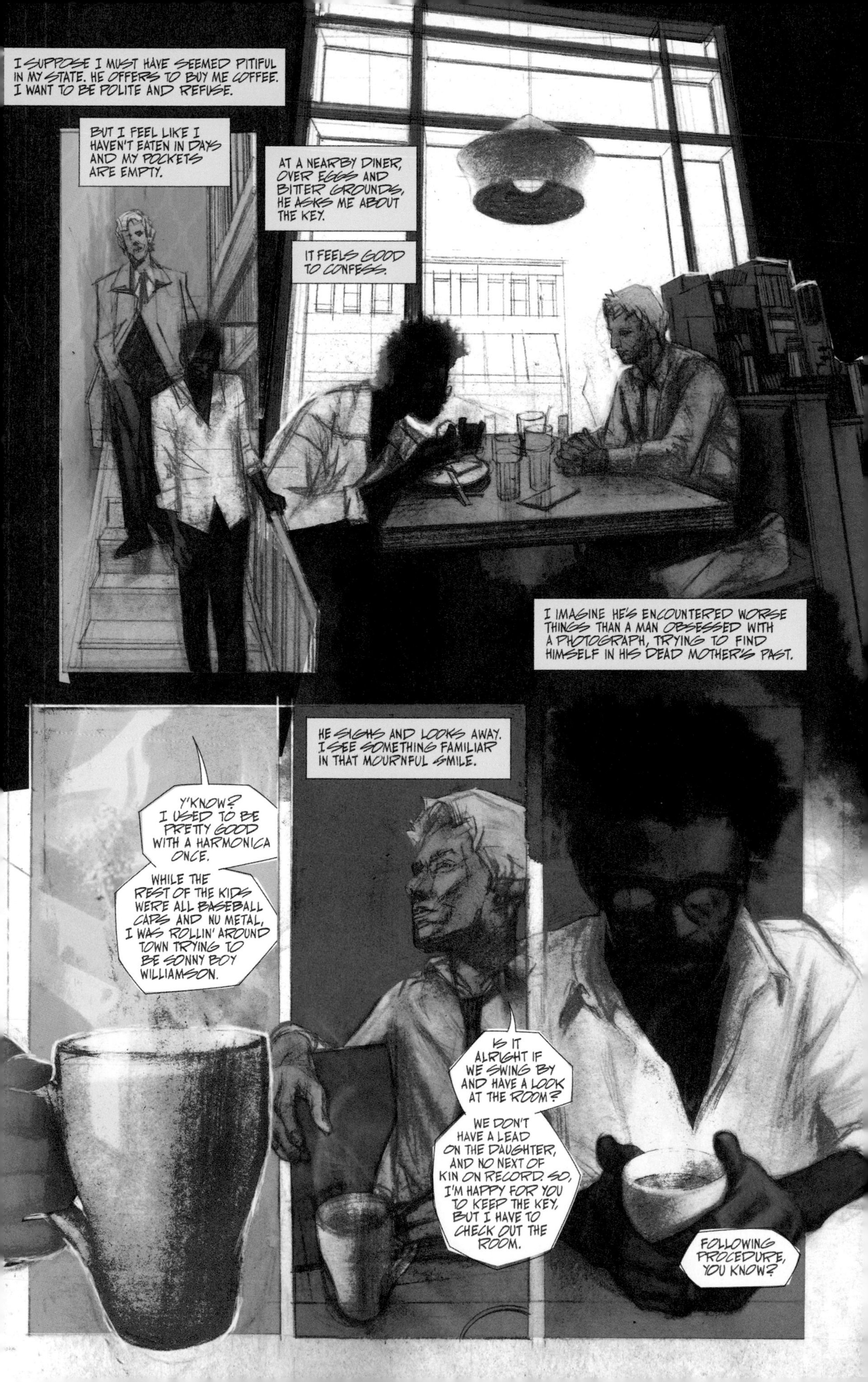
I SUPPOSE I MUST HAVE SEEMED PITIFUL IN MY STATE. HE OFFERS TO BUY ME COFFEE. I WANT TO BE POLITE AND REFUSE.
BUT I FEEL LIKE I HAVEN'T EATEN IN DAYS AND MY POCKETS ARE EMPTY.
AT A NEARBY DINER, OVER EGGS AND BITTER GROUNDS, HE ASKS ME ABOUT THE KEY.
IT FEELS GOOD TO CONFESS.
I IMAGINE HE'S ENCOUNTERED WORSE THINGS THAN A MAN OBSESSED WITH A PHOTOGRAPH, TRYING TO FIND HIMSELF IN HIS DEAD MOTHER'S PAST.
Y'KNOW? I USED TO BE PRETTY GOOD WITH A HARMONICA ONCE.
WHILE THE REST OF THE KIDS WERE ALL BASEBALL CAPS AND NU METAL, I WAS ROLLIN' AROUND TOWN TRYING TO BE SONNY BOY WILLIAMSON.
HE SIGHS AND LOOKS AWAY. I SEE SOMETHING FAMILIAR IN THAT MOURNFUL SMILE.
IS IT ALRIGHT IF WE SWING BY AND HAVE A LOOK AT THE ROOM?
WE DON'T HAVE A LEAD ON THE DAUGHTER, AND NO NEXT OF KIN ON RECORD. SO, I'M HAPPY FOR YOU TO KEEP THE KEY, BUT I HAVE TO CHECK OUT THE ROOM.
FOLLOWING PROCEDURE, YOU KNOW?

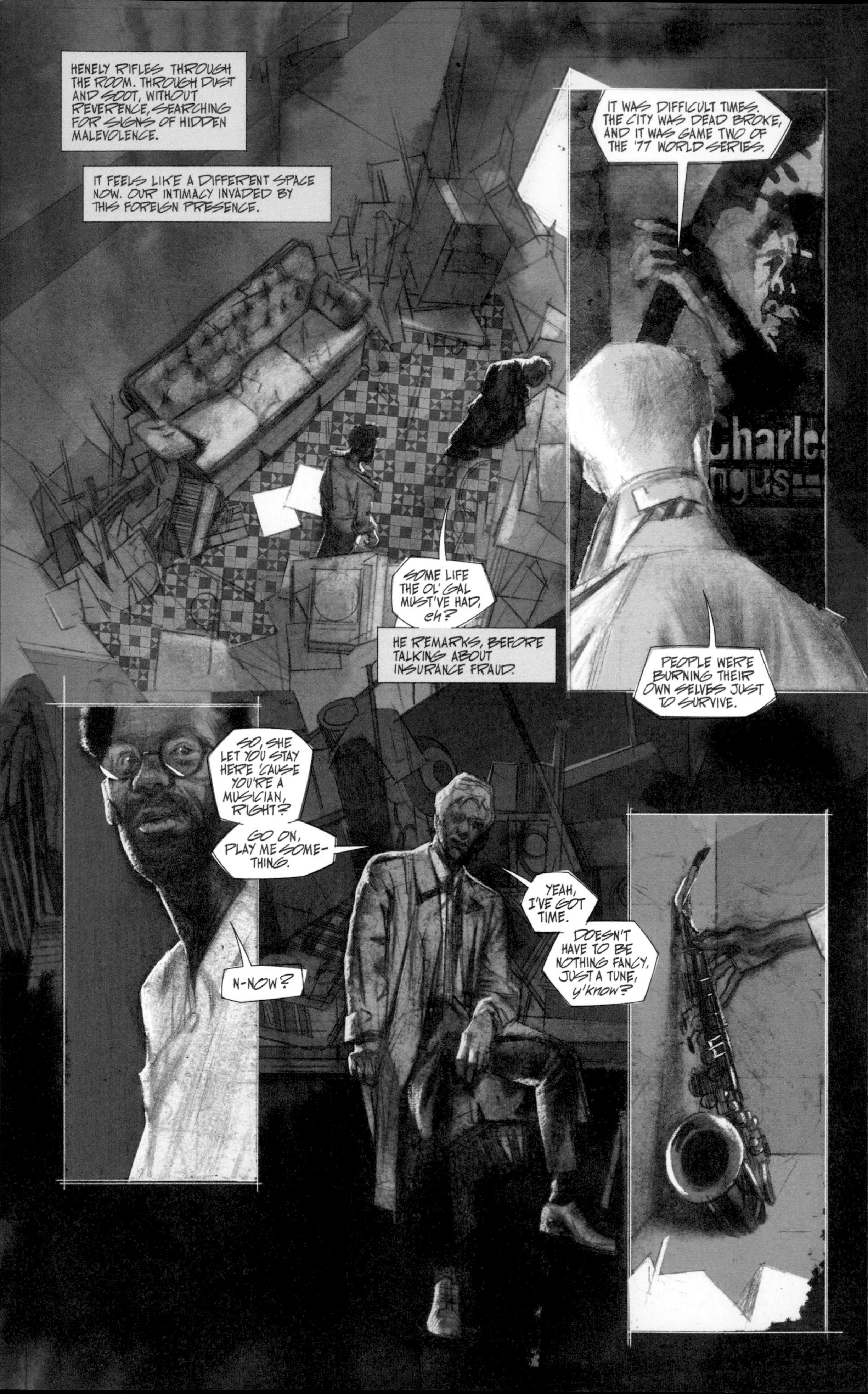
HENELY RIFLES THROUGH THE ROOM. THROUGH DUST AND SOOT, WITHOUT REVERENCE, SEARCHING FOR SIGNS OF HIDDEN MALEVOLENCE.
IT FEELS LIKE A DIFFERENT SPACE NOW. OUR INTIMACY INVADED BY THIS FOREIGN PRESENCE.
SOME LIFE THE OL' GAL MUST'VE HAD, eh?
HE REMARKS, BEFORE TALKING ABOUT INSURANCE FRAUD.
IT WAS DIFFICULT TIMES. THE CITY WAS DEAD BROKE, AND IT WAS GAME TWO OF THE '77 WORLD SERIES.
Charles
ngus
PEOPLE WERE BURNING THEIR OWN SELVES JUST TO SURVIVE.
SO, SHE LET YOU STAY HERE 'CAUSE YOU'RE A MUSICIAN, RIGHT?
GO ON, PLAY ME SOME-THING.
N-NOW?
YEAH, I'VE GOT TIME.
DOESN'T HAVE TO BE NOTHING FANCY, JUST A TUNE, y'know?

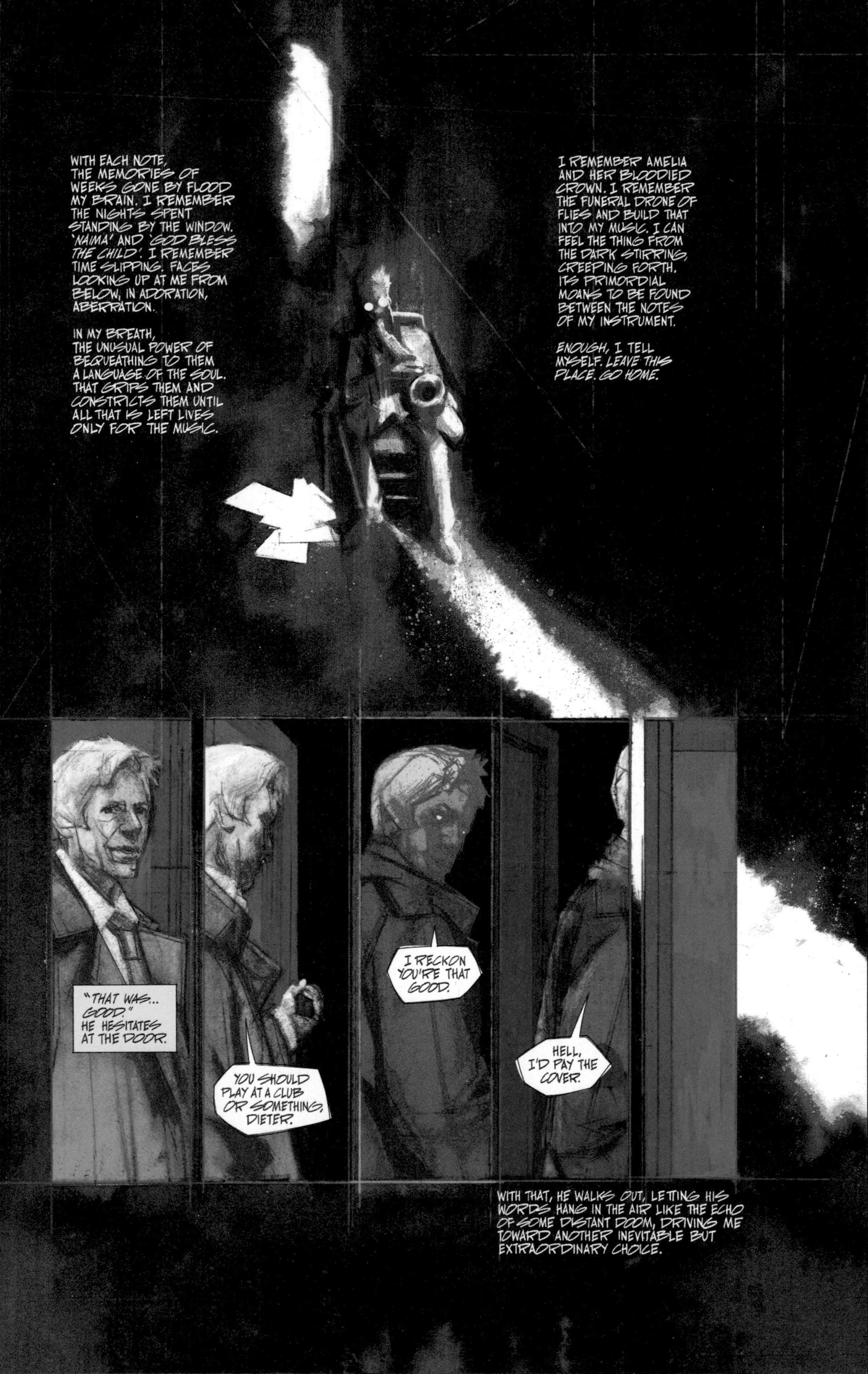
WITH EACH NOTE, THE MEMORIES OF WEEKS GONE BY FLOOD MY BRAIN. I REMEMBER THE NIGHTS SPENT STANDING BY THE WINDOW. 'NAIMA' AND 'GOD BLESS THE CHILD'. I REMEMBER TIME SLIPPING. FACES LOOKING UP AT ME FROM BELOW, IN ADORATION, ABERRATION.
IN MY BREATH, THE UNUSUAL POWER OF BEQUEATHING TO THEM A LANGUAGE OF THE SOUL. THAT GRIPS THEM AND CONSTRICTS THEM UNTIL ALL THAT IS LEFT LIVES ONLY FOR THE MUSIC.
I REMEMBER AMELIA AND HER BLOODIED CROWN. I REMEMBER THE FUNERAL DRONE OF FLIES AND BUILD THAT INTO MY MUSIC. I CAN FEEL THE THING FROM THE DARK STIRRING, CREEPING FORTH. ITS PRIMORDIAL MOANS TO BE FOUND BETWEEN THE NOTES OF MY INSTRUMENT.
ENOUGH, I TELL MYSELF. LEAVE THIS PLACE. GO HOME.
"THAT WAS... GOOD." HE HESITATES AT THE DOOR.
YOU SHOULD PLAY AT A CLUB OR SOMETHING, DIETER.
I RECKON YOU'RE THAT GOOD.
HELL, I'D PAY THE COVER.
WITH THAT, HE WALKS OUT, LETTING HIS WORDS HANG IN THE AIR LIKE THE ECHO OF SOME DISTANT DOOM, DRIVING ME TOWARD ANOTHER INEVITABLE BUT EXTRAORDINARY CHOICE.

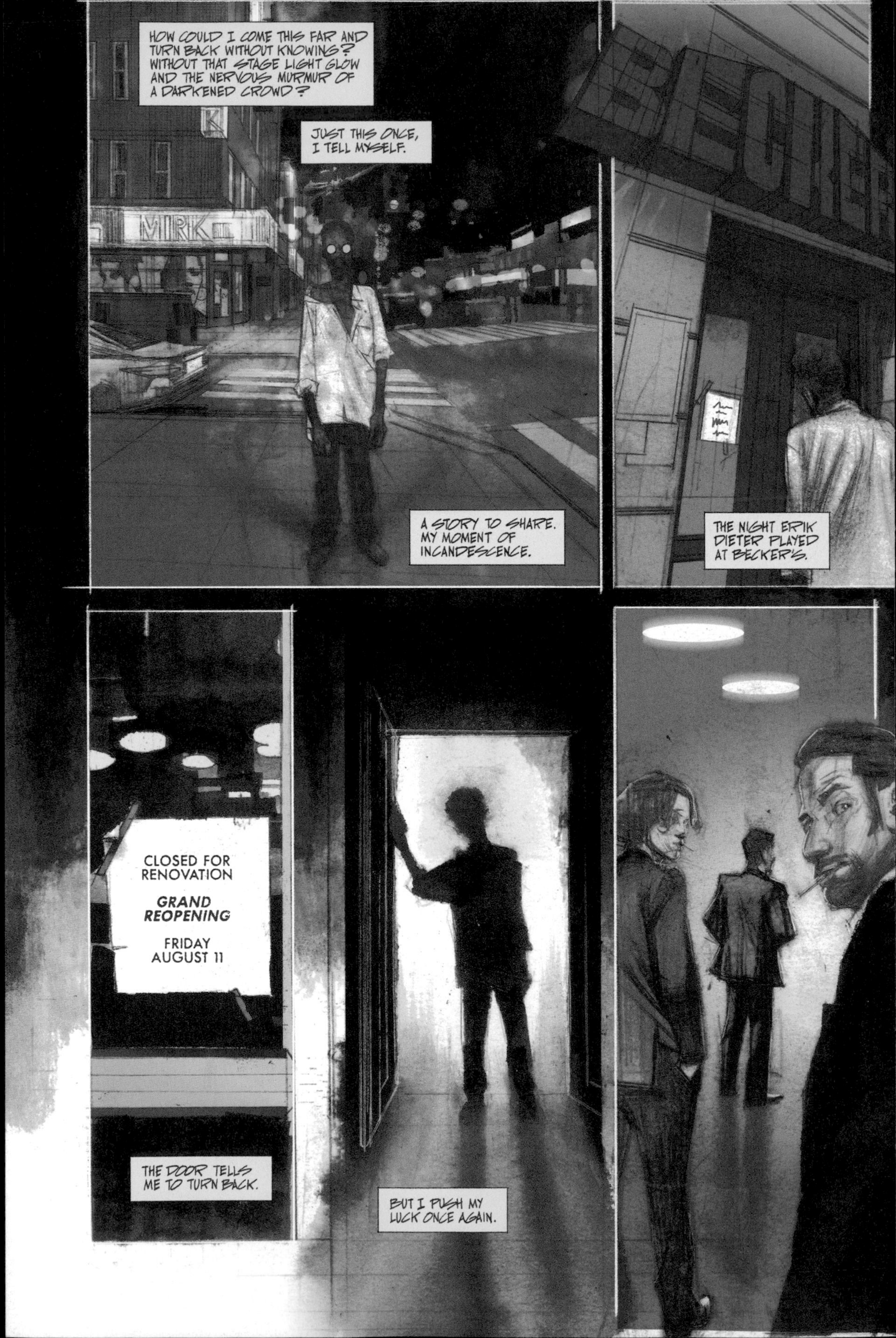
HOW COULD I COME THIS FAR AND TURN BACK WITHOUT KNOWING? WITHOUT THAT STAGE LIGHT GLOW AND THE NERVOUS MURMUR OF A DARKENED CROWD?
JUST THIS ONCE, I TELL MYSELF.
MIRK
A STORY TO SHARE. MY MOMENT OF INCANDESCENCE.
THE NIGHT ERIK DIETER PLAYED AT BECKER'S.
CLOSED FOR RENOVATION
GRAND REOPENING
FRIDAY AUGUST 11
THE DOOR TELLS ME TO TURN BACK.
BUT I PUSH MY LUCK ONCE AGAIN.

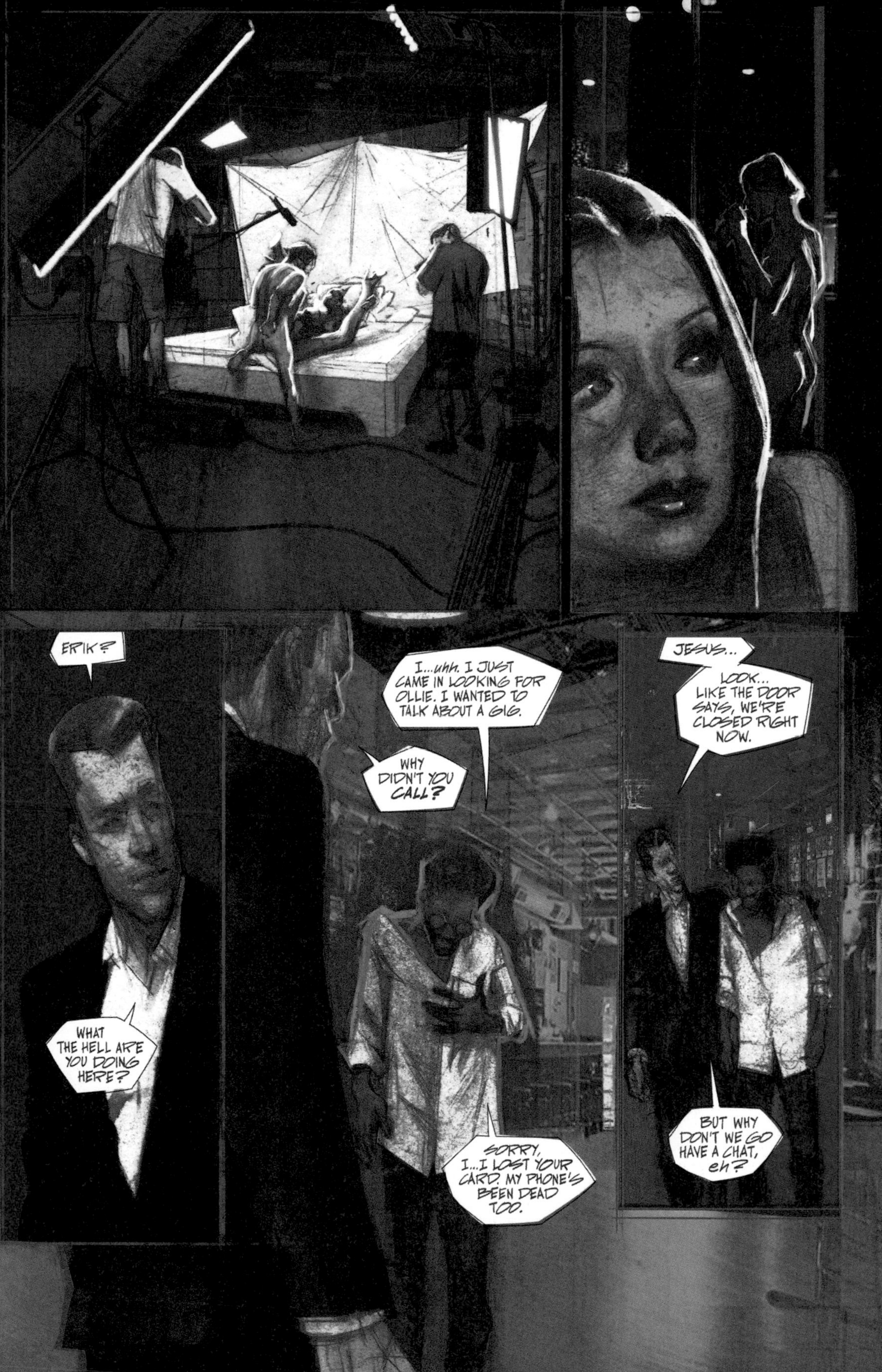
ERIK?
WHAT THE HELL ARE YOU DOING HERE?
I...uhh. I JUST CAME IN LOOKING FOR OLLIE. I WANTED TO TALK ABOUT A GIG.
WHY DIDN'T YOU CALL?
SORRY, I...I LOST YOUR CARD. MY PHONE'S BEEN DEAD TOO.
JESUS...
LOOK... LIKE THE DOOR SAYS, WE'RE CLOSED RIGHT NOW.
BUT WHY DON'T WE GO HAVE A CHAT, eh?

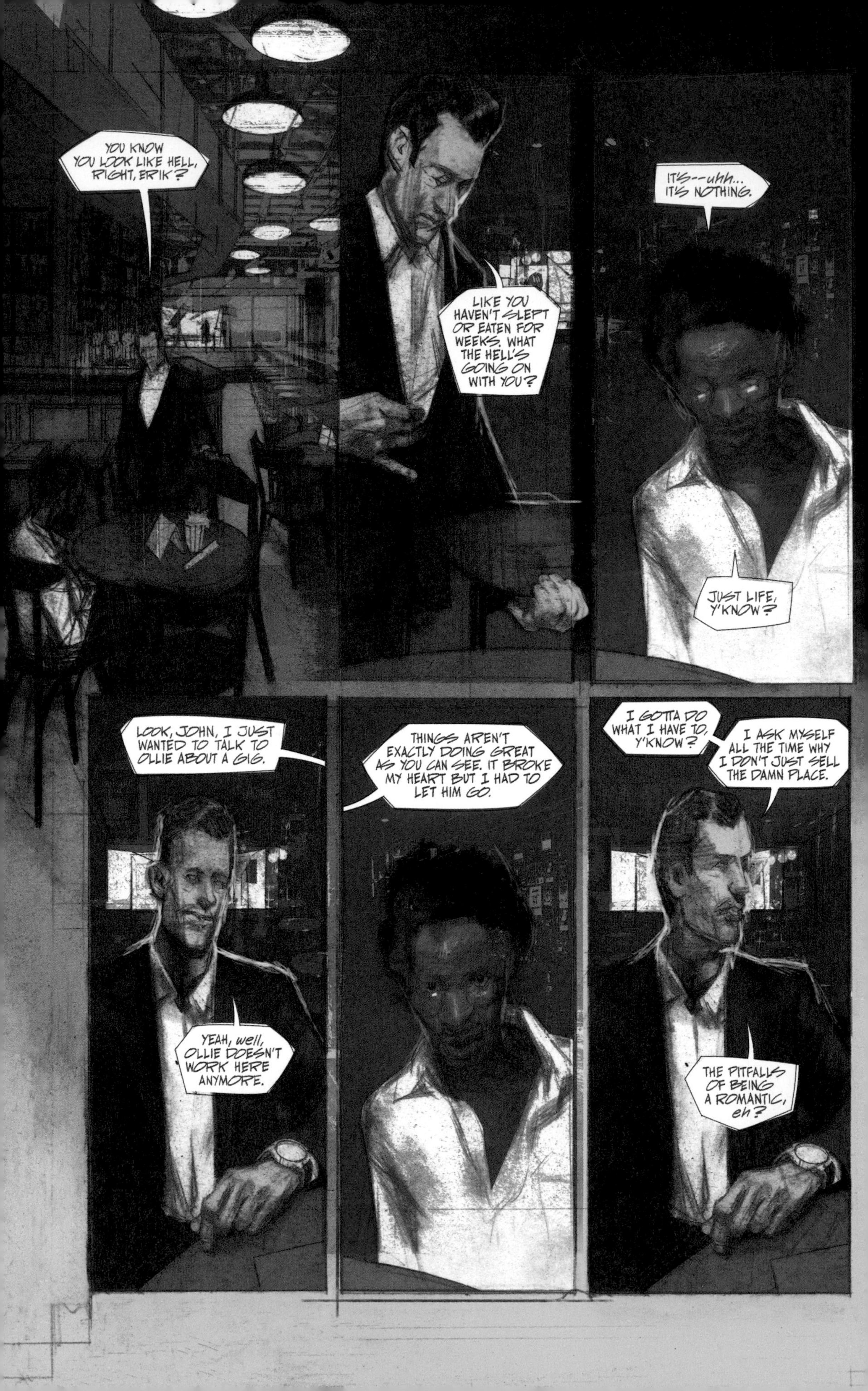
YOU KNOW YOU LOOK LIKE HELL, RIGHT, ERIK?
LIKE YOU HAVEN'T SLEPT OR EATEN FOR WEEKS. WHAT THE HELL'S GOING ON WITH YOU?
IT'S--uhh... IT'S NOTHING.
JUST LIFE, Y'KNOW?
LOOK, JOHN, I JUST WANTED TO TALK TO OLLIE ABOUT A GIG.
YEAH, WELL, OLLIE DOESN'T WORK HERE ANYMORE.
THINGS AREN'T EXACTLY DOING GREAT AS YOU CAN SEE. IT BROKE MY HEART BUT I HAD TO LET HIM GO.
I GOTTA DO WHAT I HAVE TO, Y'KNOW?
I ASK MYSELF ALL THE TIME WHY I DON'T JUST SELL THE DAMN PLACE.
THE PITFALLS OF BEING A ROMANTIC, eh?

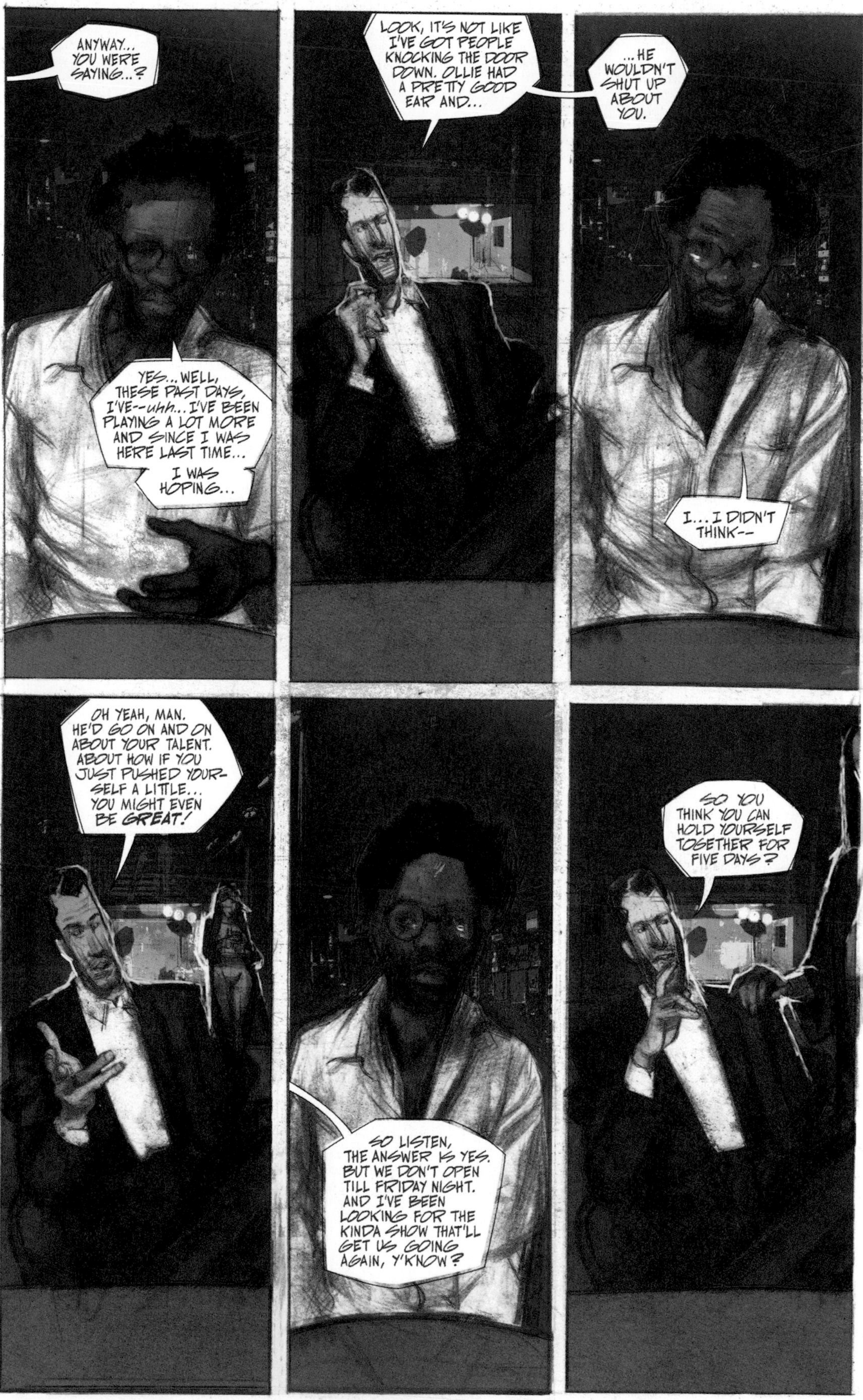
ANYWAY... YOU WERE SAYING...?
YES... WELL, THESE PAST DAYS, I'VE--uhh... I'VE BEEN PLAYING A LOT MORE AND SINCE I WAS HERE LAST TIME...
I WAS HOPING...
LOOK, IT'S NOT LIKE I'VE GOT PEOPLE KNOCKING THE DOOR DOWN. OLLIE HAD A PRETTY GOOD EAR AND...
...HE WOULDN'T SHUT UP ABOUT YOU.
I... I DIDN'T THINK--
OH YEAH, MAN. HE'D GO ON AND ON ABOUT YOUR TALENT. ABOUT HOW IF YOU JUST PUSHED YOURSELF A LITTLE... YOU MIGHT EVEN BE GREAT!
SO LISTEN, THE ANSWER IS YES. BUT WE DON'T OPEN TILL FRIDAY NIGHT. AND I'VE BEEN LOOKING FOR THE KINDA SHOW THAT'LL GET US GOING AGAIN, Y'KNOW?
SO YOU THINK YOU CAN HOLD YOURSELF TOGETHER FOR FIVE DAYS?

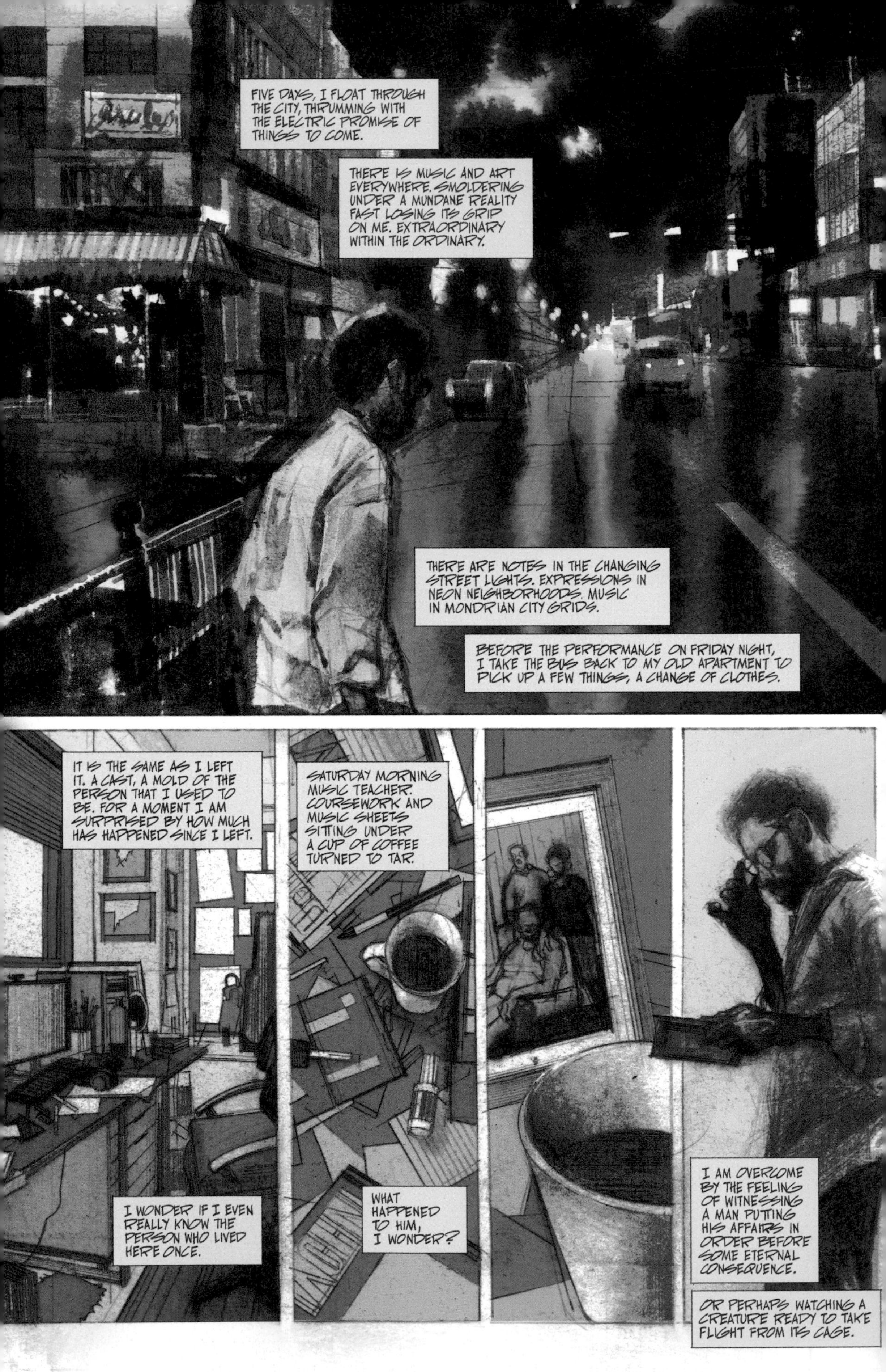
FIVE DAYS, I FLOAT THROUGH THE CITY, THRUMMING WITH THE ELECTRIC PROMISE OF THINGS TO COME.
THERE IS MUSIC AND ART EVERYWHERE. SMOLDERING UNDER A MUNDANE REALITY FAST LOSING ITS GRIP ON ME. EXTRAORDINARY WITHIN THE ORDINARY.
THERE ARE NOTES IN THE CHANGING STREET LIGHTS. EXPRESSIONS IN NEON NEIGHBORHOODS. MUSIC IN MONDRIAN CITY GRIDS.
BEFORE THE PERFORMANCE ON FRIDAY NIGHT, I TAKE THE BUS BACK TO MY OLD APARTMENT TO PICK UP A FEW THINGS, A CHANGE OF CLOTHES.
IT IS THE SAME AS I LEFT IT. A CAST, A MOLD OF THE PERSON THAT I USED TO BE. FOR A MOMENT I AM SURPRISED BY HOW MUCH HAS HAPPENED SINCE I LEFT.
I WONDER IF I EVEN REALLY KNOW THE PERSON WHO LIVED HERE ONCE.
SATURDAY MORNING MUSIC TEACHER. COURSEWORK AND MUSIC SHEETS SITTING UNDER A CUP OF COFFEE TURNED TO TAR.
WHAT HAPPENED TO HIM, I WONDER?
I AM OVERCOME BY THE FEELING OF WITNESSING A MAN PUTTING HIS AFFAIRS IN ORDER BEFORE SOME ETERNAL CONSEQUENCE.
OR PERHAPS WATCHING A CREATURE READY TO TAKE FLIGHT FROM ITS CAGE.

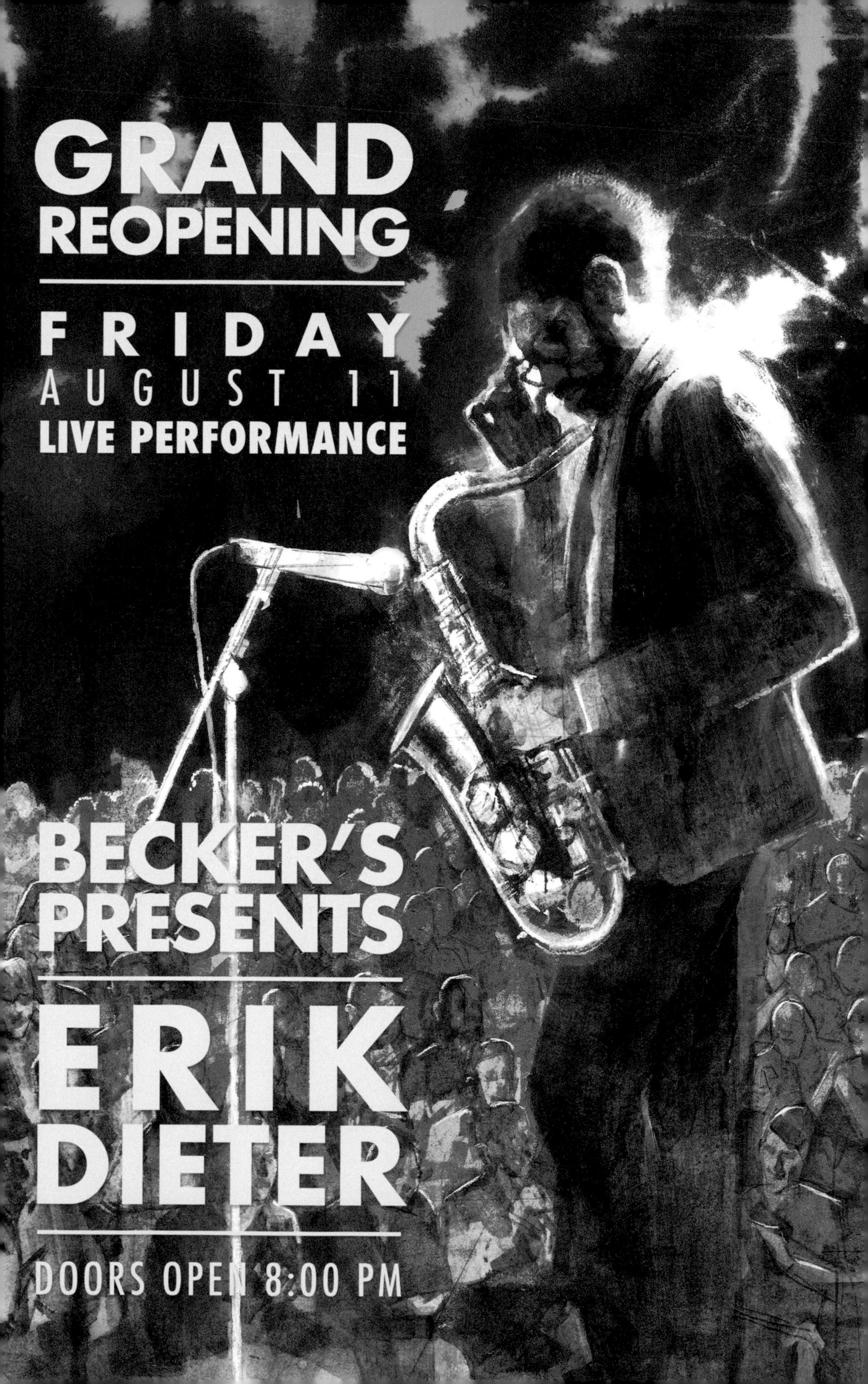
GRAND
REOPENING
FRIDAY
AUGUST 11
LIVE PERFORMANCE
BECKER'S
PRESENTS
ERIK
DIETER
DOORS OPEN 8:00 PM

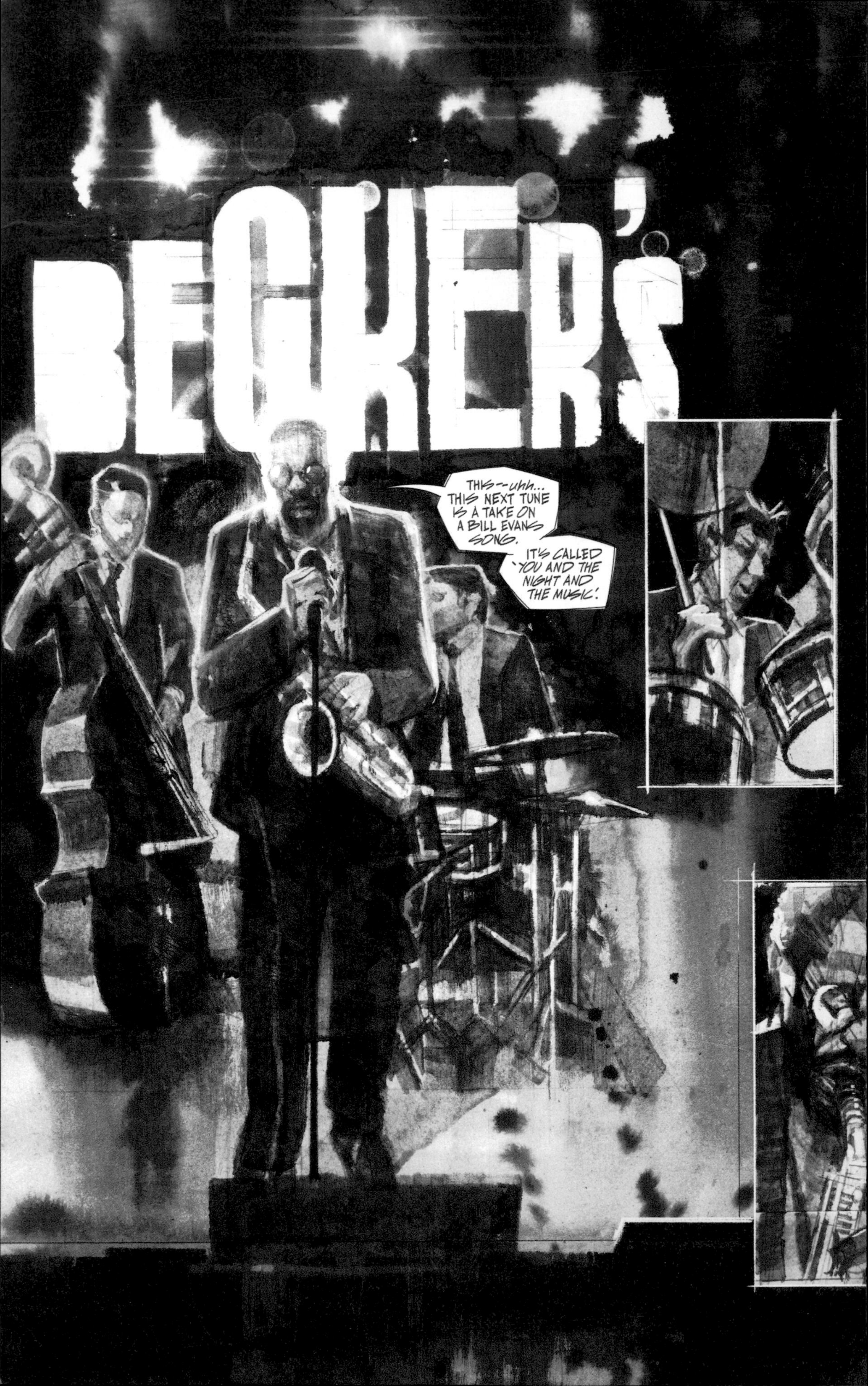
BECKER'S
THIS--uhh... THIS NEXT TUNE IS A TAKE ON A BILL EVANS SONG.
IT'S CALLED 'YOU AND THE NIGHT AND THE MUSIC'.

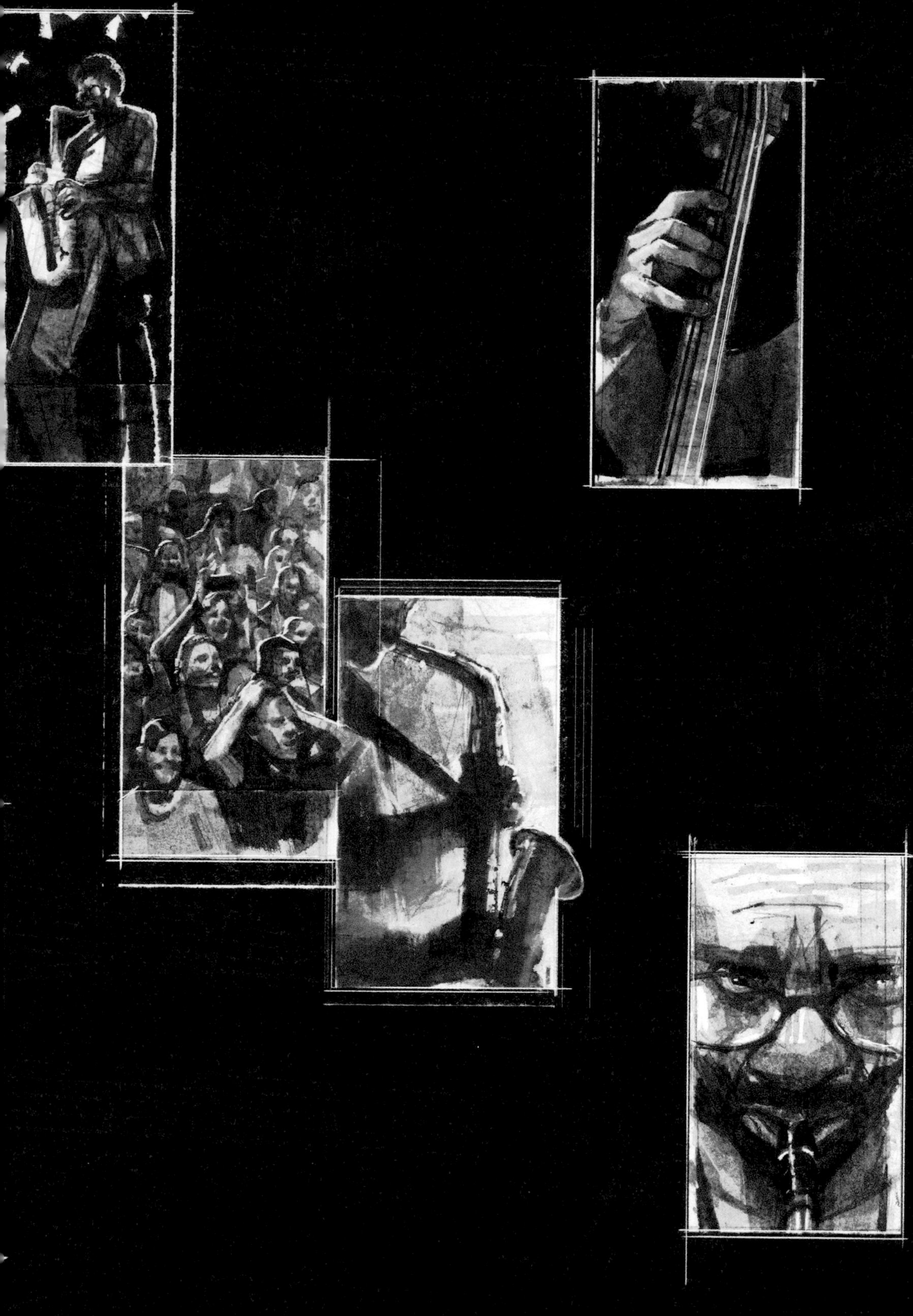

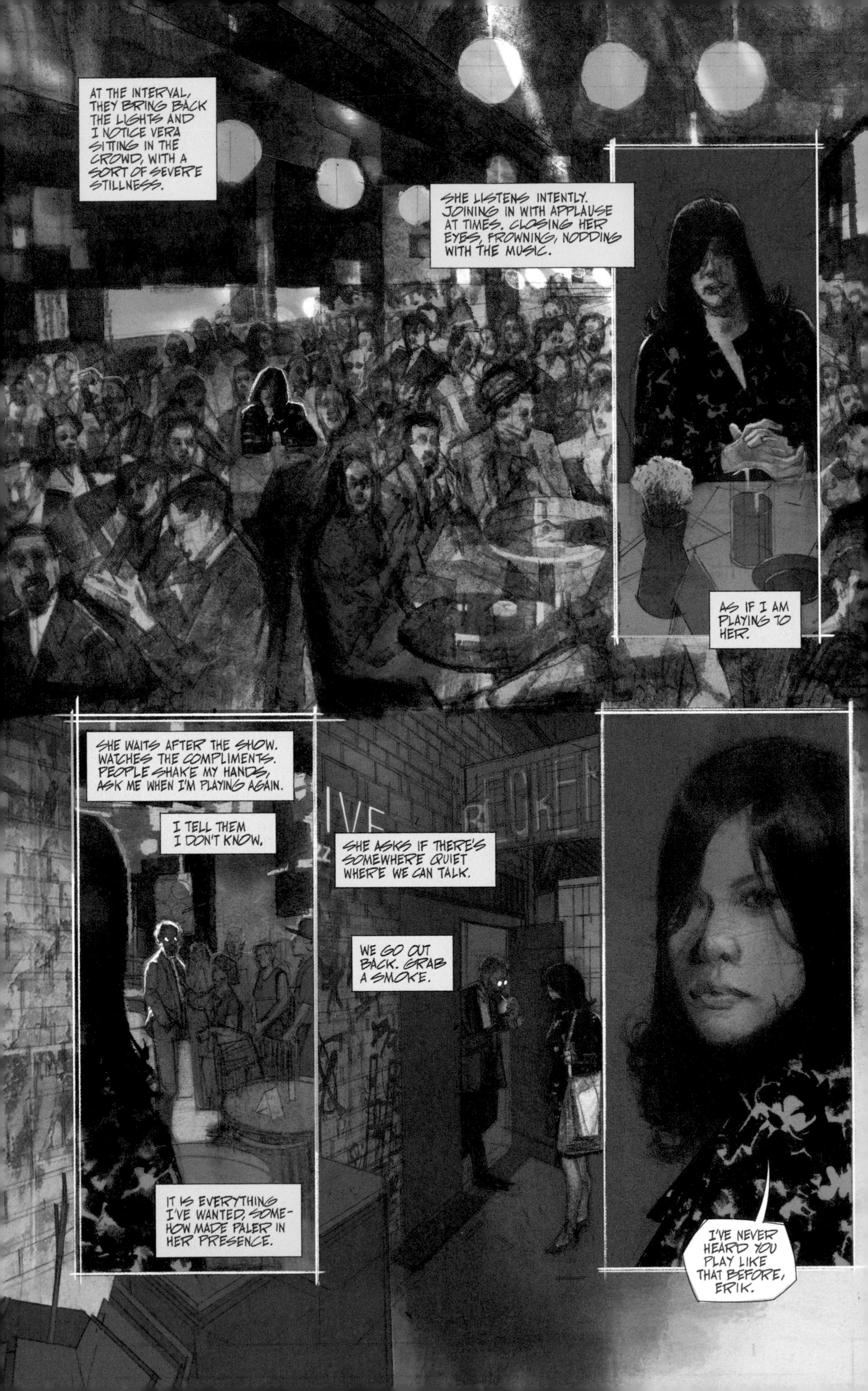
AT THE INTERVAL, THEY BRING BACK THE LIGHTS AND I NOTICE VERA SITTING IN THE CROWD, WITH A SORT OF SEVERE STILLNESS.
SHE LISTENS INTENTLY. JOINING IN WITH APPLAUSE AT TIMES. CLOSING HER EYES, FROWNING, NODDING WITH THE MUSIC.
AS IF I AM PLAYING TO HER.
SHE WAITS AFTER THE SHOW. WATCHES THE COMPLIMENTS. PEOPLE SHAKE MY HANDS, ASK ME WHEN I'M PLAYING AGAIN.
I TELL THEM I DON'T KNOW.
IT IS EVERYTHING I'VE WANTED, SOME-HOW MADE PALER IN HER PRESENCE.
SHE ASKS IF THERE'S SOMEWHERE QUIET WHERE WE CAN TALK.
WE GO OUT BACK. GRAB A SMOKE.
I'VE NEVER HEARD YOU PLAY LIKE THAT BEFORE, ERIK.

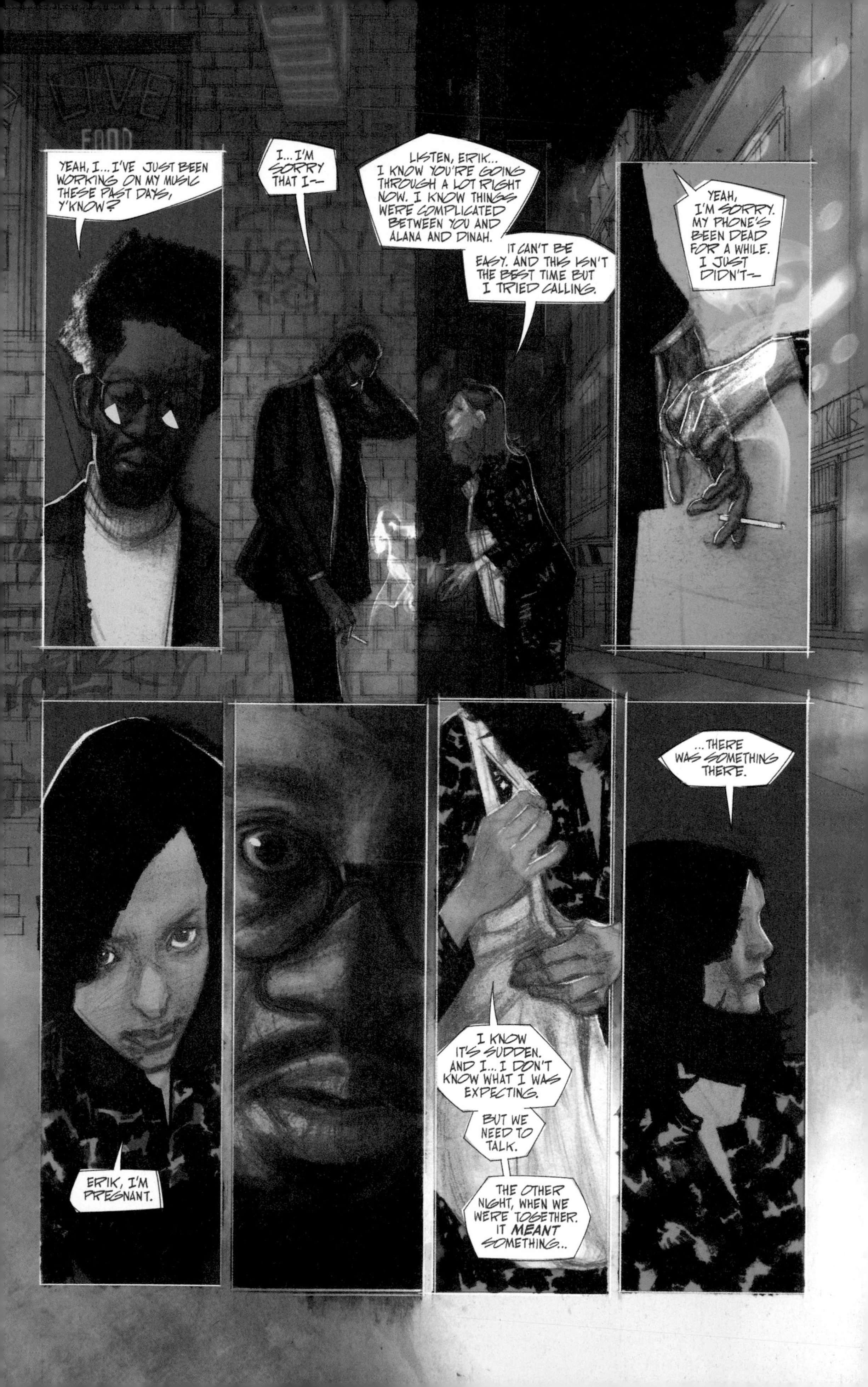
YEAH, I... I'VE JUST BEEN WORKING ON MY MUSIC THESE PAST DAYS, Y'KNOW?
I... I'M SORRY THAT I--
LISTEN, ERIK... I KNOW YOU'RE GOING THROUGH A LOT RIGHT NOW. I KNOW THINGS WERE COMPLICATED BETWEEN YOU AND ALANA AND DINAH.
IT CAN'T BE EASY. AND THIS ISN'T THE BEST TIME BUT I TRIED CALLING.
YEAH, I'M SORRY. MY PHONE'S BEEN DEAD FOR A WHILE. I JUST DIDN'T--
ERIK, I'M PREGNANT.
I KNOW IT'S SUDDEN. AND I... I DON'T KNOW WHAT I WAS EXPECTING.
BUT WE NEED TO TALK.
THE OTHER NIGHT, WHEN WE WERE TOGETHER. IT MEANT SOMETHING...
...THERE WAS SOMETHING THERE.

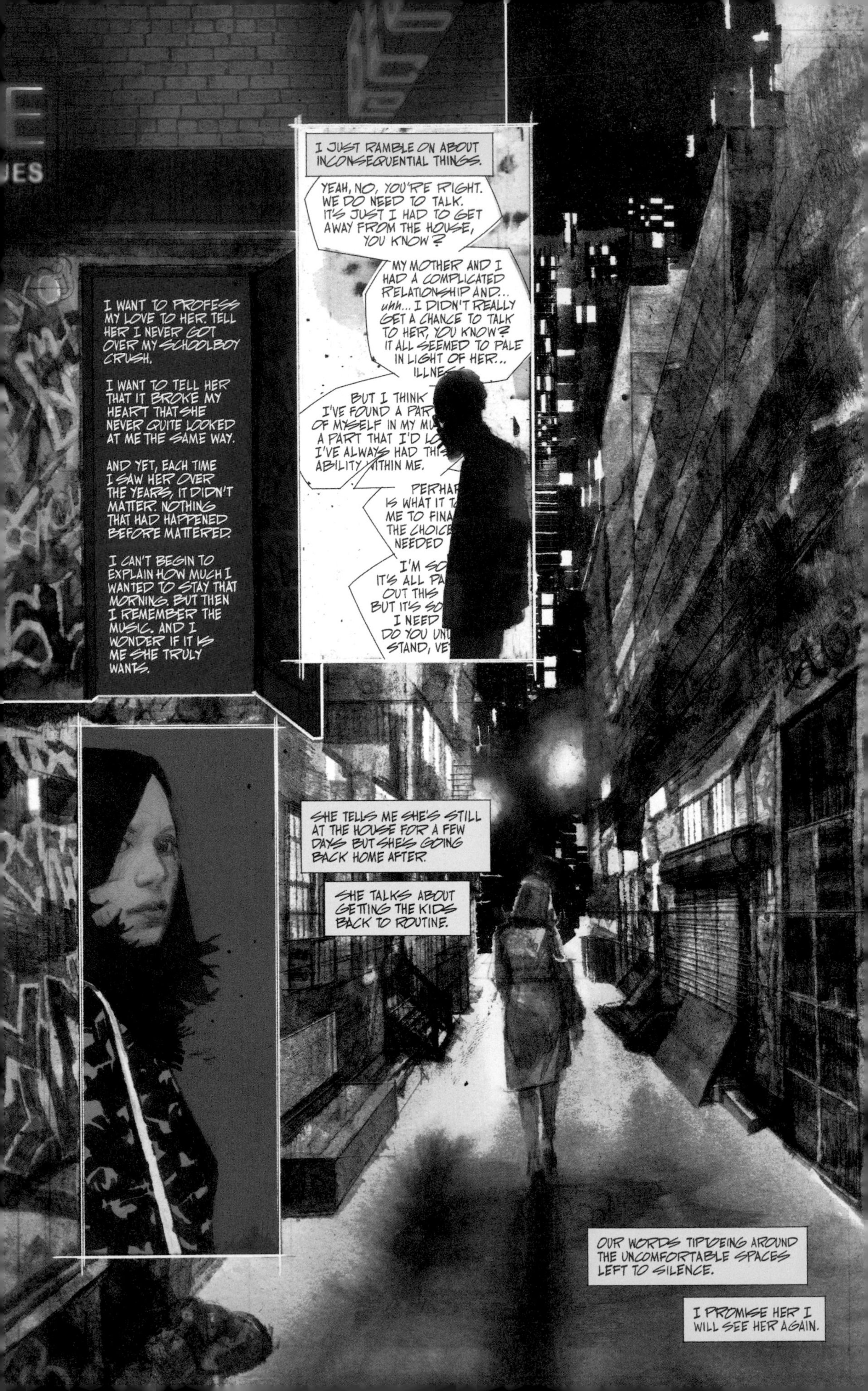

I JUST RAMBLE ON ABOUT INCONSEQUENTIAL THINGS.
YEAH, NO, YOU'RE RIGHT. WE DO NEED TO TALK. IT'S JUST I HAD TO GET AWAY FROM THE HOUSE, YOU KNOW?
MY MOTHER AND I HAD A COMPLICATED RELATIONSHIP AND... uhh... I DIDN'T REALLY GET A CHANCE TO TALK TO HER, YOU KNOW? IT ALL SEEMED TO PALE IN LIGHT OF HER... ILLNES
BUT I THINK I'VE FOUND A PAR OF MYSELF IN MY MU A PART THAT I'D LO I'VE ALWAYS HAD TH ABILITY WITHIN ME.
PERHA IS WHAT IT T ME TO FINA THE CHOICE NEEDED
I'M S IT'S ALL PA OUT THIS BUT IT'S S I NEED DO YOU UN STAND, VE
I WANT TO PROFESS MY LOVE TO HER. TELL HER I NEVER GOT OVER MY SCHOOLBOY CRUSH.
I WANT TO TELL HER THAT IT BROKE MY HEART THAT SHE NEVER QUITE LOOKED AT ME THE SAME WAY.
AND YET, EACH TIME I SAW HER OVER THE YEARS, IT DIDN'T MATTER. NOTHING THAT HAD HAPPENED BEFORE MATTERED.
I CAN'T BEGIN TO EXPLAIN HOW MUCH I WANTED TO STAY THAT MORNING. BUT THEN I REMEMBER THE MUSIC. AND I WONDER IF IT IS ME SHE TRULY WANTS.
SHE TELLS ME SHE'S STILL AT THE HOUSE FOR A FEW DAYS BUT SHE'S GOING BACK HOME AFTER.
SHE TALKS ABOUT GETTING THE KIDS BACK TO ROUTINE.
OUR WORDS TIPTOEING AROUND THE UNCOMFORTABLE SPACES LEFT TO SILENCE.
I PROMISE HER I WILL SEE HER AGAIN.

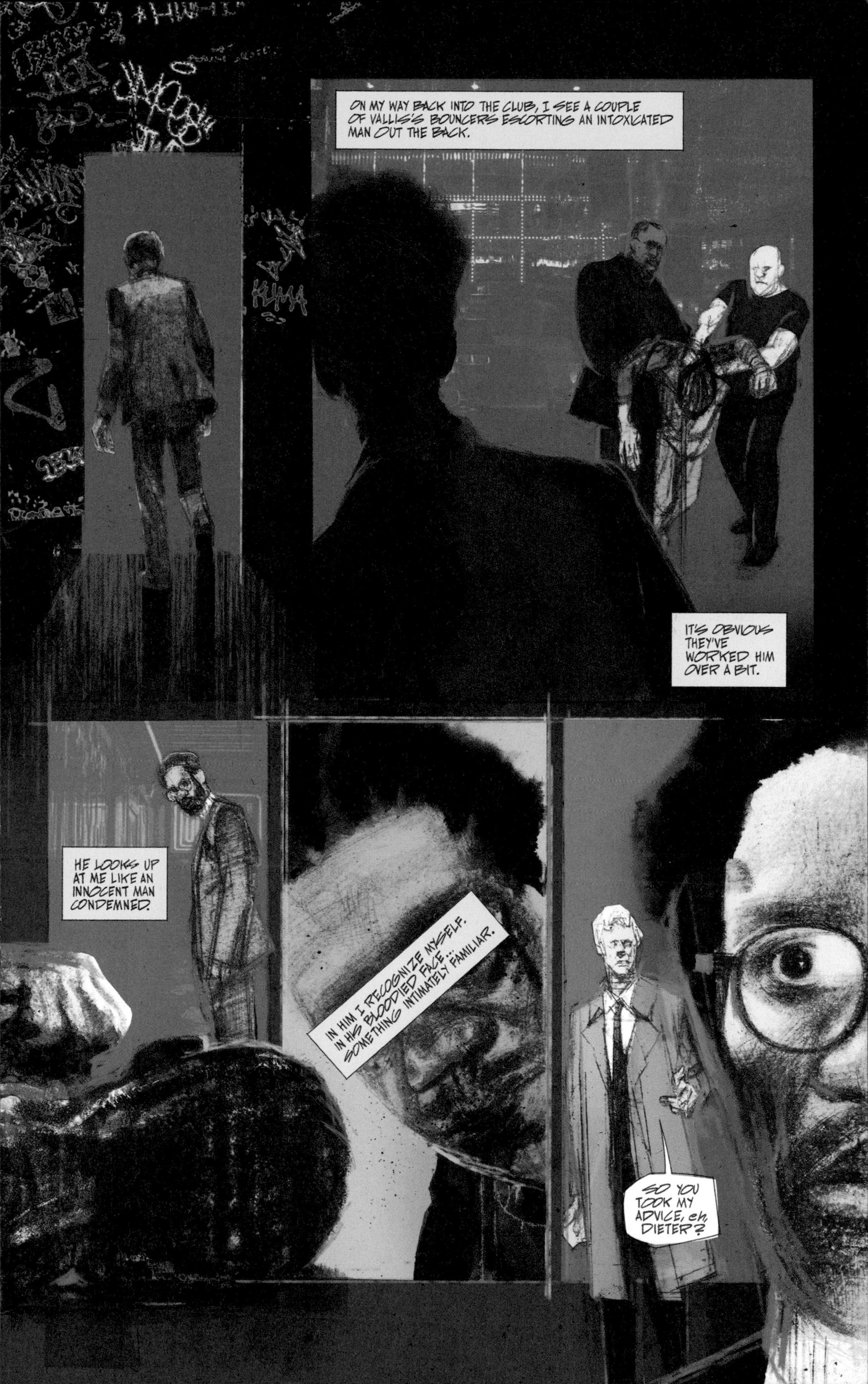

ON MY WAY BACK INTO THE CLUB, I SEE A COUPLE OF VALLIS'S BOUNCERS ESCORTING AN INTOXICATED MAN OUT THE BACK.
IT'S OBVIOUS THEY'VE WORKED HIM OVER A BIT.
HE LOOKS UP AT ME LIKE AN INNOCENT MAN CONDEMNED.
IN HIM I RECOGNIZE MYSELF. IN HIS BLOODIED FACE... SOMETHING INTIMATELY FAMILIAR.
SO YOU TOOK MY ADVICE, eh, DIETER?

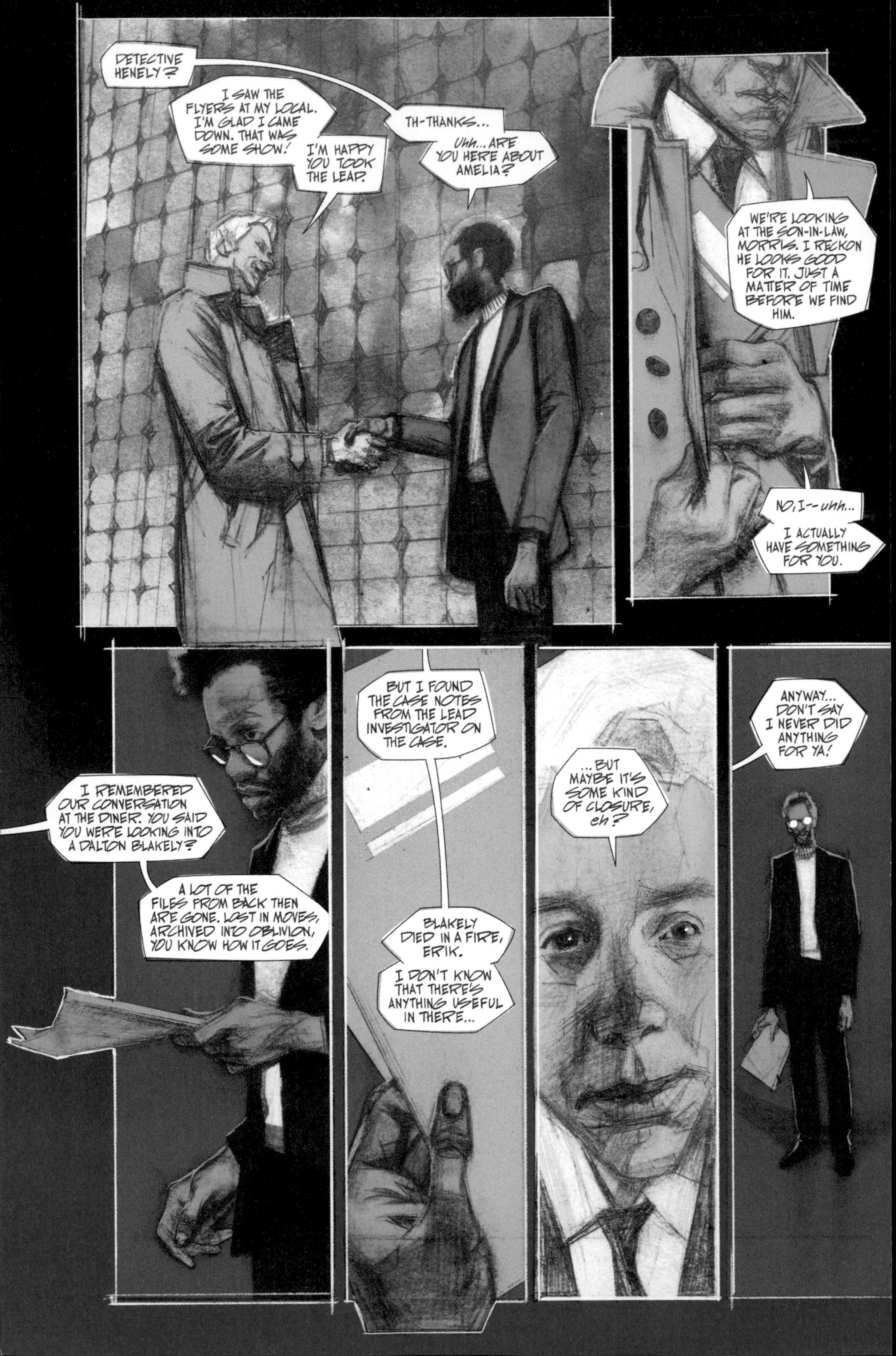
DETECTIVE HENELY?
I SAW THE FLYERS AT MY LOCAL. I'M GLAD I CAME DOWN. THAT WAS SOME SHOW!
I'M HAPPY YOU TOOK THE LEAD.
TH-THANKS...
Uhh... ARE YOU HERE ABOUT AMELIA?
WE'RE LOOKING AT THE SON-IN-LAW, MORRIS. I RECKON HE LOOKS GOOD FOR IT. JUST A MATTER OF TIME BEFORE WE FIND HIM.
NO, I-- uhh...
I ACTUALLY HAVE SOMETHING FOR YOU.
I REMEMBERED OUR CONVERSATION AT THE DINER. YOU SAID YOU WERE LOOKING INTO A DALTON BLAKELY?
A LOT OF THE FILES FROM BACK THEN ARE GONE. LOST IN MOVES, ARCHIVED INTO OBLIVION, YOU KNOW HOW IT GOES.
BUT I FOUND THE CASE NOTES FROM THE LEAD INVESTIGATOR ON THE CASE.
BLAKELY DIED IN A FIRE, ERIK.
I DON'T KNOW THAT THERE'S ANYTHING USEFUL IN THERE...
...BUT MAYBE IT'S SOME KIND OF CLOSURE, eh?
ANYWAY... DON'T SAY I NEVER DID ANYTHING FOR YA!

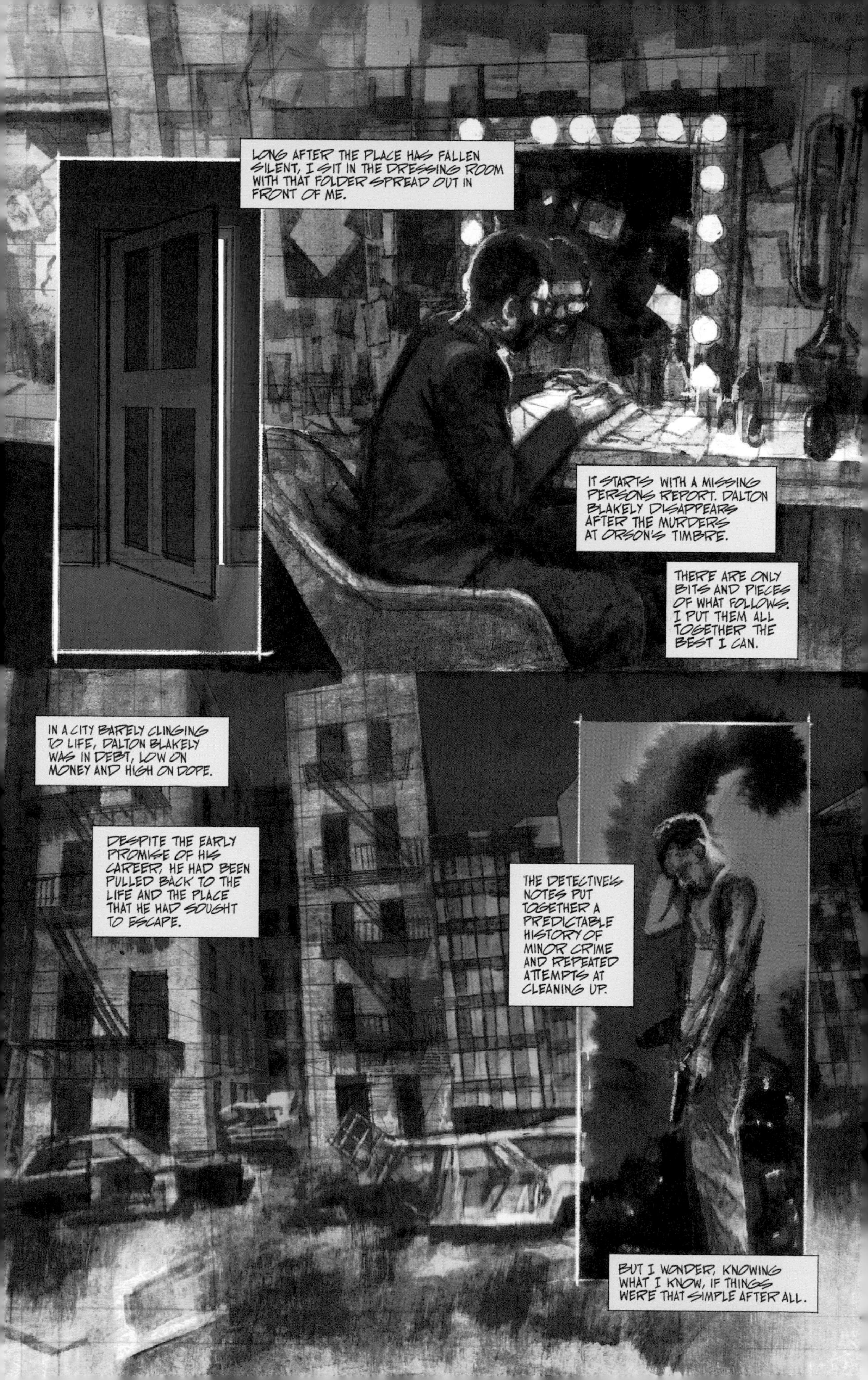
LONG AFTER THE PLACE HAS FALLEN SILENT, I SIT IN THE DRESSING ROOM WITH THAT FOLDER SPREAD OUT IN FRONT OF ME.
IT STARTS WITH A MISSING PERSONS REPORT. DALTON BLAKELY DISAPPEARS AFTER THE MURDERS AT ORSON'S TIMBRE.
THERE ARE ONLY BITS AND PIECES OF WHAT FOLLOWS. I PUT THEM ALL TOGETHER THE BEST I CAN.
IN A CITY BARELY CLINGING TO LIFE, DALTON BLAKELY WAS IN DEBT, LOW ON MONEY AND HIGH ON DOPE.
DESPITE THE EARLY PROMISE OF HIS CAREER, HE HAD BEEN PULLED BACK TO THE LIFE AND THE PLACE THAT HE HAD SOUGHT TO ESCAPE.
THE DETECTIVE'S NOTES PUT TOGETHER A PREDICTABLE HISTORY OF MINOR CRIME AND REPEATED ATTEMPTS AT CLEANING UP.
BUT I WONDER, KNOWING WHAT I KNOW, IF THINGS WERE THAT SIMPLE AFTER ALL.

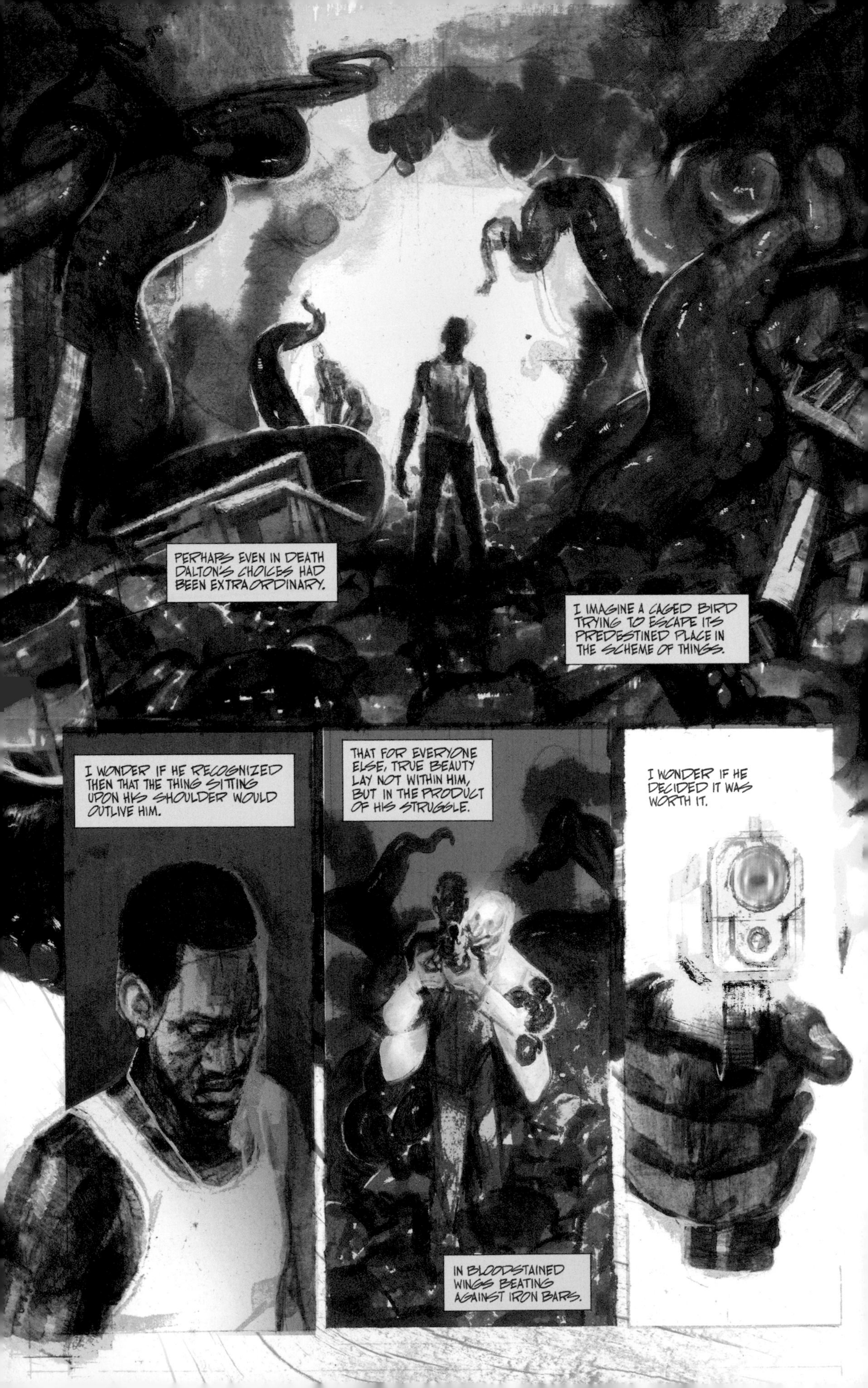
PERHAPS EVEN IN DEATH DALTON'S CHOICES HAD BEEN EXTRAORDINARY.
I IMAGINE A CAGED BIRD TRYING TO ESCAPE ITS PREDESTINED PLACE IN THE SCHEME OF THINGS.
I WONDER IF HE RECOGNIZED THEN THAT THE THING SITTING UPON HIS SHOULDER WOULD OUTLIVE HIM.
THAT FOR EVERYONE ELSE, TRUE BEAUTY LAY NOT WITHIN HIM, BUT IN THE PRODUCT OF HIS STRUGGLE.
IN BLOODSTAINED WINGS BEATING AGAINST IRON BARS.
I WONDER IF HE DECIDED IT WAS WORTH IT.

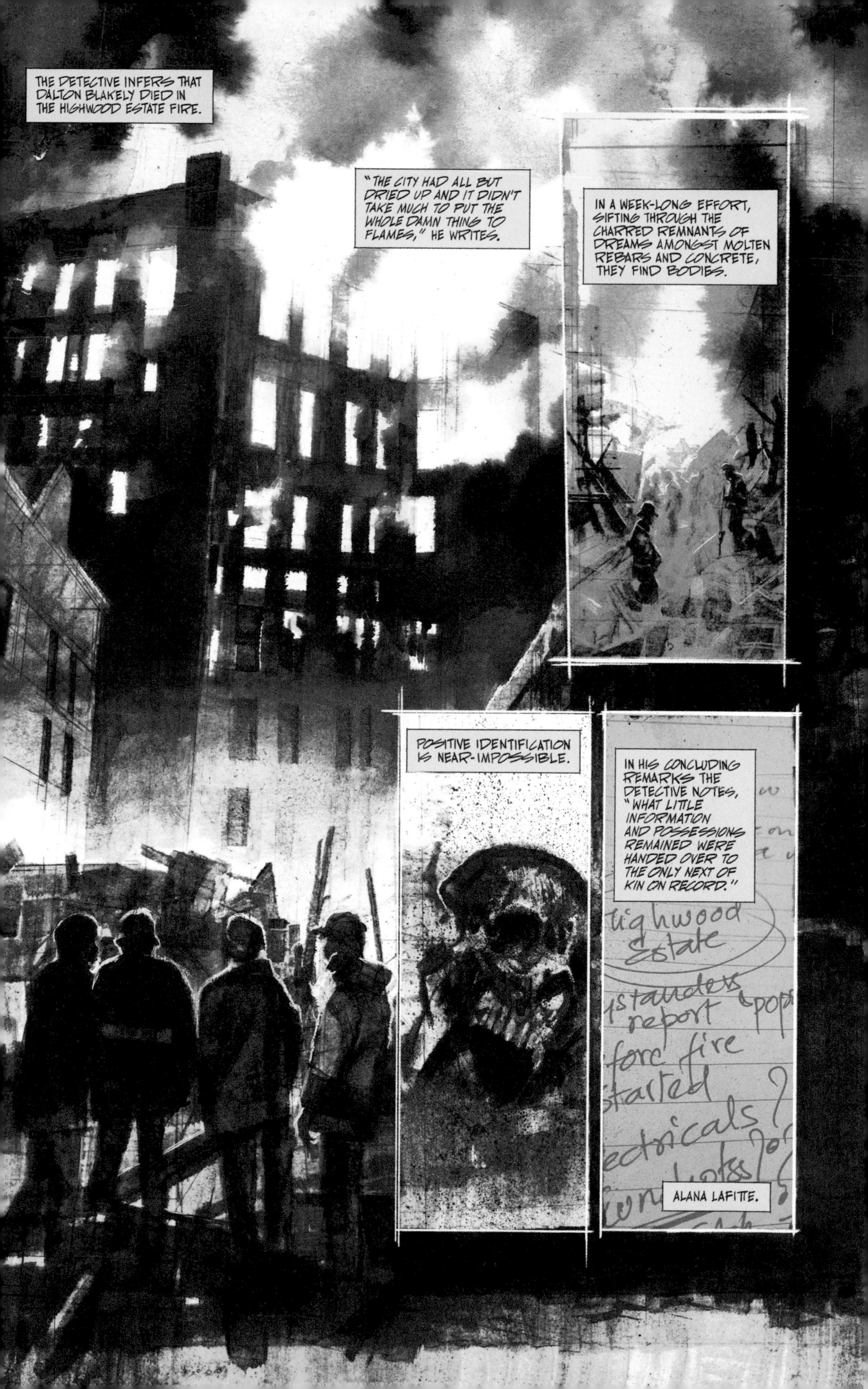
THE DETECTIVE INFERS THAT DALTON BLAKELY DIED IN THE HIGHWOOD ESTATE FIRE.
"THE CITY HAD ALL BUT DRIED UP AND IT DIDN'T TAKE MUCH TO PUT THE WHOLE DAMN THING TO FLAMES," HE WRITES.
IN A WEEK-LONG EFFORT, SIFTING THROUGH THE CHARRED REMNANTS OF DREAMS AMONGST MOLTEN REBARS AND CONCRETE, THEY FIND BODIES.
POSITIVE IDENTIFICATION IS NEAR-IMPOSSIBLE.
IN HIS CONCLUDING REMARKS THE DETECTIVE NOTES, "WHAT LITTLE INFORMATION AND POSSESSIONS REMAINED WERE HANDED OVER TO THE ONLY NEXT OF KIN ON RECORD."
Highwood Estate
ALANA LAFITTE.

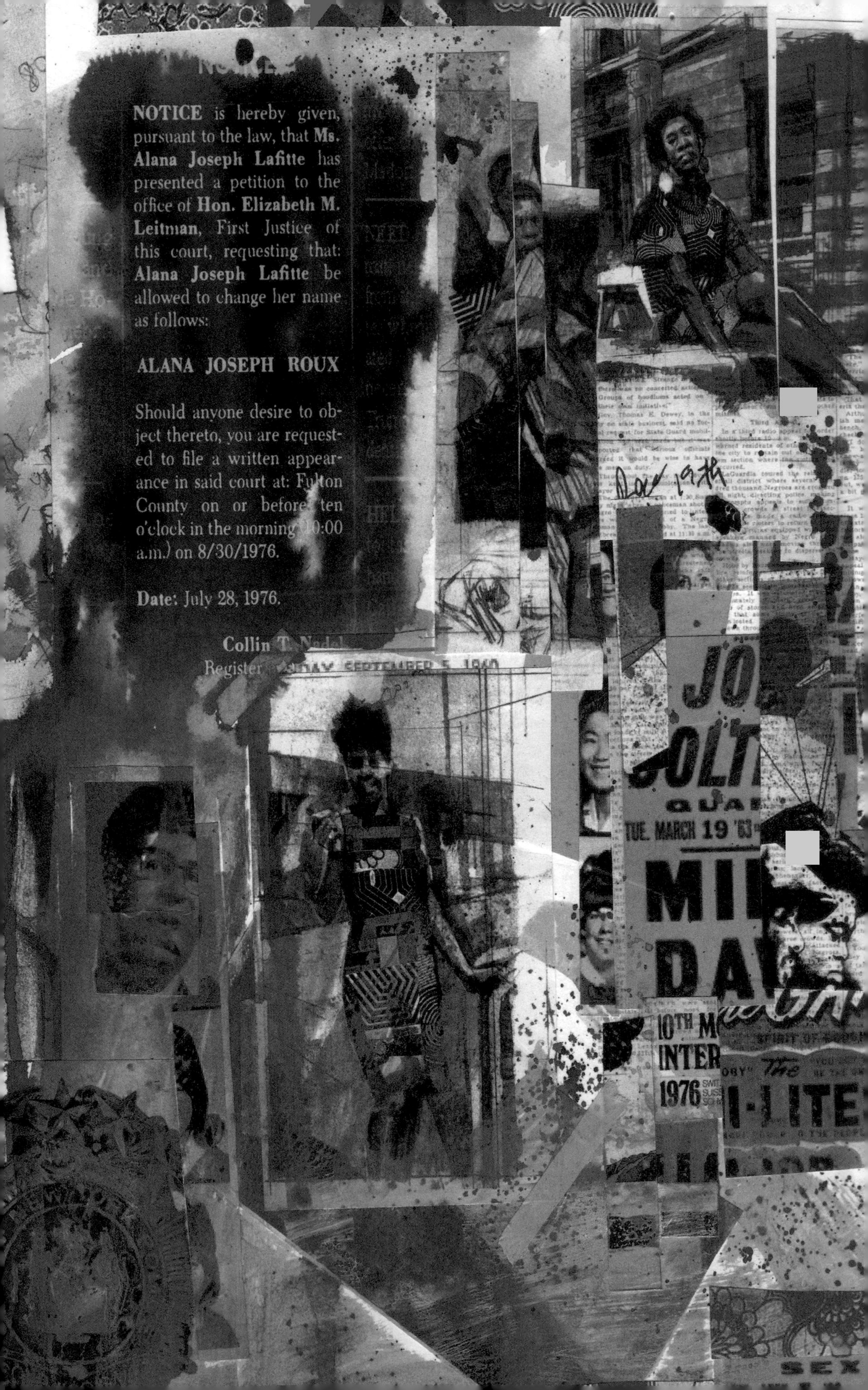
NOTICE is hereby given, pursuant to the law, that Ms. Alana Joseph Lafitte has presented a petition to the office of Hon. Elizabeth M. Leitman, First Justice of this court, requesting that: Alana Joseph Lafitte be allowed to change her name as follows:
ALANA JOSEPH ROUX
Should anyone desire to object thereto, you are requested to file a written appearance in said court at: Fulton County on or before ten o'clock in the morning (10:00 a.m.) on 8/30/1976.
Date: July 28, 1976.
Collin T.
Register
TUE. MARCH 19 '63
1976

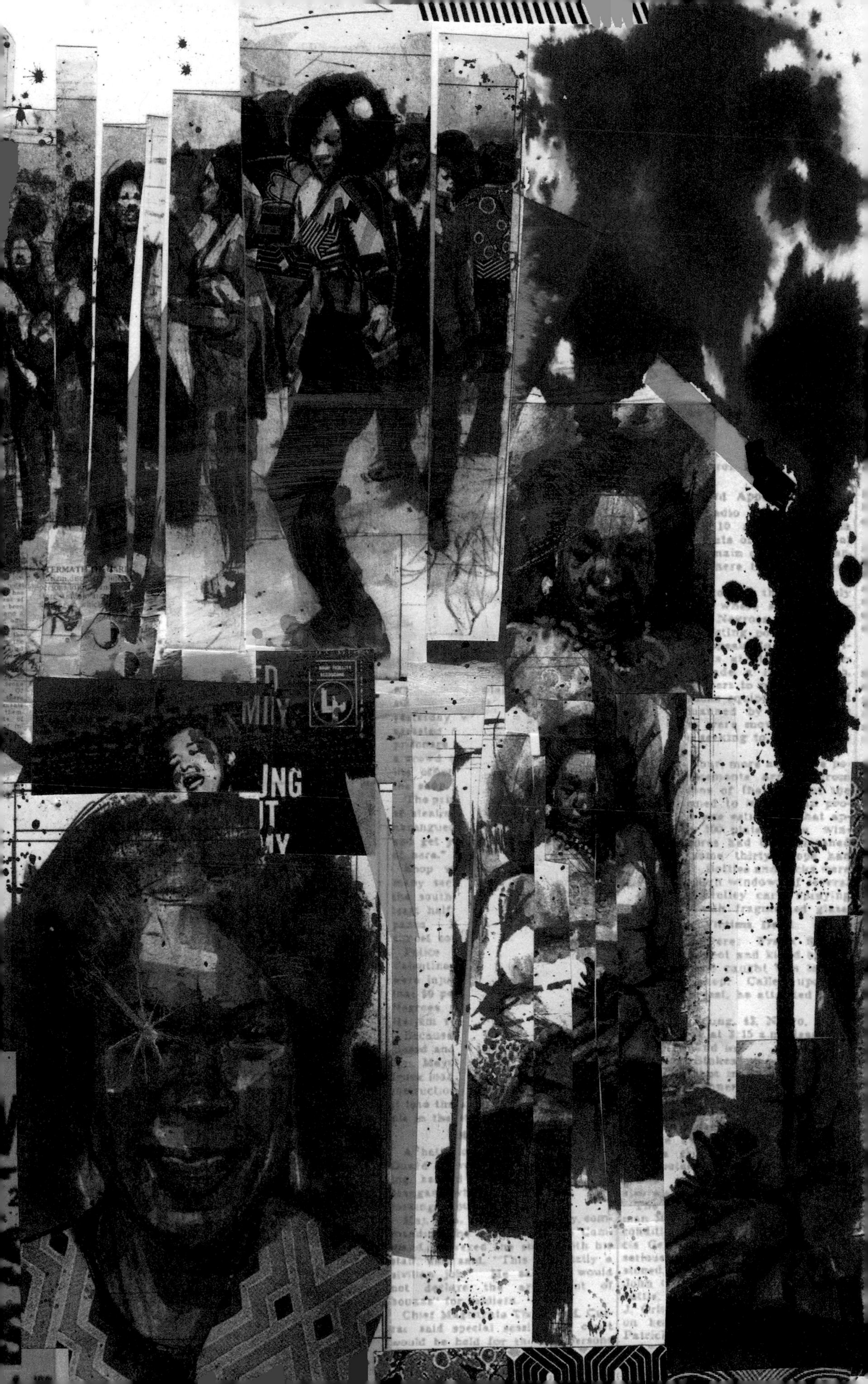

CHAPTER 4

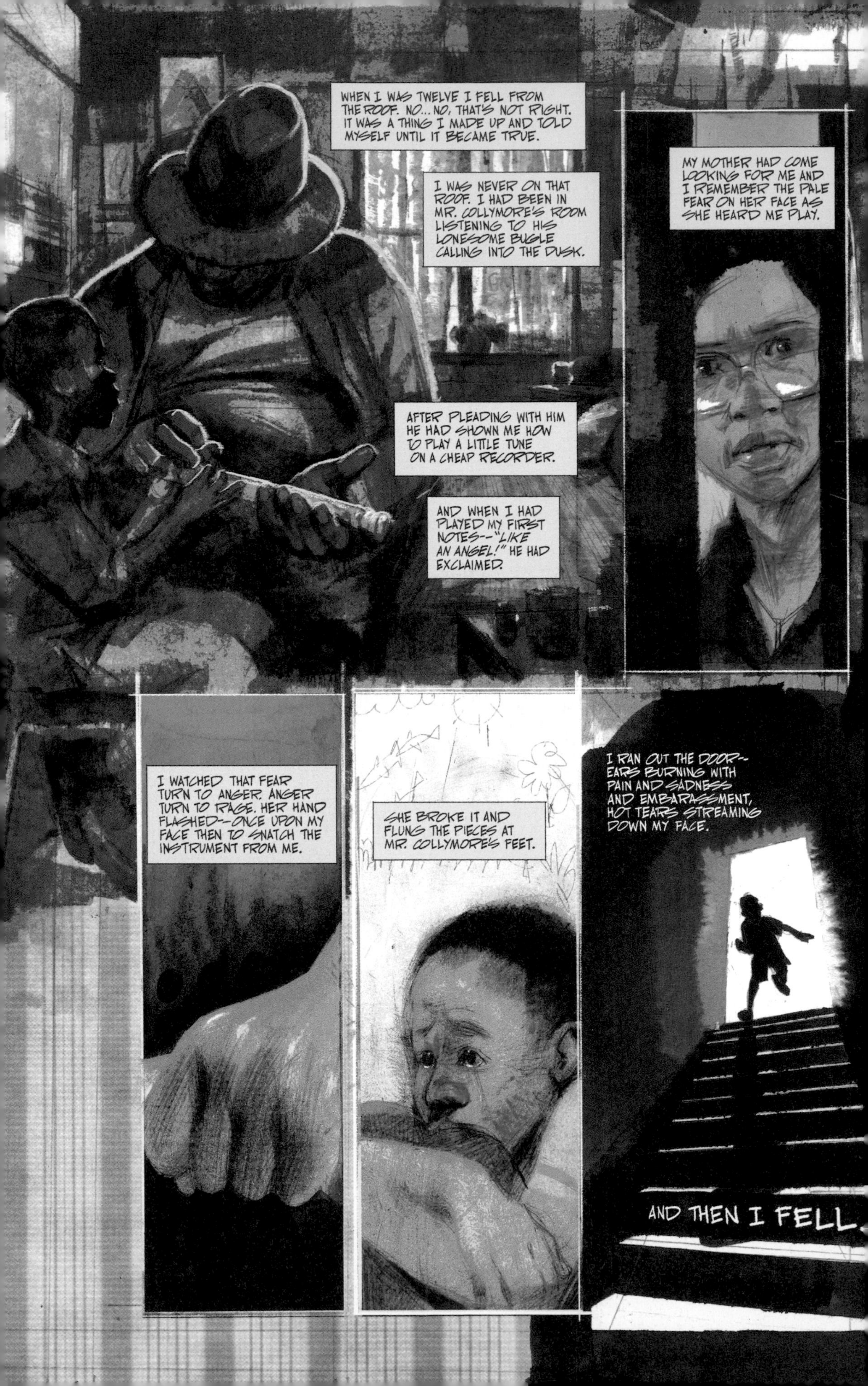
WHEN I WAS TWELVE I FELL FROM THE ROOF. NO... NO, THAT'S NOT RIGHT. IT WAS A THING I MADE UP AND TOLD MYSELF UNTIL IT BECAME TRUE.
I WAS NEVER ON THAT ROOF. I HAD BEEN IN MR. COLLYMORE'S ROOM LISTENING TO HIS LONESOME BUGLE CALLING INTO THE DUSK.
AFTER PLEADING WITH HIM HE HAD SHOWN ME HOW TO PLAY A LITTLE TUNE ON A CHEAP RECORDER.
AND WHEN I HAD PLAYED MY FIRST NOTES--"LIKE AN ANGEL!" HE HAD EXCLAIMED.
MY MOTHER HAD COME LOOKING FOR ME AND I REMEMBER THE PALE FEAR ON HER FACE AS SHE HEARD ME PLAY.
I WATCHED THAT FEAR TURN TO ANGER. ANGER TURN TO RAGE. HER HAND FLASHED--ONCE UPON MY FACE THEN TO SNATCH THE INSTRUMENT FROM ME.
SHE BROKE IT AND FLUNG THE PIECES AT MR. COLLYMORE'S FEET.
I RAN OUT THE DOOR--EARS BURNING WITH PAIN AND SADNESS AND EMBARASSMENT, HOT TEARS STREAMING DOWN MY FACE.
AND THEN I FELL.

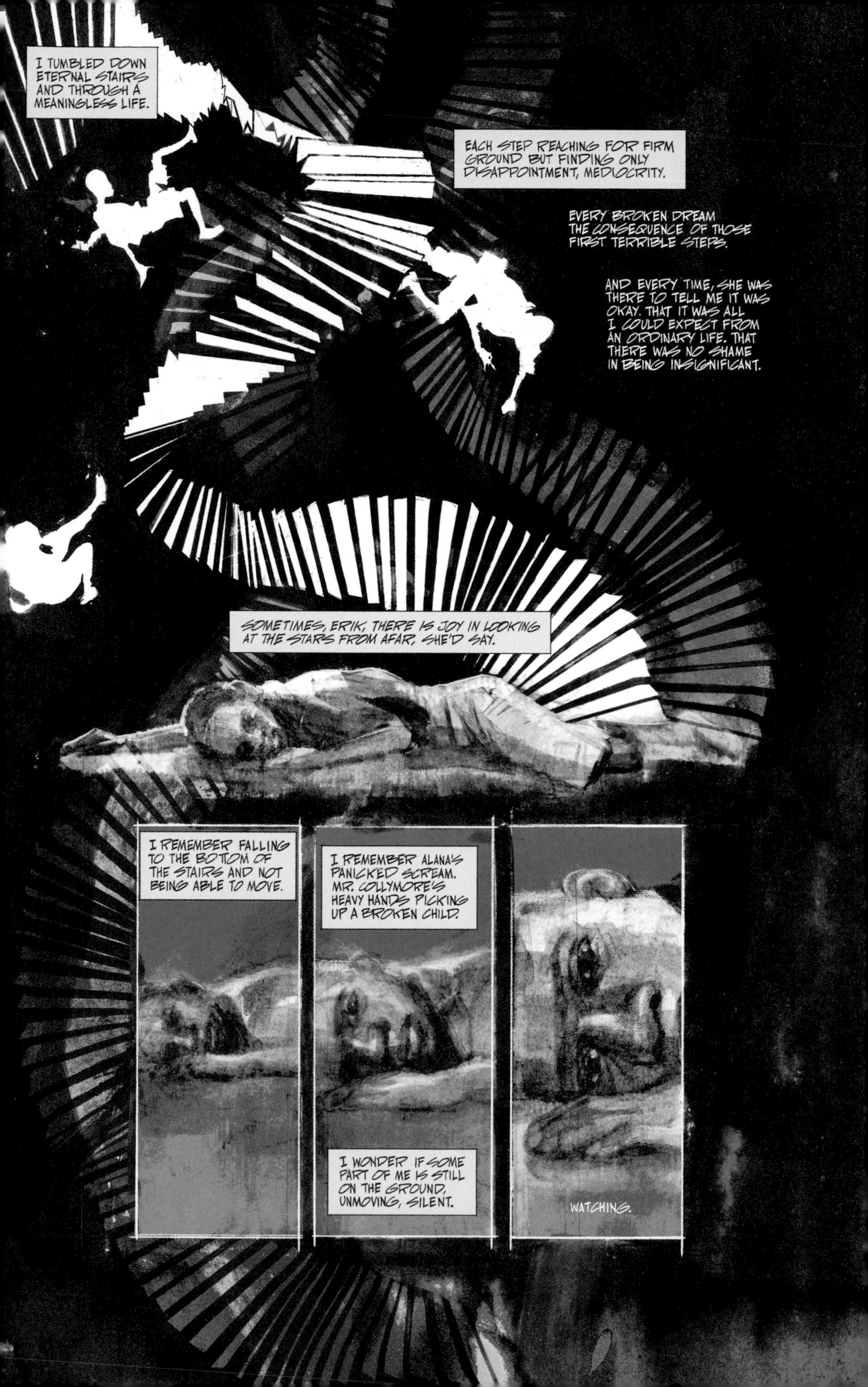
I TUMBLED DOWN ETERNAL STAIRS AND THROUGH A MEANINGLESS LIFE.
EACH STEP REACHING FOR FIRM GROUND BUT FINDING ONLY DISAPPOINTMENT, MEDIOCRITY.
EVERY BROKEN DREAM THE CONSEQUENCE OF THOSE FIRST TERRIBLE STEPS.
AND EVERY TIME, SHE WAS THERE TO TELL ME IT WAS OKAY. THAT IT WAS ALL I COULD EXPECT FROM AN ORDINARY LIFE. THAT THERE WAS NO SHAME IN BEING INSIGNIFICANT.
SOMETIMES, ERIK, THERE IS JOY IN LOOKING AT THE STARS FROM AFAR, SHE'D SAY.
I REMEMBER FALLING TO THE BOTTOM OF THE STAIRS AND NOT BEING ABLE TO MOVE.
I REMEMBER ALANA'S PANICKED SCREAM. MR. COLLYMORE'S HEAVY HANDS PICKING UP A BROKEN CHILD.
I WONDER IF SOME PART OF ME IS STILL ON THE GROUND, UNMOVING, SILENT.
WATCHING.

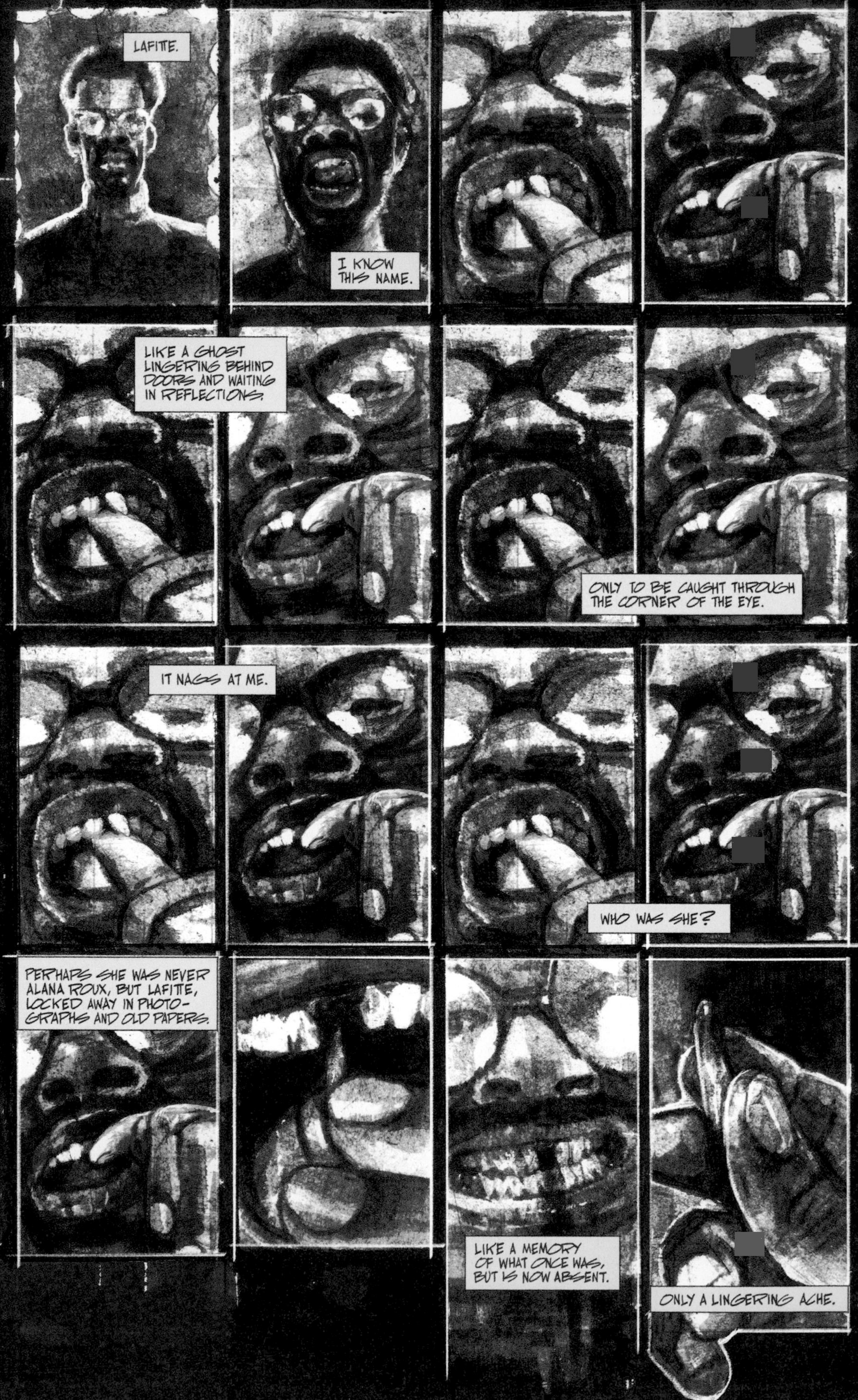
LAFITTE.
I KNOW THIS NAME.
LIKE A GHOST LINGERING BEHIND DOORS AND WAITING IN REFLECTIONS.
ONLY TO BE CAUGHT THROUGH THE CORNER OF THE EYE.
IT NAGS AT ME.
WHO WAS SHE?
PERHAPS SHE WAS NEVER ALANA ROUX, BUT LAFITTE, LOCKED AWAY IN PHOTO-GRAPHS AND OLD PAPERS.
LIKE A MEMORY OF WHAT ONCE WAS, BUT IS NOW ABSENT.
ONLY A LINGERING ACHE.

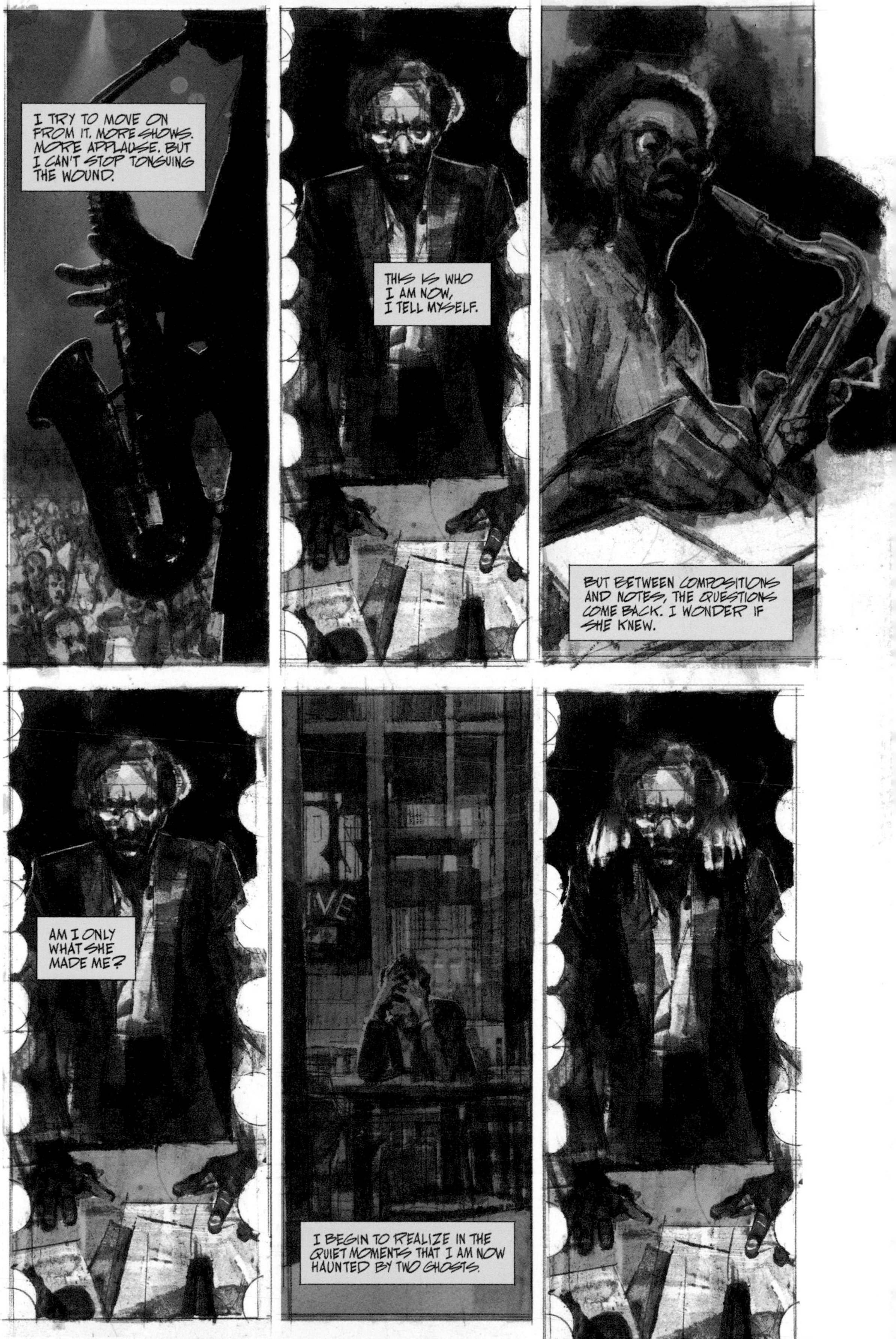
I TRY TO MOVE ON FROM IT. MORE SHOWS. MORE APPLAUSE. BUT I CAN'T STOP TONGUING THE WOUND.
THIS IS WHO I AM NOW, I TELL MYSELF.
BUT BETWEEN COMPOSITIONS AND NOTES, THE QUESTIONS COME BACK. I WONDER IF SHE KNEW.
AM I ONLY WHAT SHE MADE ME?
IVE
I BEGIN TO REALIZE IN THE QUIET MOMENTS THAT I AM NOW HAUNTED BY TWO GHOSTS.

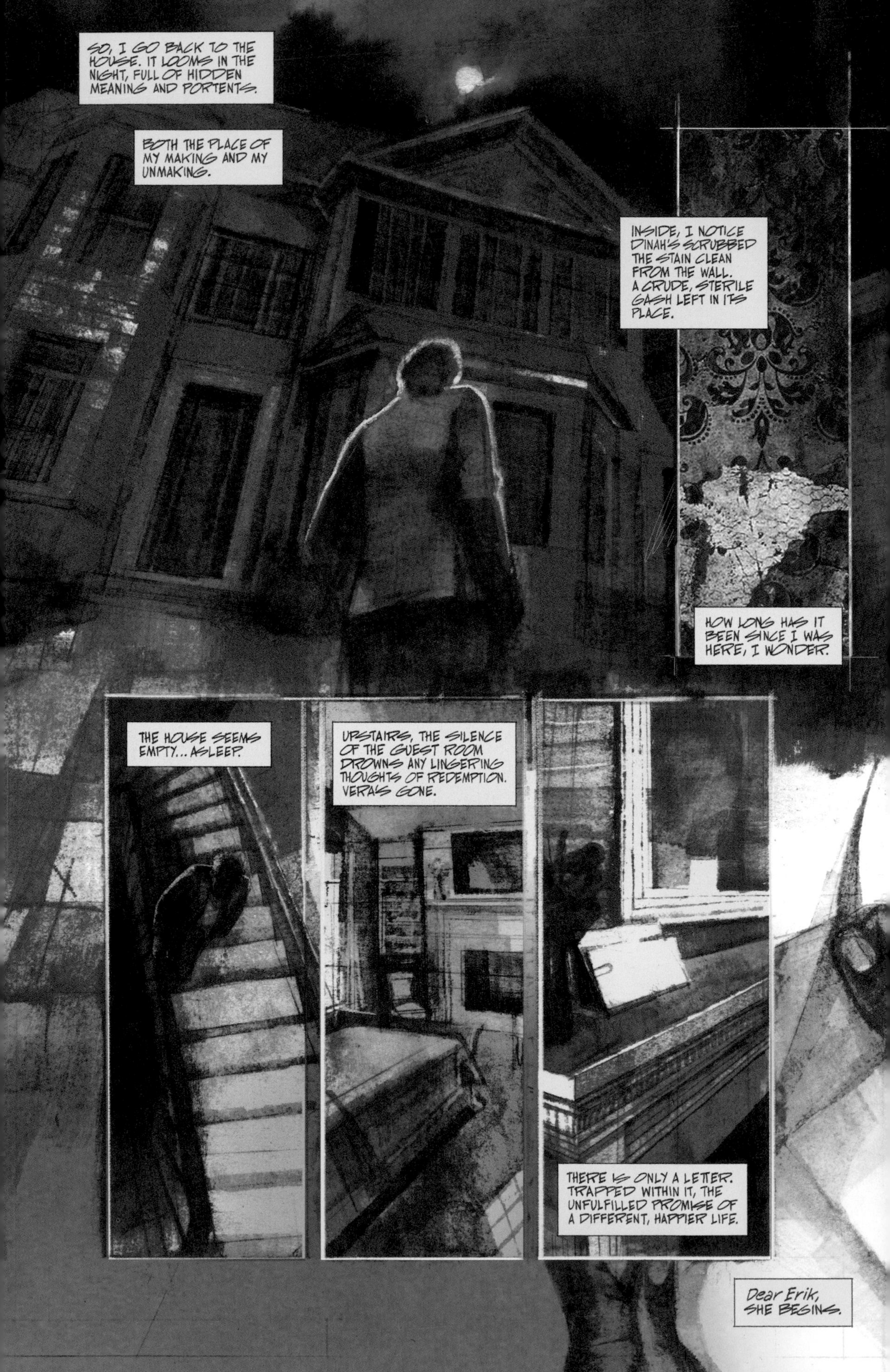
SO, I GO BACK TO THE HOUSE. IT LOOMS IN THE NIGHT, FULL OF HIDDEN MEANING AND PORTENTS.
BOTH THE PLACE OF MY MAKING AND MY UNMAKING.
INSIDE, I NOTICE DINAH'S SCRUBBED THE STAIN CLEAN FROM THE WALL. A CRUDE, STERILE GASH LEFT IN ITS PLACE.
HOW LONG HAS IT BEEN SINCE I WAS HERE, I WONDER.
THE HOUSE SEEMS EMPTY... ASLEEP.
UPSTAIRS, THE SILENCE OF THE GUEST ROOM DROWNS ANY LINGERING THOUGHTS OF REDEMPTION. VERA'S GONE.
THERE IS ONLY A LETTER. TRAPPED WITHIN IT, THE UNFULFILLED PROMISE OF A DIFFERENT, HAPPIER LIFE.
Dear Erik, SHE BEGINS.

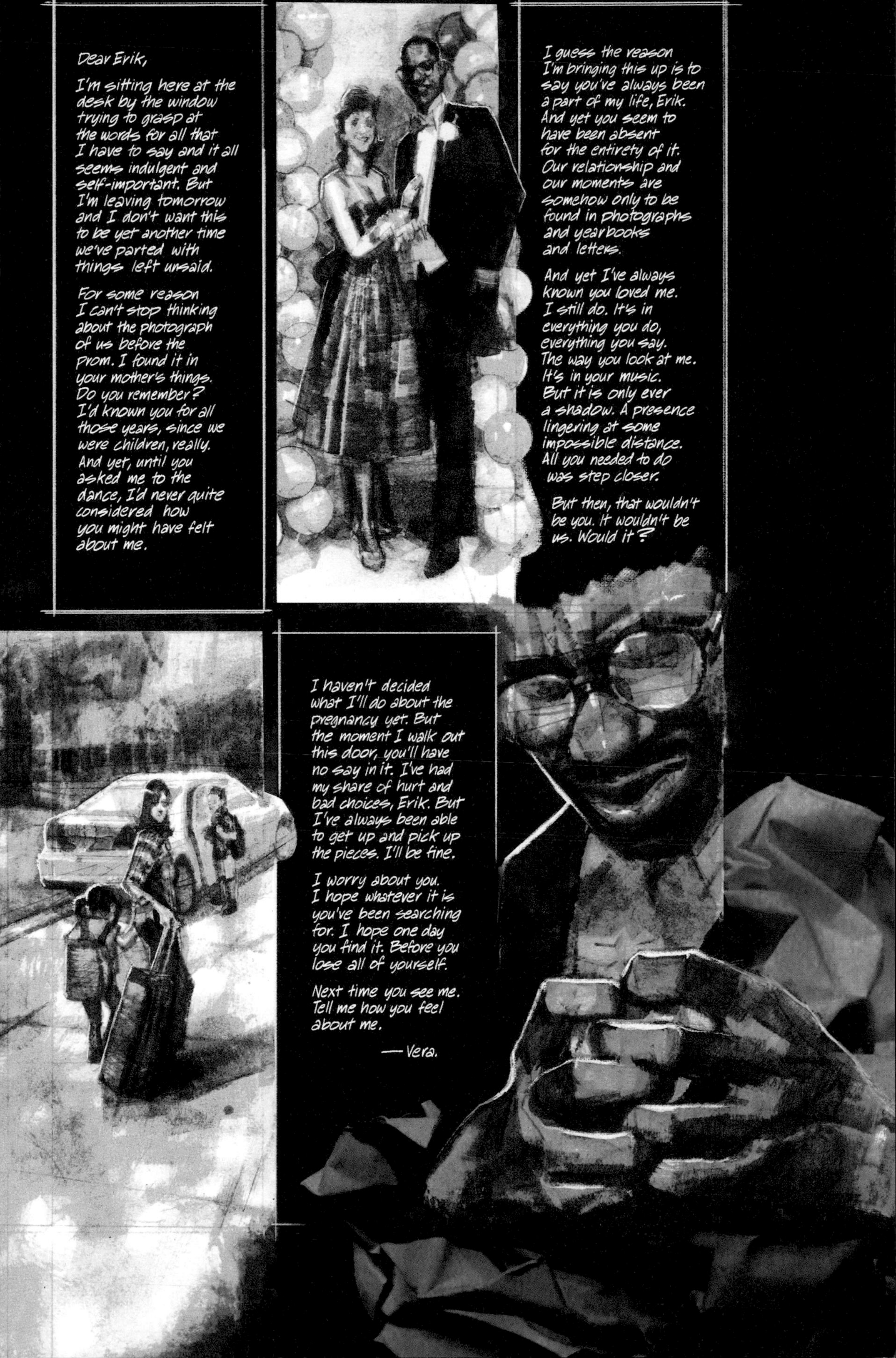
Dear Erik,
I'm sitting here at the desk by the window trying to grasp at the words for all that I have to say and it all seems indulgent and self-important. But I'm leaving tomorrow and I don't want this to be yet another time we've parted with things left unsaid.
For some reason I can't stop thinking about the photograph of us before the prom. I found it in your mother's things. Do you remember? I'd known you for all those years, since we were children, really. And yet, until you asked me to the dance, I'd never quite considered how you might have felt about me.
I guess the reason I'm bringing this up is to say you've always been a part of my life, Erik. And yet you seem to have been absent for the entirety of it. Our relationship and our moments are somehow only to be found in photographs and yearbooks and letters.
And yet I've always known you loved me. I still do. It's in everything you do, everything you say. The way you look at me. It's in your music. But it is only ever a shadow. A presence lingering at some impossible distance. All you needed to do was step closer.
But then, that wouldn't be you. It wouldn't be us. Would it?
I haven't decided what I'll do about the pregnancy yet. But the moment I walk out this door, you'll have no say in it. I've had my share of hurt and bad choices, Erik. But I've always been able to get up and pick up the pieces. I'll be fine.
I worry about you. I hope whatever it is you've been searching for. I hope one day you find it. Before you lose all of yourself.
Next time you see me. Tell me how you feel about me.
— Vera.

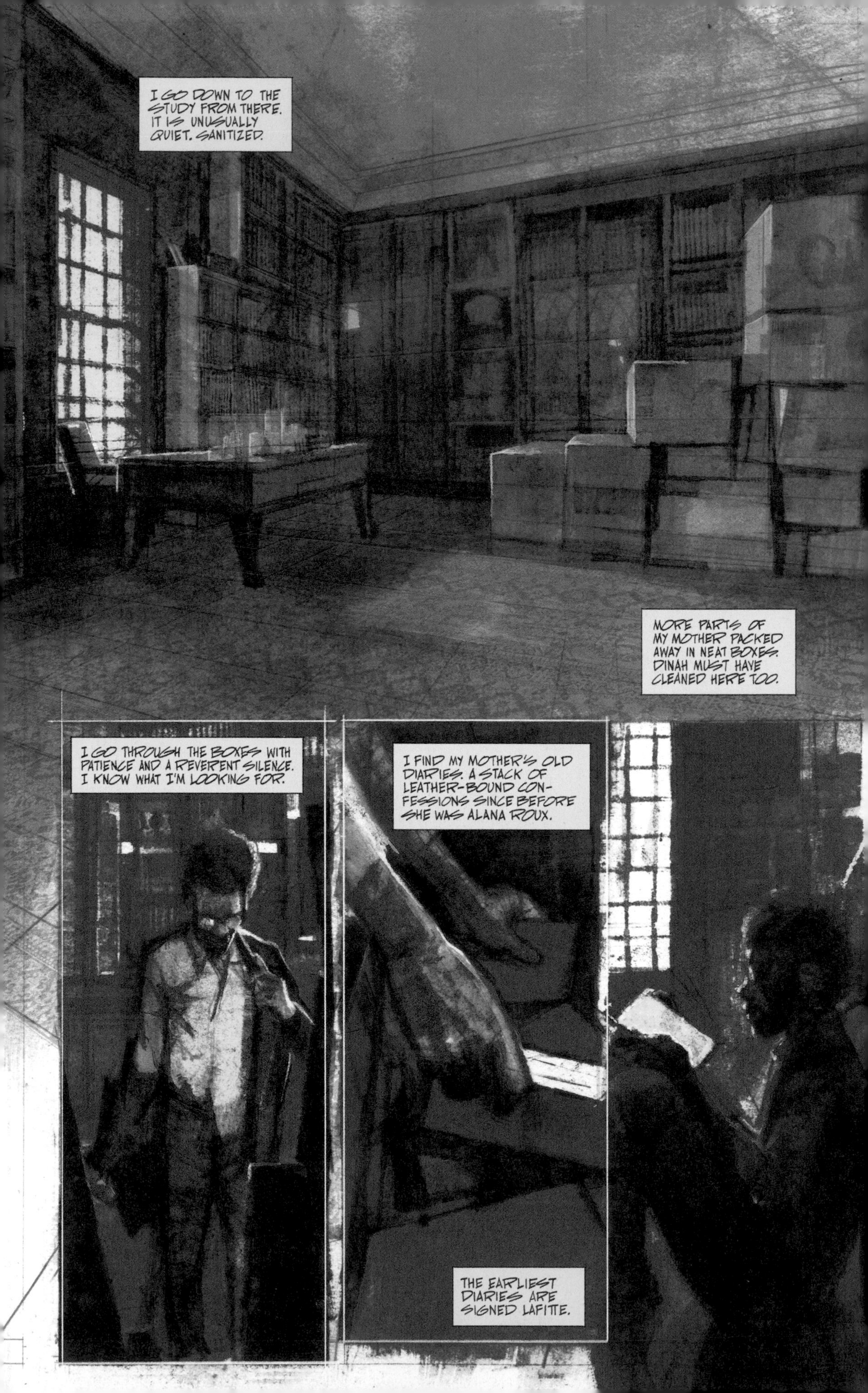
I GO DOWN TO THE STUDY FROM THERE. IT IS UNUSUALLY QUIET. SANITIZED.
MORE PARTS OF MY MOTHER PACKED AWAY IN NEAT BOXES. DINAH MUST HAVE CLEANED HERE TOO.
I GO THROUGH THE BOXES WITH PATIENCE AND A REVERENT SILENCE. I KNOW WHAT I'M LOOKING FOR.
I FIND MY MOTHER'S OLD DIARIES. A STACK OF LEATHER-BOUND CONFESSIONS SINCE BEFORE SHE WAS ALANA ROUX.
THE EARLIEST DIARIES ARE SIGNED LAFITTE.

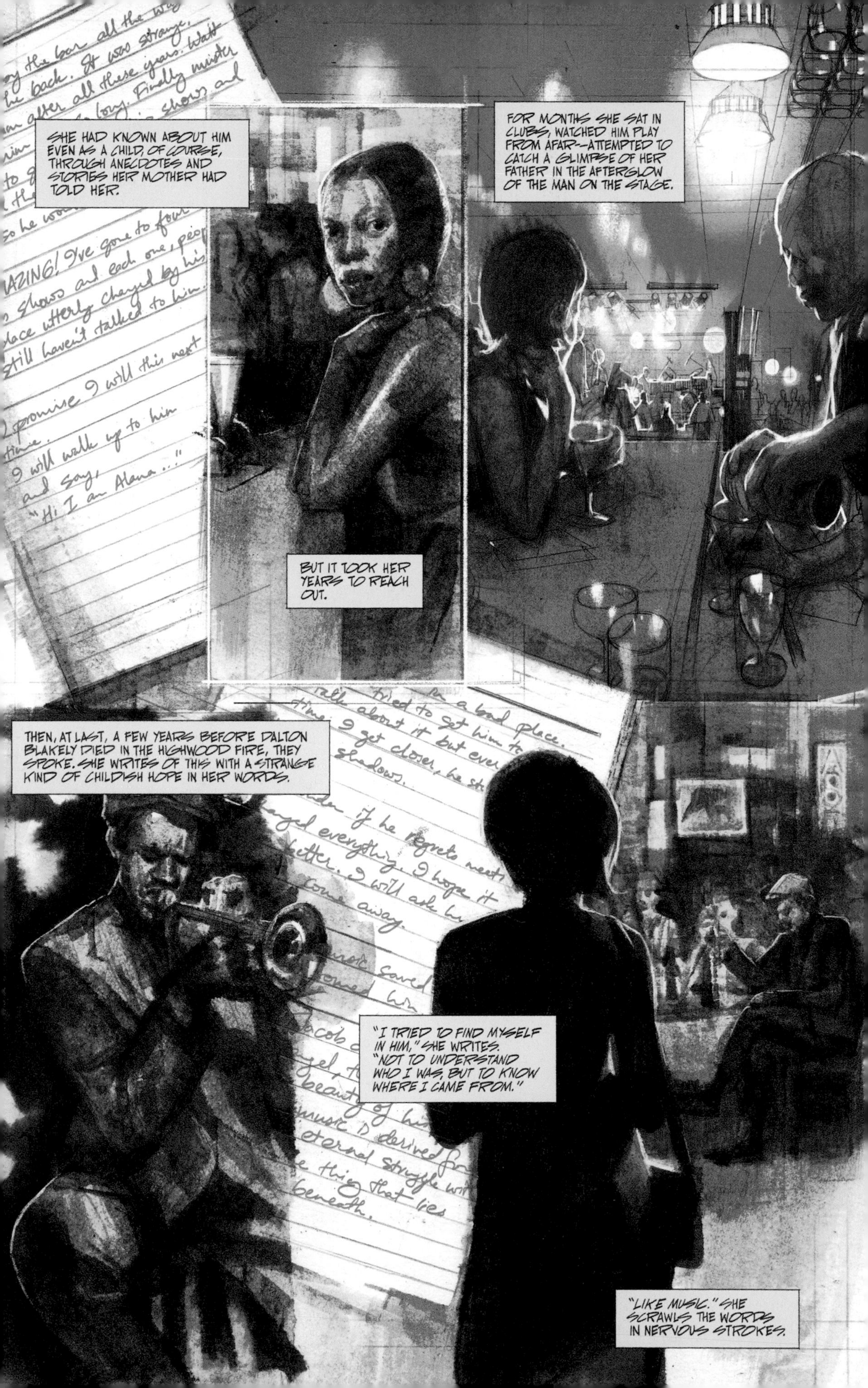
SHE HAD KNOWN ABOUT HIM EVEN AS A CHILD, OF COURSE, THROUGH ANECDOTES AND STORIES HER MOTHER HAD TOLD HER.
BUT IT TOOK HER YEARS TO REACH OUT.
FOR MONTHS SHE SAT IN CLUBS, WATCHED HIM PLAY FROM AFAR--ATTEMPTED TO CATCH A GLIMPSE OF HER FATHER IN THE AFTERGLOW OF THE MAN ON THE STAGE.
THEN, AT LAST, A FEW YEARS BEFORE DALTON BLAKELY DIED IN THE HIGHWOOD FIRE, THEY SPOKE. SHE WRITES OF THIS WITH A STRANGE KIND OF CHILDISH HOPE IN HER WORDS.
"I TRIED TO FIND MYSELF IN HIM," SHE WRITES. "NOT TO UNDERSTAND WHO I WAS, BUT TO KNOW WHERE I CAME FROM."
"LIKE MUSIC." SHE SCRAWLS THE WORDS IN NERVOUS STROKES.

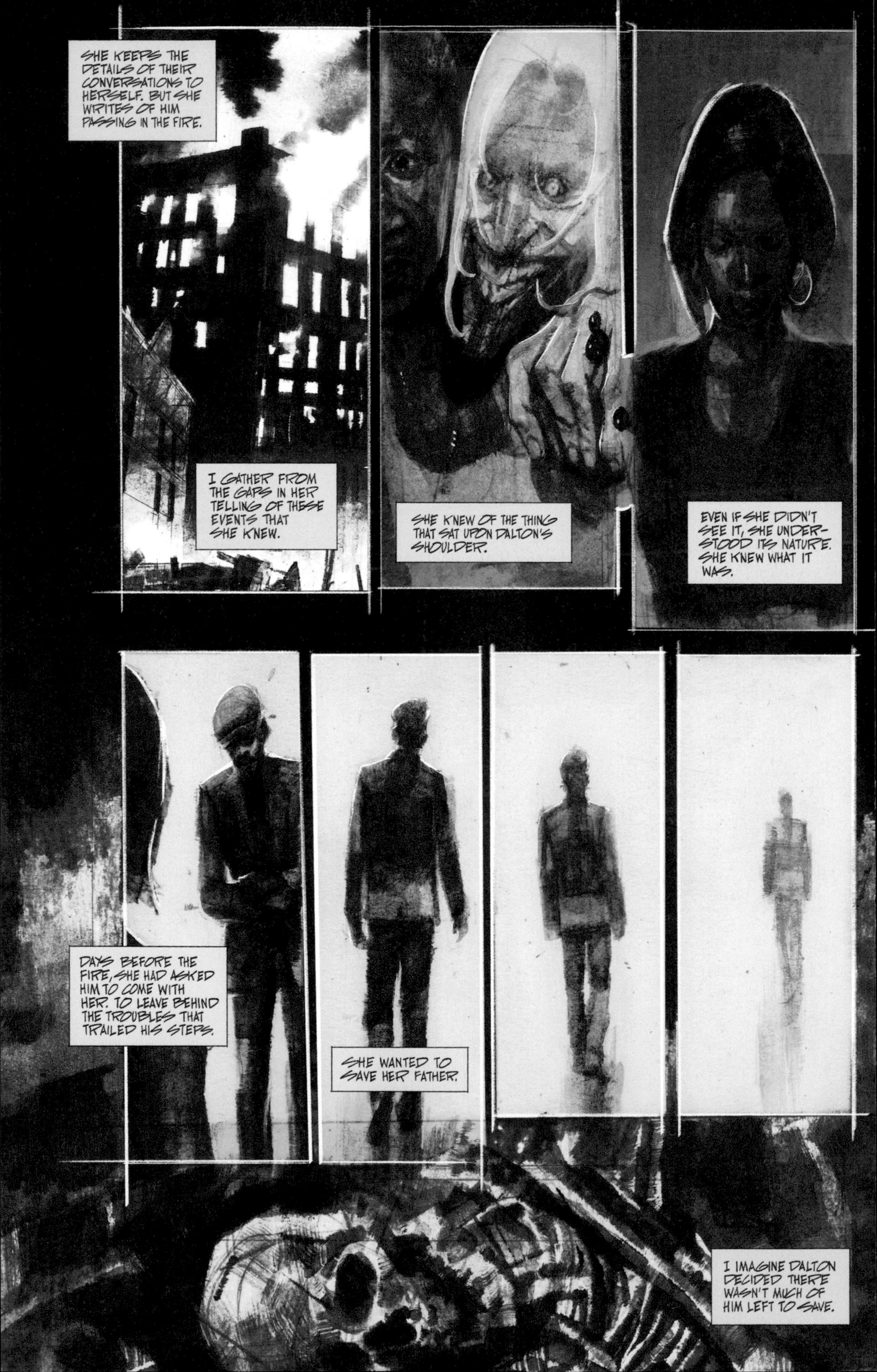
SHE KEEPS THE DETAILS OF THEIR CONVERSATIONS TO HERSELF. BUT SHE WRITES OF HIM PASSING IN THE FIRE.
I GATHER FROM THE GAPS IN HER TELLING OF THESE EVENTS THAT SHE KNEW.
SHE KNEW OF THE THING THAT SAT UPON DALTON'S SHOULDER.
EVEN IF SHE DIDN'T SEE IT, SHE UNDERSTOOD ITS NATURE. SHE KNEW WHAT IT WAS.
DAYS BEFORE THE FIRE, SHE HAD ASKED HIM TO COME WITH HER. TO LEAVE BEHIND THE TROUBLES THAT TRAILED HIS STEPS.
SHE WANTED TO SAVE HER FATHER.
I IMAGINE DALTON DECIDED THERE WASN'T MUCH OF HIM LEFT TO SAVE.

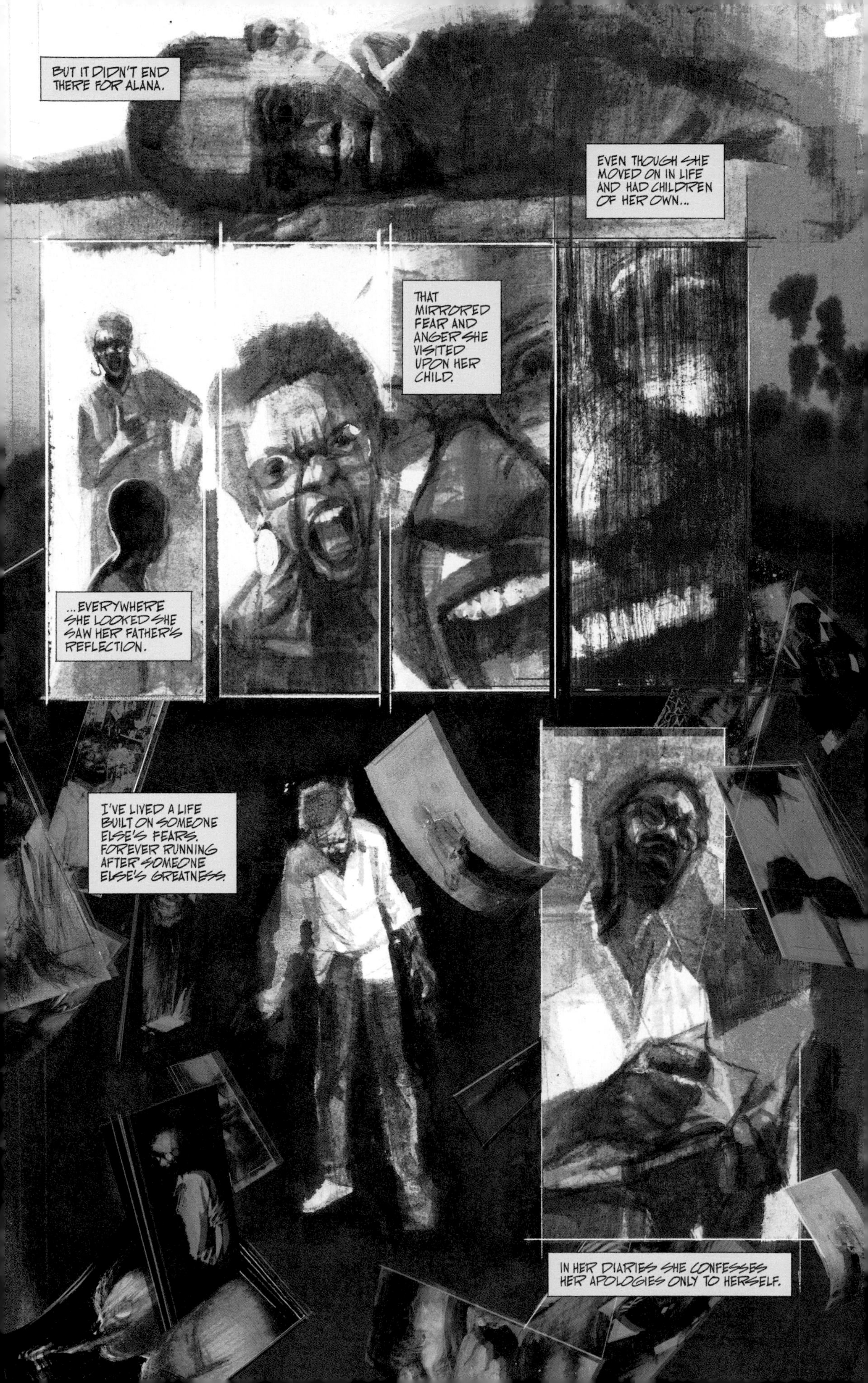
BUT IT DIDN'T END THERE FOR ALANA.
EVEN THOUGH SHE MOVED ON IN LIFE AND HAD CHILDREN OF HER OWN...
...EVERYWHERE SHE LOOKED SHE SAW HER FATHER'S REFLECTION.
THAT MIRRORED FEAR AND ANGER SHE VISITED UPON HER CHILD.
I'VE LIVED A LIFE BUILT ON SOMEONE ELSE'S FEARS. FOREVER RUNNING AFTER SOMEONE ELSE'S GREATNESS.
IN HER DIARIES SHE CONFESSES HER APOLOGIES ONLY TO HERSELF.

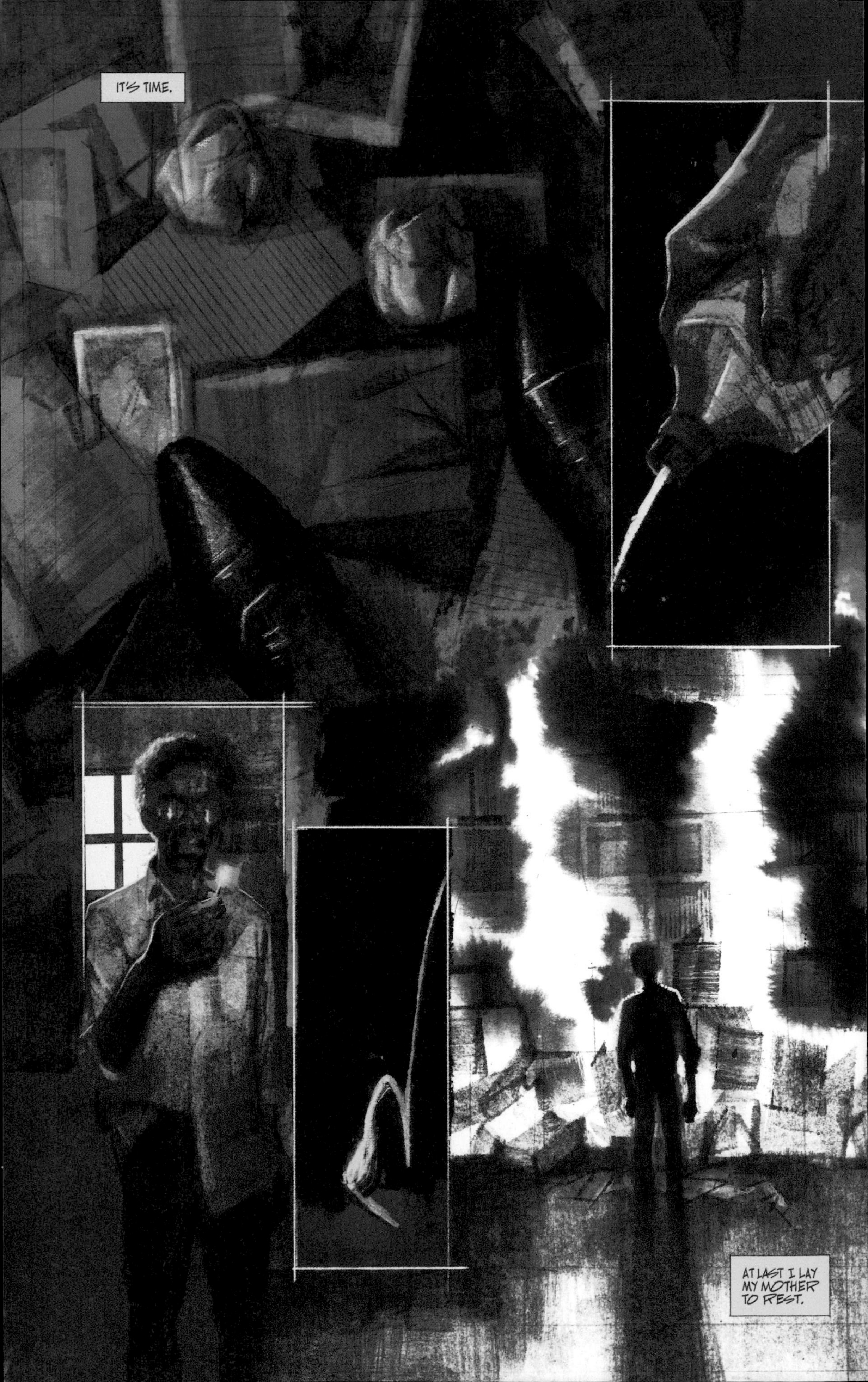
IT'S TIME.
AT LAST I LAY MY MOTHER TO REST.

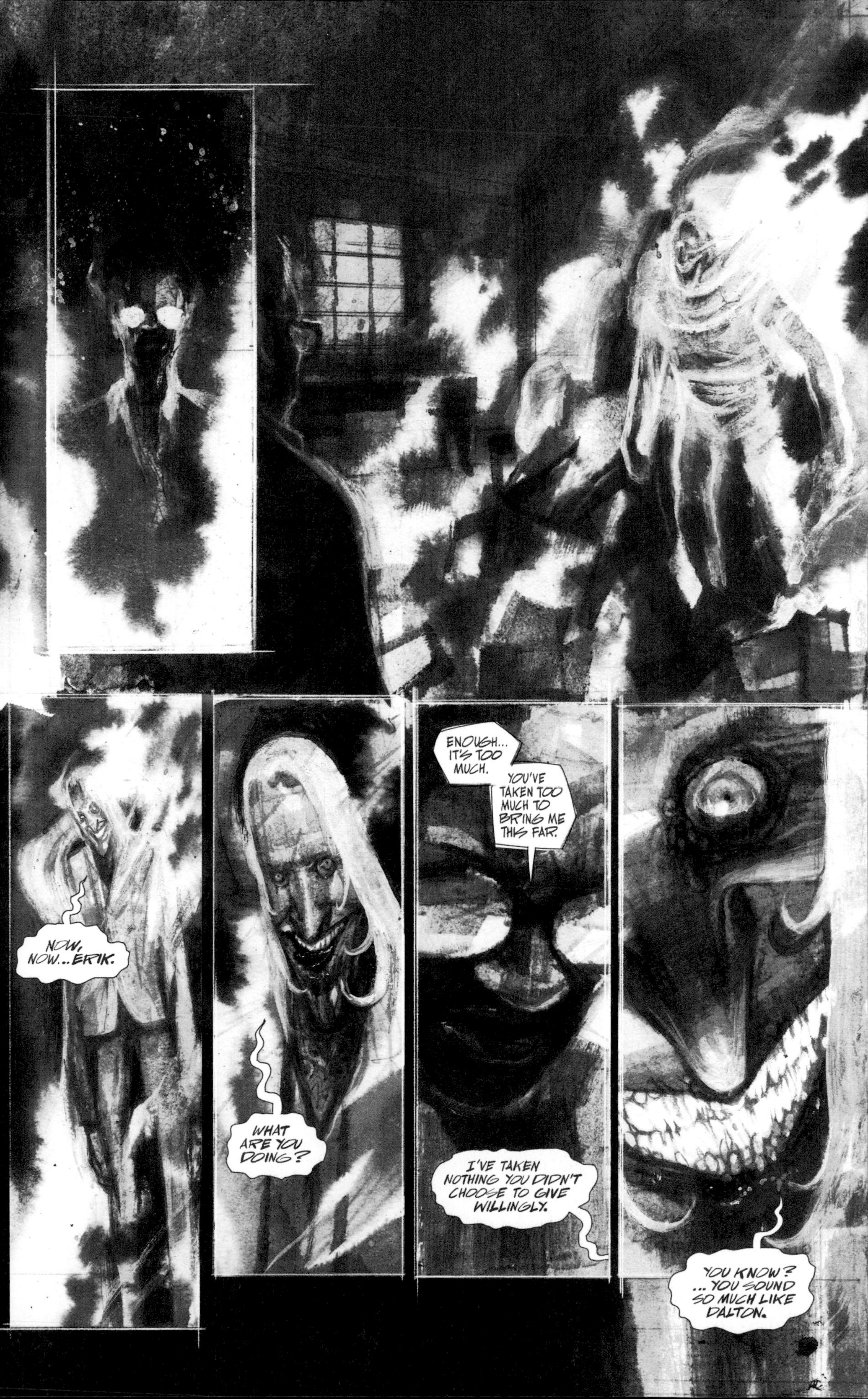
NOW, NOW... ERIK.
WHAT ARE YOU DOING?
ENOUGH... IT'S TOO MUCH.
YOU'VE TAKEN TOO MUCH TO BRING ME THIS FAR.
I'VE TAKEN NOTHING YOU DIDN'T CHOOSE TO GIVE WILLINGLY.
YOU KNOW? ...YOU SOUND SO MUCH LIKE DALTON.

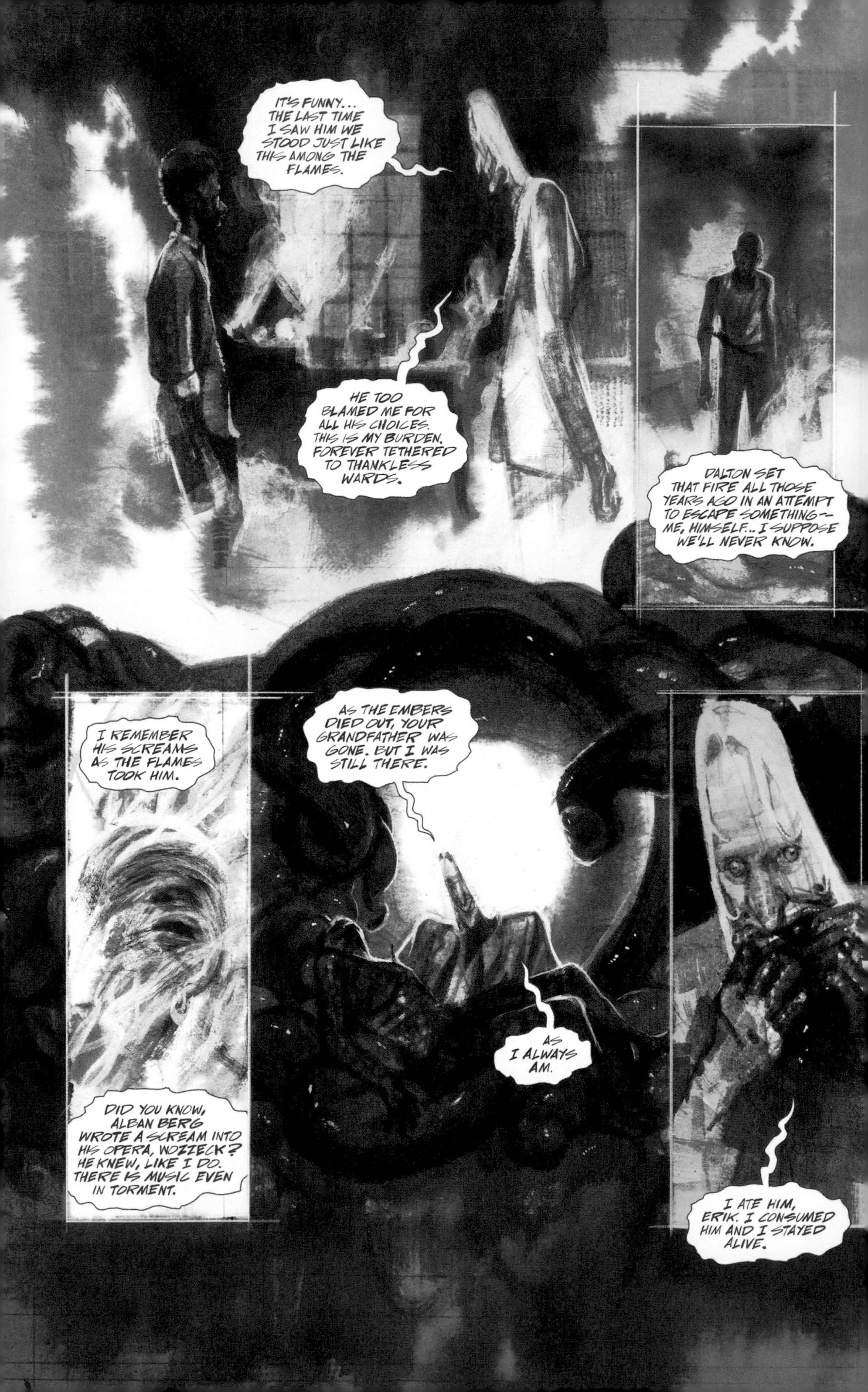
IT'S FUNNY... THE LAST TIME I SAW HIM WE STOOD JUST LIKE THIS AMONG THE FLAMES.
HE TOO BLAMED ME FOR ALL HIS CHOICES. THIS IS MY BURDEN, FOREVER TETHERED TO THANKLESS WARDS.
DALTON SET THAT FIRE ALL THOSE YEARS AGO IN AN ATTEMPT TO ESCAPE SOMETHING-- ME, HIMSELF... I SUPPOSE WE'LL NEVER KNOW.
I REMEMBER HIS SCREAMS AS THE FLAMES TOOK HIM.
DID YOU KNOW, ALBAN BERG WROTE A SCREAM INTO HIS OPERA, WOZZECK? HE KNEW, LIKE I DO. THERE IS MUSIC EVEN IN TORMENT.
AS THE EMBERS DIED OUT, YOUR GRANDFATHER WAS GONE. BUT I WAS STILL THERE.
AS I ALWAYS AM.
I ATE HIM, ERIK. I CONSUMED HIM AND I STAYED ALIVE.

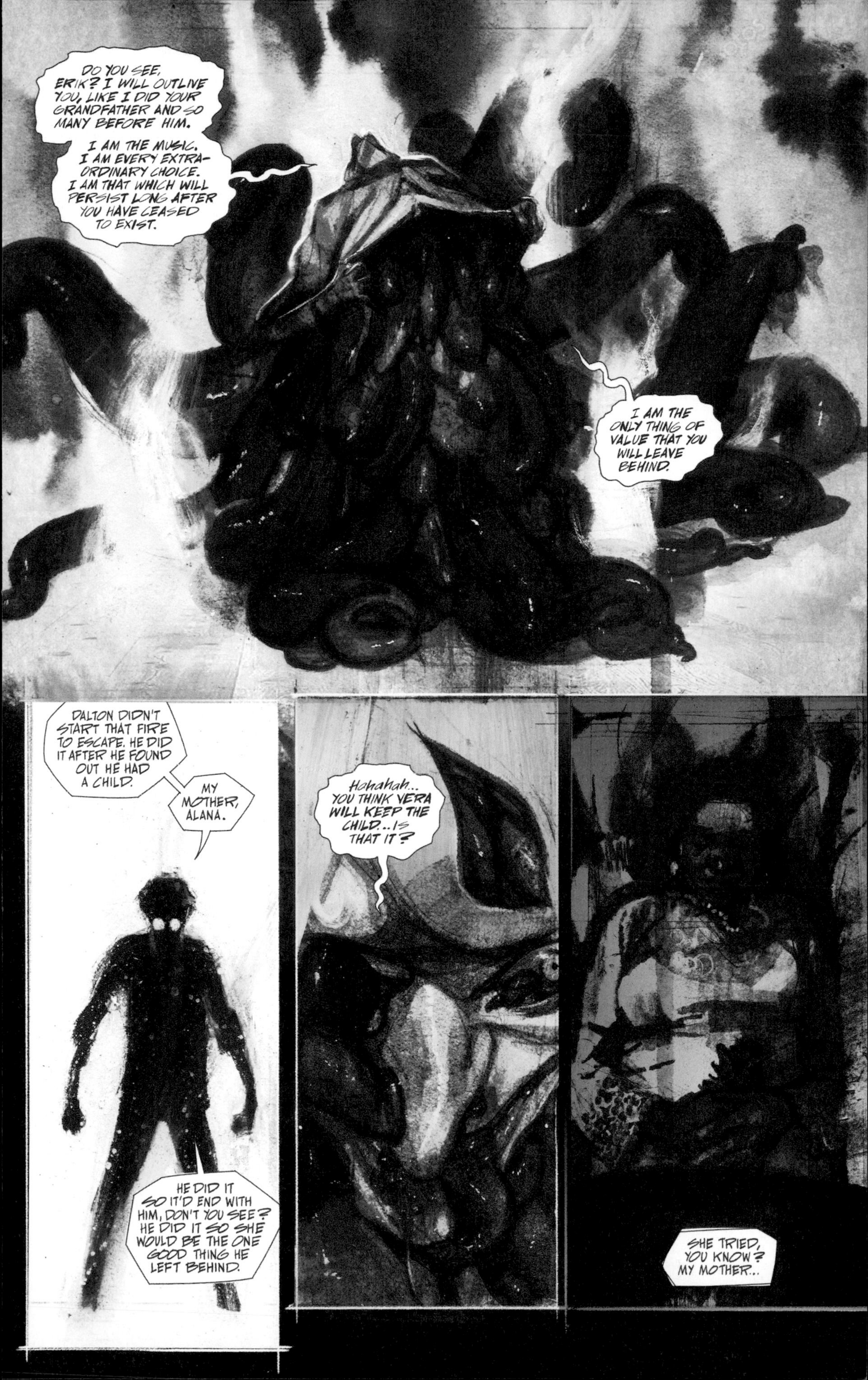
DO YOU SEE, ERIK? I WILL OUTLIVE YOU, LIKE I DID YOUR GRANDFATHER AND SO MANY BEFORE HIM.
I AM THE MUSIC. I AM EVERY EXTRA-ORDINARY CHOICE. I AM THAT WHICH WILL PERSIST LONG AFTER YOU HAVE CEASED TO EXIST.
I AM THE ONLY THING OF VALUE THAT YOU WILL LEAVE BEHIND.
DALTON DIDN'T START THAT FIRE TO ESCAPE. HE DID IT AFTER HE FOUND OUT HE HAD A CHILD.
MY MOTHER, ALANA.
HE DID IT SO IT'D END WITH HIM, DON'T YOU SEE? HE DID IT SO SHE WOULD BE THE ONE GOOD THING HE LEFT BEHIND.
Hohahah... YOU THINK VERA WILL KEEP THE CHILD... IS THAT IT?
SHE TRIED, YOU KNOW? MY MOTHER...

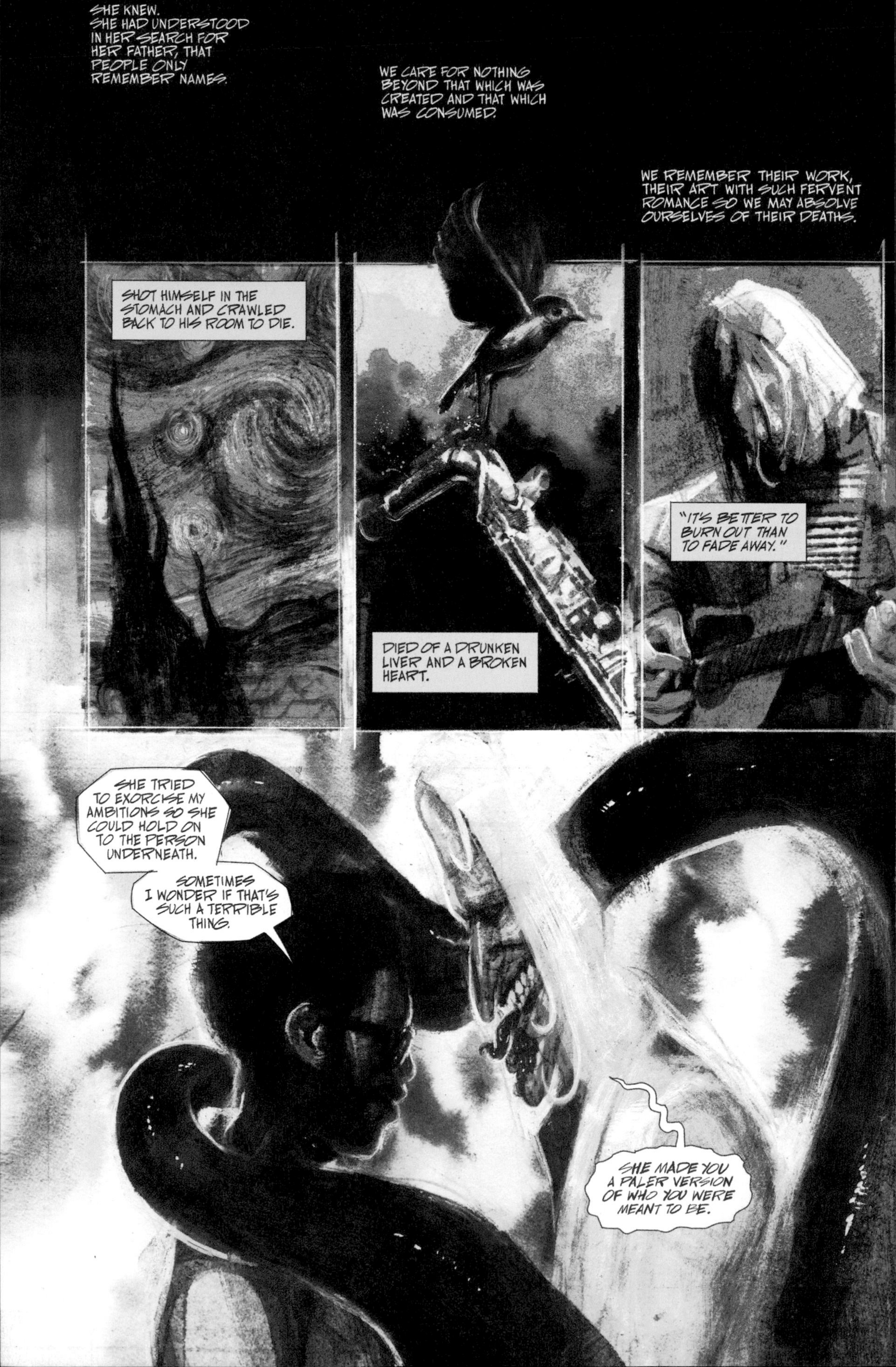
SHE KNEW. SHE HAD UNDERSTOOD IN HER SEARCH FOR HER FATHER, THAT PEOPLE ONLY REMEMBER NAMES.
WE CARE FOR NOTHING BEYOND THAT WHICH WAS CREATED AND THAT WHICH WAS CONSUMED.
WE REMEMBER THEIR WORK, THEIR ART WITH SUCH FERVENT ROMANCE SO WE MAY ABSOLVE OURSELVES OF THEIR DEATHS.
SHOT HIMSELF IN THE STOMACH AND CRAWLED BACK TO HIS ROOM TO DIE.
DIED OF A DRUNKEN LIVER AND A BROKEN HEART.
"IT'S BETTER TO BURN OUT THAN TO FADE AWAY."
SHE TRIED TO EXORCISE MY AMBITIONS SO SHE COULD HOLD ON TO THE PERSON UNDERNEATH.
SOMETIMES I WONDER IF THAT'S SUCH A TERRIBLE THING.
SHE MADE YOU A PALER VERSION OF WHO YOU WERE MEANT TO BE.

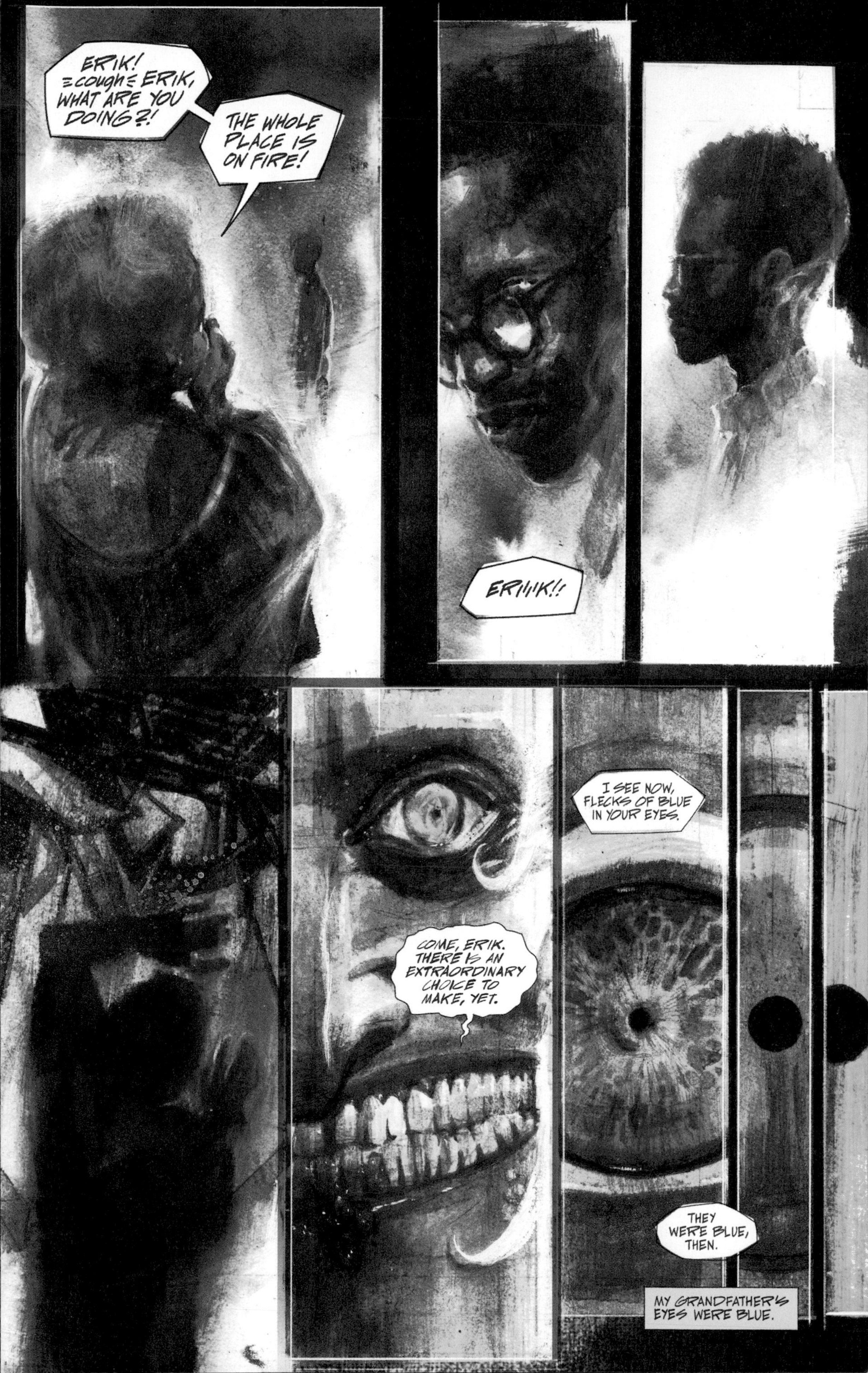
ERIK! =cough= ERIK, WHAT ARE YOU DOING?!
THE WHOLE PLACE IS ON FIRE!
ERIIIK!!
I SEE NOW, FLECKS OF BLUE IN YOUR EYES.
COME, ERIK. THERE IS AN EXTRAORDINARY CHOICE TO MAKE, YET.
THEY WERE BLUE, THEN.
MY GRANDFATHER'S EYES WERE BLUE.

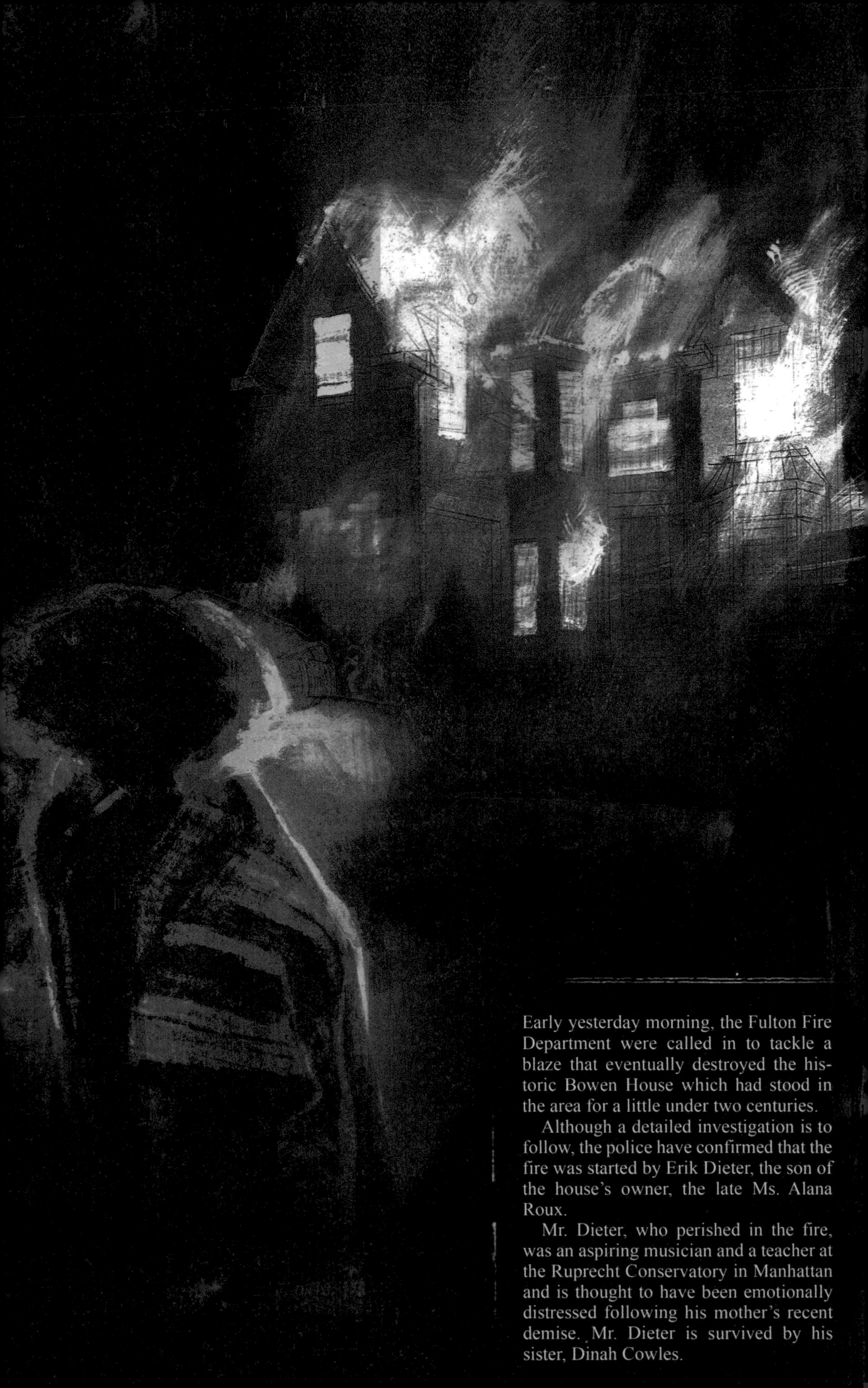

Early yesterday morning, the Fulton Fire Department were called in to tackle a blaze that eventually destroyed the historic Bowen House which had stood in the area for a little under two centuries.

Although a detailed investigation is to follow, the police have confirmed that the fire was started by Erik Dieter, the son of the house's owner, the late Ms. Alana Roux.

Mr. Dieter, who perished in the fire, was an aspiring musician and a teacher at the Ruprecht Conservatory in Manhattan and is thought to have been emotionally distressed following his mother's recent demise. Mr. Dieter is survived by his sister, Dinah Cowles.

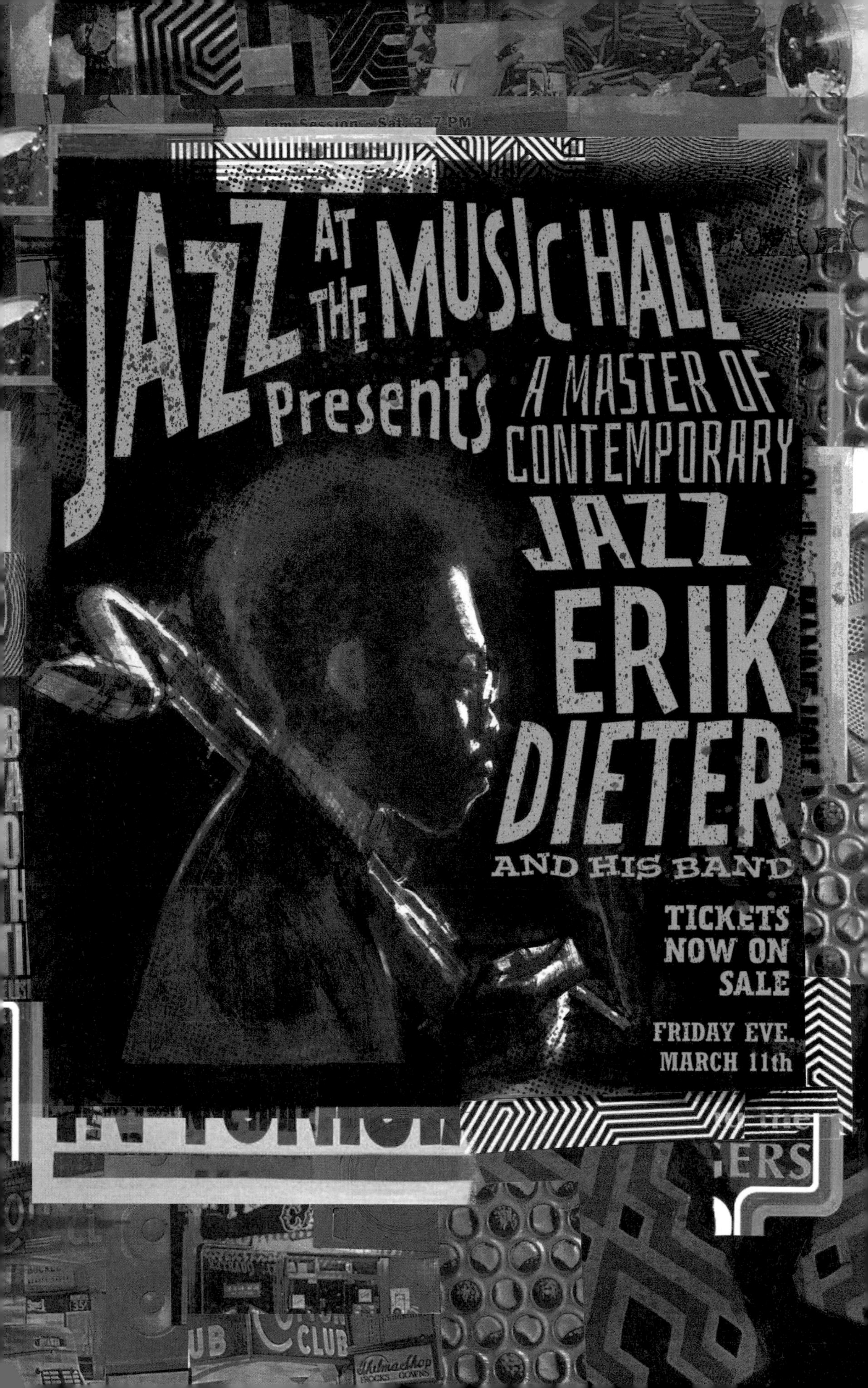
JAZZ
AT THE MUSIC HALL
Presents
A MASTER OF CONTEMPORARY JAZZ
ERIK DIETER
AND HIS BAND
TICKETS NOW ON SALE
FRIDAY EVE. MARCH 11th

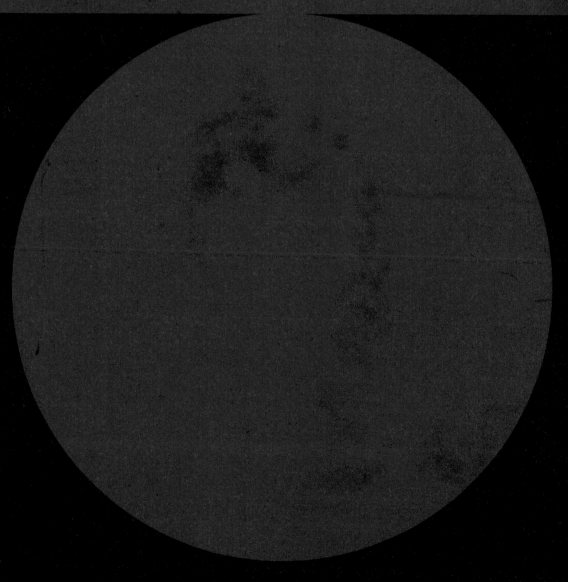

ART GALLERY

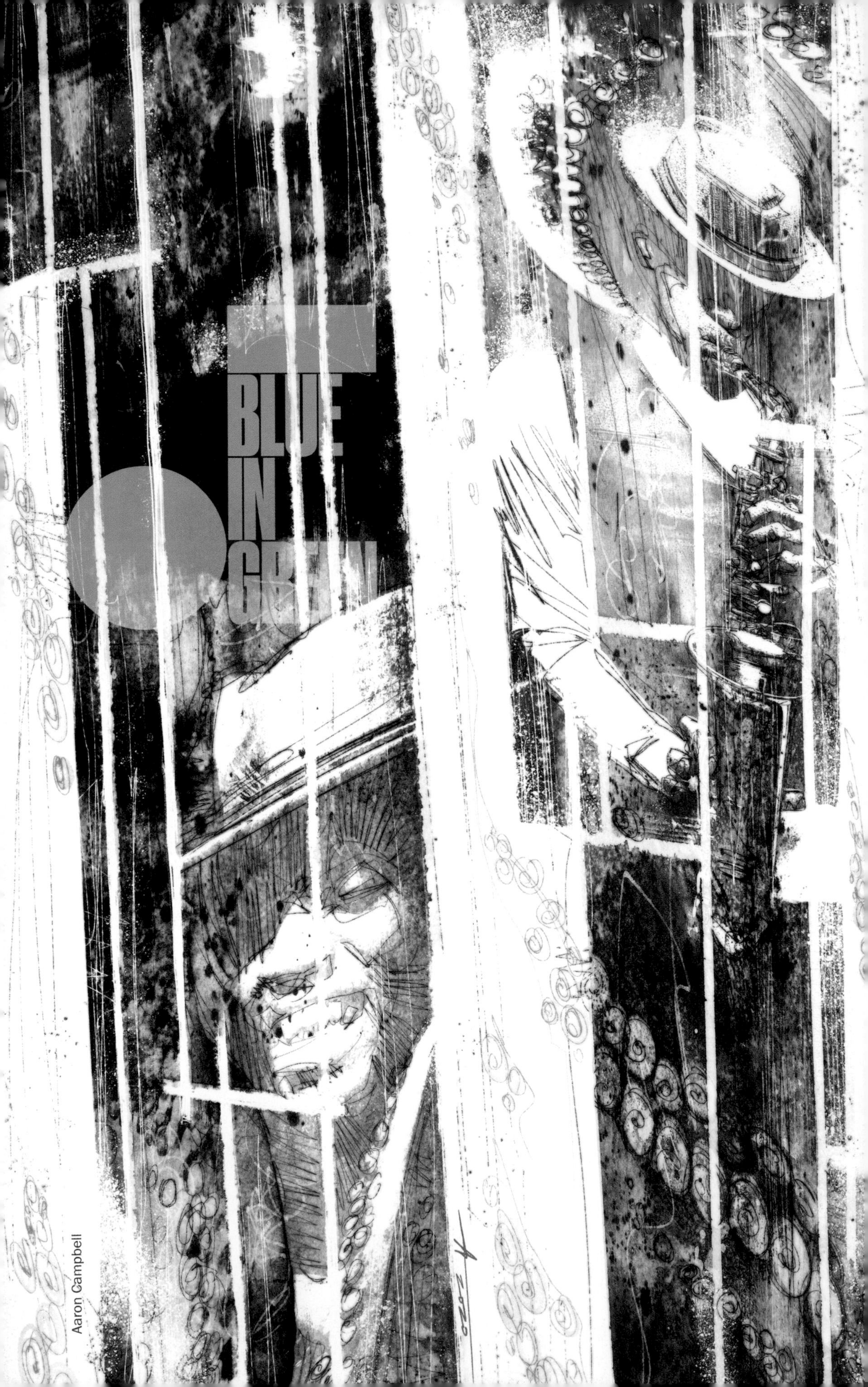
BLUE
IN
GREEN
Aaron Campbell

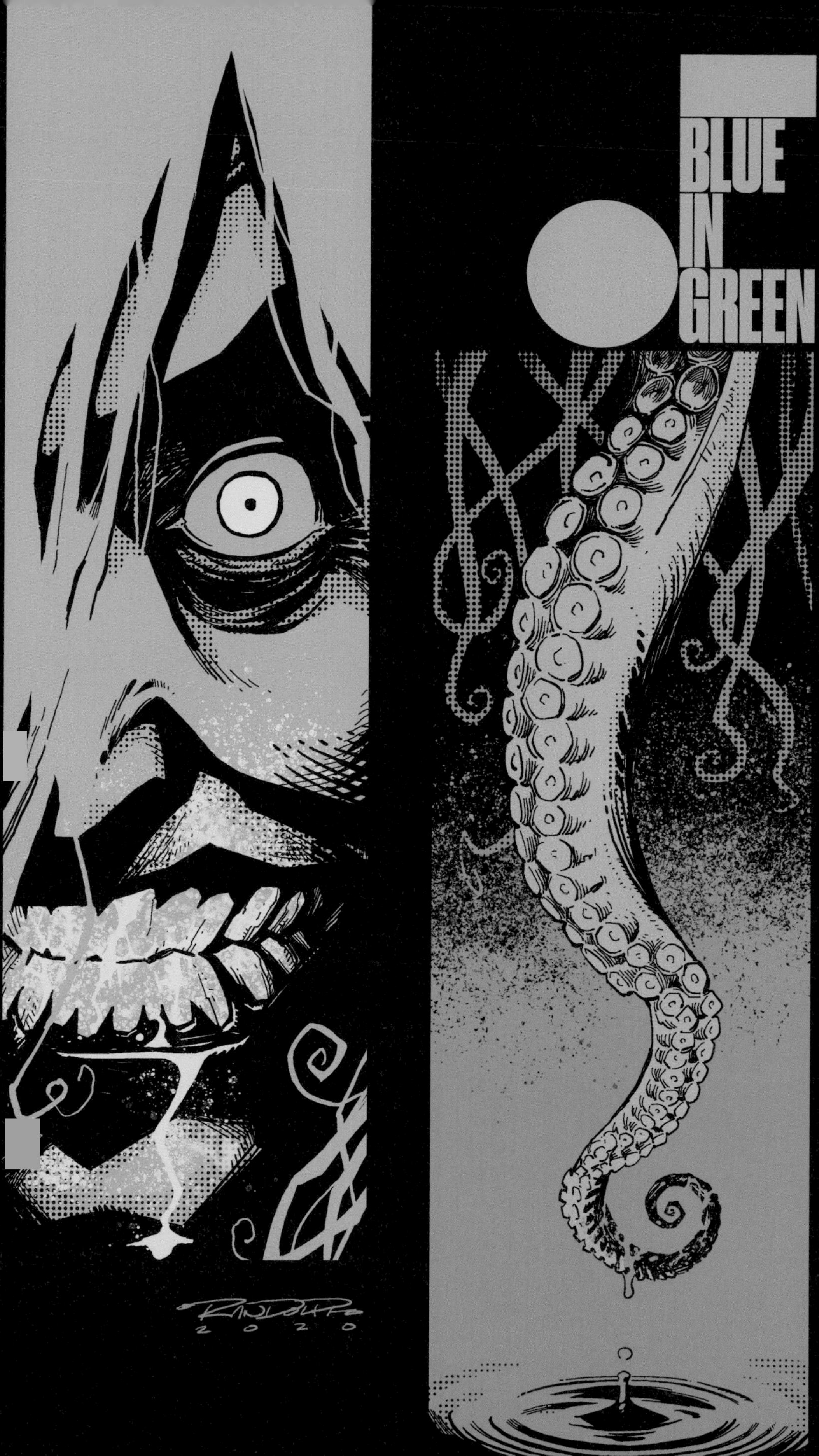
BLUE
IN
GREEN

Khary Randolph

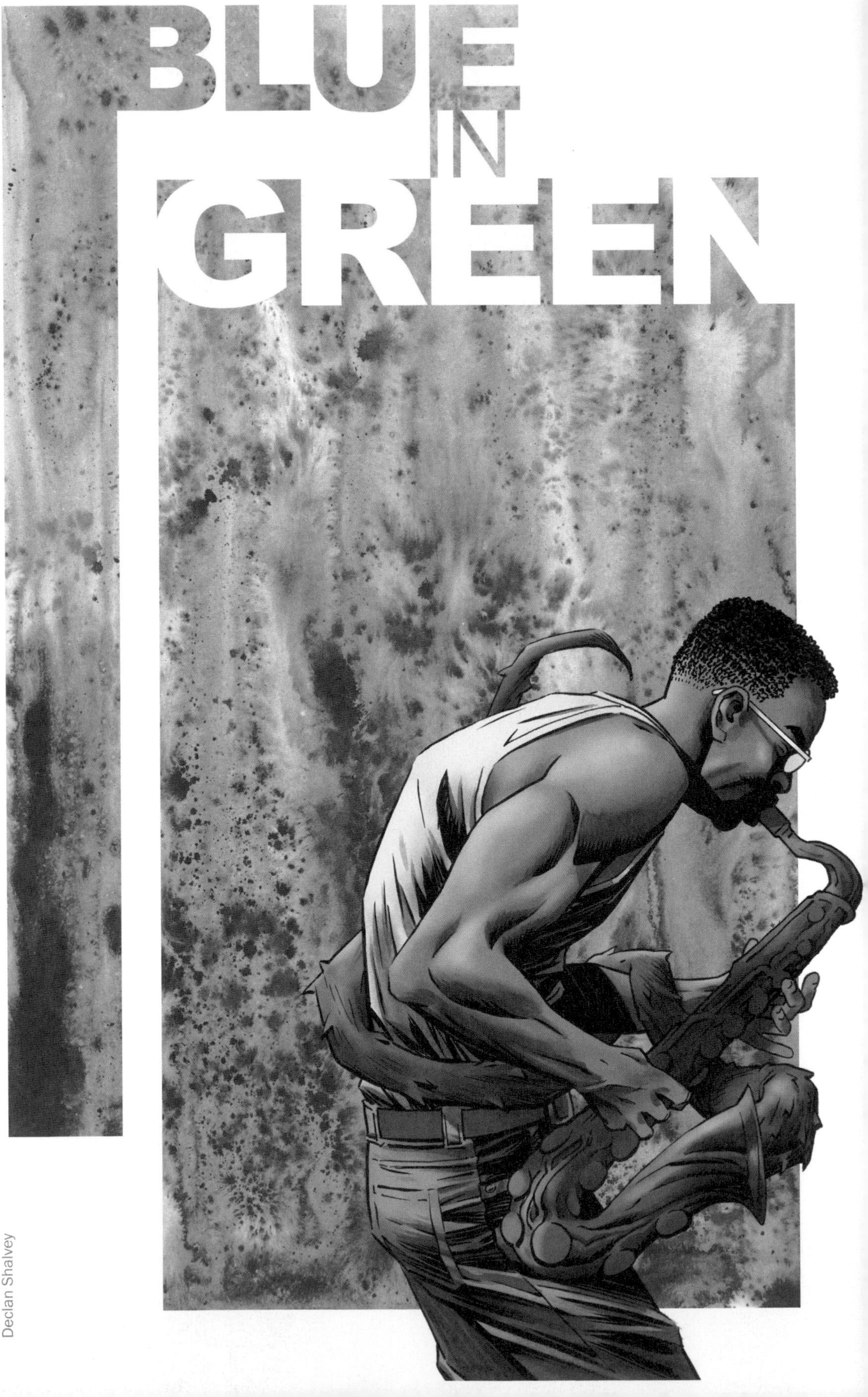
BLUE
IN
GREEN

Declan Shalvey

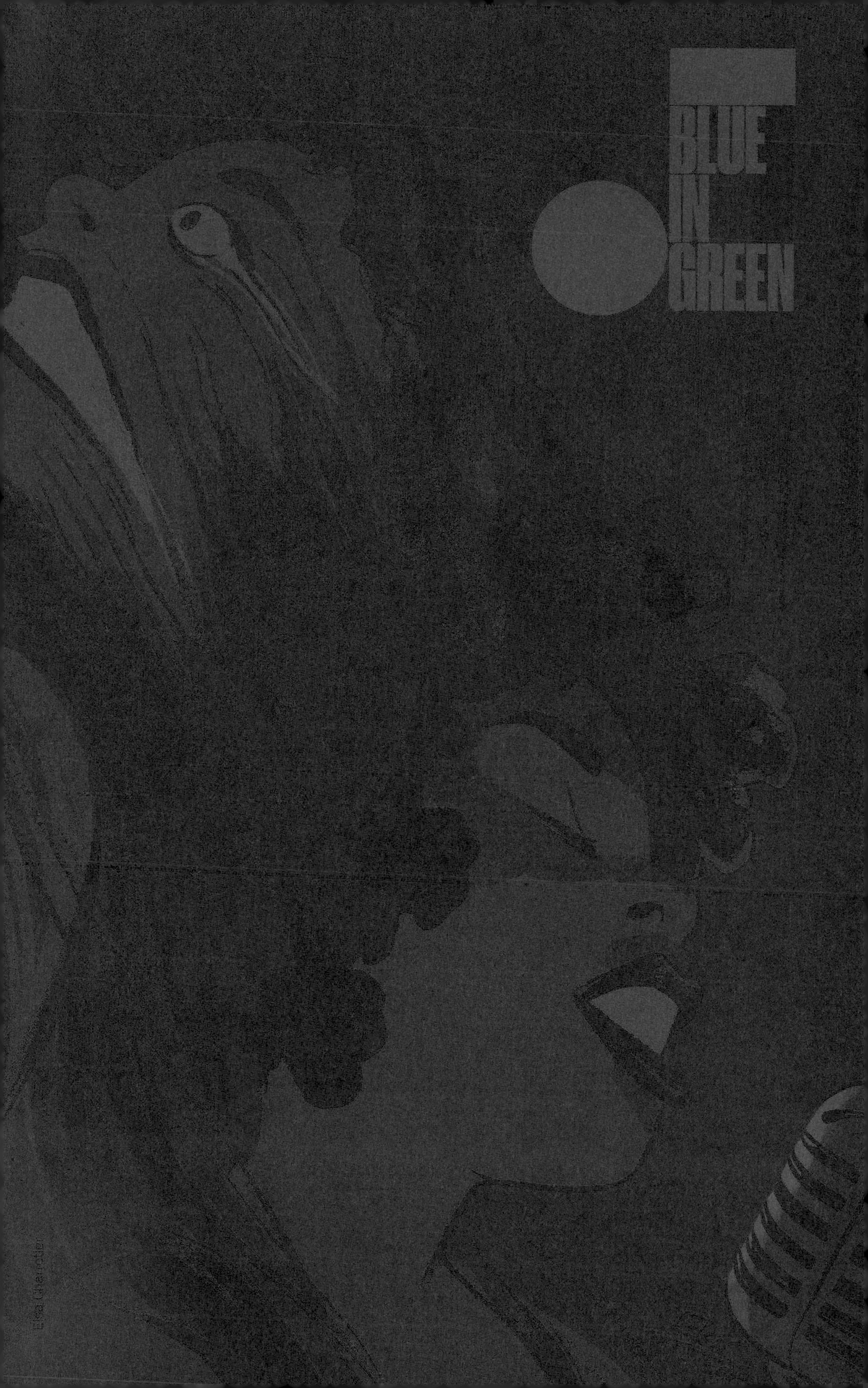
BLUE
IN
GREEN

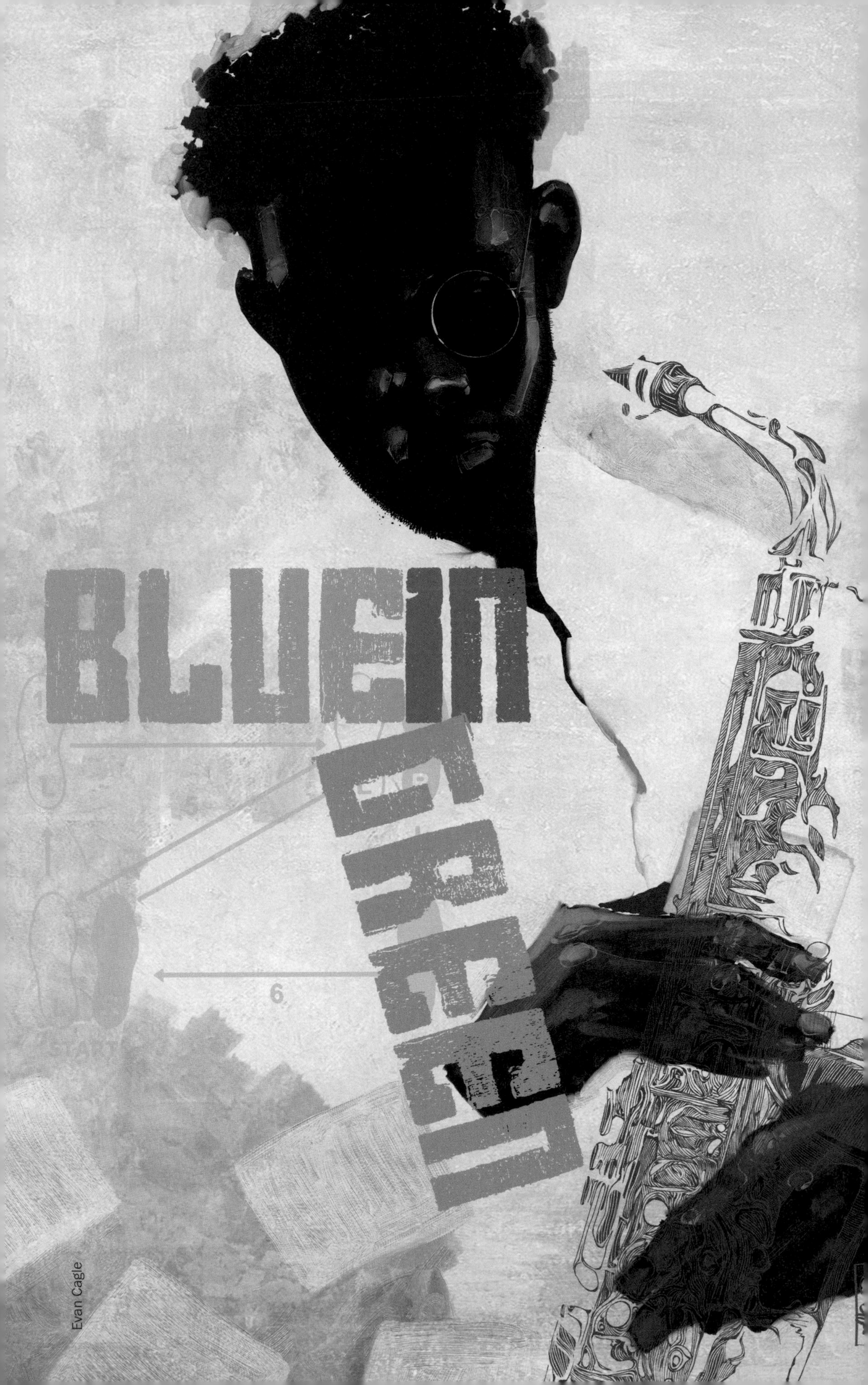
BLUE IN
GREEN
6
Evan Cagle

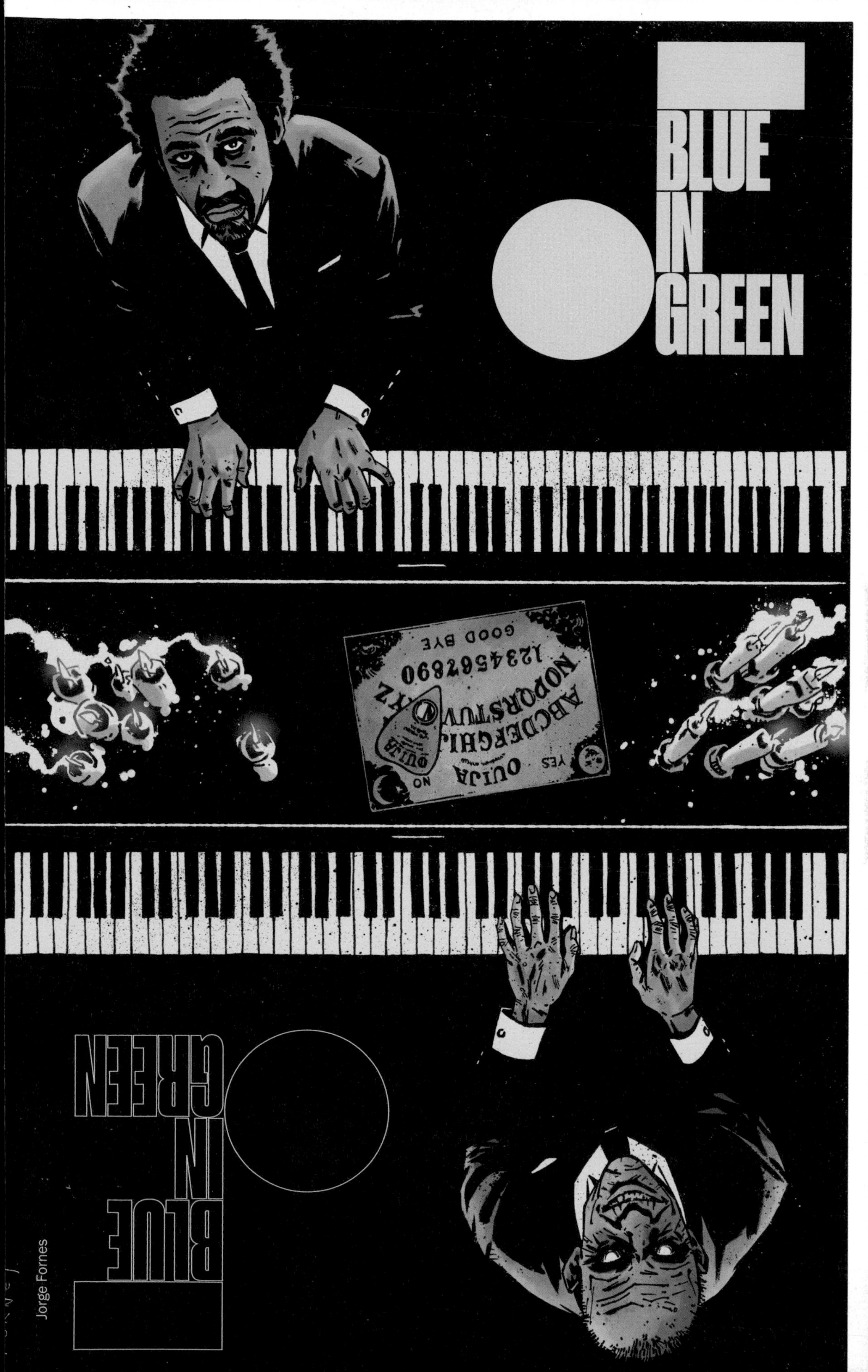
BLUE
IN
GREEN
OUIJA
YES
NO
1234567890
GOOD BYE
BLUE
IN
GREEN
Jorge Fornes

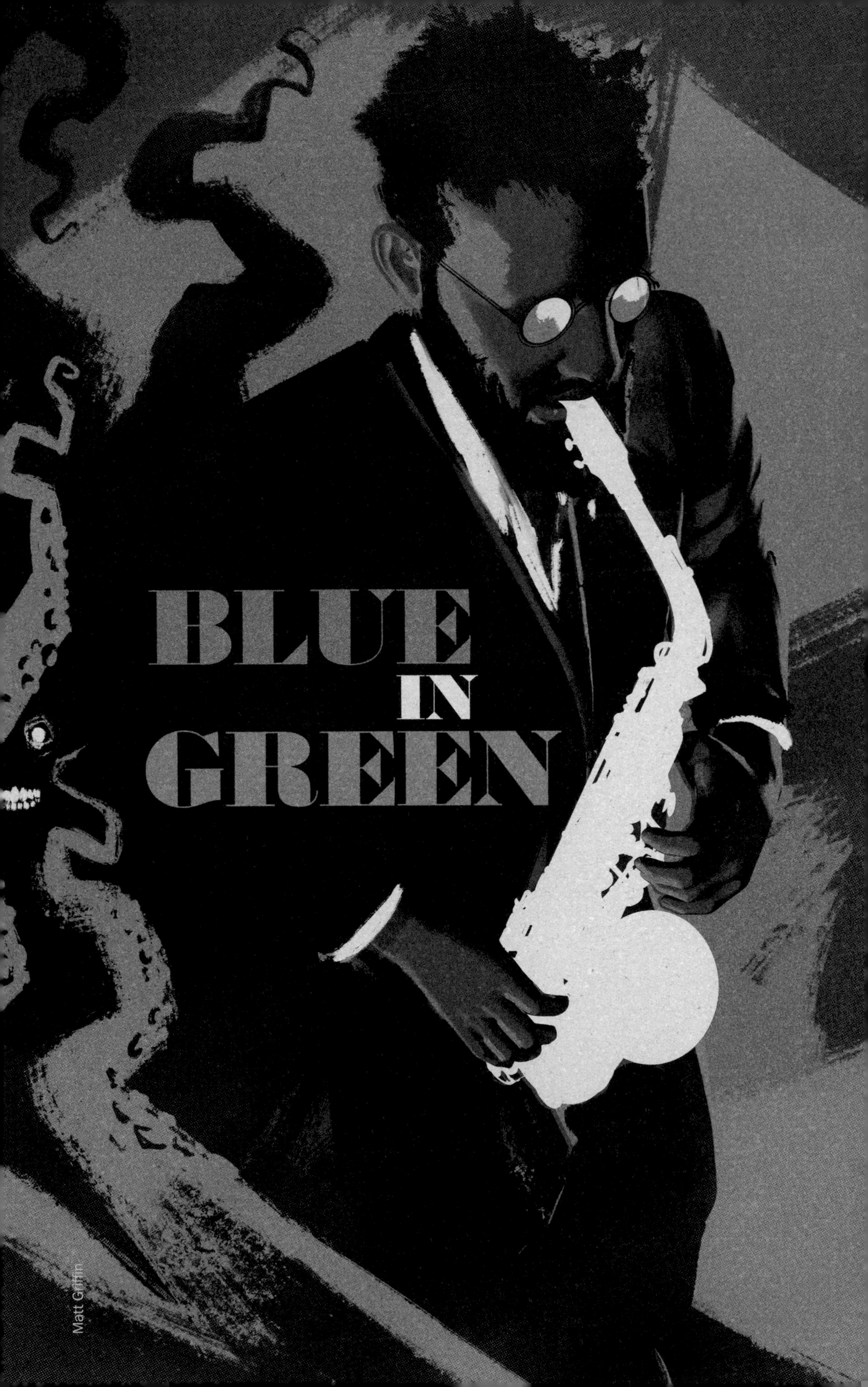
BLUE
IN
GREEN
Matt Griffin

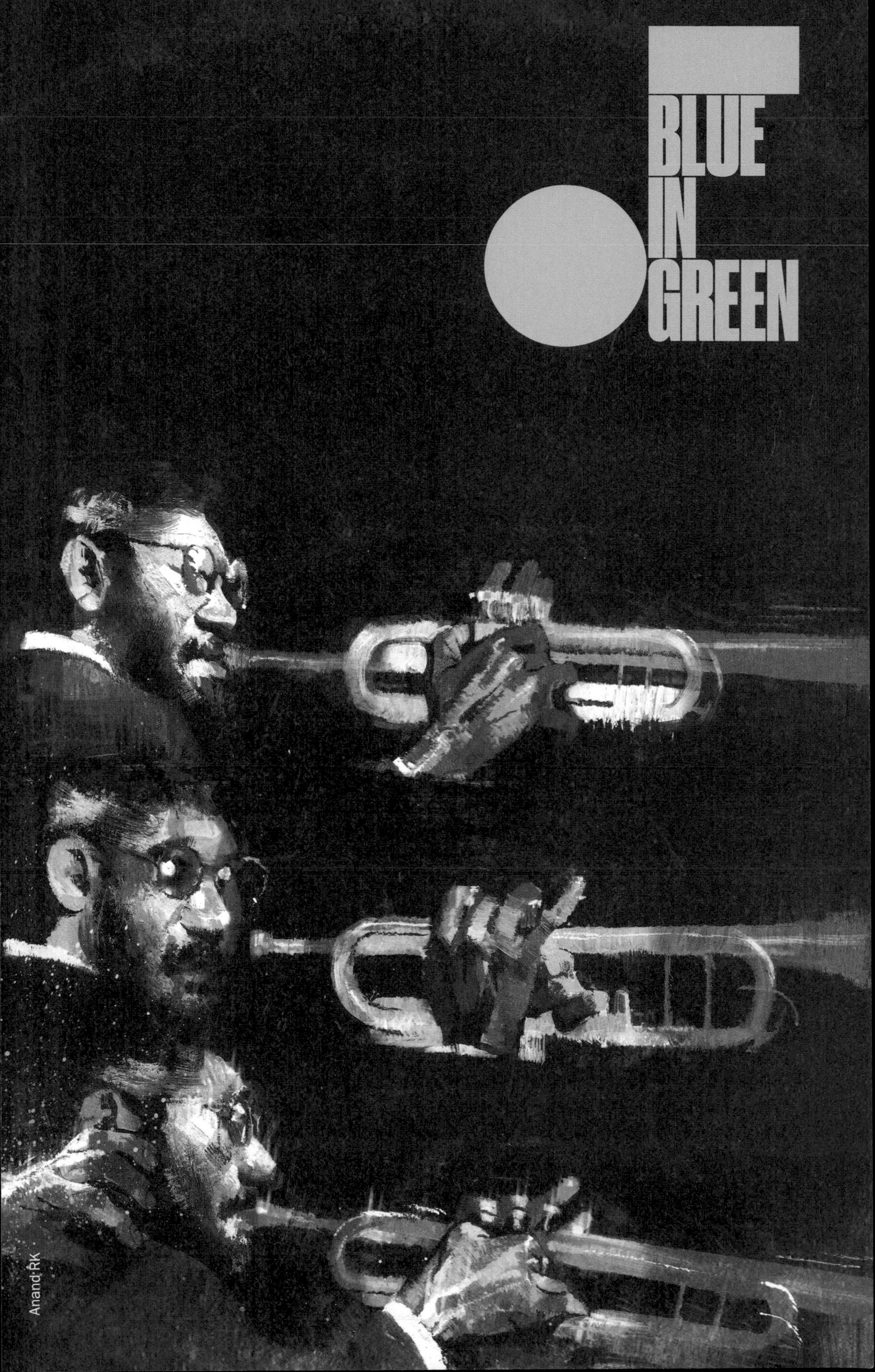
BLUE
IN
GREEN
Anand RK

[redacted]

[redacted]

[redacted]

[redacted]

[redacted]

BONUS CONTENT

SCRIPT TO PAGE

PAGE 30

PANEL 1

By the side of a lonely highway, set against the backdrop of trees beyond the edges of the road, Erik's car is halted by the side of the road. It's not parked properly. Tire track show that he has skidded to a halt.
It's raining heavily. Headlights, taillights and lighting from inside the car conspiring to create a ghostly effect.

NARRATION

It rains heavily on the drive back. Sheets pelting down from the sky.

NARRATION

Twice, I drive off the road and nearly hit a deer before I stop for the rain to pass.

NARRATION

Taillight reds click on and off , disapprovingly.

PANEL 2

A vague, ghostly, perhaps slightly more abstract or blurry shot of the flautist.

NARRATION

I can't stop thinking about the flautist. I wonder what it is about her that is so burned into my mind.

NARRATION

I come to realize it's not her. It's the music.

PANEL 3

Shot of Eric inside the car, sitting with both hands gripping the steering wheel but with his forehead resting on the steering wheel.

NARRATION

It's my heartbeat. It's the groaning wipers on my windshield.

PANEL 4

Abstract. Imagine how the windshield looks from the outside. Water pelting down on it. Little pearls of water scaterring - and flows of water streaking down the glass.
All backlit by the light from inside the car.

NARRATION

It's the rain drumming on the roof. The sound of my breath in my ears. The shuddering of my lungs.

NARRATION

I grip the leather on the steering wheel, hear it creaking in my grip.

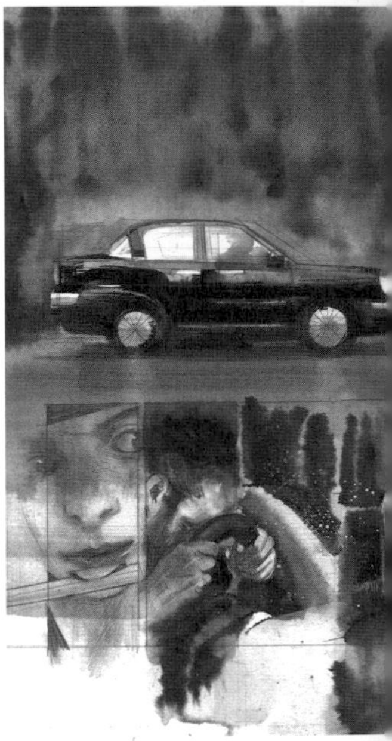

PANEL 5

Shot of the tail light of the car. A single light - blinking red.

NARRATION

Stop.

NARRATION

I want it to stop.

PANEL 6

In the dark space below the panels.

NARRATION

Then, it does. The silence exhales.

NARRATION

And I remember, just as when I fell from the roof. Just as I did on that night in Alana's study.

NARRATION

I hear it. The oily groan of something monstrous, slithering underneath it all.

PAGE 31

PANEL 1

Large full bleed. Shot of the house in the dark. It's stopped raining - just a drizzle here and there. Erik's car is parked outside. Only one light is on in the house. (pick a window.) Again, a haunting image.

> NARRATION
>
> It's late when I get back to the house. Dinah is asleep.

> NARRATION
>
> I can hear footsteps upstairs, haunting the dark. Vera's probably home.

PANEL 2

In perfect black, shot of a cigarette lighter being sparked.

> NARRATION
>
> I can't sleep.

> NARRATION
>
> So, I wander down to Alana's study.

PANEL 3

Pull out as Eric brings it to his face and lights a cigarette. He's clearly gotten a bit wet - so his hair is tousled and he's taken off his shirt.

PANEL 4

Off panel - as he clicks on a laptop it shines a ghostly glow on to his face. He exhales - his face partly obscured by the smoke.

> NARRATION
>
> I haven't smoked in years.

PAGE 55

PANEL 1

Large, bleed. Erik sits down in front of the old woman, talking to her. Leaning in that way people lean and talk slowly and exaggerated when talking to old people.

> ERIK NARRATION
>
> Morris is right. She's a ghost. I sit down on the bed in front of her. I tell her everything, who I am, why I'm there.

> ERIK NARRATION
>
> I call out her name, Amelia. But I get nothing.

> ERIK NARRATION
>
> All she does is look out of the window wearing that haunted expression.

PANEL 2

Exasperated, Eric rubs his forehead with an expression of futility.

PANEL 3

We're going to do something cool here. We're going to draw an image of Erik looking at one of her possessions in his hand, but we're going to put it in the f/g cutting across the borders of this and the next 2 panels.

In the b/g on this and the next 2 panels, we're going to put aspect shots of the things Amelia has in her room, let's discuss.

> ERIK NARRATION
>
> I take a pause and wander around her room admiring the knick-knacks strewn about.

> ERIK NARRATION
>
> They are dusty and sun-bleached. She flinches when I touch them.

PANEL 6

A stark. Haunting panel as suddenly Amelia's eye is looking right at us as she speaks with a frail voice.

> AMELIA
>
> Stop. Please don't.

PAGE 56

PANEL 1

From behind Amelia in the f/g, we're Erik, surprised and turning back to talk, even as he puts the book back in the shelf.

> ERIK NARRATION
>> I am embarrassed.

> ERIK
>> I...I'm so sorry. I didn't...

> ERIK NARRATION

Suddenly aware that I am scavenging for answers in remnants of the dusty, sun-bleached memories of her life...

PANEL 2

A shot of Amelia's wrinkled hands, she keeps them on her lap.

> ERIK NARRATION
>> ...when all she wants is to hold on to them a little longer, in silence.

PANEL 3

A shot of Erik as he puts his head down and is walking past Amelia, when she reaches out and stops him.

> ERIK NARRATION
>> It's all a mistake. I am already walking out, when she stops me.

> AMELIA
>> What did you want?

PANEL 4

On Erik,

> ERIK NARRATION
>> For a moment, I wonder if I should just keep walking, go home and

talk to Vera.

> ERIK NARRATION
>> Apologize to my sister for a lifetime of absences. And finally lay my
>> mother to rest.

PANEL 5

> ERIK NARRATION
>> But like I fool I pick out the photograph and show it to her.
>> Perhaps I'm even hoping it's another face lost to time, when she
>> says...

> AMELIA

Dalton...

> AMELIA

It's Dalton Blakely.

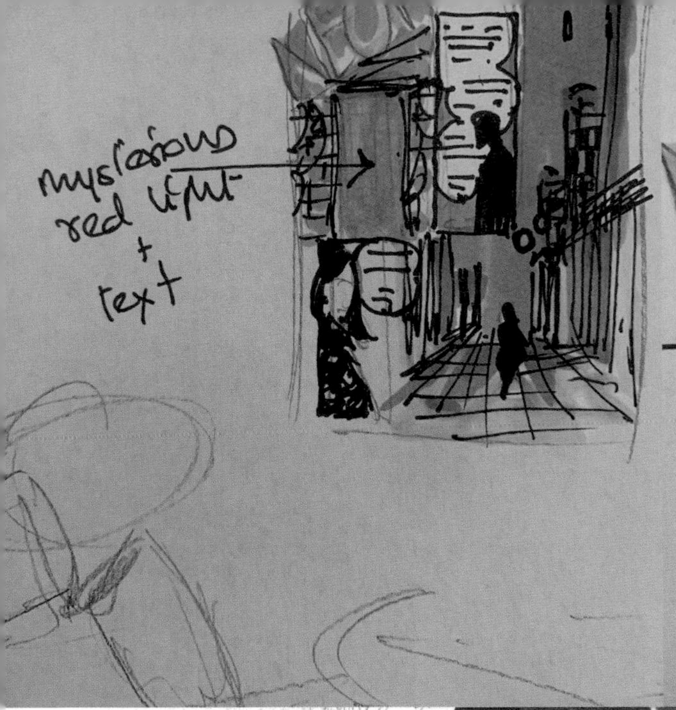
mysterious
red light
+
text

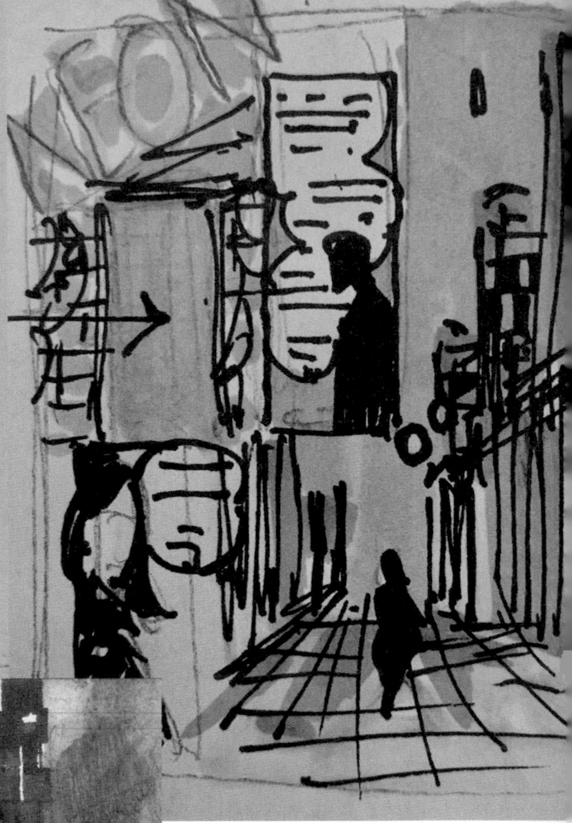

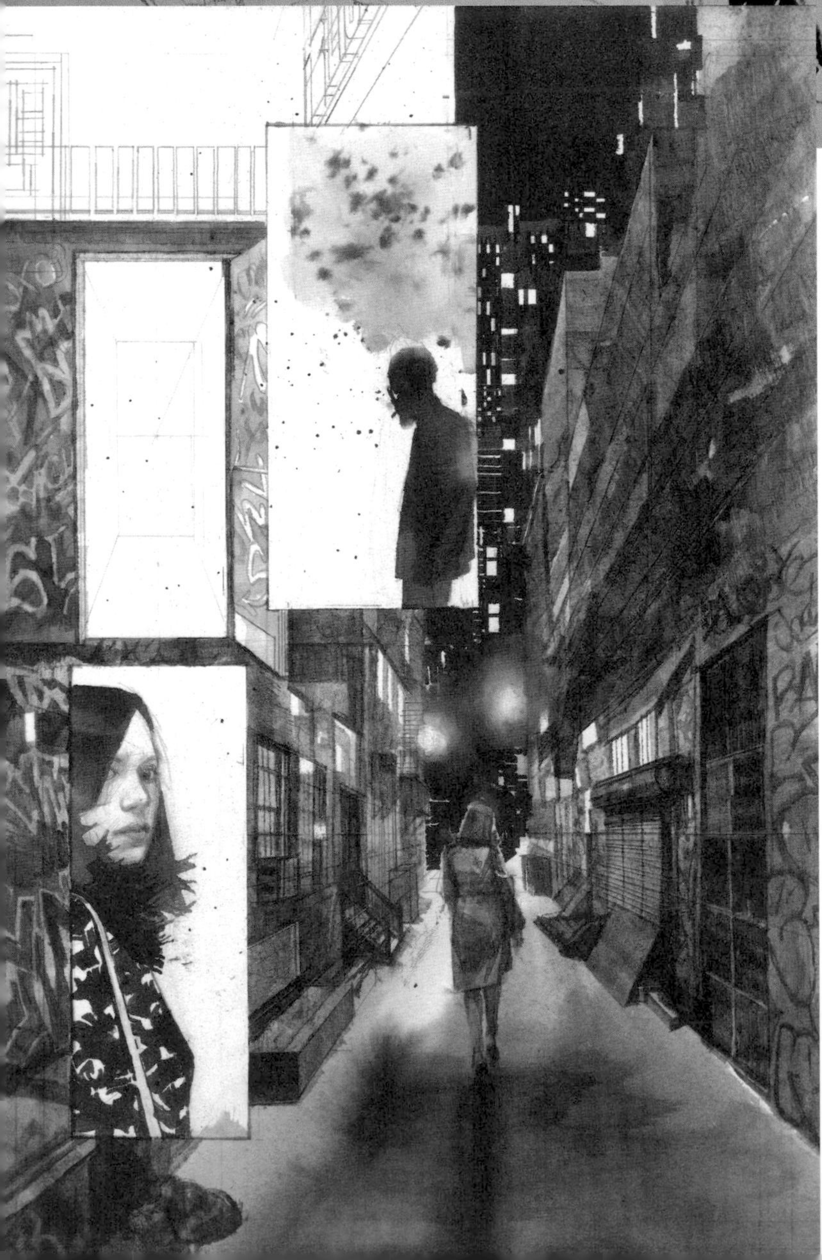

Ram Commentary:

"With this book, Anand and I eventually got to a place where it started making more sense for me to provide a thumbnail for pages where I had something very specific in mind. I particularly like how this one turned out, all the way from this little scribble to that coloured and lettered page."

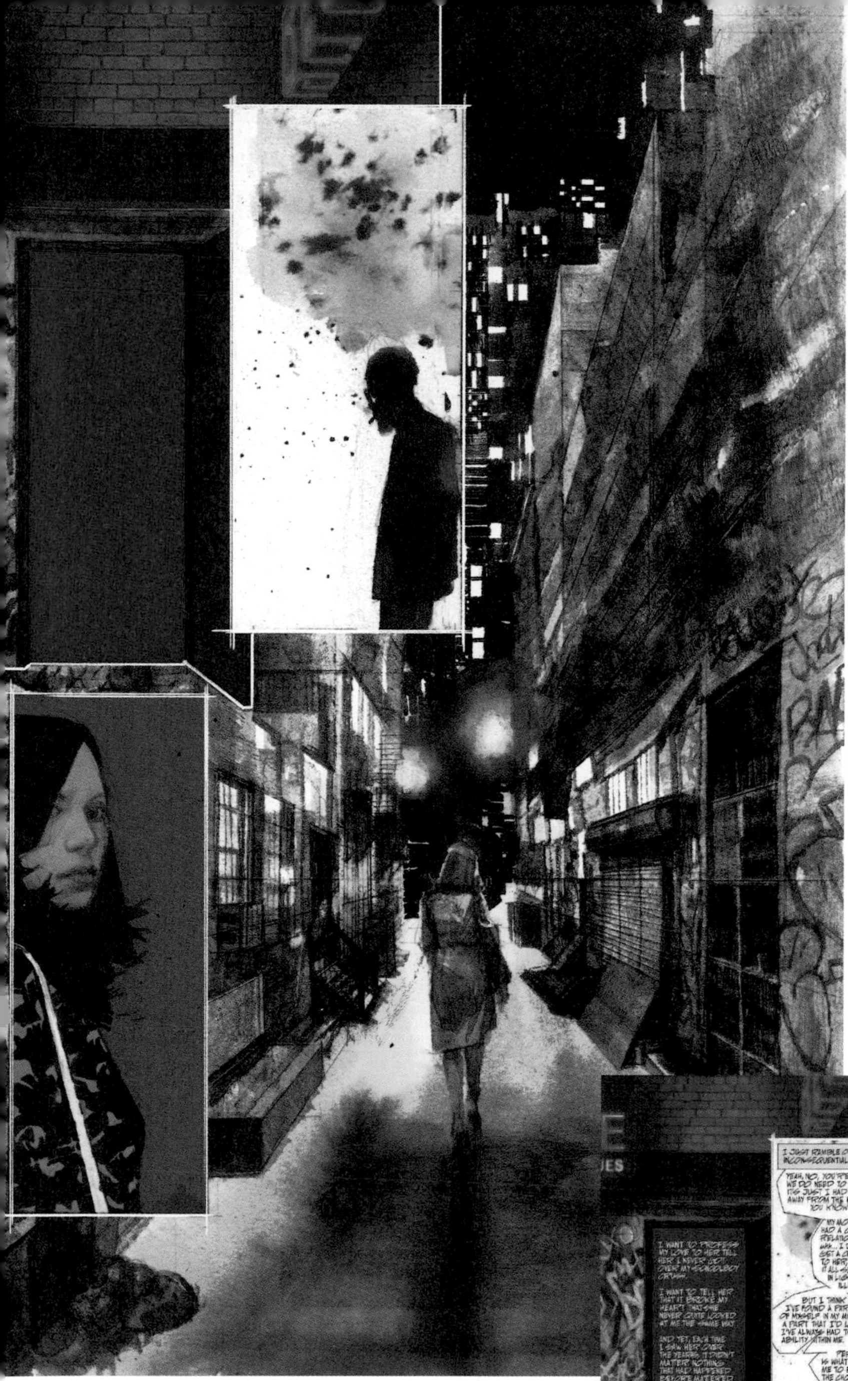

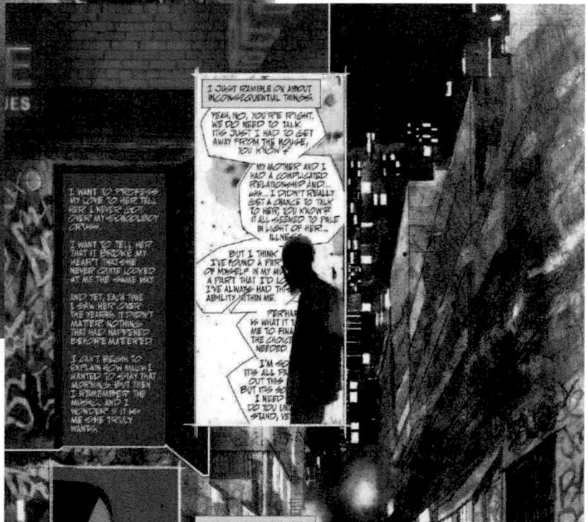

I WANT TO PROFESS MY LOVE TO HER. TELL HER I NEVER GOT OVER MY SCHOOLBOY CRUSH.
I WANT TO TELL HER THAT IT BROKE MY HEART THAT SHE NEVER QUITE LOOKED AT ME THE SAME WAY.
AND YET, EACH TIME I SAW HER OVER THE YEARS, IT DIDN'T MATTER. NOTHING THAT HAD HAPPENED BEFORE MATTERED.
I CAN'T BEGIN TO EXPLAIN HOW MUCH I WANTED TO SAY THAT MORNING. BUT THEN I REMEMBER THE MUSIC, AND I WONDER IF IT WAS ME SHE TRULY WANTS.
I JUST RAMBLE ON ABOUT INCONSEQUENTIAL THINGS.
YEAH, NO, YOU'RE RIGHT. WE DO NEED TO TALK. IT'S JUST I HAD TO GET AWAY FROM THE HOUSE, YOU KNOW?
MY MOTHER AND I HAD A COMPLICATED RELATIONSHIP AND... UHH... I DIDN'T REALLY GET A CHANCE TO TALK TO HER, YOU KNOW? IT ALL SEEMED TO PALE IN LIGHT OF HER...
BUT I THINK
SHE TELLS ME SHE'S STILL AT THE HOUSE FOR A FEW DAYS BUT SHE'S GOING BACK HOME AFTER.
SHE TALKS ABOUT GETTING THE KIDS BACK TO ROUTINE.
OUR WORDS TIPTOEING AROUND THE UNCOMFORTABLE SPACES LEFT TO SILENCE.
I PROMISE HER I WILL SEE HER AGAIN.

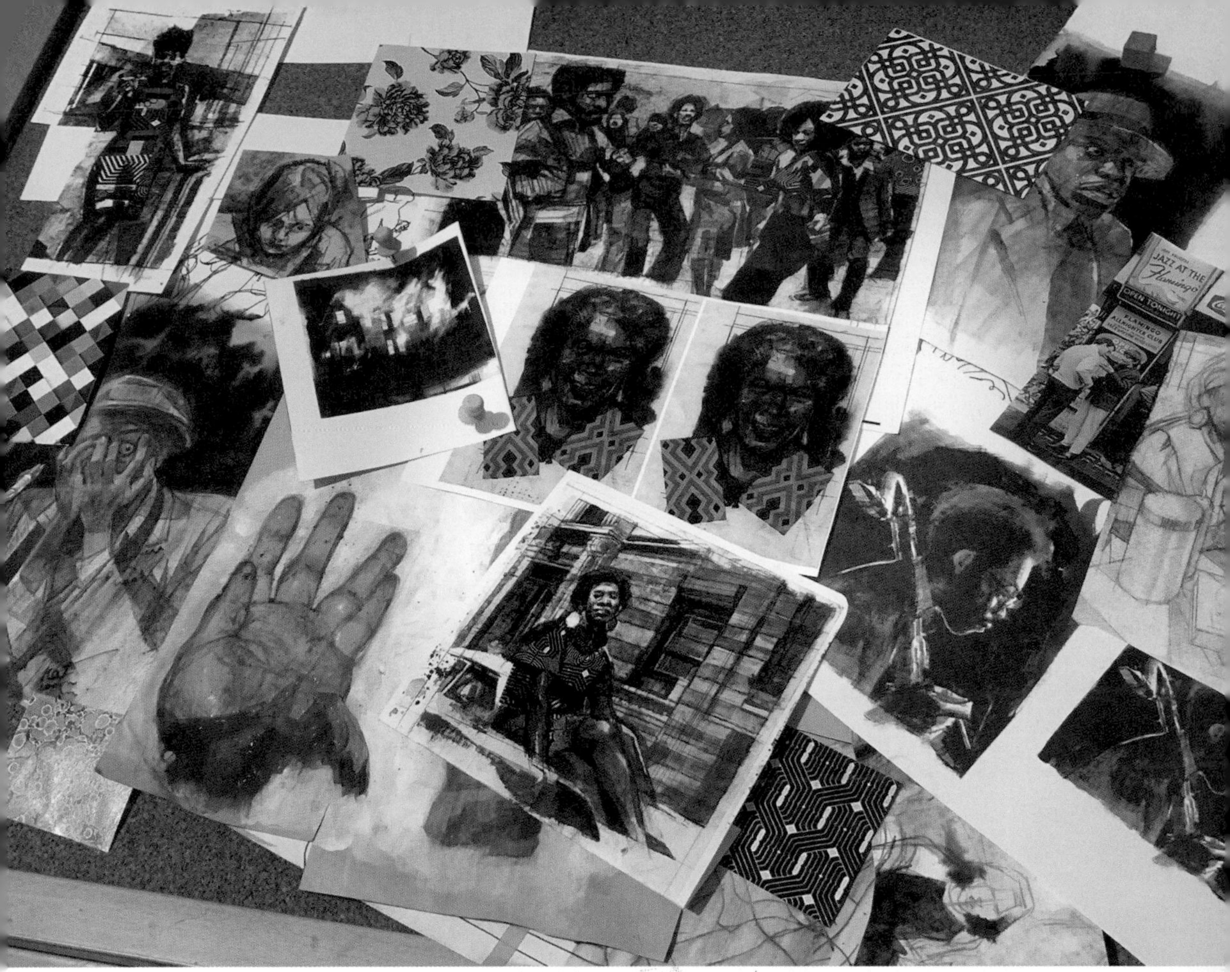
JAZZ AT THE Flamingo
OPEN TONIGHT

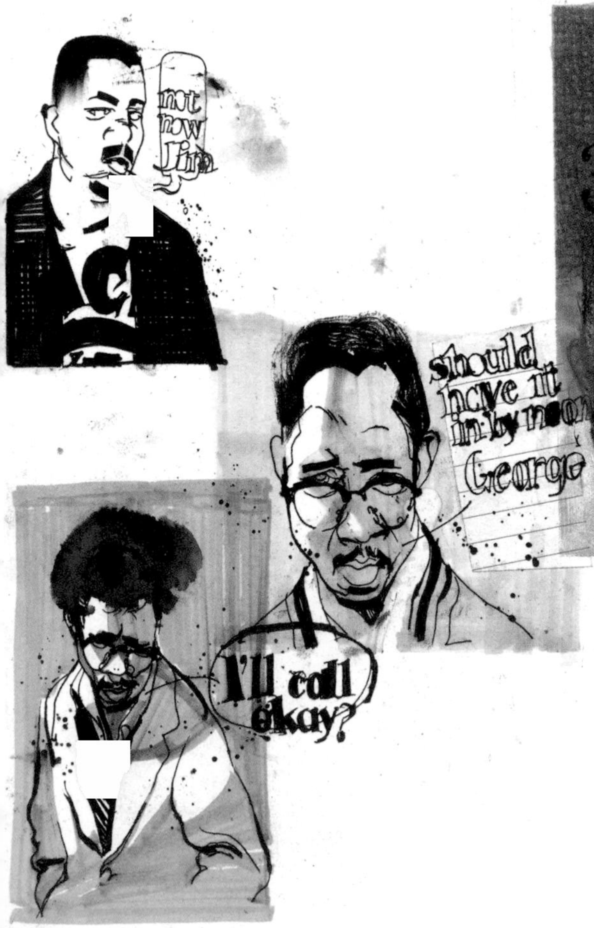
not now Jim
should have it in by noon George
I'll call okay?

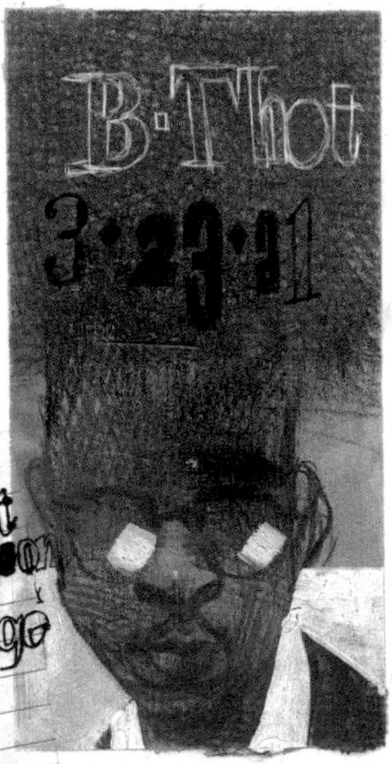

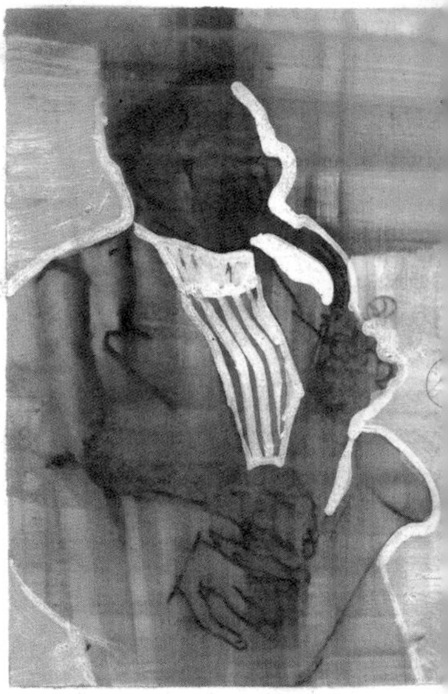

Ram Commentary:

"Anand and I took close to two months just to settle on a style for the book. There are stacks of papers where we went through trial and error to arrive at something that we both enjoyed."

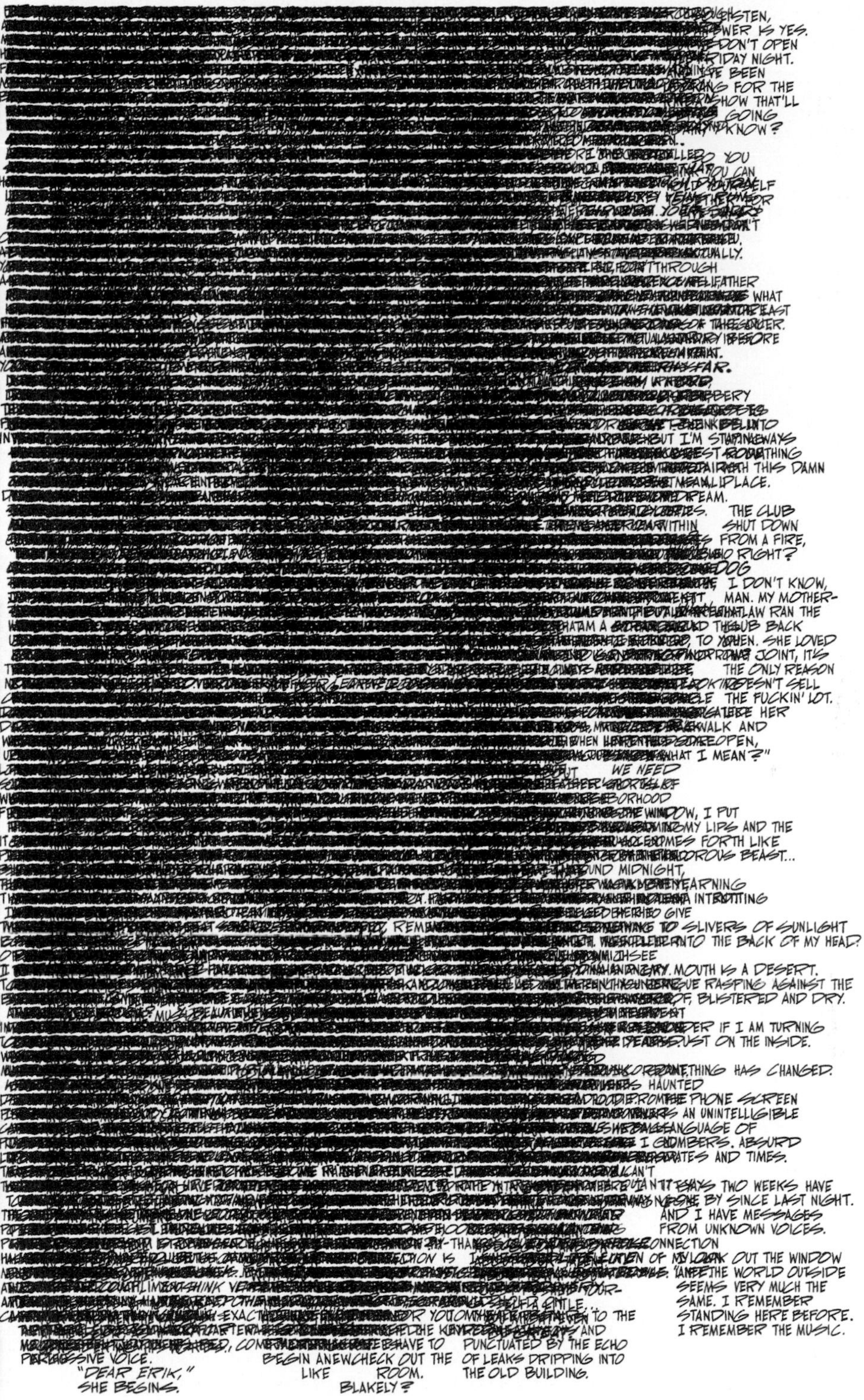
THE CLUB
SHUT DOWN
FROM A FIRE,
I DON'T KNOW,
MAN. MY MOTHER-
MOUTH IS A DESERT.
AND I HAVE MESSAGES
FROM UNKNOWN VOICES.
SEEMS VERY MUCH THE
SAME. I REMEMBER
STANDING HERE BEFORE.
I REMEMBER THE MUSIC.
PUNCTUATED BY THE ECHO
OF LEAKS DRIPPING INTO
THE OLD BUILDING.
"DEAR ERIK,"
SHE BEGINS.
BLAKELY?

Ram Commentary:

"The entirety of this book was painstakingly hand-lettered, digitized and then placed on the pages. All that extraordinary effort put onto a single page is art in itself."

BIOGRAPHIES

RAM V, is an award winning author and creator of comics and graphic novels such as *Black Mumba*, PARADISO, *These Savage Shores & Grafity's Wall*. Since publishing his first book in 2016, he's also gone on to write for iconic titles at DC and Marvel. Ram currently lives in London— dog person, doodles, argumentative melancholic.

ANAND RK, is an illustrator and artist who lives and works in Mumbai, India. His work includes an eclectic mix of illustration, painting and sequential art. His previous work includes the graphic novel *Grafity's Wall*.
In between projects, he's to be found painting murals, making zines and juggling about half a dozen personal projects on the side.

ADITYA BIDIKAR, is an award-winning letterer for comics like ISOLA, LITTLE BIRD, *These Savage Shores*, *Hellblazer* and more.
He is also, occasionally a writer and editor. He lives in India, surrounded by comics. Cat person but makes an exception for Ram's dog.

JOHN J. PEARSON, is an illustrator and artist based in Leeds, U.K. His varied portfolio includes work for Arrow Video, Warner Bros., WWE, Nuclear Blast Records and Netflix amongst many others. He is also an award-shortlisted comic book artist, working on BLUE IN GREEN, Death Sentence: London, and Megadeth: Death by Design for Image, Titan, and Heavy Metal, respectively, as well as self-publishing the ongoing folk horror webcomic *Blood Moon*.

TOM MULLER, is an award-winning designer and creative director who works in culture, entertainment and technology. In comics he's best known for the award-winning '*Dawn of X*' rebrand of Marvel's X-Men franchise and his work on numerous Image titles including VS, THE NEW WORLD, DAYS OF HATE, THE WEATHERMAN, DRIFTER and ZERO. Beyond comics he works with the likes of Sony Pictures, Wired, Hivemind, Google, StudioCanal and Mondo. He lives in London with his wife and two cats.